THE ASSASSINATION OF FEDERICO GARCÍA LORCA

IAN GIBSON

PENGUIN BOOKS

Penguin Books Ltd, Harmondsworth, Middlesex, England
Penguin Books, 625 Madison Avenue,
New York, New York 10022, U.S.A.
Penguin Books Australia Ltd, Ringwood, Victoria, Australia
Penguin Books Canada Limited, 2801 John Street,
Markham, Ontario, Canada L3R 1B4
Penguin Books (N.Z.) Ltd, 182–190 Wairau Road,
Auckland 10, New Zealand

First published in Spanish in Paris under the title
*La represión nacionalista de Granada en 1936
y la muerte de Federico García Lorca* by Ruedo Ibérico 1971
First published in Great Britain under the title
The Death of Lorca by
W. H. Allen & Co. Ltd 1973
The Death of Lorca first published in the United States of
America by J. Philip O'Hara 1973
Completely revised and rewritten edition, entitled
The Assassination of Federico García Lorca,
first published in Great Britain by W. H. Allen & Co. Ltd 1979
Published in Penguin Books 1983

LIBRARY OF CONGRESS CATALOGING IN PUBLICATION DATA
Gibson, Ian.
The assassination of Federico García Lorca.
Originally published: London: W. H. Allen, 1979.
Bibliography: p.
Includes index.
1. García Lorca, Federico, 1898–1936—Biography—Last years and death.
2. Authors, Spanish—20th century—Biography.   I. Title.
[PQ6613. A763Z64813   1983]   868'.6209   [B]   82-22308
ISBN 0 14 00.6473 7

Printed in the United States of America by
R. R. Donnelley & Sons Company, Harrisonburg, Virginia
Set in Bembo

The author and publisher gratefully acknowledge permission granted for the use of extracts from the following publications: *Death in the Morning* by Helen Nicholson (Baroness Zglinitski); Peter Davies Limited. *The Face of Spain* by Gerald Brenan; Hamish Hamilton Limited (originally published by Turnstile Press Limited). *The Spanish Labyrinth* by Gerald Brenan; Cambridge University Press. *Alfonso the Sage and Other Spanish Essays* by J. B. Trend; Constable & Company Limited.

PENGUIN BOOKS

THE ASSASSINATION OF FEDERICO GARCÍA LORCA

Ian Gibson was born in Dublin, Ireland, in 1939 and attended Newtown School, Waterford. He read Spanish and French at Trinity College, Dublin, graduating in 1961 with first-class honors. From 1962 to 1968 he was Lecturer in Spanish at the Queen's University of Belfast, and then he was Lecturer in Spanish at London University. He was awarded the Prix International de la Presse at the Nice Book Festival in 1972 for the Spanish-language edition of *The Death of Lorca,* published in Paris in 1971 and at that time banned in Spain. He has contributed articles to several scholarly journals. Married, with two children, Ian Gibson now lives in Spain.

For Gerald Brenan,
without whose example this book
might never have been written

CONTENTS

Acknowledgements to the First Edition   8

Introduction to the First Edition   9

Introduction and Acknowledgements to this Edition   11

1. Granada and Federico   13
2. The Republic   26
3. Granada Before the Terror   36
4. Lorca and the Popular Front   51
5. Ramón Ruiz Alonso   61
6. The Fall of Granada   67
7. The Repression   90
8. Granada Cemetery   104
9. Lorca at the Huerta de San Vicente   112
10. Lorca with the Rosales   125
11. Lorca in the Civil Government Building   135
12. Death at Dawn: Fuente Grande   155
13. Why Did They Kill Lorca?   168
14. Lorca's Assassination: Press and Propaganda from 1936 until the Death of Franco   183

Afterword to the Penguin Edition   211

Appendices

A. A complete list of town councillors holding office in Granada between February and July 1936 and of those executed   216
B. The Origins of a Rumour: Federico García Lorca and the Spanish Civil Guard   218
C. 'Jean-Louis Schonberg' and his 'Homosexual Jealousy' Thesis Concerning Lorca's Death   224
D. Further References by Arab Authors to Ainadamar   230
E. An Anonymous Ballad on the Death of García Lorca   233

Notes   235
Selected Bibliography   250
Index   264

Photographs appear after page 134.

ACKNOWLEDGEMENTS TO THE
FIRST EDITION

This book could not have been written without the help of many people. To begin with I must thank my parents, Mr and Mrs Cecil Gibson of Dublin, whose generosity enabled me to spend a full year in Granada. Thanks are also due to the Queen's University of Belfast, which gave me a grant to return to Spain in 1967 to complete my research. Throughout the book I draw on the work of Gerald Brenan, Claude Couffon and Jean-Louis Schonberg, and am happy to acknowledge this debt here. My friend Mr Daniel de W. Rogers of Durham University made valuable, chastening criticisms of an early draft of the book, and Mr Herbert R. Southworth kindly put at my disposal his vast knowledge of the Spanish Civil War and suggested numerous improvements. Regrettably I cannot name the many people in Granada who gave me help and encouragement: to do so might be to jeopardise their safety. Three Granadine friends whose contribution to the book was fundamental have recently died, however, and I remember them here with deep affection and gratitude: Don Miguel Cerón, Don Antonio Pérez Funes and Don Rafael Jofré García. Among the many other friends and acquaintances whose assistance made my task easier it is a pleasure to thank Mme Marcelle Auclair, Dr James Dickie, Mr Bernard Adams, Dott. Enzo Cobelli, Don Manuel Angeles Ortiz, Don Rafael Martínez Nadal, M. Robert Marrast, M. Paul Werrie, Dr James Casey, Mr and Mrs S. C. B. Elliott, Mlle Marie Laffranque, Don José Luis Cano, Mr Patrick Teskey, Mr John Beattie, Dr Roger Walker, Miss S. M. Bull of the British Embassy in Mexico, Mr Leonard Downes, OBE, of the British Council in the same city, Dr Philip Silver, Dr E. Inman Fox, Professor and Mrs Sanford Shepard, Mr David Platt, Mr Jeffrey Simmons, Mr Howard Greenfeld and Mr Adrian Shire. Mr Neville Rigg and Mr Bertie Graham did valiant work in preparing the photographs for publication, Miss Eileen Duncan kindly drew the plan and map, and my friend and colleague Professor Anthony Watson made many useful suggestions. Finally, how can I thank my wife, to whom this book is dedicated? Without her unfailing support the strain of the investigation might have proved too much.

INTRODUCTION
TO THE FIRST EDITION

In the summer of 1965 my wife and I settled down to live in Granada for a year. My intention was to write a doctoral thesis on the great Granadine poet Federico García Lorca, whose work had influenced me deeply as an undergraduate.

One evening that autumn we were invited to a party at a friend's house, during which Gerardo Rosales, a poet and painter who has since died, came up to me and exclaimed: 'You foreigners, you're all the same! You come here to find out about Federico's death, yet you don't know a damn thing about what really happened in Granada in 1936. Do you realise, for example, that there weren't even fifty Fascists in the town before the war broke out?' My embarrassment was intense, and I tried to explain that my interest lay in Lorca's poetry. But Gerardo insisted. I had come to investigate the poet's death, and that was that.

Over the following months similar situations arose until, one day, I decided to accept the inevitable. I would shelve the thesis and write the book that I was already assumed to be writing.

Before we arrived in Granada I had reached the conclusion that much remained to be said about Lorca's death. Several accounts of it had come to my attention, notably those by Gerald Brenan, Claude Couffon and Jean-Louis Schonberg, and I had been struck by the frequent inconsistencies and contradictions which a comparison of their narratives revealed. Clearly a serious reconsideration of the whole question was required.

Huge estimates for the number of *granadinos* executed by the Nationalists on the outbreak of the Civil War were constantly being suggested to me; other extraordinary claims were being put forward on all sides; dozens of versions describing how Lorca had died were circulating, and one wondered where to begin. I was convinced of only one thing: that Lorca's death would have to be studied in the general context of the repression, and not as an isolated event.

I was aware that my researches, to be successful, would have to be carried out on two levels. First, starting with the indispensable pieces by Brenan, Couffon and Schonberg, I would have to read every article, book, newspaper or other document that could throw light, however dim, on Lorca's death and the Granada repression. Accordingly I drew up as complete a preliminary bibliography as I could, and sent off for material that had appeared all over the world, often in the most inaccessible places. It was a slow business, but little by little photocopies, books and cuttings began to trickle in, leading me in turn to other publications whose existence I could not have suspected.

Secondly, I would have to track down those people who might be able to furnish me with first-hand accounts of the repression and Lorca's last days.

This, I well knew, would be more difficult, not only because of the Andalusians' vivid imaginations and gift for spontaneous elaborations of the truth, but also because I sensed that people were still afraid to talk openly with strangers about the war, and that the police were keeping a close eye on what was going on in the town.

Gradually some of these problems were overcome. Through a small group of friends who had known Lorca intimately, I met an increasing number of *granadinos* who had experienced the early months of the rising in their home town and could give me detailed, verifiable information on the period. Without a car it would have been impossible to follow up the clues that came out of these discussions: often, on being given a lead, I would drive to some village in the province in search of a vaguely remembered witness who might be willing to talk, only to discover that he or she had moved to Málaga, Madrid, South America – or the local cemetery. On other occasions I was luckier.

My investigation is introduced by an account of the political situation obtaining in Spain in the years that led up to the Civil War, for I believe that without this background knowledge the reader unacquainted with the period would be at a loss to understand fully what happened in Granada in 1936.

I have taken the opportunity here to correct the many deficiencies of the original Spanish-language edition of my book,* and have incorporated a considerable amount of new information which has come to light since 1971.

Ian Gibson
London
1973

* Ian Gibson, *La represión nacionalista de Granada en 1936 y la muerte de Federico García Lorca* (Paris, Ruedo ibérico, 1971).

INTRODUCTION AND ACKNOWLEDGEMENTS
TO THIS EDITION

Seven years have passed since the publication, in Paris, of the Spanish edition of my book on Lorca's death, and five since its appearance in England (*The Death of Lorca*). With the momentous changes that have taken place in Spain, especially since the demise of Franco in November 1975, a great deal of fresh information has inevitably become available on the Nationalist repression and its victims. Lorca is no exception, and interest in the poet, far from flagging, has grown apace and there have been many new books and articles on his work, his life – and his death.

Between 1971 and 1975 I received dozens of letters from Spain in connection with my book (which was banned in that country on publication), and several of these contained important new details about Lorca's death and the Granada repression, or suggested clues that could be followed up. All these letters I filed carefully, hoping that some day I might be able to use them. When, after Franco's death, I returned to Spain, I found that the country had changed almost beyond recognition and that people were talking quite openly about their experiences during the war. Again, more information about Lorca's death came my way, and I met several people who were only too happy to recount their first-hand experiences of wartime Granada. It was clear to me that, sooner or later, my book would need to be thoroughly revised, and I am grateful that W. H. Allen have now given me that opportunity.

Many people have helped me in one way or another with this new edition, and since it would be impossible for me to assess the relative importance of their varied and various contributions, I hope that they will forgive me if I do not particularise these. I must make an exception in the case of my wife Carole, however: she has been as supportive as ever (or more so, if that is possible), and continues to be my most constructive critic. To her and to all the following friends and acquaintances (and to those whom no doubt I have overlooked) my sincere thanks: Andrew Anderson, Cayetano Aníbal, André Belamich, José Bergamín, Josefina Cedillo, Isabel and Eduardo Carretero, José Castilla Gonzalo, Tica and Antonio de Casas, Nigel Dennis, Daniel Eisenberg, José Fernández Castro, José Luis Franco Grande, Manuel

Fernández-Montesinos García, Antonio, Nieves and María Galindo Monge, Isabel García Lorca, Clotilde García Picossi, Mario Hernández, Marie Laffranque, José Landeira Yrago, José G. Ladrón de Guevara, Antonio Márquez Villegas, Eutimio and Monique Martín, Manuel Marín Forero, William Ober, Alfredo Rodríguez Orgaz, Esperanza Rosales, José Rosales (RIP), Luis Rosales, Laura de los Ríos de García Lorca, José Rodríguez Contreras, Herbert Southworth, Daniel Sueiro, César Torres Martínez.

Ian Gibson
Madrid
December 1978

ONE

Granada and Federico

'Give him alms, woman, for nothing in
life can equal the agony of being
blind in Granada.'

F. A. DE ICAZA

Westwards from the historic Andalusian town of Granada there
stretches a fertile plain, the *vega*,* which is nourished by the rivers
Darro and Genil that descend from the snows of the Sierra
Nevada, the highest mountain range in the peninsula. The *vega*
is one of the most intensively cultivated regions in Spain, and
was described long ago by an Arab author as being 'superior in
extent and fertility to the Ghauttah, or the valley of Damascus'.[1]

With the fall of Granada to Ferdinand and Isabella in 1492
and the expulsion of the Moors from this last Islamic enclave
in Spain, the agriculture of the plain declined and it was only
at the end of the nineteenth century, with the discovery that
sugar-beet could be grown there easily and profitably, that its
exploitation began again in earnest.

Among the tracts of land in the *vega* that benefited most from
the new activity was the Soto de Roma, a huge estate along the
banks of the Genil which had been granted by the Spanish
government to the Duke of Wellington in recognition of his services in driving the French from the country. Throughout the
nineteenth century the Soto, which the Duke himself never
deigned to visit, had lain abandoned and untilled, but now it suddenly revived as its English administrators became aware of its
economic potential. Villages started to spring up all over the
estate, and after a few years it held a population of several thousand people.

* *Vega*, a watered valley between hills.

In one of these villages, Fuente Vaqueros, Federico García Lorca was born on 5 June 1898. In that same year there took place the 'Disaster' in which Spain was deprived of her last overseas colonies – Cuba, Puerto Rico and the Philippines – in a humiliatingly brief and decisive encounter with the United States Navy.

Lorca's grandparents were all natives of the province of Granada and his father, Federico García Rodríguez, a successful farmer, was one of a family of eight or nine children who grew up in the *vega* and were deeply influenced by its way of life. The poet's paternal grandfather, Enrique García Rodríguez, and his three brothers, were renowned for their artistic improvisations, pranks and somewhat extravagant personalities. Enrique is reputed to have composed a sonnet in which he warned the reader against bad translations of Victor Hugo, whom he idolised; Federico played the guitar and died in obscure circumstances in Paris; Narciso drew well and travelled among the villages of the plain teaching the peasants to read; while Baldomero, the most original character of the four brothers, had a superb voice and sang *jaberas*, accompanying himself on the *bandurria*, better than anyone in the province.* It was small wonder that the young Federico adored his 'Uncle' Baldomero and wanted to resemble him.

Of the poet's numerous aunts and uncles on his father's side, only Luis, who attended a seminary, received a college education. The Garcías were all 'naturals' and their musical and artistic abilities, which Federico inherited, derived not from formal instruction but from their assimilation of the rich traditions and rhythms of the *vega*. Before he was four Federico knew dozens of folk songs by heart (many of them would later reappear, transformed, in his poetry and plays) and had been given his first guitar lessons by his Aunt Isabel.

Unlike the ebullient Garcías, Lorca's mother, Vicenta Lorca Romero, was quiet and serious. She was born in Granada in 1870[2]

* *Jabera*, a flamenco song similar to a *malagueña*. The *bandurria* (from which the English 'bandore' derives) is a form of lute.

and had been a teacher before becoming Don Federico's second wife in 1897. Lorca was very fond of his mother, and later claimed that he inherited his intelligence from her and his passionate temperament from his father.*

The human and natural environment of these early years made an indelible impression on the future poet's sensibility. Later he would say:

I love the countryside. I feel myself linked to it in all my emotions. My oldest childhood memories have the flavour of the earth. The meadows, the fields, have done wonders for me. The wild animals of the countryside, the livestock, the people living on the land, all these are suggestive in a way that very few people understand. I recall them now exactly as I knew them in my childhood. Were this not so I could never have written *Blood Wedding* [....] My very earliest emotional experiences are associated with the land and the work on the land. This is why there is at the basis of my life what psycho-analysts would call an 'agrarian complex'.[3]

And again:

My whole childhood was centred on the village. Shepherds, fields, sky, solitude. Total simplicity. I'm often surprised when people think that the things in my work are daring improvisations of my own, a poet's audacities. Not at all. They're authentic details, and seem strange to a lot of people because it's not often that we approach life in such a simple, straightforward fashion: looking and listening. Such an easy thing, isn't it? [...] I have a huge storehouse of childhood recollections in which I can hear the people speaking. This is poetic memory, and I trust it implicitly.[4]

Unlike J. M. Synge, whose appropriation of the folk language of the west of Ireland was the result of conscious study, Federico was himself 'of the people', for in the *vega* no linguistic and few social distinctions separated wealthy and poor, peasants and

* In Spanish surnames the father's name is followed by that of the mother. Often the mother's name is dropped, but if the patronym is more common than the mother's name, as is the case with Federico García Lorca, the tendency is to use the latter.

landowners. Lorca inherited all the vigour of a speech that springs from the earth and expresses itself with extraordinary spontaneity. One has only to hear the inhabitants of the Granadine *vega* talk, and observe their colourful use of imagery, to realise that the metaphorical language of Lorca's drama and poetry, which seems so strikingly original, is rooted in an ancient, collective awareness of nature in which all things – trees, mountains, horses, the moon, rivers, flowers, human beings – are closely interrelated and interdependent. The landscape of much of Lorca's work is anthropomorphic and participates in the human action: the moon may suddenly materialise before a frightened child's eyes as a deathlike woman dressed in white, the leaves of an olive tree turn pale with fear, or the first light of morning become a thousand glass tambourines which 'wound' the dawn. It is a world of strange metamorphoses, a mythical world where mysterious voices whisper in the night, the world of the first kiss and 'the first dead bird on the branch'.[5]

In 1909 Lorca's family moved from the village to Granada to see to the children's education. This was to be the second crucial stage in the poet's development when his experience of the town, with its dense historical and literary associations, fused with the childhood vision of the world he had assimilated in the *vega* to form a unique synthesis of culture of the blood and culture of the intellect.

Although by 1909 the entrepreneurs were already at work in Granada, demolishing Moorish buildings, widening streets and generally trying to make the 'living ruin', as Baedeker had called it a few years earlier,[6] more modern and more 'European', the old quarters crowding the Albaicín and Alhambra Hills had changed little since the early nineteenth century, when Granada had caught the imagination of the Romantics, avidly in search of the exotic.

In 1829 Victor Hugo had exclaimed:

L'Alhambra! L'Alhambra! palais que les Génies
Ont doré comme un rêve et rempli d'harmonies,

Forteresse aux créneaux festonnés et croulants,
Où l'on entend la nuit de magniques syllabes,
Quand la lune, à travers les mille arceaux arabes,
Sème les murs de trèfles blancs![7]

and shortly afterwards Washington Irving settled down to live in the town. His *Legends of the Alhambra* (1832), much read at the time, was to establish the Moorish palace as one of the most admired monuments in Europe. Irving was followed by scores of other writers and aristocratic visitors, many of whom felt compelled to record their impressions in print. Among these were Henry Inglis, Richard Ford (whose famous *Handbook for Travellers in Spain* remains one of the best books on the country ever written), Dumas *père*, George Borrow, Théophile Gautier and Prosper Mérimée. The Alhambra's attractions were widely advertised in the exquisite engravings by Gustave Doré and David Roberts, and poems evoking Granada's Moorish past (with a proliferation of Lindaraxas, Zaydas, Aixas, sultans and weeping fountains) also became fashionable.

Nor did the town escape the attentions of foreign musicians. During the winter of 1845 Glinka spent several months in Granada. He struck up a friendship with a celebrated local guitarist, Francisco Rodríguez Murciano, who took the Russian to the Albaicín and introduced him to the *cante jondo* of the gypsies – the primitive form of the modern *flamenco*. Glinka, fascinated by the possibilities for his own work afforded by Spanish folk music, began the experiments that led to his *Jota aragonesa* (1845) and *Summer Night in Madrid* (1848), which in turn sparked off both a new interest in folk song in Russia and a spate of Spanish-inspired pieces by foreign and national composers. As Lorca said in a lecture during the Cante Jondo Festival which he and Manuel de Falla organised in Granada in 1922:

And so you see how the sad modulations and grave orientalism of our *cante* are imparted by Granada to Moscow, and how the melancholy of the Vela* is echoed by the mysterious bells of the Kremlin.[8]

But only the delicate impressionism of Claude Debussy, who had heard a group of Spaniards sing *cante jondo* at the Paris Exhibition in 1900, was adequate to transform the idiom into something genuinely original and subtle. However successful his orchestral *Iberia*, it is in his evocative piano compositions *La Puerta del Vino* (the prelude was inspired by a picture postcard sent to him by Falla) and particularly *La Soirée dans Grenade* that Debussy most perfectly captured the hidden essence of Spanish music.

Hugo had noted, with a *frisson* of delight, that the walls of the Alhambra were crumbling, and Richard Ford tells us that the palace was allowed to fall into ruins after it had been occupied by the French under Sebastiani. He complains that

Few *Granadinos* ever go there or understand the all-absorbing interest, the concentrated devotion, which it incites in the stranger. Familiarity has bred in them the contempt with which the Bedouin regards the ruins of Palmyra, insensible to present beauty as to past poetry and romance.[9]

Sixty years later, when the Garcías moved to the town, the average *granadino*'s attitude to his artistic heritage had changed little.

In Granada Federico worked for the examination that would afford him entry to the University, where he eventually matriculated in 1915. But he disliked bookwork and his real passion was for music, which he studied with Don Antonio Segura, an old *maestro* who admired Verdi and had himself written an opera, *The Daughters of Jephthah*, which was never produced. Don Antonio was a sensitive teacher and under his guidance Lorca

* The massive Vela Tower stands on the projecting prow of the Alhambra's fortifications and looks out over the plain. Its bell, known as 'La Vela', is rung at intervals during the night to regulate the *vega*'s complicated irrigation procedures.

became a first-rate pianist and wrote several compositions for the piano which do not, unfortunately, seem to have survived. Segura died in 1916, however, and Federico's parents decided against the musical career for which their son had seemed destined.

In the same year, and again in 1917, Lorca travelled through Castile, León and Galicia with Don Martín Domínguez Berrueta, Professor of the Theory of Art at Granada University, who encouraged him to write his first book, *Impressions and Landscapes* (Granada, 1918). This work expressed in poetic prose the author's reactions to the decaying towns, monasteries and rolling *meseta* of Old Spain. There can be little doubt that Don Martín, who died in 1920, exerted a decisive influence on his pupil by coaxing his talents into a literary channel.

The atmosphere in Granada at the time, moreover, greatly favoured the development of artistic abilities, and the town was enjoying exceptional conditions that would never be repeated. Its pattern of existence remained undisturbed by a world war that, so far as it was concerned, was being fought only on the front pages of the local newspapers; living was still cheap; there were no transistor radios, no coaches full of tourists grinding up the Cuesta de Gomeres and choking the elms of the Alhambra Wood with poisonous fumes. There was time to talk, to read, to listen to the murmuring of Granada's innumerable fountains, to contemplate the most consistently marvellous sunsets in Spain. Indeed, contemplation of beauty – what Joyce once called 'the luminous, silent stasis of aesthetic pleasure' – is the attitude of mind most readily engendered by Granada. Lorca, who perceived this better than anyone, would say:

Granada is an easy-going town, made for the contemplative life, a town in which, better than anywhere else, the lover writes his sweetheart's name on the ground. The hours are longer and sweeter there than in any other Spanish town. Granada has complicated sunsets composed of extraordinary colours which you feel will never fade [...] Granada has any amount of good ideas but is incapable of acting on them. Only in such a town, with its inertia and tranquillity, can there exist those exquisite contemplators of water, temperatures and sunsets that we find in Granada. The *granadino* is surrounded by Nature's most lavish display, but he never reaches out to it.[10]

Without the added stimulus of contact with kindred spirits, Lorca's adolescence in this contemplative paradise might have been less productive, but fortunately there was in Granada at the time a group of people passionately devoted to the arts.

Chief among them was Manuel de Falla, who had fallen in love with the gardens, perspectives and fountains of Granada in 1916 and come to live here permanently three years later in a modest *carmen** just below the Alhambra.

There was Fernando de los Ríos, Professor of Political Law in the University of Granada, a great teacher, socialist, scholar and humanist, who exerted a profound influence on his students, and whose daughter, Laura, later married Lorca's brother.

Other able university teachers in the town included Martín Domínguez Berrueta (with whom Federico made his trips to Castile), the historian José Palanco Romero, and Alfonso Gámir Sandoval, an anglophile who was a close friend of the British Consul, William Davenhill.†

There were the painters Manuel Angeles Ortiz and Ismael G. de la Serna, the art historian Antonio Gallego Burín (whose *Guide to Granada* is still one of the most useful), the sculptor Juan Cristóbal, Constantino Ruiz Carnero, who became editor of the liberal daily newspaper *El Defensor de Granada*, the poets Alberto A. de Cienfuegos and Manuel de Góngora, Angel Barrios the guitarist and founder of the well-known Trio Iberia, Andrés Segovia (who had come to Granada from his native Jaén), the literary critic José Fernández Montesinos, who died not long ago

---

* The word *carmen*, from the Arabic, denotes a hillside villa with an enclosed garden hidden by high walls from inquisitive eyes, and corresponds to the Islamic notion of the inner paradise, a reflection of heaven.
† In *South from Granada* (London, Hamish Hamilton, 1957), Gerald Brenan has given us a delightful account of the eccentric English colony in Granada in the early 1920s.

in the United States after a distinguished academic career, the engraver Hermenegildo Lanz, the brilliant aesthete Francisco Soriano Lapresa, the cultured dilettante Miguel Cerón (one of Falla's most intimate friends in Granada), the belligerent journalist José Mora Guarnido, who later wrote a vivid account of these days in his book on Lorca,[11] Miguel Pizarro and many other original and often weird figures.

The younger members of this talented group met regularly in the Café Alameda (now a farm machinery store) in the Plaza del Campillo and their *tertulia** became affectionately known as the *rinconcillo* ('little corner') because a recess at the back of the café was reserved for their use each evening. When visiting lecturers and artists arrived in Granada, the 'rinconcollistas' would take them to the Café Alameda before showing them the Alhambra, or initiating them into the delights of Granada's hidden gardens, which so few tourists ever see. Among these privileged guests were Wanda Landowska, Arthur Rubinstein, H. G. Wells, Rudyard Kipling and John Trend.

Trend, who was to become Professor of Spanish at Cambridge, met the Café Alameda confraternity in 1919 and afterwards described his introduction to Lorca. He had gone that evening with Falla to a concert at the Arts Centre, after which they were invited to a party in an Albaicín *carmen*. Late in the night a local poet was called on to recite and, to the general amusement of the guests, forgot his lines and withdrew in confusion.

Then we were hushed and a rather shy youth recited. He did not declaim, but spoke in a soft, warm, eager voice: *la obscura, cálida, turbia, inolvidable voz de Federico García Lorca*, Gerardo Diego said long afterwards. It was a simple ballad with striking but easily intelligible imagery. 'Who is it?' 'Federico García Lorca. You must meet him.' The evening ended after 4 a.m., with the poet and myself, arm in arm, helping one another down the steep streets of the Albaicín to the main street at the bottom of the Alhambra Hill.[12]

* A *tertulia* is a regular meeting of friends in a café, and an indispensable part of Spanish life.

Although Trend realised that Granada was passing through a unique period in its artistic history, he never stayed long enough in the town to form a close relationship with the 'rinconcillistas', and may not have met a member of the group who had a significant influence on Lorca: Francisco ('Paquito') Soriano.

Soriano, as has been indicated, was an aesthete, a sort of Granadine Oscar Wilde who enjoyed private means and took pleasure in offending the town's rigid Catholics by his flamboyance and easy morals. He was undoubtedly one of the cleverest men in Granada at the time, and his house in Puentezuelas Street contained a magnificent library of books on a wide variety of esoteric subjects and in many languages, which he lent generously to Lorca and the other members of the *tertulia* in the Café Alameda. Federico and Soriano became intimate friends, and the latter was one of the few people in the town to whom the young poet confided his problems.

Whatever the precise nature of these problems, there can be no doubt that Lorca's early poetry reveals a deep sexual malaise, a feeling of being rejected and isolated, nor that his work in general is concerned with the theme of frustration in one form or another. In Granada the poet was considered to be a homosexual, and this was a particular disaster in a town noted for its aversion towards unconventional sexuality. Many people, when they realised that Lorca was not 'normal' according to the canons of standard Spanish sexuality, became uneasy and distanced themselves from the poet. Miguel Cerón, who had been one of Lorca's closest friends, declared in 1971, shortly before his death:

Round about 1920 or 1921 Federico used to come to my flat every evening when he was in Granada, and we would spend hours talking and reading together. That was when I read *Riders to the Sea* to him, translating from the English. But when I realised that people were beginning to talk, I started to get uneasy. You know, it was awkward, I didn't want people to think that I was queer![13]

Spanish males are obsessed by stereotyped concepts of virility,

and homosexuals are universally treated with disdain. The uneasiness about which Miguel Cerón spoke with such honesty
could have become loathing and hatred in a less enlightened
Spaniard, and it is a fact that when the Civil War began in 1936
many people were persecuted as much for sexual as for political
reasons. Lorca was acutely aware of being *different*, and it seems
likely that his own sense of rejection lay behind his interpretation
of the personality of Granada and his identification with the
sufferings of the Moors and Jews who were persecuted by the
Christians when the town fell. As he put it once:

I believe that being from Granada gives me a sympathetic understand-
ing of those who are persecuted – of the gypsy, the negro, the Jew,
of the Moor which all *granadinos* carry inside them.[14]

Lorca felt that Granada, despite its beauty and Romantic aura,
was a town that had lost its soul in 1492, and he looked upon
the philistine descendants of the Castilian conquerors with distaste.

Soon after the meeting between Trend and Lorca the poet
moved to Madrid, where for ten years he lived at the famous
Residencia de Estudiantes, familiarly known as the 'Resi', the
nearest approximation in Spain to an Oxbridge college. In the
capital he published his first collection of poems, *Libro de poemas*
(1921), and became involved in the ferment of ideas, movements
and 'isms' which characterised Madrid at this time. Gradually
his fame spread and his *Gypsy Ballads* (1928) became the most
widely read book of poems to appear in Spain since the publication of Gustavo Adolfo Bécquer's *Rimas* in 1871. In 1921 he
accompanied Fernando de los Ríos to New York, where he spent
nine months before returning to Spain via Cuba in the summer
of 1930. *The Poet in New York*, arguably his greatest book of
poems, appeared in 1940, four years after his death.

On the advent of the Republic in 1931, the Ministry of Education appointed Lorca director of a travelling theatre company,
La Barraca, which under his inspiration performed Spanish plays

in the squares and market places of villages up and down the country. To this task Federico wholeheartedly devoted his talents and energies, and his experience with La Barraca convinced him of the educational potential of the theatre in Spain.

From October 1933 to March 1934 the poet was in South America where his play *Blood Wedding* achieved a triumphant success in Buenos Aires.

By 1934 Lorca was the most famous living Spanish poet and dramatist but, despite his celebrity, he always remained essentially *granadino* at heart. When his play *Mariana Pineda* opened in the town in 1929 he had declared:

If by the grace of God I become famous, half of that fame will belong to Granada, which formed me and made me what I am: a poet from birth and unable to help it.[15]

Granada had made him, it was true, but Lorca never subjected his work to the dictates of that facile local colour with which Granadine artists all too readily fill out their canvases. While the poets Manuel de Góngora and Alberto A. de Cienfuegos, for example, were content to express until well into this century an outmoded Romantic concern with a pseudo-oriental Granada, Federico probed deeper and perceived in the beautiful but narrowly provincial town a tragic sense of life, an anguish which belies the superficial appearances. And just as Joyce had felt the need to escape from a small, claustrophobic Dublin in 1902 before being able to create a meaningful art out of his experience there, so Lorca had to abandon Granada and its *vega*. As he said when launching the vanguardist review *Gallo* in 1928:

We must love Granada, but in a European context. Only in this way will we be able to discover our best hidden and most splendid treasures. A Granadine review for the world outside, a review sensitive to what is going on in the world in order better to understand what's going on here. A vital, lively, anti-local and anti-provincial review, belonging to the whole world, as Granada does.[16]

Although the poet often returned to Granada during the summer months to escape from the heat of Madrid, he increasingly found the town's inhabitants apathetic and reactionary, and his visits became more sporadic when his parents moved to the capital soon after the inauguration of the Republic in 1931.

It is to the Republic and the poet's activities during these troubled years that we must now turn our attention.

TWO

The Republic

On 12 April 1931 municipal elections were held throughout Spain. The results showed that the larger cities, including Granada, were overwhelmingly anti-Monarchist and pro-Republican, and two days later King Alfonso XIII left the country. From 1923 to 1930 Spain had been labouring under the yoke of an authoritarian regime imposed by the genial, erratic and philandering General Primo de Rivera, and now she wanted a change.

As is well known, the five years of the Republic's short life were marked by a turbulence in which the hatreds, passions, contradictions, hopes and fears that had been dividing Spaniards for generations came inexorably to a head and exploded in a fratricidal war that killed about 600,000 people.

The parliaments of the Republic spanned three well-defined periods. From June 1931 to November 1933 the Constituent Cortes had a strongly Republican government headed by Manuel Azaña. Then from November 1933 to January 1936 power swung to a right-wing coalition government; this period is often referred to as the 'black biennium'. Finally, from February 1936 to July 1936, when the Civil War broke out, the country was run by the Popular Front.

To understand why a Republican government that had come to power on a surge of popular enthusiasm in 1931 found itself out of office two years later, it is important to realise to what extent Spanish politics have consistently been polarised between the 'traditionalists' on the one hand and the 'progressives' on the other.

Spanish traditionalists identify Spain with the Catholic Church: Spain has been chosen by God as the torchbearer of the Faith and the guardian of Christian values in a hostile world, and virtue lies in remaining faithful to the spirit of Ferdinand and Isabella, the 'Catholic Monarchs' who unified Castile and Aragon, defeated the Moors of Granada, expelled the Jews, promoted the discovery, colonisation and conversion of the New World and imposed state Catholicism. The intensely nationalistic traditionalists have never made any secret of their distaste for the processes of democracy and have consistently supported authoritarian governments. For them to be a 'liberal' is to be an enemy of the true Spain, and as recently as 1927 the following exchange appeared in a catechism published by the Spanish Church:

What sin is committed by him who votes for a liberal candidate? Generally a mortal sin.[1]

This narrow traditionalism is found only in the ruling, propertied class, which has a vested interest in maintaining an autocratic system. It is not, certainly, an attitude of mind that was held by the majority of Spanish Catholics in the nineteenth century, a large proportion of whom were illiterate peasants and labourers. Indeed, as a result of the Church's lack of concern for social problems and of its political rigidity, attendance at mass had started to decline during the latter half of the century, and by 1931 it appears that, for example, only about 5 per cent of the villagers of New Castile carried out their Easter duties, while in Andalusia male attendance was down to 1 per cent.[2] In the cities the position was even worse.

Thus the Church and the comfortably-off minority, which together controlled the bulk of the country's resources, constituted a relatively small numerical group.

During the nineteenth century the battle between the two factions had centred on the problem of education, the liberals wanting to free the schools and universities from clerical influence while the traditionalists insisted that all teaching must be controlled by the clergy. Each swing of the political pendulum brought with it new violence and disorder, and the party that acceded to power inevitably dismantled almost everything that had been done by the previous government. 'Spain', complained the journalist Larra in 1836, 'is like a new Penelope. She spends all her time weaving and unweaving.' The comparison was apt, and from Larra's day to the 1920s the fabric of Spanish political life had undergone little essential modification.

In 1931 the Republic inherited not only many problems that had been bedevilling Spanish life for centuries but a host of immediate difficulties. The economy was in a disastrous condition after the seven years of General Primo de Rivera's rule, and the situation was exacerbated by the world slump; there was chronic unemployment; there was, particularly, the agrarian question, most urgently demanding the attention of the new government, which had promised to effect a more just land distribution; there was opposition from the Army and all the forces of the right[3]; there were bitter quarrels between the various left-wing parties; and, not least, there was the lack of political experience on the part of the liberal Republicans who had now to guide the country on a democratic course through the troubled waters of extremism on both the Left and the Right.

Azaña's government, in its eagerness to carry out sweeping reforms, antagonised the Right to a greater extent than it need have done. But even more instrumental than the Right's hatred in hastening the government's downfall was the stubborn refusal of the left-wing parties to compromise on their individual policies and form an electoral alliance that would enable them to benefit from the provisions of the 1932 Electoral Law. Since it was this law, enacted by the Azaña government, that regulated the 1933 election from which the Right emerged victorious, it will be worth our while to consider it here briefly.

Under the new law Spain was divided into sixty constituencies, corresponding to (1) each of her fifty provinces, (2) the eight cities which had a population in excess of 150,000 inhabitants (Madrid,

Barcelona, Málaga, Seville, Murcia, Valencia, Bilbao and Zara-
goza) and (3) her two sovereign cities in Morocco, Ceuta and
Melilla. Each constituency was to return one member for every
50,000 inhabitants resident within it (with the exception of Ceuta
and Melilla, which would return one each): thus Madrid would
return seventeen members while Granada (capital and province
together) would return only thirteen.

Voting was to be for lists of candidates, and the Electoral Law
established that, in each constituency, a fixed number of seats
would be allocated to both the winning candidature (the
mayoría, majority) and the losers (the *minoría*, minority). In
Madrid, thirteen out of the total of seventeen seats would go to
the majority and the remaining four would be distributed among
the minority; in Granada the majority would obtain ten seats,
the minority three; and so on.

The law also laid down that no candidature receiving less than
40 per cent of the total vote in any constituency could be elected
to the Cortes. In other words it encouraged the formation of
coalitions, the intention being to force political extremism of
all kinds to come to terms with more moderate opinion in the
interests of its own parliamentary viability. No small party
standing separately could hope to win an election under the new
law: only a sudden and massive increase in extremism among
voters, from either the Right or the Left, could propel a hither-
to minority grouping to power, and no such contingency was
envisaged.[4]

The resounding success of the Right in the 1933 election was
a direct result of its determination to benefit from the advantages
of the Electoral Law enacted by the Azaña government, and of
the Left's inability to do so.[5] The Right went to the country
in a coalition that united the leading conservative parties
throughout Spain, while the Left, torn by internal dissension,
failed to form a unified front. The result of the election, con-
sequently, gave the Right a large majority in the Cortes, a
majority increased by the law's provision that the winning side
would automatically receive a bonus of seats. In spite of this the

number of votes cast for the left-wing parties together totalled more than those polled in favour of the right-wing coalition. It was the failure of the left-wing parties to stand shoulder to shoulder that cost them the election.[6]

By far the largest of the right-wing groups to emerge from the 1933 election was the new middle-class Catholic party, the CEDA (Confederación Española de Derechas Autónomas). This was a coalition of several smaller Catholic organisations built around Acción Popular, a party founded in 1931, of which Gerald Brenan has written that it

represented the reaction of the Church and especially of the Jesuits to the Republic. It was a superficial imitation of the German Catholic party and was intended by its founders to be, not simply the party of the *caciques*,* the Army and the aristocracy, but of the Catholic masses as well. It accepted the Republic, but not the anti-Catholic laws, and the main part of its programme consisted in a demand for the revision of the Constitution.[7]

The mind behind Acción Popular was that of Angel Herrera Oria, a Madrid lawyer who edited *El Debate*, the most widely read Catholic daily newspaper in Spain. Herrera (who later entered the priesthood and became a cardinal in 1965) promoted as leader of Acción Popular a young lawyer working on the staff of *El Debate*, José María Gil Robles, who had been educated by the Salesians in Salamanca. A marriage was 'arranged' between Robles and the daughter of the Conde de Revillagigedo, one of the richest men in Spain, and the couple spent their honeymoon in Germany, where Robles found that he greatly admired Hitler. He disapproved of the Nazi persecution of the Church, however, and eventually decided that the best model for the new Spain was Dollfuss's corporate state in Austria.[8]

Although Gil Robles never became Prime Minister, he held

* The Indian word for the chieftains through whom the Spaniards ruled their American colonies. In Spain the word was applied to the provincial landowners whose position gave them political power over the peasants.

several important ministerial posts up to the election of February 1936 (from which he confidently expected to emerge as Premier of the next government), and exerted considerable influence on the course of events during the 'black biennium'. He was the classical Spanish traditionalist and the CEDA demonstrated all the perennial characteristics of the Right. It was financed by rich landowners and businessmen, and as a result was both unable and unwilling to embark on any programme of reform that might benefit the working classes, to which it was openly hostile. It was the party of stolid reaction, and increasingly attracted the allegiance of the Catholic middle class and moneyed groups throughout the country, who realised that the growing power of the proletariat was threatening their security.

Despite its success in the 1933 elections the CEDA failed to achieve an absolute majority in the new Cortes, the first government of which was extremely vicious in its dismantling of the legislation introduced by the Azaña administration and showed a determination to suppress the rights of the working classes in favour of the privileges of the Right. Larra's Penelope was still busily at work.[9]

On 1 October 1934 the Cabinet fell, deprived of the CEDA support which it had enjoyed for ten months. Gil Robles, the leader of the CEDA, now demanded his party's participation in the new Cabinet. The President of the Republic, Alcalá Zamora, distrusted Gil Robles but gave in under pressure, entrusting Alejandro Lerroux with the formation of a coalition government. When it was announced that the CEDA had been allotted the Ministries of Agriculture, Labour Relations and Justice – three particularly sensitive areas – the reaction on the part of the working class was immediate and hostile. For, as Gabriel Jackson has observed, CEDA participation in the government 'appeared both to the middle-class liberals and to the revolutionary Left as equivalent to fascism in Spain'.[10]

The rising of the Asturian miners, which broke out four days later, on 4 October 1934, was a direct reaction to the CEDA's elevation to government. The rising was put down with extreme brutality, although at the time rigid censorship prevented the facts from being widely known in Spain. García Lorca must have been fully aware of them, however, for his friend Fernando de los Ríos was a member of the team of MPs appointed to investigate what had happened.

The CEDA was in reality a pretty amorphous and soft-spined party, with no dynamic aims or decisive leadership, and one minority group on the Right rapidly lost patience with Gil Robles's ineffectiveness and began to look for a new approach. These men were attracted by the rise of Fascism in Italy and Germany and by the political activities of José Antonio Primo de Rivera, son of the dictator, who had founded the Falange Española (Spanish Phalanx) in 1932. In 1934 the Falange merged with another Fascist group, the JONS (Juntas de Ofensiva Nacional-Sindicalista), and the new party was named Falange Española de las JONS.

Up to the general election of February 1936 the Falange had only a small following and the Catholic middle class gave it very little support, infatuated as it was with the personality of Gil Robles. Moreover the Catholics were not yet prepared to give their allegiance to a semi-military organisation that openly preached violence. It was only after the defeat of the CEDA in the 1936 election that the Falange really became important, and we shall be looking at its development in Granada in the next chapter. For the moment it is sufficient to stress that the CEDA and the Falange, while positively disliking each other, were nonetheless the outward embodiment of an attitude of mind that varied only in its degree of intensity and in the lengths to which it was prepared to go in pursuit of its aims. Although the CEDA claimed to speak for Spanish Catholics, it was the Falange that adopted as its symbols the yoke and arrows that had been the device of Ferdinand and Isabella, the 'Catholic Monarchs'.

During the first two years of the Republic, Granada, whose fall to Ferdinand and Isabella in 1492 has always held particular significance for the traditionalists, witnessed frequent clashes between the rich landowners who controlled the sugar industry in the *vega* and the peasants, now strongly organised by the Socialist UGT. The former, seeing in the Republic a serious threat to their privileged position, quickly threw their support behind the local branch of Acción Popular, which had founded the Granada daily newspaper *Ideal* in 1931. *Ideal* became a vital factor in the political struggle now developing in the town, and in its columns were expressed all the most deeply entrenched attitudes of the Spanish Right. Meanwhile the left-wing *El Defensor de Granada*, launched in 1879, continued its struggle against what it considered to be the obscurantist forces that were afflicting the life of the province.

These forces were powerful enough to ensure that the right-wing coalition won the elections in Granada in 1933 and 1936. As we have seen, the thirteen Granada deputies were elected over the province as a whole, and while the Socialists were strong in the capital the Right was always successful in the rural areas of the province, where the landowners could bully the peasants into electoral submission. Thus in the 1933 election the Right had an easy victory even though the Socialists topped the poll in the capital.[11] Such a situation was intolerable to the Left.

Republican bitterness became intense when, following the Asturian insurrection of October 1934, the Socialist workers' clubs and Anarchist Syndicates were closed throughout the country and left-wing councillors deposed. In Granada the corporation that had been freely elected in April 1931 was sacked and its place taken a few days later by conservative councillors appointed by the 'authorities'. Many of the left-wing councillors were imprisoned, which explains the tremendous fervour with which the Republican council was reinstated after the victory of the Popular Front in February 1936.

On 21 December 1934, shortly after these turbulent events, *El Defensor de Granada* published an article entitled 'The poet García Lorca talks about the theatre and the artistic vocation'. This reproduced the most lively part of an interview given by Lorca some weeks earlier to the Madrid daily *El Sol*, in the course of which he clarified his attitude to the problems afflicting post-Asturias Spain:

I will always be on the side of those who have nothing, of those to whom even the peace of nothingness is denied. We – and by we I mean those of us who are intellectuals, educated in well-off middle-class families – are being called to make sacrifices. Let's accept the challenge.

Spoken only a few months after the massacre of the Asturian miners, at a time when the average income in Spain was pitifully low, the poet's words left little room for misunderstanding: he was for the poor against the rich, for the workers and peasants in their fight against oppressive and anti-democratic forces which were determined to maintain them in a position of economic subservience.

The Right did not miss the underlying attitudes revealed in Lorca's statement of solidarity with the ordinary people of Spain. When his rural tragedy *Yerma* was staged a week later in Madrid, the reactionary press refused without exception to acknowledge the author's talent and claimed that his work was immoral, anti-Catholic, irrelevant to Spain's problems and lacking in verisimilitude. During the opening moments of the première a group of noisy young men tried to disrupt the performance by shouting political slogans against Azaña and barracking the actors, but the angry audience quickly silenced them.[12]

Yerma was a triumph for the poet and on 30 December 1934 *El Defensor* announced with pride that the staging of the new play had met with 'fantastic success'. The newspaper described the events of the first night and ended by reaffirming its admiration and friendship for the Granadine poet who was bringing glory to the town.

García Lorca's name was by now firmly connected with liberalism in the broadest sense of the word, with Manuel Azaña and Fernando de los Ríos (who had become Minister of Education in the Azaña government) and, as far as Granada was concerned, with *El Defensor*. Over the next two years leading up to the elections of February 1936, when the Popular Front swept to power, other reports in the local press of the poet's actions and words made his passionately democratic sympathies widely known.

In the event of a right-wing revolution Lorca's love of Granada would be no guarantee of his safety in the town.

THREE

Granada Before the Terror

On Sunday, 16 February 1936, Spain went to the polls. In Granada, as elsewhere throughout the country, the day passed off quietly enough, although there was some momentary excitement in one of the polling stations when a right-wing supporter, piqued by the high spirits of the proletariat, smashed the urn in an access of electoral despair.[1] It was a different story in the rural areas of the province, however, and *El Defensor de Granada* gave detailed accounts of electoral outrages committed by the *caciques*. In the little village of Güevéjar, for example, many of the electors were forced at gunpoint to stay away from the polling station,[2] and similar events occurred in Motril, the Alpujarras and elsewhere in those districts where the population was dependent on the big landowners for its livelihood.[3]

The final results of the election gave the Popular Front a narrow majority, the figures usually accepted as the most reliable being:

Popular Front	4,700,000
National Front	3,997,000
Centre	449,000
Basque Nationalists	130,000[4]

In considering these figures it is important to remember that the distribution of seats in the Cortes, in accordance with the 1932 Electoral Law, did not correspond exactly to the proportion of votes cast and that the victorious side automatically acquired a much increased parliamentary representation. In fact the Popu-

lar Front obtained 267 seats in the new Cortes and the Right only
132; just as in November 1933 the Right had won a large majority
of seats in spite of the fact that less votes were cast for it than
for the Left.[5]

On 21 February both *El Defensor de Granada* and *Ideal*
published the final results of the voting in Granada (capital and
province). The Right had won a resounding victory. Infuriated
by this outcome, which they attributed to the bullying of the
caciques throughout the rural districts of the province, the left-
wing organisations decided to press for the annulment of the
Granada election when the new Cortes met in Madrid.

Resentment about the tactics used by the Right came to a head
on Sunday 8 March, when a protest meeting was held by the
Popular Front in Granada's Cármenes sports stadium. This was
attended, according to the *Defensor*'s probably exaggerated estimate, by 100,000 people. The meeting was addressed by such
well-known speakers as the Socialist Fernando de los Ríos, and
when it ended the vast crowd moved in a demonstration along
the town's main thoroughfares: the Avenue of the Republic (later
renamed Calvo Sotelo by the Nationalists), Gran Vía, Reyes
Católicos and the Puerta Real. They handed a protest note to
the Civil Governor, demanding that the government call new
elections in Granada, and then dispersed.[6]

It was the most gigantic left-wing demonstration that Granada
had ever seen, and it is not difficult to imagine the effect it must
have produced on the minds of the town's well-off Catholic bourgeoisie.

While the results of the parliamentary elections had not been
satisfactory for the Left in Granada, the Popular Front could have
little complaint with the state of its municipal affairs. On 20
February Torres Romero, the Civil Governor, had resigned as
an automatic consequence of the change of government,* and

---

* Each Spanish provincial capital had (and has) its Civil Governor and Civil
Government Building (I refer to the latter throughout as the 'Civil Government').
Before Franco's victory the Civil Governors were the official representatives of
the government in office and, as such, at the mercy of political change.

his place was taken by Aurelio Matilla García del Campo, a member of Martínez Barrio's Republican Union party.[7] Similarly the hated town council was forced to resign *in toto*, and was replaced by the Republican one pushed out of office in October 1934. These were the men originally elected on 12 April 1931 on the inauguration of the Republic, and their return now in February 1936 was greeted with jubilation by Republican supporters.

The short speech pronounced on the occasion of the opening session of the reinstated town council by Constantino Ruiz Carnero, the acting mayor and editor of the *Defensor*, expressed the elation of these moments:

Gentlemen of the Council. People of Granada. With no more authority than the fact that I hold this office in an interim capacity I want, first of all, to offer heartfelt greetings to Granada. Here we are again after the parenthesis into which we were forced. This is not a taking of office, it is a *re*taking of office, a renewal of functions. Republican legality has been restored with the triumph of the people. Sixteen months ago we councillors, who had been elected by the people of Granada, were arbitrarily stripped of our office, not for having squandered public money, but because we were Republican councillors, for which reason they threw us out, while at the same time affording us the repellent spectacle of a bunch of fake councillors playing around with the town's affairs.

At this time I only want to speak words of peace and restraint. I recommend restraint and serenity, because the Republic must stand for restraint and serenity.

At this solemn moment we say to the town that we are here to defend its interests, to occupy ourselves with its problems and to seek its aggrandisement.

And to the people of Granada we say that we return to this Chamber with more Republican fervour than ever and are ready at all times to defend the Republic.

People of Granada! Let us work together for Granada and for the Republic.[8]

But, given conditions in Granada, the idealism of Ruiz Carnero and his colleagues was to prove inadequate to deal with the realities of the situation. Conservative opinion was hardening and there were daily encounters between rival political factions.

Widespread violence flared up just two days after the mass meeting in the Cármenes stadium. The demonstration had enflamed not only left-wing passions, and on the Monday after the meeting various cases of right-wing provocation occurred in Granada. That evening a group of Falangist gunmen opened fire on a crowd of workers and their families gathered in the Plaza del Campillo, and several women and children were wounded. The trade unions decided there and then to hold an immediate twenty-four-hour strike.[9]

When the *Defensor* appeared next morning, Tuesday, 10 March 1936, by special permission of the strike committee, it carried a prominent notice addressed to the workers by the local heads of the CNT, UGT, the Syndicalist Party and the Communist Party, informing them of the reasons for the strike and expressing uncompromising demands for the dissolution of right-wing organisations and the dismissal from the armed services of all known 'subversive' elements. Such a strike was bound to lead to further exacerbation of the already dangerous situation, and in fact the day turned out to be one of unparalleled violence in Granada's recent history.

On 11 March the *Defensor* printed a detailed account of what took place. The first action of the workers was to burn down the premises of the Falange in the Cuesta del Progreso. This occurred at 9.30 in the morning. Half an hour later another group set fire to the Isabel la Católica theatre, which had played an outstanding role in Granada's cultural life for many years. At 10.15 the crowd wrecked the 'bourgeois' Café Colón, making a bonfire of its tables and chairs and then setting the building alight. Then another café, the Royal, went up in flames. When the police tried to intervene the crowd milled around and prevented them from being effective, and at this point right-wing elements took advantage of the disorder to fire on the demonstrators and the police from the surrounding rooftops and balconies. The *Defensor* states that both police and firemen were subjected throughout the day to non-stop aggression from anti-Republican gunmen, who were doubtless grateful for this opportunity for violence afforded them by the workers.

The next building to burn was the premises of the Catholic newspaper *Ideal*, so hated by the Popular Front in Granada. The printing presses were smashed to pieces, the place was soaked in petrol and, under the very eyes of the police, set on fire. The *Defensor*'s claim that the police were surrounded by women who 'prevented them from intervening' is hardly convincing and it seems that the Republican authorities may have given orders that the workers were not to be attacked.

Meanwhile other establishments were receiving the attentions of the crowd. The premises of Acción Popular were burning, as were those of Acción Obrerista (the Catholic Workers' Organisation). The chocolate factory owned by the local leader of Acción Popular, Francisco Rodríguez, had also been set alight, along with several shops owned by 'conservatives'. Even the tennis club (doubtless an offensive symbol for the workers) was wrecked. Faced with such destruction of its property, the middle class reacted with a hatred that would vent itself at the outbreak of the Nationalist rising, when the most brutal members of the assassination squads were often from well-off families.

To round off the day's work, two churches in the Albaicín were set on fire; the convent of San Gregorio el Bajo and the church of El Salvador, the latter being completely gutted. It is hard to be sure who was responsible for these two acts of destruction, and the intervention of *agents provocateurs* cannot be ruled out. The *Defensor* reported that fire brigades were prevented from reaching the blazing buildings in time by the ferocity of the gunfire directed against them as they tried to climb the steep, narrow streets of the Albaicín, and it may well be that hired gunmen were involved. It is easy to set a church on fire and such an act would be immediately ascribed to the 'Reds' by the Catholic middle class, whose fear of the Popular Front would be increased as a result. Indeed, the *Defensor* published a warning note the following day addressed to the workers by the Popular Front Committee, in which it was claimed that the parties of the Left had been infiltrated by *agents provocateurs* in the service of reaction', who were seeking to stir up hatred and violence in order to make matters increasingly difficult for the government. Certainly when the Nationalists gained control of Granada some months later many of the most vociferous Communists and Anarchists of the town suddenly appeared wearing their true colours: Falangist blue.

The events of 10 March made impossible any reconciliation between the Right and Left in Granada. As the ultra-reactionary Gollonet and Morales comment in their book:

The revolutionary strike of March made a profound impression on the town. For many days there was an extraordinary lack of animation in the streets. The only people circulating were the forces of law and order and groups of workers with instructions to harass anyone wearing a collar and tie. These were, apparently, the symbols of honour and probity and as such could not be tolerated by the shameless Marxists.[10]

Many arrests were made on and after 10 March, not so much in connection with the burning of the various premises as with the numerous shooting incidents which had occurred. More than 300 people were detained and numerous weapons were discovered in house-to-house searches.[11]

It may seem odd that there was no military intervention in the events of 10 March, so it will perhaps be useful at this point to consider the garrison and its relation to the political situation in Granada at the time.

One essential fact about the constitution and organisation of the Granada garrison must be grasped: Granada was not in 1936 a Captaincy-General (that is, the head of a military region) but a Military Commandery, whose Commander received his orders from the Captain-General in Seville. From this it follows that a military upheaval in Seville would cause automatic confusion in Granada, which is precisely what happened when the Nationalist rising began in July 1936.

The Granada garrison was made up of the Lepanto Infantry

Regiment (300 men) and the Fourth Light Artillery Regiment (180 men). To this should be added the 40 officers and men of the paramilitary Civil Guard. The *Historia de la cruzada española*,[12] which gives these figures, states that when the war started the garrison had at its disposal only 300 rifles, 2 mortars 'which had not even been tested', 72,000 cartridges and 4 artillery batteries which were almost without shells. The same source adds that 14,000 guns and rifles allegedly collected by the Assault Guards in the aftermath of the 10 March disturbances also became available to the Nationalists when the rising started.[13] The *Cruzada* forgets to mention that the garrison also had several machine-guns, which were used in the early hours of the rebellion with great effect.

If these factors are borne in mind it will be easier to understand not only the role of the garrison in subsequent events but also the whole course of the war in Granada.

How, then, did the military react to the 10 March disturbances? According to Gollonet and Morales, the Military Commander, General Elíseo Alvarez Arenas, highly indignant about what was happening, presented himself during the day in the Civil Government, where a meeting was in progress between the Governor and the strike committee. He stated that the garrison would intervene to re-establish order if the strike were not terminated at once. Gollonet and Morales believe that it was this act of defiance that brought about the General's speedy transfer to another command. He was replaced by General Llanos Medina, a man of conservative opinions who was 'ready to support, at the head of the Granada garrison, any attempt to save Spain'.[14] The Civil Governor himself was dismissed shortly afterwards, doubtless for his clumsy handling of the events of 10 March, and his place was taken on 21 March by a fellow member of the Republican Union party, Ernesto Vega, who was believed to be a particularly bitter enemy of the Right.[15]

Four days after the events of 10 March 1936 in Granada, the government banned the Falange and imprisoned most of its leaders, including José Antonio Primo de Rivera.

The Falange had been numerically unimportant up to the 1936 elections, and its violent tactics had alienated Catholic support. But the Popular Front victory in February terrified the Catholic middle class which, disillusioned by the CEDA's ineffectiveness, increasingly threw in its lot with the extremists. Accordingly, there was a considerable swelling of the Falangist ranks in these months and the party rapidly became the most efficient and ruthless right-wing organisation operating in Spain. As Herbert Rutledge Southworth has written:

Now was the great moment come for the Spanish Fascists. For the first time in Spain the conjuncture was favourable for Fascist development. The conservative elements were panic-stricken by the Popular Front victory, and had, in the course of forty-eight hours, lost their faith in the capacity of the political groups which had in the past defended their interests. Catholic youths who but a few days before had been screaming '*Jefe! Jefe! Jefe!*' at every appearance of Gil Robles, now abandoned in droves the catholic youth organisation, the JAP, and for the first time viewed with interest and wonder the fascist solution in the 'dialectic of fists and pistols', for their 'justice' and their 'Patria' had been insulted by the victory of the Left.[16]

Another historian of Spanish Fascism, Stanley Payne, quotes the local chief of the Falange in Seville, who recalled:

After the elections of February, I had absolute faith in the triumph of the Falange because we considered the Right, our most difficult enemy, ruined and eliminated. Its disaster constituted for us a fabulous advance and the inheritance of its best youth. Furthermore, we held the failure of the Popular Front to be an absolute certainty, because of its internal disorganisation and its frankly anti-national position, openly opposed to the feelings of a great mass of Spaniards. Our task consisted simply in widening our base of support among the working class.[17]

The Falange, in Granada as elsewhere, attracted its members almost entirely from the well-to-do middle class, who saw in the liberated proletariat a huge threat to their own security. Before the February elections the handful of Falangists in Granada had been the laughing-stock of the Left, and nobody took them seriously. Now the position had changed, and the Popular Front's victory in February, the post-election disturbances and the banning of the Falange on 14 March all helped to shift a considerable proportion of right-wing opinion firmly behind José Antonio Primo de Rivera's party.

Another important factor in this process was the annulment by the Cortes, on 31 March 1936, of the result of the February election in Granada. On 1 April *El Defensor de Granada* published full details of the previous day's debate in the Cortes which had led to the majority decision in favour of annulment, a debate in which Fernando de los Ríos had played a prominent part. The newspaper noted the furious reaction of the right-wing deputies (many of whom had stormed out of the Chamber before the vote was taken) and informed its readers that the new election would be held on 3 May 1936.

During April the National Front agreed on the composition of its list of candidates: four Falangists, five members of the CEDA and one 'Independent Nationalist'. By joining in this coalition the Granada CEDA now lost whatever scant respect it still commanded among serious-minded supporters of the Popular Front. Previously the CEDA had remained aloof from the Falange and its violent methods, preferring legally acceptable modes of procedure and protest. But things had changed and the party had shifted its ground. It was obvious to everyone that Catholic opinion in Granada was hardening fast.

As was to be expected, the National Front's electoral campaign met with constant interference. Its candidates received threats and were sometimes physically assaulted, and its propaganda was censored by the Republican authorities. According to Gil Robles, the CEDA leader (whose account of the Granada election is inadequately documented), the Civil Governor attempted to dissuade the National Front from contesting the election, claiming that their insistence on doing so would cause serious disturbances throughout the province.[18] Whether this was so or not, the fact remains that the National Front soon realised that the campaign was a waste of time and that success at the polls would be impossible. When the results of the election became known it was obvious that there had been a massive abstention on the part of conservative voters. The Popular Front won a resounding victory and not a single right-wing candidate was returned. Indeed, if the *Defensor*'s report is accurate, no National Front candidate polled more than 700 votes.[19] The *Cruzada*, whose information on the election is extremely tendentious, comments:

The last legal attempt at resistance in Granada had failed. The enemy wanted only war, war with all its consequences (p. 272).

But it would be a mistake to attribute the failure of the National Front in Granada solely to left-wing intimidation. The Popular Front was in power and it was natural that the election should favour the Left more than the Right, particularly in the rural areas, where the *caciques* could no longer bully the peasants into electoral submission without risking legal sanctions.

The *Defensor* failed to realise, in its satisfaction with the outcome of the new election, that the complete absence of right-wing representation in the Cortes (as well as on the town council) could only be damaging to Granada's best interests in these dangerous moments. Forced into the political wilderness, conservative discontent now began to express itself clandestinely and there is no doubt that some, at least, of the Granadine right-wing deputies who lost their seats in May became involved in active plotting against the Republic.

The political situation in Granada had now become very unstable and relations between the Civil Government and the garrison grew worse daily. It seems that the government, aware of the anti-Republican feelings of many of the officers, instructed Ernesto Vega to keep a close eye on their behaviour and movements. This interference led to strong resentment. A series of confrontations occurred between the civil and military authorities of the town, the outcome of which was the eventual dismissal of the Civil Governor, on 25 June 1936.

The new Civil Governor, César Torres Martínez, arrived the following day. Born in 1905, Torres was one of the youngest Civil Governors in Spain. Galician, lawyer, sincere Catholic, member of the Left Republican party and an intimate friend of the Prime Minister, Casares Quiroga, Torres had been Civil Governor of Jaén since April 1936. The day before his arrival in Granada, Casares Quiroga's secretary, Ossorio Tafall, had telephoned him from Madrid. 'César', he said, 'we're sending you to Granada. Vega's being transferred and there's a hell of a mess there which you'll have to clear up.'

On arrival in Granada, Torres Martínez discovered that it was true: the town *was* in a hell of a mess. In the first place, dissension was rife in the town council. For months the different left-wing groups had been arguing among themselves about whom to appoint mayor. A decision was only reached on 10 July 1936, when the socialist doctor, Manuel Fernández-Montesinos, husband of Concha García Lorca, the poet's sister, was elected. Fernández-Montesinos would only hold office for eight days: he was arrested in his office when the rising began and executed a few weeks later.

Given the lack of cohesion of the town council, Torres Martínez (who hardly knew anyone in Granada) had to struggle almost single-handed to resolve a double strike of binmen and tram operators which had been bedevilling the life of the town for weeks. He was successful. Then he intervened to prevent a recurrence of certain anti-clerical abuses which had been taking place in some parts of the province, where the priests had been prevented from ringing the church bells. Again the mild, persuasive methods of the new Civil Governor were effective. Soon the life of Granada returned to normality, or relative normality. Torres was to be Civil Governor of Granada for only twenty-five days, and he had little inkling of the plotting against the Republic that was taking place all about him. He was fortunate to escape execution when the war broke out. Torres is still alive, and later we shall hear his version of the events that took place in Granada on 20 July 1936.[20]

Ideal, which had reappeared on 1 July after three and a half months' enforced absence from the political scene in Granada, was scathing in its comments on the current situation. Within the limits imposed on it by the censor, the newspaper made its political aspirations quite clear. 'We have not returned too late to join the ranks of those who have undertaken the noble task of freeing the country from its present disorder,' its editorial exclaimed. 'There is still time for us to unite with those who are fighting to preserve Spain's traditionalist principles, and to return to a system which will enable the Holy Spirit to dominate the social hierarchy.'

Ideal well knew that by this time the conspiracy to overthrow the Republic was in an advanced state of preparation. What role did the Granada Falange play in that conspiracy?

With Primo de Rivera in gaol it had become more difficult for the Falange to maintain contact with the party's central organisation. Towards the end of April 1936, however, José Díaz Pla and José Rosales Camacho managed to visit their leader in the Model Prison in Madrid and received instructions from him which they took back to their comrades. Primo de Rivera promised to send a delegate to help with plans, and at the end of May the architect José Luis de Arrese arrived in Granada, where the following Falange appointments were made:

Provincial Chief	Dr Antonio Robles Jiménez
Chief of Militia	José Valdés Guzmán
Provincial Secretary	Luis Gerardo Afán de Ribera
Provincial Treasurer	Antonio Rosales Camacho
Local Chief	José Díaz Pla
Local Secretary	Julio Alguacil González

Arrese returned to Granada on 25 June to make definitive arrangements for the Falange's role in the military rising that was shortly to take place. The town was divided into three sectors, each of which was to be controlled by a squadron of Falangists under the command, respectively, of Enrique de Iturriaga, Cecilio Cirre and José Rosales Camacho.

The *Cruzada*, from which these details are taken, asserts that in Granada the Falange now had 575 members.[21] Presumably this figure refers to the province as a whole, for in the capital itself the party is unlikely to have had 300 members before the war began.

Of the Falangist officers listed above, special attention should be drawn to José Valdés Guzmán, for it was he who became Civil Governor of Granada on the outbreak of the Nationalist rising on 20 July. Valdés was born in 1891 in the town of Logroño in northern Spain. His father was a General in the Civil Guard and the son inherited his military interests. Valdés joined the Army and fought in the Moroccan war during the years 1918–23. Having sustained serious injuries during an offensive, he was forced to spend seven months recuperating in a Seville hospital. He underwent an operation for a duodenal ulcer in 1929 and seems to have been unwell for the rest of his life (he died later of tuberculosis or cancer of the intestine). On the inauguration of the Republic in 1931, Valdés was sent to Granada in the capacity of War Commissioner (*Comisario de guerra*), a position he held until the outbreak of the rising.[22] The fact that Valdés was an 'old shirt' member of the Falange* as well as an army officer explains the influence he exerted during the preparations for the rising and the position he assumed once it began. While military commanders and civil governors had come and gone regularly since 1931, Valdés had retained his post, and thus by 1936 must have had his finger on the political pulse of all his fellow officers in the Granada garrison.

José Rosales has spoken of his meetings with Valdés and the other conspirators in these last few weeks before the war. In order to avoid suspicion they met in an empty flat in San Isidro Street, and on several occasions were almost caught redhanded with incriminating papers and materials.[23]

* *Los camisas viejas*, the nickname by which the original, pre-Civil War members of the Falange are known.

It should be clear that, while Valdés and José Rosales were close associates, the former nevertheless held a position of far greater authority within the hierarchy of the Nationalist conspiracy in Granada. To state, as Claude Couffon has done, that the Rosales brothers were 'chefs tout-puissants de la Phalange' in Granada and that José was the 'chef suprême de la Phalange'[24] – a claim also made by Schonberg[25] – is to fail to grasp the realities of the situation. Rosales was merely one of the three Falangist sector chiefs, while Valdés was supreme commander of the Falangist militia in Granada, as well as being an Army officer and, once the rising began, Civil Governor. Rosales, unlike Valdés, was a civilian, and the Falange, without the military rising, would never have been in a position to impose itself on the community. This is stressed here because, as we shall see, the Rosales family found itself much involved in the circumstances surrounding the arrest of Federico García Lorca.

Valdés had become the leading conspirator in Granada when the government sacked General Llanos Medina, who had been deeply committed to the rebellion, on 10 July 1936. When General Queipo de Llano visited Llanos Medina at the beginning of the month to inform him of the progress of plans for the rising, Llanos had reaffirmed his allegiance to the Cause and assured Queipo that he could count on the support of the Granada garrison. The government was informed of the meeting and immediately dismissed General Llanos, thereby causing an unexpected blow to the conspirators. 'Granada', comments the Cruzada, 'had lost the brains behind the insurrection' (p. 276).

The new Military Commander was General Miguel Campins Aura. Campins had a fine military record and was known to be friendly with General Franco. He turned out to be a staunch Republican, however, and the rebel officers soon realised that they could expect no collaboration from their new chief. Plotting continued behind the General's back and he seems to have been quite unaware of what was happening until it was too late.

Among the conspirators, Colonel Basilio León Maestre, commanding officer of the Lepanto Infantry Regiment, his subordinate Commandant, Rodriguez Bouzo, and Colonel Antonio Muñoz Jiménez of the Fourth Light Artillery Regiment, were actively plotting against the Republic and were to play a vital role in the rising.[26]

They were supported by several of their officers, among whom Captain José María Nestares was outstanding. Nestares had attended the Military Academy in Toledo and was a handsome young man with a liking for women and the other prescribed pursuits of the Andalusian *señorito*. In this, as in his rabidly anti-Republican sentiments, he was out of the same stable as José and Antonio Rosales and had joined the Falange in its early days. Although Nestares was a Captain of Infantry, he was chief of the police security department until being dismissed after the events of 10 March 1936, and this experience was to prove particularly useful to him when the rising started. He was then appointed 'head of public order' and became one of the most dedicated organisers of the repression. At the end of July Nestares took command of the Falangist position in Víznar, a little village five miles to the north-west of Granada below the Sierra de Alfacar. We shall hear more of him and of Víznar.

One other notable conspirator against the Republic who should be mentioned here is Lieutenant Mariano Pelayo, of the Civil Guard. Under Pelayo the Civil Guard sided with the rebels from the start and vindicated the reputation for brutality by which they are known in Spain.

These, then, were some of the more prominent Nationalists who dedicated themselves during the summer of 1936 to making preparations for the rising in Granada. Before tracing the development of events in the town, however, some consideration should be given to the activities under the Popular Front of the poet who is the principal concern of this book.

FOUR

Lorca and the Popular Front

During the long years of Franco's dictatorship it was customary to maintain that Lorca was 'apolitical', and that his death was due to strictly non-political causes. It is indisputable, however, that Lorca identified himself closely with the aspirations of the Republic and, in the last months before the civil war, with the Popular Front. Lorca never joined a political party and had little interest in the mechanics of politics: it is impossible to imagine him as an active party member. But there can be no doubt whatsoever that his views came close to those of liberal Socialism nor that, from the point of view of the Right, he was a 'Red intellectual'.

As early as 1933 the poet had made his position on Fascism clear by signing a manifesto condemning the Nazi persecution of German writers.[1] And when, in 1935, Mussolini invaded Abyssinia, he cancelled a projected visit to Italy and signed another anti-Fascist manifesto.[2]

In the weeks leading up to the general election of February 1936 the atmosphere in Madrid was extremely tense. Politics and the arts had become inextricably mixed, and political significance was given to the smallest word or most trivial action on the part of well-known artists and writers. Keenly aware of the threat of Fascism to Europe, the majority of these openly voiced their support for the Popular Front – the alignment, remember, of all the progressive forces in Spain – and used their influence as public figures to attack the Right. Lorca was no exception.

On 9 February 1936, the last Sunday before the election, a banquet was offered to the Communist poet Rafael Alberti and the writer María Teresa León on their return from Russia. Federico delivered the speech of welcome (the text of which, unfortunately, seems not to have been preserved) and read a manifesto drawn up by a group of intellectuals in support of the Popular Front. Full reports of the banquet appeared in the Communist newspaper *Mundo obrero* and in *El Socialista*.[3]

On 14 February a celebration in memory of the Galician playwright Ramón del Valle-Inclán, who had died in January, was organised in Madrid's Zarzuela Theatre by Alberti and María Teresa León. Federico took part in this gathering of markedly political flavour, and read two sonnets in praise of Valle-Inclán and his work by the Nicaraguan poet Rubén Darío.[4]

On Saturday 15 February 1936, the day before the election, *Mundo obrero* published a manifesto which seems to have been that read by Federico at the Alberti banquet. The first signatory was Lorca, and I reproduce the document here in translation as proof that, far from being apolitical, the poet was publicly and explicitly a supporter of the Popular Front:

Intellectuals in Favour of the Popular Front

Political parties separated by considerable theoretical divergences, but united in defence of freedom and the Republic, have wisely joined forces in the formation of a broadly-based Popular Front. We intellectuals, artists and members of the liberal professions would fail in our duty if, at this time of undeniable political gravity, we refrained from making public our opinion on a situation of such importance. We all feel the obligation of joining our well-wishes and our best hopes to what is undoubtedly the aspiration of a majority of the Spanish people: the necessity for that free and democratic government whose absence has been so lamentably obvious in Spanish life during the last two years.

We reaffirm our support for the Popular Front not as individuals but as a numerous group of representatives of Spanish intellectual life, and we do so because we want liberty to be respected, the standard of living raised and culture brought to the widest possible range of Spaniards (p. 3).

On 23 February shortly after the triumph of the Popular Front, *El Sol*, one of Spain's leading newspapers, published the manifesto of the Universal Union of Peace on behalf of its Spanish committee. It was signed by the great poet Antonio Machado, Teófilo Hernando, Manuel Azaña, Angel Ossorio and Julio Alvarez del Vayo, and among the dozens of writers and prominent people who publicly expressed their support for the document was García Lorca.

At the end of March 1936 the news reached Spain that Luis Carlos Prestes, the Brazilian Communist leader, had been imprisoned by the dictator Getulio Vargas and was in danger of being executed along with thousands of workers. International Red Aid, whose Spanish section had been systematically hounded by the authorities between October 1934 and the victory of the Popular Front, decided immediately to organise a protest meeting in support of Prestes, to be held in the Madrid Casa del Pueblo, the Socialist workers' HQ. Federico promised to take part, perhaps feeling that, on account of his fame in South America, his voice might have particular influence. The event took place on 28 March and received full coverage in the left-wing press.[5] Lorca read revolutionary poems composed by South American poets and some of the compositions of his own *Poet in New York*. He was applauded with wild enthusiasm by the large audience, and a photograph showing him reciting was published on 31 March in *Mundo obrero*. In those days of extreme political tension could anyone of right-wing views doubt that Lorca was politically committed?

During April and May the poet signed several other documents in connection with the imprisonment of Prestes, joined a new society called the Friends of Latin America which was dedicated to the struggle against the dictators, and then another one called the Friends of Portugal which had similar aims.[6]

On 7 April the Madrid newspaper *La Voz* published an

important interview with the poet in which he talked about his concern for social justice and his feelings about the responsibility of the artist at a time when the world was in turmoil:

As long as there is economic injustice in the world, the world will be unable to think clearly. I see it like this. Two men are walking along a river bank. One of them is rich, the other poor. One has a full belly and the other fouls the air with his yawns. And the rich man says: 'What a lovely little boat out on the water! Look at that lily blooming on the bank!' And the poor man wails: 'I'm hungry, I can't see anything. I'm hungry, so hungry!' Of course. The day when hunger is eradicated there is going to be the greatest spiritual explosion the world has ever seen. We will never be able to picture the joy that will erupt when the Great Revolution comes. I'm talking like a real Socialist, aren't I?[7]

Then, on 1 May, Federico's connection with the Spanish section of International Red Aid was further underlined when he published the following brief text in the organisation's magazine ¡Ayuda! (Help!):

I send my affectionate and enthusiastic greeting to all the workers of Spain, united on the First of May by the desire for a more just and cohesive society.

On 22 May Lorca attended an impressive banquet given in honour of three French writers who were visiting Madrid as representatives of the French Popular Front: André Malraux, Jean Cassou (a friend of Lorca) and the dramatist Henri-René Lenormand. Two hundred distinguished guests, including several Cabinet ministers, were present at this eminently left-wing gathering, during which the Marseillaise and the Internationale were sung by the banqueters. The event received wide coverage in the Madrid press.

Lorca had been increasingly concerned, since returning from his first trip to America, with the social mission of the theatre in

Spain. The formation of the travelling company La Barraca gave him a marvellous opportunity to bring Spanish classical drama to the *pueblo*, and he devoted tremendous energy to ensuring the success of the project. This sharpened social concern was reflected in his ideas about what modern drama should seek to achieve, and he came to feel that the playwright could no longer afford not to identify with the social realities of his time. In the last interview published before his death he said:

The idea of art for art's sake is something that would be cruel if it weren't, fortunately, so ridiculous. No decent person believes any longer in all that nonsense about pure art, art for art's sake.

At this dramatic point in time, the artist should laugh and cry with the people. We must put down the bunch of lilies and bury ourselves up to the waist in mud to help those who are *looking* for lilies. For myself, I have a genuine need to communicate with others. This is why I knocked at the doors of the theatre and why I now devote all my talents to it.

In the same interview, Lorca was asked for his opinion on the fall of Granada to Ferdinand and Isabella in 1492. His reply, which in itself could have been sufficient to endanger his life in the town once the civil war got under way, is final proof that his attitude to Spain was utterly unlike that of the Granadine conspirators who were at this very moment plotting against the Republic:

It was a disastrous event, even though they say the opposite in the schools. An admirable civilisation, and a poetry, architecture and delicacy unique in the world – all were lost, to give way to an impoverished, cowed town, a wasteland populated by the worst bourgeoisie in Spain today.

After this outburst Federico proceeded to define his feelings about being a Spaniard:

I am totally Spanish, and it would be impossible for me to live outside my geographical limits. At the same time I hate anyone who is Spanish just because he was born a Spaniard. I am a brother to all men, and I detest the person who sacrifices himself for an abstract, nationalist ideal just because he loves his country with a blindfold over his eyes. A good Chinaman is closer to me than a bad Spaniard. I express Spain in my work and feel her in the very marrow of my bones; but before this I am cosmopolitan and a brother to all. Needless to say, I don't believe in political frontiers.[8]

El Sol, where this interview appeared, was one of the most widely read newspapers in Spain and the piece did not miss the attention of that Granadine middle class characterised by the poet as 'the worst in Spain today'.[9]

And then it was July. Federico had announced in April that he was planning a trip to Mexico, where he would see his plays performed and give a lecture on the seventeenth-century poet Quevedo;[10] it seems that he intended to take a short holiday with his parents in Granada, and then to set off on his trip. He was bubbling over with ideas and literary projects, and in an interview given to the journalist Antonio Otero Seco on 3 July (but not published until 1937, several months after his death) he said that he had six books of poetry ready for the press and three new plays, one of which was to be an Andalusian drama set in the *vega* of Granada and the other 'a social play ... in which the audience and people in the street take part; a revolution flares up and the theatre is taken by force'.

Antonio Otero Seco had accompanied Federico that day to the Buenavista courthouse, where the poet was required to sign some documents in connection with an unexpected accusation which had recently been made against him. Before they arrived there, Federico explained to Otero:

You're not going to believe this, it's so absurd. But it's true. Not long ago I was surprised to receive a summons. I couldn't imagine what it could be about, no matter how hard I tried, it made no sense. I went to the courthouse, and do you know what they told me? Neither more nor less than that a certain character in Tarragona, quite unknown to me, had denounced me for my "Ballad of the Spanish Civil

Guard", published eight years ago in the *Gypsy Ballads*! Apparently
the bloke had suddenly felt an urge for revenge – an urge which had
lain dorment for such a long time – and would be satisfied with little
less than my head. Naturally I explained to the prosecutor exactly
what the poem is about, my idea of the Civil Guard, of poetry, of
poetic images, of surrealism, of literature and I don't know what else.
He was very intelligent and of course was quite satisfied about it all.[11]

This seemingly unimportant event indicates that Lorca's work
was capable of arousing extreme hostility among traditionally-
minded Spaniards, as we saw earlier when referring to the
première of *Yerma* in Madrid in 1935.

Two days later, on 5 July, Federico's parents returned to
Granada for the summer. The poet saw them off at the station.
He was accompanied by his old schoolteacher Antonio Rodrí-
guez Espinosa, who wrote later in his memoirs:

On 5 July 1936 Federico García Lorca's parents returned to Granada
to spend the summer, as they always did, in their country house, 'Villa
Vicenta'. Various friends went to the South Station to see them off.
Federico was also there to say goodbye to his parents. When I asked
him why he wasn't going too, he said: 'I've invited some friends to
come and hear me read a play which I'm finishing, *The House of Bernarda Alba*, because I want to know their opinion of it.'[12]

A few days later Federico dined at the house of his friend Carlos
Morla Lynch, of the Chilean Embassy. The Socialist minister Fernando de los Ríos was present and expressed himself much disturbed by the political situation. 'The Frente Popular is falling
apart,' he said, 'and Fascism is growing apace. We mustn't
deceive ourselves. The situation is extremely grave and great
sacrifices need to be made.' Carlos Morla Lynch noted in his diary
that night that Lorca had not been in his usual lively form:

Federico said very little; he's almost disembodied, absent, miles away.
Not his normal self – brilliant, witty, luminous, brimful of confidence
in life and bursting with optimism.[13]

On Saturday 11 July, Federico and some other friends, among them the Socialist deputy for Extremadura, Fulgencio Díez Pastor, dined with the Chilean poet Pablo Neruda. Díez Pastor, like Fernando de los Ríos, was extremely worried about the political situation, and Lorca assailed him with question after question. 'What was going to happen? Would there be a civil war? What should he do?' Finally Federico burst out: 'I'm going to go back to Granada!' 'Stay here,' replied Díez Pastor. 'You'll be safer in Madrid than anywhere else.'[14] It seems that the Falangist writer Agustín de Foxá gave similar advice to the poet: 'If you want to leave Madrid, don't go to Granada. Go to Biarritz,' he said. 'What would I do in Biarritz?' exclaimed the poet. 'In Granada at least I can work.'[15]

On Sunday 12 July, at nine in the morning, four Falangist gunmen assassinated Lieutenant José Castillo of the Assault Guard, in revenge for the death of one of their comrades. The situation was explosive.[16]

It may have been on the night of the 12th that Federico read *The House of Bernarda Alba* to his friends at the flat of Dr Eusebio Oliver. Among those present were the poets Jorge Guillén, Dámaso Alonso and Pedro Salinas, and the critic Guillermo de Torre. Dámaso Alonso would recall that, as they were leaving the flat, a lively discussion was taking place about a certain writer (Dámaso Alonso doesn't tell us his name) who had become deeply involved in politics. 'He'll never write anything worthwhile now', was Federico's comment. 'I'll never be political. I'm a revolutionary, because all true poets are revolutionaries – don't you agree? – but political, never!'[17] One must assume that these words, quoted *ad nauseam* by those writers who have insisted that Lorca was 'apolitical', expressed simply the poet's determination not to become actively involved in a political party.

A few hours later, at three in the morning of 13 July, Calvo Sotelo, the Monarchist leader, was kidnapped and assassinated. 'Ominous date,' wrote Morla Lynch that night in his diary:

Federico didn't come and his absence surprised us. We haven't seen him for days, but he can't have left yet for Granada.[18]

But that very night, as Morla was writing up his diary, Federico was travelling to Granada.

There has been some confusion about the date of Lorca's last day in Madrid. What is certain is that he spent a good part of it in the company of his friend Rafael Martínez Nadal, who called for him at the family flat at around 2 p.m. and took him to lunch. Afterwards the two friends caught a taxi to the Puerta de Hierro, on the outskirts of Madrid, and there, quite suddenly, Federico took the decision to leave that evening for Granada, exclaiming: 'Rafael, these fields are going to be strewn with corpses. My mind is made up. I'm going to Granada, come what may.' According to Martínez Nadal, they went immediately to Thomas Cook's to buy the train ticket, returning then to the flat in Alcalá Street where Martínez Nadal helped Federico to pack.[19]

Martínez Nadal does not mention in his account the farewell visit that Federico paid that evening to his old schoolmaster Antonio Rodríguez Espinosa, who wrote in his memoirs:

On the night of the 13th of that month [July] he came to my flat at 9 o'clock; he rang the bell and when the servant opened the door asked: 'Is Don Antonio in?' 'Yes, Sir.' 'Well, tell him that Don Homobono Picadillo is here.' I knew his jokes and moreover recognised his voice, and appeared saying: 'And what does this wretched Don Homobono want now?' 'Only to touch you for 200 pesetas; at 10.30 tonight I'm off to Granada. There's a thunder storm brewing and I'm going home where the lightning can't strike me.'[20]

Did Don Antonio make a mistake over the date of Federico's last visit to his flat? It is difficult to be sure about this, although the details he provides in his account suggest that he did not.

Martínez Nadal forgets a visit that Federico certainly paid that evening before catching the train to Granada – to the Ladies' Residence in 8, Miguel Angel Street, where his sister Isabel and Laura, daughter of Fernando de los Ríos, were living at the time. While the poet said goodbye to them, Martínez Nadal waited for him in the taxi.[21]

Martínez Nadal has always insisted that Federico left Madrid on the night of 16 July 1936. The Granada newspapers show beyond any doubt, however, that the poet arrived there on the morning of 14 July which means that he must have left Madrid on the night of 13 July.

On 15 July *El Defensor de Granada* announced the poet's arrival in the centre of its front page:

García Lorca, in Granada
The Granadine poet Don Federico García Lorca has been in Granada since yesterday.

The illustrious author of *Blood Wedding* intends to stay briefly with his parents.

Constantino Ruiz Carnero, editor of *El Defensor de Granada*, was a close friend of Federico and, like him, would be killed during the repression. It is probable that Ruiz Carnero himself wrote the note about Federico's arrival. The Madrid train was scheduled to arrive at 8.20 a.m., which would have given Ruiz Carnero plenty of time to see his friend during 14 July. Moreover, the small detail about the poet's intending only to stay *briefly* in Granada catches one's attention. From whom could this information have come if not from Federico himself? It seems likely that the poet was still thinking about joining Margaritu Xirgu in Mexico after spending a few days or weeks with his parents in Granada, and that he explained this to Ruiz Carnero.

On 16 July the Catholic daily newspaper *Ideal* also announced the arrival of the poet, albeit with less enthusiasm than *El Defensor*: 'The Granadine poet Federico García Lorca is in Granada.' And, on the 17th, *Noticiero Granadino* – an un- committed, liberal newspaper – announced on its front page: 'Our dear Granadine friend, the great poet Federico García Lorca, is spending some time in Granada with his family.'

It was well known, therefore, that Lorca was in Granada. It was also well known that, a few days previously, another celebrated person had returned to the town: Ramón Ruiz Alonso, the ex- deputy of the CEDA. We must now take a close look at this man, who is to play an important part in our narrative.

FIVE

Ramón Ruiz Alonso

On 4 November 1933, in the middle of the election campaign, *El Defensor de Granada* published the following note on its front page:

Last night we learnt that the coordinating committee of the Right Union had agreed to modify its list of candidates for the Radical–Right coalition. Don Alfonso García Valdecasas has been dropped from the list, and his place has been taken by the compositor Ramón Ruiz Alonso. Señor Valdecasas has been dropped, we understand, in consequence of his Fascist-style declarations during the meeting in the Comedia Theatre in Madrid.[1]

Ramón Ruiz Alonso was born at the turn of the century in the village of Villaflores, in the province of Salamanca. His parents were well-off landowners, and the villagers remember that they had a marked predilection for gambling – a predilection which seems to have led to their financial ruin.[2]

Ramón was educated at the Salesian college in Salamanca, and in 1967 he recalled his teachers with great affection, adding that for several years he had presided over the Old Boys' Association.[3] One of his schoolmates was José María Gil Robles, later to become the head of the CEDA. Robles would play a significant part in the development of Ruiz Alonso's political career, and in 1937 wrote a prologue to the latter's book *Corporativism*, published in Salamanca.

Before the advent of the Republic, Ruiz Alonso had worked as a draughtsman for the Company of Aerial Photogrammetry in Madrid, as well as doing private work of the same kind. At this period his life was prosperous. Under the new Republic, however – as we learn from his book – he found himself converted into a menial bricklayer, earning only eight pesetas a day. Such a change in his fortunes had come about, not because of bad luck or chance, but on account of his refusal to join the Socialist trades union, the Association of the Art of Printing, presided over by Ramón Lamoneda. Or, at least, that was Ruiz Alonso's own explanation of what had happened, an explanation challenged by Lamoneda in the Cortes.[4] Ruiz Alonso never forgot this experience, which filled him with loathing for the Socialists. He referred to it on several occasions during debates in the Cortes between 1933 and 1936, and it is mentioned, too, in his book:

SIX conservative (?)... Catholic (?)... right-wing (?)... companies THREW ME into the street because the Socialists demanded it.
How vile!!
I went hungry, very hungry... and so did my family (pp. 132–3).

Given Ruiz Alonso's hatred for Socialism and Communism (he scarcely distinguishes between them in his book), his scorn for the work of the left-wing trades unions and his aggressive personality, it comes as no surprise to learn that he should have been attracted by Fascism. Thanks to the enthusiastic study which Tomás Borrás has made of the Fascist thinker Ramiro Ledesma Ramos, we know that Ruiz Alonso joined the latter's organisation, the JONS (Juntas de Ofensiva Nacional-Sindicalista) in 1933. Writes Borrás:

The JONS had an 'infantry' section. Ramiro was fortunate to find a collaborator for this genuinely 'offensive' undertaking in Ramón Ruiz who succeeded, with his gift for leadership and his military spirit, in getting 100 carefully chosen members of the JONS, divided into patrols of five men, to obey his commands.
The combat unit of the JONS disputed the control of the streets with the Socialistic *pistoleros*. It was vital to have shock troops at a moment when Marxist despotism – and in Barcelona, Marxist-separa-

tist despotism – was trying to create that panic which deadens the vital reactions and facilitates the victory of terrorism. It was necessary to react and to win. It was Ramiro, and the leader of his 'ready for everything' men, Ramón Ruiz, who hurled against the forces of the aggressors their own 'offensive' defensive troops. The first militia of the new young Spain! [...] Ramón Ruiz and his men equipped themselves with blankets, which they threw over the heads of their victims. By this method their cries were stifled while a good drubbing was administered to their sides.[5]

One of the most talked-about feats of the JONS at this time was their attack on the HQ of the Association of the Friends of the Soviet Union, which took place on 14 July 1933. Having tied up the officers of the Association who happened to be on the premises, three *jonsistas* proceeded to destroy numerous documents and then bore away the card index giving the names and addresses of all the members of the Association.[6] Although there is no definite proof that Ruiz Alonso was one of the three *jonsistas* who took part in the raid, his participation seems likely. And there can be no doubt that he quickly familiarised himself with the names of the members of the Association of Friends of the Soviet Union filed on the cards. Was Lorca's among them? Again we cannot be certain, but we do know that by 1936 the poet was a member of the organisation.

We have seen that Ruiz Alonso and Gil Robles attended the same school in Salamanca. Their relationship continued later. Gil Robles was on the staff of *El Debate*, the most influential Catholic newspaper in the country, which had been founded by Angel Herrera Oria, one of the leaders of Acción Popular, and it is likely that it was due to Gil Robles's recommendation that Ruiz Alonso obtained a position as compositor on the newspaper. Gil Robles seems, moreover, to have sensed immediately that Ruiz Alonso would make an effective Acción Popular militant, and it was probably due to his persuasion that the compositor left the JONS. In the autumn of 1933 he was sent to Granada to work on the newspaper *Ideal*, which had been founded in 1931 and which was controlled, like *El Debate*, by Herrera Oria.

Things were now looking up for Ruiz Alonso, and his satisfaction must have been complete when the CEDA decided to include him on their list of candidates to contest the 1933 election.

The Right, as we know, won an overwhelming victory at the polls, and Ruiz Alonso became an MP for Acción Obrerista, the Catholic workers' union that formed part of the larger CEDA organisation.

During his first year in the Cortes the 'domesticated worker' (*obrero amaestrado*) as he had been nicknamed, allegedly by José Antonio Primo de Rivera, failed to distinguish himself on behalf of Acción Obrerista, over whose central committee he now presided. On 18 November 1934, shortly after the bloody repression of the Asturian miners, he published an open letter in the Madrid daily *ABC* in which he formally dissociated himself from the party, claiming that politics were vilifying the soul of the proletariat and that the class struggle should be divorced altogether from party politics and restricted to the trade unions, where it belonged. Acción Obrerista reacted furiously to its leader's treachery and published a rejoinder in *ABC* on 20 November in which it deplored the underhand method chosen by Ruiz Alonso to announce his resignation, reminding him that he should now relinquish the seat in the Cortes which he was occupying on its behalf.

Far from giving up his seat, however, the 'domesticated worker' now chose to ally himself more closely with the activities of Acción Popular, in whose ranks he militated during the two years leading up to the elections of February 1936 and the triumph of the Popular Front. But he lost his seat in the Cortes as a result of the annulment of the Granada election, and his defeat in the reconvened election of May 1936 confirmed him in his already aggressive loathing of democracy and threw him into the arms of the conspirators. Later he wrote in his book:

The Parliament was all lies, all deceit.

It was necessary to destroy it, to shake its very foundations, to leave not a stone standing, in order to build anew, to construct, to preserve.

And a Parliament which did not want to die threw me from its midst so that I should not be a witness to its shameful downfall nor read its death sentence on its face. Before this it had proposed the annulment of my election and the acceptance of its own candidates for Granada....

How disgusting! How disgusting! How disgusting!

And how proud I was!

By this time people were talking about a revolution. I returned to the people, I identified with the people and became again what I had been before.

The people!

I breathed again with expanded lungs. I learned what it was like to conspire, because I became a conspirator ... (pp. 249–50).

Ruiz Alonso's book is little more than an unoriginal Fascist manual and, having attempted to describe what a Spanish corporative state would be like, he appends a translation of 'The Corporative Laws of Italian Fascism', headed with the words: 'The complete text of the documents necessary to study the Italian regime.' The attitude of mind revealed on every page is a Fascist one, and Ruiz Alonso shows himself to be an implacable enemy of democracy and the political freedom of the Spanish people. Between his political objectives and those of the Falangist and military conspirators in Granada, with whom he collaborated, there can have been little essential difference. Ruiz Alonso's Fascist attitudes attracted the dislike of the left-wing *El Defensor de Granada*, which barracked him with unfailing zest during the months that led to the rising, and there is no doubt that the town's Republicans regarded him as one of their most unpleasant enemies.

On 10 July 1936 Ruiz Alonso left Madrid by car for Granada. He knew, doubtless, that a military rising against the Republic was about to take place; and it seems fair to surmise that he wished to be in Granada when the shooting began. But just outside Madridejos, in the province of Toledo, Ruiz Alonso met with a piece of bad luck, in the form of a lorry which pulled across his path. On 12 July *Noticiero Granadino* announced on its front page:

Señor Ruiz Alonso received severe bruises in a motorcar accident.

As he was returning from Madrid in a motorcar driven by himself, and at great speed, the ex-deputy of the CEDA for Granada, Señor Ruiz Alonso, had to swerve to avoid a lorry which pulled out in front of him. After turning over four or five times the vehicle ended up in a ditch.

The car was completely destroyed, and Señor Ruiz Alonso received bad bruises all over his body.

In the same lorry that caused the accident Señor Ruiz Alonso was taken to Madridejos, where he was attended by political and personal friends.

The Granada branch of Acción Popular, informed of what had happened to their colleague, sent a motorcar to bring him to Granada, and Señor Ruiz Alonso is now at home and is being carefully looked after by Doctor Guirao who, as a precaution, has recommended that visits to the victim of the accident should be limited.

Yesterday the patient was feeling somewhat better, although he complained of considerable pain.

Ruiz Alonso's family ask us to express their gratitude to all those who have inquired after his state of health and who have been so kind to them.

Ruiz Alonso's bruises were not sufficiently serious to prevent him from participating in the events that took place in Granada once the rising began on 20 July. And, as we shall see, the role played by this proud, violent, ambitious man in those events would be a relevant one, particularly at a time when the life of Federico García Lorca hung in the balance.

SIX

The Fall of Granada

For well over a century the Army has been a decisive factor in Spanish politics, and the military coup or *pronunciamiento* a much abused means of effecting political change. This was so throughout the nineteenth century and in the case of Primo de Rivera's accession to power in 1923; and it was so with the Nationalist insurrection in July 1936, although Franco had to wait two and a half years for the eventual fall of Madrid.

The rebellion began on 17 July 1936 with the revolt of a small group of officers of the Melilla garrison in Spanish Morocco who, supported by troops of the Foreign Legion, soon took the city. Similar risings in Ceuta and Tetuan were equally successful and, by midnight, the insurgents had gained almost complete control throughout the area and were pushing ahead their preparations for the military offensive on the Spanish mainland.[1] Let us now consider the development of the rising, in particular as it affected Granada.

Granada: Saturday 18 July 1936
In the early hours of 18 July Generals Franco and Orgaz seized control of Las Palmas in the Canary Islands, and at 5.15 a.m. that morning Franco's famous Manifesto announcing the Nationalist Movement* and calling on the support of 'loyal' Spaniards was broadcast to the mainland from Canary and Moroccan radio stations.[2]

---

* *El Movimiento (Nacional)*, the name given by the rebels both to the rising and to the subsequent political system.

That same morning the Madrid Government transmitted a bulletin in which it informed the Spanish people that a military rising against the Republic had taken place in Morocco but that everything was quiet on the mainland.[3] The broadcast came too late for the morning newspapers in Granada, however, and the only indication in *Ideal* on 18 July that all was not normal appeared in an announcement on the front page that 'causes beyond our control have prevented us from obtaining our customary general news'.

But everything was *not* quiet on the Spanish mainland, despite the government's assurances, and that morning General Queipo de Llano seized command of the Sevillan garrison in a coup of the greatest audacity. Queipo, who had been sent to Seville as Director of Customs Police, arrested almost single-handed the Captain General, General Villa-Abrille, and the Colonel of the Regiment, and with the help of as few as one hundred soldiers and fifteen Falangists gained control of the city centre by nightfall. Joined now by the Civil Guard and the artillery section of the garrison, Queipo's success was certain; the workers, demoralised and weaponless, could only barricade themselves into the populous quarters on the outskirts of the city and await the inevitable repression.[4]

During 18 July the government continued to broadcast inaccurate bulletins on the course of what it refused to admit was a full-blooded military rising.

In Madrid the government floundered in a state of extreme confusion and seemed unable to decide what should be done or even to grasp the significance of what was happening. Precious, irrecuperable time was lost in prevarication and until 19 July the government stubbornly refused to distribute arms to the people. Indeed the Prime Minister, Casares Quiroga, announced that anyone who did so without his permission would be shot: a warning that was heeded by the majority of Civil Governors throughout the country, including Granada, and that facilitated more than anything else the easy Nationalist successes of 18 July.

Finally, at 7.20 p.m., the government announced that Queipo de Llano had proclaimed martial law in Seville, adding that 'various seditious acts have been perpetrated there by rebel military elements which have now been crushed by Government forces. Cavalry reinforcements have just entered the city. . . . The rest of the Peninsula remains loyal to the Government, which is in complete control of the situation.'[5]

One and a half hours later Queipo broadcast from Radio Seville the first of what was to be a long series of nightly harangues notable for their fiery rhetoric, misrepresentations and gruesome fanaticism. The General announced that the Nationalist rising had triumphed everywhere in Spain except in Madrid and Barcelona; that the transportation of troops from Africa was being effected at that very moment; that columns would advance immediately on Granada, Córdoba, Jaén, Extremadura, Toledo and Madrid and that the Marxist scum (*canalla*) would be exterminated like wild animals.[6]

The General's account of the military situation on the night of 18 July had been intentionally misleading, for in fact the rising had so far been restricted to Andalusia, where resistance from the Republicans had been more or less overcome in all the main cities except Málaga, which remained in the hands of the Popular Front.[7]

Queipo's bulletin threw the people of Granada into confusion, and both the garrison and the civilian population of the town displayed extreme uneasiness in the face of the disturbing, and incompatible, reports being broadcast from different radio stations. The garrison, it will be remembered, was at this time subordinate to the Captaincy-General in Seville, and Queipo's assumption of command there inevitably challenged the loyalties of Granada's soldiery.

General Campins, Granada's Military Commander, had only been in the town six days when the rising began. He was a loyal Republican but, from all accounts, extremely naïve politically. Campins seems to have been unaware of the plotting that was taking place around him, and expressed his firm belief in the loyalty of his officers, despite the fact that he hardly knew them. The right-wing historians Gollonet and Morales state that Campins assembled his officers on the morning of 18 July to explain the situation to them and demand their loyalty:

The Minister [said Campins] had authorised him to take whatever measures he deemed necessary in order to prevent any attempt to join forces with the 'rebels'. He, for his part, would be inflexible with anyone who attempted to rise against 'the legally constituted Government'. But 'he was certain' that no commanding officer or officer of the Granada garrison would support the rising and that every man would 'do his duty'. (And so each one would; but his duty as a Spaniard, as a patriot.) (p. 80.)

The same authors record that throughout 18 July there was feverish activity in the Civil Government, where César Torres Martínez, the Governor, was besieged by the representatives of the trades unions and left-wing political groups.

Torres Martínez was in constant contact with Campins. As he explained to the author:

From the moment of Calvo Sotelo's death, when the situation began to grow very tense, we were in permanent touch. Some days we talked two or three times on the telephone. And he came to the Civil Government two or three times, I don't remember exactly how many. We were constantly talking on the telephone.*

Torres Martínez recalls that Campins (whom he had not known previously) expressed complete confidence in the Republican loyalty of his officers:

I don't know what promises Campins received from the two colonels. But what is evident is that he believed that the garrison would not

* All the declarations by Torres Martínez quoted in this chapter are taken from our tape-recorded conversation of 15 October 1977.

rebel unless there were a grave disturbance of public order, with people taking to the streets; that it wouldn't intervene unless something really serious happened. He believed this until the very end. He told me that he would answer for the Army so long as we guaranteed that the civil population didn't get out of hand.

Torres Martínez, like other civil governors up and down the country, obeyed the orders of the Prime Minister, Casares Quiroga, and refused to consider distributing firearms to the Republicans in order to prevent a possible military rising. This is beyond any doubt, and I stress the fact here in order to disprove the lie, put out by the Granada rebels, that they rose to prevent a Marxist revolution made possible through the widespread distribution of arms to the workers. Not only have I found no evidence whatsoever that the Granada authorities carried out such a distribution, but the survivors of the repression almost always criticise Torres Martínez for not having disregarded Casares Quiroga's orders. Further proof that the workers were unarmed can be found in the fact that, when the rising occurred, there was virtually no opposition to the garrison. Torres Martínez comments:

Yes, I spoke several times on the telephone to Casares Quiroga. He told me that by no account were arms to be distributed, that the rising would be over in eight days and that it would be madness to arm the people in such circumstances. Moreover all the Republican and left-wing leaders in Granada who were with me in the Civil Government agreed with this policy. Campins had convinced all of us that we could trust both him and the garrison and that there was no reason whatsoever to arm the people. Everybody was pleased, thinking that things were all right, and nobody asked me to distribute arms. Nobody. Moreover, how could I have asked the military to give arms to the people when, according to Campins, the officers were insisting on their loyalty to the Republic? And another thing: if arms *had* been distributed, what civilians would have been capable of handling them effectively in the event of a military rising?

Torres Martínez and the Popular Front leaders were convinced, moreover, that the Granada Assault Guard – 150 well-armed and rigourously trained men, commanded by Captain Alvarez – would do its duty to enforce Republican legality. Torres Martínez continues:

When I ask myself now, after the event, how we could have trusted the *asaltos*, I reply: 'But how could we have failed to trust them in view of the fact that the Assault Guard was the only force created by the Republic and was considered to be absolutely loyal?' There could be no doubt that we had good friends there, nor that the officers were loyal ... had it been otherwise they would not have been appointed. Moreover, Captain Alvarez had come to Granada after Nestares was sacked – if Nestares had still been in command we would have known that it was a waste of time to try and protect even the Civil Government with the *asaltos*. This is absolutely certain, because the Popular Front would have told us 'watch Nestares, he's an enemy, a Falangist, a conspirator, a man who's going to rebel'. But no-one in the Popular Front told me that Alvarez was suspicious, not a single person.

The Governor also trusted the Civil Guard. This force, like the Assault Guard, was subordinate to the civil authority, not the military, and Torres Martínez, in his experience as a Civil Governor in various provinces, had never had the slightest trouble with the *civiles*. Moreover, was it not a fact that the head of the Granada Civil Guard, Lieutenant-Colonel Fernando Vidal Pagán, had given him his word of honour that he was loyal to the Republic?:

Nobody connected with the Popular Front told me that I should distrust the *asaltos*. But they were certainly suspicious of the Civil Guard. I thought the opposite, I thought that the Civil Guard would remain loyal. They have such iron discipline, such respect for their commanding officer, that I never believed that the Civil Guard would rebel. And moreover it's a fact that they rebelled hardly anywhere in Spain.

But the sad truth was that, in both forces, rebel officers were busy conspiring against the Republic. Captain Alvarez turned out to be a traitor. And, behind Vidal Pagán's back, Lieutenant Pelayo was preparing the Civil Guard's contribution to the rising.

During the night of 18 July few *granadinos* can have slept soundly. The local radio station continued to relay government bulletins and to broadcast exhortations from Popular Front spokesmen, while from Radio Seville came the ranting voice of Queipo de Llano and reports of Nationalist victories all over the country.

What would happen in Granada? Would the garrison rise in arms against the people? With such thoughts the citizens anxiously awaited the new day.

Granada: Sunday 19 July 1936

On Sunday morning Granada received confirmation that Queipo de Llano was indeed in control of Seville. The headline on the front page of *Ideal* read THE GOVERNMENT DENIES THE EXISTENCE OF A MILITARY RISING, but the subtitle IT SAYS THAT THE RISING IS RESTRICTED TO MOROCCO AND SEVILLE showed that things were much more serious than the government allowed. *Ideal* had been unable to receive information from Madrid through the normal channels and had been forced to rely on official government bulletins for news of what was happening throughout the country. It had also been subjected to censorship. No-one could doubt that Spaniards were engaged in civil war.

Ideal had managed to obtain an early morning interview with the Civil Governor, who had declared that all the necessary steps had been taken to prevent the outbreak of any disturbance in Granada. But plans for the capture of the town were already well advanced.

According to the *Cruzada*, Colonel Antonio Muñoz of the Artillery Regiment had visited his colleague Colonel Basilio León Maestre of the Infantry Regiment at 4.00 that morning to discuss tactics for the rising. They had been unable to reach a firm agreement about the final details, and meetings between the various rebel officers continued during 19 and 20 July until the Movement began.[8]

The same source states that General Campins received an urgent telephone call from the government at 11.00 that morning. He was to organise immediately a column to relieve Córdoba, which had fallen to the insurgents. Campins summoned his two Colonels and explained the position, ordering them to prepare their men at once for the expedition. Muñoz and León were now in a quandary. If they obeyed the General's instructions the garrison, already depleted by leaves of absence, would not be strong enough to guarantee the success of the rising. So they decided to play for time, and throughout the day the General was fobbed off with one excuse after another: the officers were unhappy about leaving Granada, the equipment was being checked and so on.

It was also about 11.00 when an urgent meeting took place at the HQ of the Left Republican party. Doctor José Rodríguez Contreras has recalled:

It was a Sunday. Although I no longer belonged to the Left Republican party I used to give them advice, without being a militant any more. They sent for me. All the officers of the party were there – the mayor, Fernández-Montesinos, Vigilio Castilla (President of the Provincial Deputation) and lots of other people. They were all there, with the exception of the Governor, Torres Martínez. I said to Montesinos: 'Listen, a decision has got to be taken. Here you all are, sitting around with your arms folded! You're crazy. You've got to act, it's very serious!' Montesinos said: 'No, no, we'll see what happens.' 'No', I said, 'not at all. Measures have got to be taken. You know as well as I do, as well as everybody does, who the leaders of a possible rebellion here are.' More vacillations. 'Look,' I said, 'tonight you can arrest them all and that's it. There'll be no rising here despite the military rebellion in Seville.' But they wouldn't listen.[9]

In the early hours of the afternoon Captain Nestares visited the artillery and infantry barracks to convince Muñoz and León of the necessity of assuming immediate command of the situation. His movements were noticed and reported to the Civil Governor, who rang Campins to inquire about Nestares's behaviour. Torres Martínez, who had been receiving contradictory telephone calls from the government all day long and was mentally exhausted, was told by an equally harassed Campins that he would look into the matter. The General telephoned the artillery barracks and was once again put off with a vague explanation. He was clearly quite out of touch with the situation.

Meanwhile the workers were becoming uneasy. They had noticed the comings and goings between the barracks, and had been listening to the radio bulletins that gave evidence of bitter fighting all over the country. It seems that they still trusted the garrison, however, for they now decided to form a column of their own to relieve Córdoba, and a call for support was put through to Madrid. Shortly afterwards Lieutenant-Colonel Fernando Vidal Pagán of the Civil Guard received orders from the government to collect weapons for the provision of the workers' column from the arsenal in the artillery barracks. But the artillerymen under Muñoz had already decided that they would refuse to hand over the arms. More telephone calls to and from Madrid. Eventually, at 9.00 p.m., Campins decided to visit the barracks himself.

Once there he delivered a lecture to his officers and ordered them to supply the necessary arms to the Civil Guard. He returned to the Military Commandery, apparently still unaware that he no longer held effective control of the garrison and that his orders were being disregarded.

That night further instructions were received from Madrid that the firearms were to be collected from the artillery arsenal, and at this point Vidal Pagán delegated responsibility for carrying out these orders to Lieutenant Mariano Pelayo who, unknown to his commanding officer, was one of the leaders of the conspiracy. From now on events in Granada were to move rapidly against the Republic.[10]

Granada: Monday 20 July 1936
At 1.30 a.m. on Monday 20 July, Pelayo arrived at the artillery

barracks with a government order demanding the provision of 3,000 weapons for the Córdoba column. The decision to with-hold them was ratified, and Campins was informed once more that the arms were still being prepared and would be ready within a few hours.[11]

José Valdés Guzmán spent most of that night in the Military Commandery, unknown to Campins. Gollonet and Morales tell us:

Valdés and the other rebel officers put the night to good use. The conversation revolved around the new times that were beginning in Spain and on the means of proclaiming the state of war in Granada.

It was agreed that civilian collaboration would be more effective if allied to the military.... At seven in the morning Valdés drove to the Artillery barracks (pp. 105–6).

There the final details for the rising were drawn up. A few moments later, Commandant Rodríguez Bouzo was sent by Muñoz to sound out Captain Alvarez of the Assault Guard.[12] Although we know nothing of the conversation that took place, there can be no doubt that Alvarez immediately promised his support. It was a decisive moment, for with the *asaltos* on their side the rebels could not fail to take Granada. Torres Martínez has put it in these terms:

I believe that, if the Assault Guard had resisted, had refused to join the conspiracy, the rebellion could not have succeeded in Granada. I would go further: I believe that if the officers of the Assault Guard had refused to truck with the conspirators (we knew nothing of these contacts, of course), and if the military had not been confident of their support, then the soldiers would not have left their barracks. They wouldn't have left their barracks because they simply didn't have enough men – I don't think they even had 200 men.

But the Assault Guard *did* join the rebels and, in the early hours of 20 July, the latter knew that Granada was in their grasp. It was clear, however, that they had to act rapidly and decisively, since there was always the possibility that the workers might at any moment storm the barracks and, by sheer superiority of numbers, nip the rising in the bud. It was decided, therefore, that the troops would take to the streets at 5 p.m.

That afternoon various Republican and left-wing leaders were with Torres Martínez in the Civil Government, among them Vigilio Castilla, President of the Provincial Council, and Antonio Rus Romero, secretary of the Popular Front committee. Also with the Governor was Lieutenant-Colonel Fernando Vidal Pagán, head of the Civil Guard, who had reaffirmed his loyalty to the Republic.

At about 4.30 p.m. someone telephoned Rus Romero: 'The troops are drawn up in the courtyard of the Artillery barracks,' he said. 'They're going to leave soon, something's got to be done quickly!'

Torres Martínez, who telephoned Campins there and then, remembers the conversation clearly:

When I told him that we had been informed that the troops were about to leave the Artillery barracks he said to me, on the telephone, that it wasn't possible, that he had heard nothing of the sort and that the officers had given their word that they would not rebel. He said he was leaving immediately for the Artillery barracks and that he would telephone me back in a half an hour to tell me that nothing was wrong.

But Campins did not telephone, and Torres Martínez never saw him again.

When Campins arrived at the barracks he was dumbfounded to find that the troops were indeed drawn up, in full battledress, in the courtyard. With them were sixty civilians, the majority of them Falangists, under the command of José Valdés Guzmán. The inevitable confrontation between Campins and Colonel Muñoz now took place and it must have come as an appalling shock to the General to realise that his subordinate had been lying to him and plotting behind his back. Informed that the Infantry Regiment, the Civil Guard and the Assault Guard, had also thrown in their lot with the rebels, the incredulous, gullible

Campins was escorted by Muñoz to the infantry barracks. Here, too, Campins found that the troops were also drawn up and ready for action. Shortly afterwards the General, now a prisoner, was driven back to the Military Commandery and forced to sign the proclamation of war which had been prepared for him by the rebel officers:[13]

PROCLAMATION

I, DON MIGUEL CAMPINS AURA, Brigadier-General and Military Commander of this Region, ANNOUNCE:

First article. Given the state of disorder prevailing throughout the country for the past three days and the lack of initiative on the part of the central Government, and with the purpose of saving Spain and the Republic from the present chaos, a STATE OF WAR is hereby proclaimed from this moment throughout the province.

Second article. All officials who fail to use every means at their disposal to maintain the public peace will be automatically dismissed from their positions and held personally responsible for their actions.

Third article. Anyone who, in order to disturb the public peace, to intimidate the inhabitants of a town or to carry out any retaliation of a social character, uses explosives or inflammable material or any other means or appliance adequate and sufficient to cause serious damage, or accidents to trains or other terrestrial or aerial modes of locomotion, will be punished with the maximum penalties prescribed under present laws.

Fourth article. Anyone who, without the necessary authorisation, fabricates, has in his possession or transports explosives or inflammable material, or possessing these legitimately, delivers or facilitates them without previous guarantees to persons who proceed to use them to commit the crimes defined in the previous articles, will be punished with a sentence ranging from 4 months to 12 years.

Fifth article. Anyone who, while not directly inducing others to commit the offences punishable under the first article, should publicly encourage others to commit it, or justify the same infraction or anyone committing it, will be punished with a sentence ranging from 4 months to 6 years.

Sixth article. Robbery with violence or intimidation carried out by two or more malefactors, when one of these is in the possession of arms and when murder or injuries listed in the first article of this law result, will be punished with death.

Seventh article. Anyone possessing arms of whatever sort, or explosives, must deliver these before eight o'clock this evening to the nearest Civil Guard post.

Eighth article. Groups of more than three persons will be dissolved with maximum energy by the troops.

CITIZENS OF GRANADA: For the sake of the peace that has been disrupted, for order, love of Spain and the Republic, for the re-establishment of the labour laws, I expect your collaboration in the cause of order.

Long live Spain. Long live the Republic.[14]

The *Cruzada*, published two years after the end of the Civil War, states that this document reflected the confusion in which Campins now found himself.[15] Doubtless this is true but it must also have reflected the confusion of the rebel officers who had drawn it up and who can have had no clear ideas about the political system envisaged by the insurrectionary generals.

Campins's declaration to *Ideal* on the night of 20 July also had the flavour of a document prepared for him by the rebels:

I have sought consistently to remain within the bounds of legality; but faced with the manifest state of abandon in which the Government was leaving us, and the lack of response from the Civil Governor, with whom I have tried at all times to maintain contact, I have deemed it expedient to proclaim a state of war throughout the province.

Moreover, the extremist elements in the town were actively engaged in inciting the soldiers by distributing leaflets in which they urged them to rebel against their officers, and other things: this in spite of the Army's gentlemanly behaviour.

I informed the Governor of what was happening but he did nothing to prevent these disgraceful incidents from taking place.

As a result the Army was showing signs of great uneasiness. The extremist elements had also asked the Civil Governor to allow the arms in the Artillery barracks to be handed over to them. This is what really decided me to take the decision adopted, since I could not allow these arms to fall into the hands of such elements, even though the Governor had assured me that they would not be used against us but against military units from other capitals. As you will appreciate, I could not hand over weapons to be employed against our brothers-in-arms. Another very alarming rumour circulating in the town was that there was a plan afoot to attack the Infantry barracks....[16]

If Campins's confusion was great, so too was that of the civil population of Granada when, at 5 p.m., the troops took to the streets, to the cry of 'Long live the Republic!' Many people were fooled into believing that the garrison was acting to *prevent* the occurrence of a Fascist rebellion, as the ultra right-wing Gollonet and Morales observe with satisfaction:

From a street-corner a group of extremists watch as the troops pass. They don't know what to make of it. They hadn't counted on this happening. Somebody says that the troops have been brought out by the General to crush the Fascists, and the group of revolutionaries begin to salute the troops with their fists raised (pp. 112-13).

The *Historia de la cruzada española* puts it more sarcastically:

Even the Reds, tricked into believing that the troops have left their barracks to 'fraternise with the people', applaud the march past. They soon learn their mistake. The troops open fire on them and the Reds, battered and in disarray, flee in panic up the Carrera del Darro (p. 284).

Batteries of artillery were now being placed in position at strategic points throughout the town: in the Plaza de Carmen, opposite the Town Hall; in the Puerta Real, the town's hub; in the Plaza de la Trinidad, behind the Civil Government; and overlooking Granada on the road to El Fargue.[17]

A lorry stopped in front of the Assault Guard barracks in the

Gran Vía and 'all the *asaltos* came out to greet the troops and shout "Long live Spain!" '[18] It seems that Captain Alvarez, who that morning had given his word to Commandant Rodriguez Bouzo that he would not join the rebels, had convinced his brother officers, or a majority of them, to support the rising.

Meanwhile, another artillery section drove to Armilla aerodrome, a few miles outside Granada on the road to Motril. The rebels took the aerodrome without meeting any resistance, since the officers had fled,[19] and this base would prove to be of the utmost importance in the war, assuring the easy maintenance of contact with Seville and the rest of Nationalist Spain and serving as a jumping-off place for planes attacking Republican positions.

At the same time another military group took the explosives factory at El Fargue, a few miles outside the town on the road to Murcia.[20] This was the largest explosives factory in Andalusia, and its role was to be crucial in the war. El Fargue produced large quantities of explosives for the Nationalist Army, including TNT for making bombs, and the Republicans never succeeded in blowing it up. The factory proved particularly useful to the rebels in the early weeks of the war: at that time General Queipo de Llano's stock of explosives was running low, and the first train to reach Seville from Granada after the outbreak of the war (on 22 August 1936) carried a huge consignment of munitions from El Fargue.[21]

The news that the troops had left their barracks reached Torres Martínez immediately. Still with him in the Civil Government were Virgilio Castilla, Antonio Rus Romero and the head of the Civil Guard, Fernando Vidal Pagán. Torres Martínez recalls:

We were still waiting for Campins to phone, but of course he never did. While we waited we heard that the troops were in the street. But we didn't yet know if Campins had joined them or not.

The Civil Government was protected by a section of Assault Guards – 20 or 25 men – under the command of Lieutenant Martínez Fajardo. As soon as he heard that the troops were drawn up in their barracks, Torres Martínez had spoken to Martínez Fajardo:

I gave orders to the Assault Guards downstairs to defend us and to shoot if necessary. And I also ordered the men in the doorway, the doorway of the Civil Government, to open fire.

Shortly before 6 p.m. Captain Nestares arrived at the Police Commissary in Duquesa Street, across the road from the Civil Government. The police immediately joined the rebels.

Just as Nestares arrived at the Commissary, six Republicans from Jaén, who had arrived that morning in Granada with an official order for the collection of a consignment of dynamite in the Commissary, were loading their vehicle with the dangerous explosives. Realising that the Nationalist rising had begun, the Republicans opened fire on the police, being wounded and arrested shortly afterwards.[22] They were to be the first men executed in Granada, dying in the cemetery on 26 July.

A few moments later an artillery section arrived in front of the Civil Government, under the command of Captain García Moreno and Lieutenant Lainez and supported by Valdés and his Falangists. Nestares joined them, as did, shortly afterwards, an infantry section with machine guns.[23]

The Assault Guards entrusted with the defence of the Civil Government realised at once that resistance would be useless. Or was their commanding officer, Martínez Fajardo, in the conspiracy? Certainly the asaltos must have learnt that Captain Alvarez, head of the force in Granada, and other officers had already thrown in their lot with the rebels. It was a situation which made their position invidious. Not a shot was fired, and the rebels entered the Civil Government without meeting the slightest obstacle.

A few seconds later they were in Torres Martínez's office. 'My greatest surprise', he recalls, 'was to find that the very Assault Guards whose duty it was to defend us were the first to aim their guns at us.' Virgilio Castilla alone offered some resistance to the rebels, pulling out a pistol and apparently (the versions differ) firing a shot. He was immediately arrested. Lieutenant-Colonel Vidal Pagán of the Civil Guard behaved with a dignity which Torres Martínez has never forgotten:

When the *asaltos* pointed their guns at me and Valdés and the other troops came into my office in the Civil Government, Vidal said: 'I want to take the consequences along with the Civil Governor.' Not that it was a statement of loyalty to me personally; he wanted to show that he was loyal to the word of honour he had given to defend the Republic.

Vidal Pagán, Castilla and Rus Romero were then taken to the Police Commissary, while Torres Martínez was committed to house detention in his own quarters in the Civil Government.

Valdés now assumed the post of Civil Governor. The first thing he did was to instal a machine-gun at the entrance to the building, a weapon whose use in such a narrow street would have been devastating. Then he telephoned the mayors throughout the province and ordered them to hand over their authority to the local Civil Guard. About this time hundreds of middle-class *granadinos* started to arrive at the Civil Government to declare their loyalty to the Nationalist cause and offer their services to the new Governor.

Meanwhile the rebels had entered the Town Hall. They met with no resistance here either, and the municipal guards joined them immediately. Several Republican functionaries, fearing for their lives, managed to escape by the back door of the building. The mayor was not among them: Manuel Fernández-Montesinos was arrested in his office, his place being taken by Lieutenant-Colonel Miguel del Campo of the Infantry Regiment.[24]

At about the same time another group, commanded by Commandant Rosaleny and Captains Miranda and Salvatierra, occupied the Radio Granada building, which was situated in the Gran Vía opposite the Assault Guard barracks.[25] At 6.30 p.m., and subsequently at half-hourly intervals, the proclamation of war drawn up for Campins's signature by the insurgents was read over the radio.

By nightfall the whole centre of Granada had fallen to the rebels. Hundreds of 'undesirables' were already in gaol. Virtually no resistance had been offered to the troops and *Ideal*, referring next day to the large numbers of civilians who flocked to put themselves at the disposal of the Military Commander, observed:

People commented on the complete ease with which all the official centres had been taken, without there having been the least resistance and without any violence at all having been necessitated....

Indeed, *Ideal* insists on the facility with which the centre of the town was occupied, and comments later in the same report:

Not a single person wounded by the troops has entered any charitable establishment, in spite of the fact that some shots were fired in different parts of the capital, either at suspicious individuals who ignored the order to raise their arms as they walked down the street or in answer to the very occasional pistol shots fired at the troops....[26]

These details are confirmed by the official Nationalist chroniclers of the Granada rising, Gollonet and Morales:

The night is peaceful, disturbed only by an occasional shot. There had been only one victim during this glorious day, a Security Guard shot as he rode in a motorcar beside Captain Nestares and other companions (p. 117).

Only in the old quarter of the Albaicín, with its labyrinth of steep and easily-barricaded streets, had there been any opposition to the Nationalists, and it was here that the Republicans, almost without arms, now prepared as best they might to resist the inevitable rebel onslaught. Later that night another bulletin, allegedly from Campins, assured citizens listening to Radio Granada that the garrison was determined to serve the best interests of Spain and of the Republic ('the faithful expression of the will of the Spanish people') and went on to warn of the penalties awaiting those whose who failed to comply with the wishes of the authorities:

The maximum rigours of martial law will fall on any misguided individual who fails to do everything in his power to prevent disturbances to the normal life of this town. Likewise, I demand that every attempted disturbance be denounced to me personally, and I assure you that I have taken every precaution to see that martial law, which is not to interfere in any way with the life of the town, means inflexibility with those who disregard my orders.[27]

For the people of the Albaicín the meaning of what was happening had become abundantly clear. Everyone knew that an offensive against the quarter was imminent, and feverish attempts were now made to prepare its defences.

The main access to the Albaicín from the centre of Granada runs along the narrow Carrera del Darro to the Paseo de los Tristes and then up the sharply-angled Cuesta del Chapiz. It was essential that this entrance to the Albaicín should be barricaded and accordingly a deep trench was cut across the bottom of the Cuesta del Chapiz to prevent vehicles from climbing the hill. Similar trenches and makeshift barriers quickly sealed off the many other, narrower streets.

Seeing these preparations the Nationalists made plans to crush the workers' opposition. First, two artillery batteries were placed in strategic positions overlooking the quarter: one just below the Church of Saint Christopher above the Albaicín on the road to Murcia, and the other on top of a bastion of the Alhambra directly facing the Republicans across the gorge of the river Darro. Night had by now fallen and the rebels decided to take no action till the following morning. There was some sporadic shooting, however, which claimed two Nationalist deaths and probably many more Republican ones.[28]

Granada: Tuesday 21 July 1936
On 21 July both batteries opened fire on the Albaicín and violent

shooting took place between the rebels (Infantry, Assault Guards and Falangists) and the scantily-armed workers who, from the windows and balconies of their tightly-packed houses, were in an advantageous position to attack the troops with the few pistols and rifles at their disposal. But the Nationalists soon managed to penetrate the Albaicín at several points and many arrests were made. No accurate figures for casualties are available. Radio Granada, meanwhile, continued to broadcast appeals from the rebel authorities to the 'loyalty' and 'good sense' of the people, and made it quite clear that as much force as was necessary would be used to crush all resistance in the Albaicín:

The criminal conduct of a band of outlaws who, in the last death-rattle of their attempt to devour our country, have been disturbing the life of Granada from the Albaicín, is about to come to an end; following the norms of the last decree, with which Granada is already familiar, our valiant troops of Assault Guards, Infantry and Artillery have now gone to attack the wild beasts in their lairs. I rely on the good sense of the citizens of Granada not to be alarmed by our resolution that the town shall be able, at last, to enjoy again the calm of its incomparable nights.

Your Military Commander joins with you in a vibrant 'Long Live Spain! Long Live the Republic! Long Live Granada!'[29]

The new military decree to which this note refers had been issued earlier that evening, when León Maestre had officially taken over from General Campins as Military Commander of Granada.* Maestre was now the supreme military authority in the province, and his decree reflected the ruthless intransigence with which enemies of the Nationalists could henceforth expect to be treated:

I call on all those Granadine patriots who love the one, noble and glorious Spain, and ask them to give their whole hearts and serene self-discipline to the carrying out of my orders.

* The unfortunate General Campins was flown to Seville and executed by firing squad on 16 August 1936 on the orders of Queipo de Llano. His death was announced by *Ideal* on 18 August.

1. The capital and province are now under martial law and every offence will be dealt with by military tribunals.

2. Anyone committing aggressive acts and hostilities against the Army and the forces of law and order will be given a summary trial and executed.

3. Anyone caught carrying arms, or who within three hours has not handed over any arms in his possession to the Civil Guard, Assault Guard or Police, will be given a summary trial and executed.

4. Groups of more than three people are strictly forbidden and will be dissolved by the troops without previous warning.

5. From the moment this decree is promulgated the driving of all vehicles of whatever kind by civilians is strictly forbidden.

6. The right to strike has been abolished and strike committees will be executed.

7. Anyone committing sabotage of whatever kind, and especially against communications, will be given a summary trial and executed.

Given in Granada on this 21 July 1936, to be scrupulously obeyed.

LONG LIVE SPAIN. LONG LIVE THE REPUBLIC. LONG LIVE GRANADA.[30]

Granada: Wednesday 22 July 1936
In the early hours of the following morning, 22 July, an ultimatum clarifying the implications of the previous night's bulletin was read over Radio Granada to the inhabitants of the Albaicín. Within three hours the women and children were to leave the quarter and assemble at places designated by the authorities; the men were to stand in the doorways of their homes with their arms up, having first thrown their weapons into the centre of the street, and white flags were to be hung on the balconies of all the houses that surrendered. In the event of non-compliance with these orders the Albaicín would be bombarded at 2.30 p.m. that day from the artillery emplacements and also from the air.[31]

Shortly after the announcement, long lines of frightened women and children started to wind their way down the narrow streets and make for the assembly points. There they were questioned and searched by female rebel supporters, and taken to a provisional concentration camp outside the town. The men of the Albaicín refused to capitulate. Shooting soon broke out again between them and the rebels, who then retired to allow the artillery the freedom to bombard the quarter in earnest. This it did, supported by three fighter planes captured that morning at Armilla,[32] which now flew low over the Albaicín and opened fire with machine-guns on the pockets of resistance. Hand-grenades were also dropped.[33] Many buildings were badly damaged in the bombardment, but in spite of this the workers had still not been dislodged from their 'lairs' when night fell.[34] The end, however, was near.

Granada: Thursday 23 July 1936
On the following morning, 23 July, the artillery bombardment was intensified, and this time it met with success. Improvised white flags began to appear at windows and balconies and the firing dwindled to occasional outbursts. The little ammunition the workers possessed had run out and it was clear that further resistance was impossible.

At this moment waiting bands of soldiers and Falangists invaded the Albaicín, and soon it was all over.[35] Those workers who were lucky managed to escape from the back of the town across-country to the Republican lines near Guadix; others less fortunate were caught trying to get away, while many were cornered in their own homes. All of these were led away for interrogation at official centres and the majority were shot soon afterwards. As the *Cruzada* comments: 'The last hope of the Reds in Granada had vanished.'[36]

On 22 July *Ideal* exultantly announced the extinction of resistance in the Albaicín and published a piece by one of its reporters who had visited the quarter after the surrender. 'The power of modern weaponry has left evidence of its irresistible efficacy,' he comments. 'The walls of many houses are pitted with fire from rifles, pistols, machine-guns and artillery.' Several buildings had been completely gutted, and the journalist sneers at the pathetic efforts of the workers to defend themselves behind makeshift barricades against the superior equipment of the troops. *Ideal* was now showing its true colours.

Resistance had ended. Other small pockets of opposition in the town had also been crushed and on the night of 23 July the rebels could congratulate themsleves on having so easily gained complete control of Granada. They had lost no more than half a dozen men.

As was mentioned earlier, the workers in Granada were almost without arms. Nationalist documentation itself proves this. A handful of pistols and rifles without ammunition is no answer, as the *Ideal* reporter reminds us, to modern artillery, aeroplanes, grenades and machine-guns. Granada fell to the rebels because, quite simply, they had the weapons and the training to use them effectively. One cannot forget, either, the credulity of the Civil Governor, Torres Martínez, or the ineptitude of General Campins, nor the lack of decisive leadership on the part of the Popular Front organisations. If arms had been distributed to those members of the left-wing groups capable of using them, or if the workers had had the enterprise to seize them by force, the rising in Granada might have been averted and the course of the war altered in favour of the Republic. But none of this happened. The 'resistance' which the Nationalists crushed with such facility was, in reality, no resistance at all, and it is this fact, continually stressed by *Ideal*, that made the subsequent repression of Granada one of the outstanding crimes of the war.

SEVEN

The Repression

Although the rebels had gained control of Granada without difficulty, and virtually without losses, they knew that their position was far from secure. The rising had failed in Malaga, and Granada was surrounded by loyal, Republican territory. At some points the 'Reds' were less than fifteen miles away, and Granada itself was alive with enemies. At any moment, in theory, a counter-attack might be launched.

In view of this situation the Nationalists decided to create new civilian militia and expand those that already existed; to undertake the immediate pacification of the province; and to arrest and shoot as many 'enemies of the Movement' as could be identified or fabricated.

In connection with the creation of the new militia, on 25 July 1936 – Saint James's Day, Spain's great national holiday – General Orgaz Yoldi arrived in Granada from Tetuan, touching down at Armilla airport in a German Junkers.[1]

On 29 July the first Republican bombing of Granada took place.[2] It was a timid, ineffectual affair, like those which followed it, and no military target was destroyed. The Republican bombings were of use only to the rebels, who made much capital out of the damage caused to the Alhambra and of the various deaths occasioned among the civilian population. Moreover, each time the Republicans bombed the town a batch of prisoners was shot in reprisal. It is difficult to credit the ineptitude of the Republican airmen, who seem to have made no concerted effort to bomb the two barracks of the garrison or blow up the vital explosives factory at El Fargue.

On the day following the first bombing, 30 July, a strong contingent of Republican militia attempted to enter Granada from Huétor Santillán, on the road to Guadix. They were repelled by rebel troops supported by a group of Civil Guards under the command of Lieutenant Mariano Pelayo. The Republicans left behind numerous dead and a considerable quantity of arms.[3] It was to be the only serious attempt to recapture Granada. If the Republic had succeeded in organising a full-scale operation against the Granada rebels in the opening weeks of the war, it is difficult to see how it could have failed to recoup the situation. But after 18 August 1936, when General Varela broke the 'siege' of Granada and re-established road and rail communications between it and Seville, such an operation would have been very much more complicated.

It may now be found helpful if we identify the principal military groups, civilian organisations and other bodies active in Granada during the war, always bearing in mind that, in practice, they and their functions tended to overlap.

1. *The Military Commandery.* As has been explained, the Granada garrison was made up of an artillery and an infantry regiment, both of which were considerably depleted when the war began owing to the fact that many of the men had been granted holiday leave. The acting Military Commander after General Campins's arrest, Colonel Basilio León Maestre, was replaced on 29 July 1936 by General Antonio González Espinosa, who arrived by aeroplane from Seville.[4] It should be recalled at this point that the Granada Military Commandery was subordinate to the Captaincy-General in Seville, which meant in fact that, from 20 July 1936, the supreme authority in Granada was General Queipo de Llano.

The Military Commandery, as one would expect, was mainly concerned with military operations, and left the general running of the town's affairs to the Civil Government, but this demarcation was by no means definitive, and the Military Commandery was as concerned as the Civil Government with the drawing up of lists of those 'undesirables' who were to be arrested and shot. A judge, Francisco Angulo Montes, was put in charge of these activities. He was assisted by Sergeant Romacho of the Civil Guard. Both men (now dead) are remembered for their brutality during the repression.

In the early days of the war various courts-martial were held in the Commandery, and dozens of Republicans were condemned to death, among them several Army officers who refused to join the rebels.

During the night of 31 July and 1 August 1936 the Civil Governor, César Torres Martínez, was court-martialled, along with the two members of the Popular Front who were with him in his office when the rising began, Virgilio Castilla and Joaquín Rus Romero, the trades unionist José Alcántara, the lawyer Enrique Marín Forero and the engineer Juan José Santa Cruz.

The sentence against Torres Martínez was ludicrous: he was accused of having abused his position as Civil Governor in order to promote 'a widespread subversive movement in readiness for the one which was being prepared throughout Spain and which would attempt to implant in our city, and by means of a campaign of terror, the most advanced Russo-marxist doctrines'; of having distributed arms to the 'Marxists'; of having ordered the latter to open fire on the troops; of having helped to organise the column that was to march in relief of Cordoba; and of several other acts of 'military rebellion'.[5]

Torres Martínez was lucky: the improvised military judges, knowing that almost all the charges against the Civil Governor were false and that moreover, as a Republican official, he could hardly have been expected to act otherwise than as a Republican, decided not to condemn him to death. It seems that the Archbishop of Granada may also have intervened on his behalf. Torres Martínez was sentenced to life imprisonment and, in the event, would spend eight years in gaol.[6]

Castilla, Rus Romero, Alcántara, Marín Forero and Santa

Cruz were less fortunate: they were condemned to death and shot on 2 August 1936.[7]

Courts-martial only took place in Granada in the opening weeks of the rebellion. After that the rebels decided that they were an unnecessary complication, a mere waste of time, and proceeded to shoot their enemies without formalities.

2. *The Civil Government.* Commandant Valdés was surrounded by a mixed group of Falangists, policemen, Army officers and thugs who devoted themselves to organising the Granada repression. Prominent among these men were the Jiménez de Parga brothers; Julio Romero Funes (the hated policeman who was responsible for the deaths of hundreds of people and who was killed later by the notorious Quero brothers in a gunfight in Granada); a brutal lout nicknamed Italobalbo for his likeness to the Italian Fascist leader; the ex-deputy of the CEDA, Ramón Ruiz Alonso, and other members of Acción Popular; Antonio Godoy Abellán (a rich landowner and old guard Falangist who regularly participated in the shootings in the cemetery) and a certain Captain Fernández. During the interrogations in the Civil Government torture was often used. An instrument known as the 'aeroplane' had been set up in one of the rooms. On this, victims with their arms tied behind their backs were hoisted to the ceiling by their wrists. The screams of men being tortured were often heard by the concierges (with whom I have spoken) and on several occasions prisoners threw themselves from top windows in an effort to kill themselves.

Valdés had a radio in the Civil Government, which had been installed in the early days of the rising, and he was in constant contact with Queipo de Llano in Seville. We can be quite certain that the new Governor received direct orders from Queipo.

When they had finished interrogating a prisoner in the Civil Government he was handed over to the assassins. As a rule such victims were not transferred to the gaol but killed there and then on the outskirts of the town or in the cemetery. We shall deal later in this chapter with the activities of these assassins, known collectively as 'The Black Squad'.

3. *The Civil Guard*. According to the *Historia de la cruzada española*, there were only forty Civil Guards in Granada when the war began.[8] The Lieutenant-Colonel of the force, Fernando Vidal Pagán, was loyal to the Republic, as has been said, and the role of conspirator fell to his subordinate, Lieutenant Mariano Pelayo. Pelayo was a brave, hard man, and shortly after the rising took place he was appointed Public Order Delegate. A good friend to his friends, Pelayo could be implacable with his enemies, as he proved during the repression.

The Civil Guard – long famous for its marksmanship – frequently took part in the executions in the cemetery.

4. *The Assault Guard*. The *asaltos* were considered to be particularly loyal to the Republic, which did not prevent their chief in Granada, Captain Alvarez, from joining the rebels. Several less treacherous Assault Guards were shot, and those who escaped did what they were told, which often included taking part in the shootings in the cemetery and elsewhere in the villages around Granada.

5. *The Municipal Police*. The Police HQ was in Duquesa Street, opposite the Civil Government, where it continues today. During the repression there was constant coming and going between the two buildings. The dungeons of the Commissary witnessed atrocious scenes, some of which have been described to me by survivors (including a freemason who is still alive in Granada). Reference has already been made to the Chief of the Granada police, Julio Romero Funes, one of Valdés's right-hand-men, whose cruelty became legendary in the town.

6. *The Falange*. It was stated earlier that the Falange had very few members in Granada before the rising. According to a note published in *Ideal* on 22 July 1936, the organisation was now prepared to enlist anyone who could be vouched for by an 'old shirt' member of the party.[9] The recruitment office in the Civil Government was soon inundated with requests for membership: the *Cruzada* claims that 900 recruits were enlisted in a few days, while Gollonet and Morales put the figure much higher and state that 2,000 were enrolled in twenty-four hours.[10] The new recruits

were organised, according to Falangist practice, into two 'lines': the first line would fight along the combat fronts with the Army, while the second would be based in the capital and help with the running of essential services. An article on the Granada Falange, published in *Ideal* on 1 September 1936, states that the second line 'is obliged to denounce all those cases which it knows of that are contrary to the Fatherland and to the Spanish Falange'. The Falange was directly responsible for the deaths of many hundreds of *granadinos*.

7. *Militia of Acción Popular*. It has been pointed out that, as a result of the victory at the polls of the Popular Front in February 1936, many members of the Juventudes de Acción Popular (JAP) joined the Falange. Not all did, however, and in Granada, as elsewhere, an attempt was made at the beginning of the war to form an Acción Popular militia. This was to be led by Ramón Ruiz Alonso, the ex-deputy of the CEDA. But, as we shall see later, the attempt failed and the *accionpopulistas* joined other groups.

8. *The Requetés (Carlists)*. In *Ideal* on 22 July the Carlists pledged their full support for the Movement: 'Our Communion offers its services to the Army, that is to say to Spain herself, asking God and His Holy Mother to protect our forces.' All members were ordered to report immediately to the organisation's HQ, where they would 'make out lists and help in the most useful way possible'. While there were few *requetés* in Granada before the rising (the organisation was strongest in the north of Spain), it was nevertheless soon possible to form a complete battalion.

9. *The Pérez del Pulgar Battalion*. During the siege of Granada by Ferdinand and Isabella in 1491 a Spanish nobleman, Hernán Pérez del Pulgar, distinguished himself one night by scaling the walls of the town and fixing a scroll bearing the words 'Ave Maria' to the front door of the chief mosque. The battalion named after him was formed at the end of August 1936[11] by Ramón Ruiz Alonso, who spoke to me of it in these terms: 'The battalion was formed to give political prisoners, who would otherwise have been shot, a chance either to redeem themselves on the field or else die with honour before enemy fire. In this

way their children would not suffer the stigma of having had Red fathers.'[12] The battalion, which played no part at all in the repression, recruited about 500 men, and Ruiz Alonso has shown me a photograph of himself proudly leading them out of Granada to the front at Alcalá. He forgot to mention, however, that the battalion's behaviour on the field lacked enthusiasm and that one night, perhaps in emulation of the original Pérez del Pulgar, many of the men slipped across the lines to join their Republican brothers. The battalion was disbanded shortly afterwards.

10. *The 'Españoles Patriotas'.* This was the first civil militia formed by Orgaz, and within a few days it numbered 5,175 men under the command of 29 officers and 150 NCOs.[13] Its quarters were established in the bull ring. The Españoles Patriotas first served as a kind of municipal police but later several of its sections fought in the field. On 29 December 1936, *Ideal* announced that the Españoles Patriotas were to merge with the Falange.

11. *Defensa Armada de Granada.* Formed in September 1936, Defensa Armada – its members were popularly known as the 'mangas verdes' ('green-sleeves') because of their green armbands – was composed of civilians unfit for military service through age, infirmity or other causes. Its men were ordered to spy on their neighbours and to denounce any suspicious activities which came to their notice. Defensa Armada divided Granada into three sectors, each with its own head who in turn appointed area chiefs and street chiefs within his sector. Each house in Granada was expected to have at least one member, and it was planned that the organisation should eventually assume the municipal functions of the Españoles Patriotas, thereby freeing these for military action. By 6 September 1936 Defensa Armada had 2,086 members, plus 4,000 applications which were being carefully screened in order to eliminate all those with even a suggestion of leftish inclinations or past history.[14] In an atmosphere worthy of Orwell's *1984*, Defensa Armada was responsible for the deaths of a huge number of innocent people, often for reasons of personal animosity, jealousy and other non-political factors.

12. *The Spanish Foreign Legion.* General Orgaz had become

aware during his short visit to Granada that, even with the aid of the newly formed militia, the town would not be sufficiently protected to withstand a concerted Republican attack. He decided, therefore, that the garrison should be quickly strengthened with professional military reinforcements.

Accordingly, at 10.30 a.m. on 3 August 1936, a three-engined Junkers transport landed at Armilla airport from Tetuan with the first twenty men of the Sixth Battalion of the Foreign Legion. Other transport planes followed, and that afternoon a complete company of the Legion marched through the streets of Granada. Their presence was greeted with jubilation and immense relief by Nationalist supporters, for it was clear that a Republican recovery of the town would now prove much more difficult.[15]

Over the next few days other legionaries arrived and soon the Battalion was complete. It was employed in numerous offensives against Republican pockets throughout the province, notably in the taking of Loja – a crucial position on the road from Granada to Malaga – on 18 August 1936.[16]

13. *The 'Regulares'*. As a consequence of the fall of Loja to the Nationalists, road and rail contact was re-established with Seville. A few days later Queipo de Llano sent a contingent of several hundred *regulares* – Moorish troops from Morocco – to Granada.[17] The *regulares* fought side-by-side with the Granada garrison and the Legionaries, and it is said that they perpetrated many barbarities in the villages of the province. Their presence in Granada greatly strengthened the position of the Nationalists.

14. *The 'Black Squad'*. We come finally to the notorious 'Black Squad' about which so much has been said in books on Lorca. It is important to understand that this squad of killers did not constitute a tightly-knit organisation such as, for example, the Falange or the *requetés*. The 'Black Squad' was little more than a loose collection of individuals who enjoyed killing for the sake of killing and to whom Valdés, in order to reduce the population of Granada to the greatest possible state of panic, had given *carte blanche* to carry out assassinations. They worked in close collaboration with the Civil Government, and many of those who

operated with the squad were thugs who had joined the Falange in the first days of the Movement, often middle-class thugs. Others saw in the squad an opportunity for working off long-standing grudges against society. All took positive pleasure in killing. Men such as Francisco Jiménez Callejas (known familiarly as 'El pajarero'), an expert throat-slitter who, until his death in 1977, ran a thriving timber business in Granada; José Vico Escamilla, who owned a small shop in San Juan de Dios Street and died not long ago; Perico Morales, a night-watchman who had been a member of the Anarchist CNT before the rising; the López Peralta brothers, one of whom, Fernando, later committed suicide; the brothers Pedro and Antonio Embíz, Cristóbal Fernández Amigo, Antonio Godoy Abellán (already mentioned in connection with the Civil Government), Miguel Cañadas, Manuel García Ruiz, Miguel Hórques, Carlos Jiménez Vílchez (who worked until recently in the Town Hall in Granada) and the individuals nicknamed 'El Chato de la Plaza Nueva', 'El cuchillero del Pie de la Torre', 'El afilaor' and 'Paco el motrileño'. Few members of the squad are alive today: many of them later met violent deaths, and those who survive are shunned by the local populace.

The 'Black Squad', as befitted its office, functioned mainly by night and Claude Couffon has graphically described its methods:

The mopping-up operations practised by the Black Squad have an evocative name: *el paseo*. They are carried out to such a characteristic pattern that one can talk of a method. For the men singled out by the killers the first thing (usually in the small hours of the night) is the noise of a car pulling up outside the front door. There are shouts, laughter and curses; if the victim inhabits one of the lower-class districts where families live crammed on all the floors, this is followed by steps on the staircase. And then the terrible scene: the mother clinging to her son, pleading with the killers, who push her away with their rifle-butts; the children and weeping wife at whom the guns are now pointed; the husband, dressing hurriedly, is jostled and bundled out into the stairs. An engine starts up and the car speeds away. Behind the closed shutters the neighbours, waiting, wonder if it will be their turn tomorrow.... Sometimes the reports ring out at the corner of the street or, still nearer, on the pavement. And the mother or wife goes downstairs, knowing that she'll find a corpse. But she must be careful not to go out into the street too quickly or else more shots might ring out, tumbling her on top of the body she had gone to recover.[18]

Every morning the bodies of the dead and dying were collected in lorries and taken to the San Juan de Dios Hospital. Before he died in 1971, Dr Rafael Jofré (a close friend of Lorca and an expert on *cante jondo*), who was on duty in the hospital during the repression, told me about his sickening experiences there. He was in charge of the ward where wounded prisoners were brought. Often members of the murder squads would arrive and drag dying men out into the streets to shoot them. In particular he remembered the visits of a brutal sergeant of the Civil Guard who on one occasion shot a father and son who had been admitted to the hospital months before the rising began. He also recalled the arrival of a batch of foreign prisoners wounded in the famous Barranco de Buco offensive: these were removed and shot almost immediately, as was a boy of fourteen who was arrested while defending the Albaicín.

These, then, were the principal groups and organisations responsible for the military affairs of the province and the repression of the civil population. No information at all about the Granada killings is provided by *Ideal*, Gollonet and Morales, the *Cruzada* or any other Nationalist publication on the war. It is as though they never took place.

As soon as the town fell to the rebels, lists began to be drawn up of those 'undesirables' considered, for whatever reason, to be enemies of the Movement. Before long the provincial gaol, situated on the road to Jaén on the outskirts of the town and originally designed to accommodate a maximum of 400 men, contained 2,000 prisoners in the most deplorable conditions. Those who survived this imprisonment speak with horror of their experiences in the gaol. Nobody knew when it might be his turn to die, for every evening the lists came from the Civil Government and Military Commandery and the names were read out of the men to be shot before sunrise. And frequently members of the 'Black Squad' would arrive and drag someone away, or batter their victims senseless in the cells. The condemned men were herded into the prison chapel and more or less forced to make their last confession. There they spent the night and then, an hour or two before dawn, the scene was always the same: the prisoners were taken from the chapel, roped or wired together and bundled into the lorries waiting to drive them to the slaughter.

As can readily be imagined, the morale of the prisoners was extremely low. César Torres Martínez recalls:

It was so terrible that one's personality cracked. I can never forget it. There were some exceptions – there always are – but in general we were sick with fear, constantly worried, constantly anxious. It was impossible to be one's true self.

Yes, there were some outstanding exceptions. I was told about a young lad – 20 or 21 he would have been – who was shot one night. It happened to be a day when his mother had sent him a melon. And this lad, there, in the chapel, said: 'Would you mind bringing me the melon from my cell? My mother has sent it to me and I'm going to eat it before I die.' This is an absolutely true story. And he ate his melon in the chapel.

I am convinced that 99 per cent. of the prisoners were terrified, utterly terrified. Otherwise I can't explain how it was that, since there were thousands of us there, we didn't do anything to get out, knowing as we did that they were capable of killing us all. Even if we ourselves had had to kill, or die in the attempt! But of course the truth was that you never knew if they were going to shoot you or not, there was always a question mark. And fear! Fear! There is no doubt that everyone was terrified.

According to Torres Martínez (and his story was confirmed by the account given to me by the Socialist lawyer Antonio Pérez Funes, who shared Torres Martínez's cell), the staff of the prison behaved in an exemplary fashion. But they had to be very careful, since in the event of any disobedience the rebels were quite capable of shooting them too. Torres Martínez continues:

For the most part the gaolers were positively horrified by what was happening. Horrified. They were professional prison staff, and had no option but to do as they were told. It pained them, since most of them were kind people. In those appalling circumstances it would have been difficult not to be compassionate, moreover. It was so dreadful, so brutal, so crazy, that it would have been impossible for anyone with any humanity not to feel compassion.

The prisoners had very little contact with the outside world, at least in the early days of the repression. For this reason a letter written by a group of them and published on 8 August 1936 in *Ideal* has great interest. The letter was concerned with the Republican bombings of Granada which, as has been said, caused several deaths among the civilian population and many reprisals among the prisoners of the gaol:

Dear Military Commander,

The undersigned, on their own behalf and that of all the political prisoners in the Provincial Gaol, wish to bring to your attention that they protest forcibly about the repeated bombings to which Granada is being subjected.

We voiced our protest from the first moment when the airmen caused victims among the civilian population, which is in no way involved in the disastrous struggle at present afflicting us: witness to our protests is the Head of the prison, to whom we have repeatedly voiced our indignation.

Our sorrow reached the limit when we learnt from the newspapers this morning about the unforgiveable bombing of the Alhambra and the victims this outrage occasioned.

The signatories to this letter are enemies of such acts of destruction and death, enemies of violence and cruelty, and we wish to say so publicly from this gaol where we are passing anxious days, quietly confident in the chivalry of Spanish Army officers. For all of which, Dear Sir, we write to you and authorise you to use this document signed by us in whatever way you may deem most beneficial, including broadcasting it over the radio so that everyone may see that we in no way identify ourselves with such acts.

Let us hope that all Spaniards will share our feelings and that, for the good of Spain, an end may be put to the shedding of so much innocent blood. We wish you long life.

Granada, 7 August 1936. Signed: Francisco Torres Monereo, Pablo Casiriai Nieva, José Villoslada, Fernández-Montesinos, Joaquín García Labella, José Megías, Luis Fajardo, Melchor Rubio, Arturo Marín Forero, Miguel Lozano, José Valenzuela, Rafael Vaquero, Maximiano Hernández, Plácido E. Vargas Corpas and other illegible signatures (p. 4).

Three days later, and after several of these men had been shot, despite their faith in the 'chivalry of Spanish Army officers', Manuel Fernández-Montesinos, horrified by what was happening in the gaol, wrote an urgent letter to his brother Gregorio, like him a doctor. The letter shows the appalling conditions in which Fernández-Montesinos and many hundreds of other innocent prisoners were living:

My Dear Gregory,

I'm writing to you absolutely shocked by what has been taking place here for several days, and tonight as well: the shooting of prisoners in reprisal for the victims of the bombing. With tonight's batch that makes sixty, chosen I don't know how, but from the Republican prisoners, that is to say from those who have not been formally charged with any crime. There's no way of communicating with the outside world, which is why I'm writing to you via a sure channel in order that this cry for help should reach you. The first executions were so monstrous that we never thought it could be repeated, but tonight it did happen again despite everything. I don't know what to ask you to do. All I can tell you is that if this continues we're all going to die more or less quickly, and one doesn't know what to wish for, since if it's terrible to die this terrible, tragic waiting is even worse, when you don't know whose turn it's going to be the next night. You've got to do something to see if this torment can be brought to an end. Make an arrangement with Diego and go and ask Uncle Frasquito if they can talk to Rosales, who's one of the leaders of the Falange. Talk to del Campo about it without telling him that I have written to you. In this business it's not the degree of political undesirability of the prisoner that counts, since up to now none of those shot has been significant in any political sense. The last was Luis Fajardo, which tells you everything.[19]

Five days later, on 16 August 1936, Manuel Fernández Montesinos was executed in the cemetery.

There was a great deal of talk in the gaol about the activities of an informer known as 'The Lady with the Fan'. This woman, Alicia Herrero Vaquero, had been sent to Granada from Jaén with her husband Luis Tello as a Republican spy and, apparently, with instructions to organise resistance to the rebels. She was soon unmasked by Mariano Pelayo of the Civil Guard – by then Delegate of Public Order – who spared her life on condition that she carry out counter-espionage and denounce left-wing 'agitatores'. To this end Pelayo set up a bar for his informer at 11, Puentezuelas Street, where numerous left-wing people began to meet. Before they realised that their conversations were being relayed to Pelayo, it was too late: they were rounded up and shot.

In the autumn of 1938 a letter-bomb was sent to 'The Lady of the Fan'. It was intercepted by Pelayo. The bomb exploded and the Civil Guard lost one of his arms. In reprisal sixty prisoners were executed, on 4 October 1938.

Given the conditions that prevailed in Granada gaol, it is not surprising that there took place there during the repression an extraordinary flowering of religion or religiosity. Since the Nationalists proclaimed themselves to be soldiers in a Christian crusade against Marxism, it seemed wise for the prisoners to feel themselves, and to show themselves, to be good Catholics. But their Catholicism did them little good, for it is a proven fact that the rebels took over 2,000 prisoners from the gaol and shot them without mercy.

EIGHT

Granada Cemetery

The Granada rebels shot most of their victims, and all the prisoners condemned to death, against the outside face of the walls of the municipal cemetery. Civilian access to the cemetery and its surroundings was prohibited once Granada fell to the Nationalists, and a Civil Guard post was set up a few hundred yards from the entrance to ensure that this ruling was enforced. In the case of deaths from 'natural' causes the rebels made things difficult too: only a limited number of close relatives were allowed to attend funerals and it was understood that these should be expedited with alacrity.

To reach the cemetery, which stands behind the Alhambra to the south-west in a position of great beauty, the lorries had first to cross the centre of the town and then climb the steep Cuesta de Gomeres. At the top of the hill stood the British Consulate, and every morning the Consul, William Davenhill, and his sister Maravillas, would hear the vehicles labouring up the slope and try not to listen. But one morning Maravillas peeped out of the window as two lorries turned past the house. 'It was ghastly,' she told me in the summer of 1966. 'In each lorry there must have been twenty or thirty men and women piled on top of each other, trussed like pigs being taken to the market. Ten minutes later we heard shooting from the cemetery and knew that it was all over. It was terrible.'

Other foreigners were witness to this sinister traffic, among them a group of Americans who happened to be in Granada when the rising began. One of these tourists was Robert Neville, the bridge editor of the *New York Herald Tribune*. Neville, a liberal and an admirer of the Spanish Republic, kept a meticulous day-by-day account of his experiences in Granada from the date of his arrival on 18 July 1936 until he was flown out to Seville on 12 August. Within two weeks he was back in New York, and on 30 August he published his diary in the *Herald Tribune*.

It made gripping reading. Neville had stayed in the Pensión Americana near the Alhambra, and each day walked down to see his compatriots in the Hotel Washington Irving, which stands just on the corner where the road to the cemetery twists sharply to the right. On 29 July he wrote in his diary:

We have solved the meaning of the outburst of shots we hear every morning about sunrise and every evening about sunset. We have also been able to correlate it with the truckloads of soldiers that go by the Washington Irving Hotel just a few minutes before we hear those shots and which return just a few minutes after. Today four of us were playing bridge in a room on the second floor of the hotel when two truckloads went by. On the ground it would seem that all the men in those huge trucks were soldiers, but today we got a glimpse of them from above, and we saw that in the centre of each truck was a group of civilians.

The road past the Washington Irving goes to the cemetery. It doesn't go anywhere else. The trucks today went up with those civilians. In five minutes we heard the shots. In five more minutes the trucks came down, and this time there were no civilians. Those soldiers were the firing squad and those civilians were on their way to execution. The men were being hauled alive to the cemetery.[1]

On the afternoon of 30 July Neville managed to pay a brief visit to the cemetery (he does not explain how). That morning some Republican bombs had fallen, and the rebel authorities announced that henceforth they would shoot five prisoners for every bomb dropped. In the cemetery Neville 'saw a squad of twelve grave diggers hard at work'.[2]

Another American witness to these events was the writer Helen Nicholson, who was spending the summer at the house of her son-in-law Alfonso Gámir Sandoval near the Alhambra. In a little-known book, *Death in the Morning*, published in London in 1937, Helen Nicholson described her experiences in Granada during the first month and a half of the war. Referring to the early-morning executions in the cemetery, she wrote:

On Sunday, August the second, we had our early [air-]raid at half-past four, and the second one at eight o'clock, after which we break-fasted downstairs in dressing-gowns. I remember that we were all feel-ing rather grumpy, for four and a half hours' sleep is an insufficient ration in wartime, when one is under a constant nervous strain. After breakfast we all dragged ourselves rather wearily upstairs, and my daughter and her husband said they were going to Mass. Not being a Catholic myself, I went to my room hoping to snatch another hour's sleep, but there seemed to be an unusual number of soldiers' lorries rattling past our house, and what with the noise they made, sounding their horns every other minute, and the clatter from the servants' *patio*, it was difficult to doze for more than a few minutes at a time. Also I was haunted by an uneasy memory of the night before. About two o'clock I had been awakened by the sound of a lorry and several cars going up the hill towards the cemetery, and shortly afterwards I had heard a fusillade of shots, and then the same vehicles returning. Later I became all too familiar with these sounds, and learned to dread the early morning, not only because it was the enemy's favourite time for bombing us, but also on account of the executions that took place then.[3]

During August Miss Nicholson was to witness the growing in-tensity of the Nationalist repression of Granada, and the fact that her own right-wing sympathies are evident on every page of her narrative makes her testimony doubly convincing. One final quotation from her account illustrates the horror of the shoot-ings:

For some time the executions had been increasing, at a rate that alarmed and sickened all thinking people. The concierge of the ceme-tery, who had a modest little family of twenty-three children, begged my son-in-law to find him some place where his wife and his twelve younger children, who were still at home, might live. Their home in the lodge at the cemetery gates had become unbearable to them. They could not help hearing the shots, and sometimes other sounds – the cries and screams of the dying – that made their lives a nightmare, and he feared the effect they might have upon his younger children.[4]

Robert Neville also heard about the plight of this family, noting in his diary on 4 August:

The caretaker of the cemetery went mad today and was taken to the insane asylum. His family fled to the Pensión Alhambra, near us. We counted thirty-seven civilians making their last trip up to the cemetery yesterday afternoon.[5]

In August 1978 I was introduced to a man who had been a guard in the cemetery during the first months of the repression, José García Arquelladas. His story confirmed the printed accounts given by Robert Neville and Helen Nicholson. According to García Arquelladas, the official executions took place twice a day before dawn and at sunset, and the *unofficial* ones at all hours of the day and night. The latter victims, unlike those proceeding from the gaol, were not entered in the cemetery register, which explains why the total figure given there for the executions, and which we shall consider in a moment, is much lower than the true one. García Arquelladas, whose declaration I tape-recorded, cannot forget his experiences in the cemetery:

The grave diggers arrived at nine in the morning, which means that the corpses lay where they fell from six o'clock or earlier onwards, alone and abandoned. The gates of the cemetery were locked until it was opened at nine o'clock. It was dreadful. At all hours of the day and night. Up and down all day long, private cars, the lot. They would round up people as they went to work, carrying their lunch in a bag or handkerchief, and bundle them into the lorries. Straight into the lorries and off with them!
    I was there for the first few months, but then I had no option but to join up. All day long, a flood. Cars going up, cars going down,

all day and all night. Women on their knees begging for mercy, the killers – bang! bang! bang! – and that was it. Some shouted 'Long live the Republic!' others 'Long live Communism!' Others were already half dead with terror (they weren't all as brave) and dragged themselves along on their knees begging for mercy.

In the first few months, when I was there, it went on all day with the Civil Guard taking people up, then more people, loading them into lorries and shooting them there and then. A flood, day and night. At night, too, by the headlights of the cars, there against the walls. You've got to realise what it was like, day and night, there were no rules – 8 people, 9 people, 15, 14, in the first months 50 every day, day and night, a flood. I'm telling you, when I was there, in the opening months, it was a flood, day and night, that's the truth, and the women screaming for mercy....

How many people were shot in Granada cemetery? A grave-digger told Gerald Brenan in 1949 that 'the list of those officially shot shows some eight thousand names',[6] but this figure, which has been widely repeated, seems to be inaccurate. And, moreover, such a 'list' is unlikely ever to have existed.

In 1966 I succeeded in gaining access to the cemetery register for the years 1936–1939 in which, side by side with the 'natural' deaths of the period, I counted the names of 2,102 men and women executed by the rebels between 26 July 1936 and 1 March 1939. In the 'cause of death' column for the early victims the euphemistic phrase 'killed by detonation of firearm' was habitual, but this was soon replaced by 'order of military tribunal'. It was unfortunately impossible to obtain a photocopy of the register, for which reason it was necessary to copy all the details by hand. My figure may be slightly inaccurate, but only slightly.

Since 1966 the register has disappeared from the cemetery office, having been removed by the police. According to information which I have received from officials in Granada Town Hall, the mayor of that time, Manuel Pérez Serrabona, ordered it to be destroyed.

It must be stressed that the figure of 2,102 victims killed in the cemetery is an official one taken from the burial records. We can be absolutely certain, therefore, that it is an accurate *minimum* total of Nationalist killings in Granada.

The true figure would be much higher. We know from the evidence of José García Arquelladas and other witnesses that many victims of the 'Black Squad' whose names were not inscribed in the register were shot and buried in the cemetery. To these unknown dead should be added the numerous corpses picked up in the streets of Granada and taken to the cemetery for burial, and, more importantly, the many hundreds of victims of the assassination squads operating in Víznar and other villages on the outskirts of Granada. At a conservative estimate it is unlikely that the number of people shot in Granada and the nearby villages could be less than 5,000.

Even if the figure of 2,102 were to be taken as the sum of all the killings in the capital, however, it would still be an appalling one. The greatest number of executions took place in August 1936, for which month the burial records list no less than 572 names. One appreciates Miss Nicholson's alarm. The figure for September 1936 is 499, for October 190, for November 88. Apart from 143 executions in February 1937, 96 in March and 90 in April, the figures decrease month by month with only occasional sharp rises, as when a batch of prisoners was shot in reprisal for a Republican air-raid or, as was the case on 4 October 1938, for the injury caused to the hated Civil Guard Mariano Pelayo by a letter-bomb meant for the notorious 'Lady with the Fan'.

The daily executions created serious problems for the staff of the cemetery. Bodies were interred in twos and threes wherever room could be found, and eventually the cemetery had to be extended. Brenan writes:

Since the labour of interring so many bodies was considerable, they were bundled into shallow cavities from which their feet and hands often stuck out. An English friend of mine who, at some risk to himself, visited the place a number of times, told me that he saw the bodies of boys and girls still in their teens.[7]

Whatever the risk to Brenan's friend, Nationalist sympath-isers, at least, were sometimes allowed to witness the executions. One man whom I met in 1965 at the house of the British Consul told me, with perfect equanimity and quite unaware of my re-action, that he had taken his young children several times to the cemetery to see how 'the enemies of Spain paid for their crimes'.

The flower of Granada's intellectuals, lawyers, doctors and teachers died in the cemetery, along with huge numbers of ordi-nary left-wing supporters. The more eminent victims, particu-larly the town councillors, were allowed preferential treatment in the matter of burial, and their families were permitted to inter them privately. Today only the tomb of Manuel Fernández-Mon-tesinos can be located with any facility.*

Some of these victims should be mentioned briefly. One of the graves seen by Brenan in 1949 belonged to a 'famous specialist in children's diseases'; this was Rafael García Duarte, Professor of Paediatrics in Granada University, a much-loved man who treated his poorer patients free of charge. His crime was to have been a freemason.[8]

Constantino Ruiz Carnero was editor of the left-wing *El Defensor de Granada*. He was an obvious target for the rebels' hatred and they arrested him on the first day of the rising. Ruiz Carnero suffered from very deficient eyesight and wore glasses with thick lenses. On the night before his execution a prison guard smashed these into his eyes with a rifle-butt. Medical assist-ance was refused and Ruiz Carnero lay in agony all night. Next morning he was bundled into a lorry with other victims, but when they arrived at the cemetery he was already dead.[9]

Also shot in the cemetery in these early days of the repression was the engineer Juan José de Santa Cruz, who had constructed the marvellous road to the top of the Sierra Nevada (today the pride of the Spanish Tourist Board). The night before his execu-tion Santa Cruz was allowed to marry the gypsy girl with whom he had lived for many years. The charge against the engineer,

* A complete list of the executed town councillors is provided in Appendix A.

trumped up by his enemies, was that he had mined the River Darro where it flows under the streets of Granada.

Other distinguished men shot in the cemetery included the Rector of Granada University, Salvador Vila, a noted Arabist; Joaquín García Labella, who held the Chair of Political Law at the University and was once the youngest professor in Spain; Jesús Yoldi Bereau, Professor of Pharmacy at the University, who with García Labella had been forced in the first weeks of the rising to dig the graves of the victims despatched by the killers in Víznar; José Palanco Romero, Professor of History at the University; José Megías Manzano, Assistant Professor in the Faculty of Medicine; Saturnino Reyes, a well-known doctor; the lawyer José Villoslada (who had tried to kill himself in the prison by slashing his wrists); and even the gentle Protestant pastor, José García Fernández. Names of other notable victims of the firing squads would make the list interminable. Enough has been said to demonstrate that in Granada, as elsewhere throughout Nationalist Spain, the so-called 'Red' intellectuals were hunted down with fanatical zeal, accused of having subverted the masses by preaching liberalism and democracy, and eliminated.

Little trace can now be found, thirty-seven years after the beginnings of the Civil War, of the last remains of these unfortunate people, for a few years after their death most of the bodies were disinterred and removed to the ossuary at the western edge of the cemetery, near the spot where the Moorish palace of Alixares once stood. The ossuary is a wide, uncovered pit enclosed within high walls, full of a revolting heap of bones, skulls, tattered shrouds and even complete skeletons still wearing their boots.

When Brenan visited the place in 1949 the skulls of the executed men, shattered by the *coup de grâce*, were pointed out to him by a helpful grave-digger. But by 1965, when I scaled the ossuary walls, the exhumed bodies of the victims had already been buried under new layers of bones and shrouds. I took my photographs (the visions of Bosch and Goya came to mind) and left.

NINE

Lorca at the Huerta de San Vicente

If one walks into the *vega* and looks back towards Granada, one observes that the town stands on a gentle slope that drops down from the base of the Albaicín and Alhambra Hills to the edge of the fertile plain. The view is spoiled, however, by a line of immense, badly-proportioned buildings that stretch along at the foot of the town and stand between it and the *vega*. These blocks of flats have been thrown up along an ugly new thoroughfare, the Camino de Ronda, which enables traffic coming from the south to bypass the centre of Granada and join the road to Jaén and Madrid. When the Camino de Ronda was constructed a few years ago it ran several hundred yards away from the edge of the town, but since then the space has been almost entirely filled in with a maze of new streets and buildings, leaving only occasional patches of open ground. Virtually no control has been exerted over this rapid expansion, the result of which has been to cut off the prospect of the *vega* previously enjoyed by the houses on the rising ground behind.

Before the road was built this whole area was a paradise of orchards, farms, villas and gardens through which little lanes picked their way out into the *vega*. Off one of these, the *callejones de Gracia*, Federico's father had bought a charming country house in 1926 which, in honour of his wife Vicenta, he renamed Huerta de San Vicente.

The Huerta, which still belongs to the family, is typical of the dwellings that dot the *vega*, and seems to grow with a complete naturalness out of the exuberant vegetation that surrounds its white walls. Federico's bedroom was upstairs, and from his balcony he could look across the fields to the snow-covered peaks of the Sierra Nevada. 'I'm now at the Huerta de San Vicente,' he wrote to the poet Jorge Guillén in 1926, just after the house had been acquired. 'There's so much jasmine and night-shade in the garden that we all wake up with poetic headaches.'[1]

It was to this pleasant retreat that Federico returned on the morning of 14 July 1936, and we have seen that his arrival in Granada attracted the attention of the three newspapers *El Defensor de Granada*, *Ideal* and *Noticiero Granadino*. On 10 July *El Defensor* had also noted the arrival of Federico's parents from Madrid a few days earlier: 'Our dear friend the landowner Don Federico García Rodríguez has returned to Granada, where he will spend the summer accompanied by his family.' (p. 1.)

On St Frederick's Day, 18 July, it was customary for the family to hold a special celebration, since both Lorca and his father were named after the saint. But, this year, news of the rising in Morocco on 17 July, followed by disturbing reports of Queipo de Llano's putsch in Seville, cast a dark shadow over the day.

Then, on 20 July, in the opening moments of the Movement in Granada, Manuel Fernández-Montesinos, Lorca's brother-in-law, was arrested in his office at the Town Hall and imprisoned in the provincial gaol along with hundreds of other Republicans. His wife Concha and her three young children Vicenta, Manuel and Concha, were staying at the Huerta de San Vicente, where the family received news of his arrest.

We have very little trustworthy information about what happened at the Huerta from this date onwards. It seems that no member of the family noted down dates, conversations or details of events, either at the time or later, and, if Federico made any such notes, they have not survived. With the passing of the years memories have faded, and several of the key witnesses have died: among them Federico's sister, Concha, and his parents. Despite this it is possible to reconstruct fairly accurately some of the decisive moments that the inhabitants of the Huerta lived through during the first weeks of the war, thanks mainly to the account given to the author in 1966 by Angelina Cordobilla González. Angelina was the Fernández-Montesinos's nanny and was living with them at the Huerta when the rising began. When I finally located her she was not at first willing to talk about her experiences in 1936, but once her understandable reluctance was overcome she became intimate in her confidences. Already an octogenarian, she retained a marvellous vitality in spite of her years and a memory astonishing in its clarity. All my conversations with Angelina, who has since died, were tape-recorded.

During one of these (her daughter was also present) Angelina told me about Federico's terror when the Republican bombs began to fall:

Angelina: Señor Federico was a funk.
Daughter: He was scared.
Angelina: Scared. He wasn't brave. When they were beating and shooting, do you know what he said to me?: 'If they killed me, would you cry a lot?' And I used to say to him: 'Go on with you, always on about the same thing!'
Author: 'If they killed me, would you cry a lot?'
Angelina: Yes, if we'd weep a lot.
Daughter: He was a very kind person.
Angelina: He was a very kind person. When he was around nobody went hungry. And when the bombs started to fall, at night, Señorita Concha and I would go down and hide under the grand piano.
Daughter: They hid under the piano.
Angelina: When we heard them coming we hid under the piano. Then he, poor creature, used to come down in his dressing gown and he'd say: 'Angelina, I'm terrified, let me in beside you, I'm scared stiff', and he'd come in underneath the piano with us.

On 9 August 1936 the Madrid architect Alfredo Rodríguez Orgaz saw Federico briefly. Knowing that he was in danger of his life, Rodríguez Orgaz had been in hiding since the beginning of the war. He now realised that he had to escape from Granada, and made his way secretly to the Huerta to ask for the poet's father's advice. Don Federico immediately promised his support, and assured the architect that some friends of his would take him that very night to the Sierra Nevada, from where he could easily walk over into the Republican zone.

The poet was optimistic, Rodríguez Orgaz recalls, about the course of the war. He had just been listening to a talk on the radio by the Socialist leader Indalecio Prieto, and was convinced that it would soon be finished. 'Granada is surrounded by the Republicans,' Federico said, 'and the rising has to collapse any minute.'

Shortly after Rodriguez Orgaz's arrival at the Huerta the family saw a group of Falangists approaching down the path. 'Alfredo, they're coming for you!' exclaimed Federico. 'Off you go and hide, quickly!' In a flash the architect had disappeared behind the Huerta and hid about a hundred yards away under a thick bush. He stayed there until nightfall and, without returning to the Huerta, set off on foot across country in the direction of Santa Fe and reached Republican territory safely.

Rodríguez Orgaz is certain that, when he saw Federico, the poet had no idea that the rebels wanted to kill him. But what happened that afternoon convinced Lorca that he was in danger.[2]

The Falangists who went to the Huerta were not looking for Rodríguez Orgaz but for the brothers of Gabriel Perea, the caretaker.

Isabel Roldán, Federico's cousin (the daughter of his Aunt Isabel), who lived close to the Huerta, has spoken to me about this visit. Although she did not witness personally what happened, she received a full account from the family shortly afterwards:

They were from Pinos Puente. One of them was 'El Marranero', I don't remember his surname. He later became mayor of Pinos. He was a pig, a killer, and the first new mayor in Pinos after the rising. He was a *protégé* of my cousins the Roldanes, the local bosses of Valderrubio.

The eldest of my cousins was a lawyer called Horacio, he's dead now. I'm not sure if Miguel is still alive. 'El Marranero' went to the Huerta and so did my cousin Miguel. I didn't see him myself – I wasn't there – but they saw him. He didn't dare to enter himself, he stayed in the path, but Gabriel's sister saw him. They were looking for

Gabriel's brother because it seems that he was one of the men who killed the brothers-in-law of 'El Marranero'. In Valderrubio two people had been killed, brothers-in-law of 'El Marranero'. The men were really after 'El Marranero', they wanted to bump him off. But he locked himself into his house, and, when his brothers-in-law appeared at the street corner, they killed them instead. It was ridiculous, because they'd done nothing and were decent people, not like 'El Marranero' who was a killer and, as I say, a *protégé* of my cousins the Roldanes.

Anyway, since one of the men who had killed 'El Marranero's' brothers-in-law was Gabriel's brother, they went to the Huerta to see if he was hiding there.[3]

Angelina Cordobilla's account ties in with Isabel Roldán's, and adds some new details. According to Angelina, Gabriel's mother, Isabel, had been wet nurse to the head of the band of Falangists who went to the Huerta:

They were looking for the caretaker's brother, for Gabriel's brother. They were looking for him and they searched the house. One of them was from Pinos, they were from Pinos. They clubbed Gabriel and his mother Isabel with the butts of their guns. On their knees they were, really beaten up. Then they went to Señorita Concha's house next door. As you know there's a wide terrace in front of the house, there was a seat there and flower pots and the rest. That's where they used to have their meals in the open. They got hold of Gabriel and began to whip him. They beat up Isabel, his mother, and threw her and me down the stairs. And then they lined us up there in front, to shoot us. And then Isabel, the mother, said to the man: 'For the sake of the breast I gave you as a child, which nourished you. . . .' And he replied: 'If you breast-fed me it was for the money, nothing else. I'm going to make you suffer and I'm going to kill you all.' They said to Señor Federico, who was there inside, that he was a queer, the lot. And they threw *him* down the stairs too and beat him up. They didn't touch his father, the old man. Just him.

Manuel Fernández-Montesinos García, son of Concha García Lorca and Manuel Fernández-Montesinos, was then four years old. Until recently a Socialist MP for Granada, he lives in the Huerta de San Vicente when in the town and has a clear memory of that afternoon:

I remember perfectly that one day I was having my siesta upstairs when I was suddenly awakened by the noise of cars stopping at the gate. Since this was quite unusual in those days, I looked out through the lattice window and saw several uniformed men getting out of the cars. They grabbed the caretaker, Gabriel, tied him to a cherry tree (more or less where the palm tree is today) and whipped him. I didn't really understand what was happening.

I also remember – although I don't know if it was the same day – that they made us all go downstairs and started pushing my grandfather and another man about. The other man, who must have been my uncle Federico, was knocked down. Then, as they were leaving, one of the men in uniform said to my grandfather: 'Eh, Don Federico, aren't you going to give us a glass of wine?' And my grandfather slammed the door in his face.[4]

Angelina, realising that things were taking a very nasty turn, contrived to hurry the three Montesinos children across the field behind the Huerta to the safety, or relative safety, of a neighbouring villa. Isabel Roldán again confirms Angelina's account:

Yes, she took the children and went to Encarnita's house. Encarnita was unmarried then, and lived directly behind the Huerta. I don't remember her surname. Angelina went to Encarnita's villa – it was only a few yards away – to get the children away from it all. Because really the spectacle was atrocious.[5]

The accounts given by Angelina Cordobilla, Isabel Roldán and Manuel Fernández-Montesinos receive further confirmation – documentary this time – from a note published in *Ideal* on 10 August 1936, which appeared in the middle of a list of recent arrests:

Detained on suspicion of withholding information
For being suspected of concealing the whereabouts of his brothers

José, Andrés and Antonio, who have been accused of the murder of José and Daniel Linares in one of the villages of the province on 20 July, a retired sergeant of the Civil Guard yesterday arrested Gabriel Perea Ruiz at his house in Don Federico García's *huerta* in Callejones de Gracia. After interrogation he was released (p. 4).

Angelina believed that someone telephoned the Falangist HQ in Granada from a nearby house (perhaps Encarnita's villa) to say what was happening at the Huerta and ask for help. Manuel Fernández-Montesinos García thinks this unlikely in view of the fact that the neighbouring houses did not have telephones. Either way it is certain that a second, more official, group did arrive at the Huerta and prevent any killings from taking place, and it is logical to assume, on the basis of the note published in *Ideal*, that this was the one headed by the 'retired sergeant of the Civil Guard'.

The *Ideal* note proves conclusively that Federico was still at the Huerta de San Vicente on 9 August, because we know from the first-hand accounts of Lorca's cousin and Angelina that the poet was bullied on the same day as Gabriel. It also confirms that the first visitors to the Huerta were not looking for the poet. While the identity of the Civil Guard remains obscure, it does not seem unreasonable to assume that it was he who now informed the rebel authorities in the Civil Government of Lorca's presence at the Huerta. However, we know for a fact that the Civil Guard was accompanied by several other men, and any one of them could have spread the news.

A clarification is called for at this point. Couffon has written that, on the same day that Gabriel was beaten up, Federico received a threatening letter.[6] This detail was copied by Schonberg[7] and other writers, who added their own embellishments, and has almost acquired the status of historical fact. But Isabel Roldán, the source of Couffon's information concerning events at the Huerta, has denied the existence of such a letter.[8]

Federico was now worried. While the thugs had not been looking for him personally, he had been pushed around and insulted, and it was quite clear that they knew who he was. Might they not decide to return and beat him up more seriously? Federico decided to appeal for help to some right-wing friend. But to whom? Then he remembered the poet Luis Rosales who, like him, had returned to Granada from Madrid shortly before the rebellion. Luis's brothers José and Antonio were prominent Falangists, surely they could help? Federico telephoned Luis, who arrived at the Huerta shortly afterwards by car.

Luis Rosales picks up the story:[9]

They telephoned me on about 5 August. I don't remember the date exactly but it was about 5 August. Federico telephoned me. He said that he was worried and would like me to go to the house. Which I did. I went with my brother Gerardo, or at least I think that Gerardo went with me, I'm not quite sure.[10] Anyway I went to the house, and once there Federico explained to me that they had been back that day a second time threatening him, hitting him, going through his personal papers and generally treating him badly.

In view of this, and in order to avoid further trouble – if we'd known that they were going to kill him we would have acted differently, but none of us thought that they would kill him – in view of this we felt that the best thing to do would be to get him out of the way. So we had a family discussion of which I am the only survivor – Conchita, her parents, Federico, they're all dead.

Well, we discussed the various possibilities open to Federico and I put myself at his disposal to do whatever they felt best. Various possibilites were suggested, including taking Federico to the Republican zone. I could have done this fairly easily and had already done it with other people – and brought people back from the Republican zone. But Federico refused. He was terrified by the thought of being all alone in a no-man's-land between the two zones. Nor would he consider going to seek refuge in Manuel de Falla's *carmen*. Federico had had a bit of a row with Falla over his *Ode to the Holy Sacrament*, which he had dedicated to him. It's a rather unorthodox poem and Falla, who was very Catholic, didn't like it. Federico said that he would prefer to be in my house. And that's what we did. He came that very day and was there for eight days or so.

Shortly after Federico arrived at the Rosales's house (I believe on 9 August) another group of rebels went to the Huerta de San Vicente. This time they were looking for the poet and no one else. They returned soon afterwards. Both Couffon and Schonberg assume that Ramón Ruiz Alonso was the leader of this group. Couffon writes:

The first day he went to the Huerta to arrest his victim the latter had already flown. The house was too small, too simply constructed, for anyone to be able to hide there satisfactorily. Thus the poet was no longer at the Huerta. In spite of this he returned two of three times, ransacking the house and bullying García Rodríguez. On his last visit he was unable to resist the pleasure of threatening him:

'If you don't tell me where your son is hiding, I'll take *you* away instead'.

He struck the old man, who staggered under the blows. The poet's sister, in an attempt to discourage him, replied:

'But he's not in hiding. He's gone out, that's all. He's gone to read some poetry at a friend's house.'

Ruiz Alonso, pondering Conchita García Lorca's words, realised that the only poet in Granada with whom Federico could be hiding was Luis Rosales. He made enquiries and found that his hunch was correct.[11]

Schonberg, whose account is almost certainly based on Couffon, also takes it for granted that it was Ruiz Alonso who went to the Huerta,[12] yet there are several difficulties about accepting such an assumption. In the first place, if Ruiz Alonso had really been looking for Federico, why would it have been necessary for him to return *two or three* times to the Huerta, when he could have bludgeoned the family into revealing the poet's whereabouts on his first visit? Secondly, and more importantly, no member of Lorca's family has ever been prepared to implicate Ruiz Alonso in what happened at the Huerta. Concha Montesinos, who was present when the house searches took place and who allegedly gave the CEDA ex-deputy the clue that led him to Angulo Street, never connected his name with these events.[13] Nor did Lorca's relatives in Granada when I questioned them about Ruiz Alonso.

On the other hand, there is no doubt that someone did go several times to the Huerta after Federico had left. Close relatives of the poet have described these visits to me. The house was turned upside down by a group of individuals who searched through the poet's papers, claiming that they were looking for letters from the Republican minister Fernando de los Ríos (whose friendship with the family was common knowledge), and even the grand piano was subjected to scrutiny in case it might conceal some secret cache of incriminating documents. These visits must have taken place between the date of Federico's removal to the Rosales's house (on or about 9 August) and 16 August, the date of his arrest, but we simply cannot be certain that Ruiz Alonso was involved in them.

In spite of this, Luis Rosales insisted during our conversation in 1966 that the 'domesticated worker' did indeed go to the Huerta to detain the poet, whom he had placed under house arrest:

Ruiz Alonso went the last time, yes, that's certain, absolutely certain. The third time he went to arrest him at the Huerta. It had all been pre-arranged and, moreover, he said to the family: 'Didn't I tell him that he was under house arrest and that he wasn't to leave the Huerta?' Then he threatened them and Conchita said: 'Oh, all right. He's in his great friend Señor Rosales's house.' So it's certain that it was Ruiz Alonso who went the last time to the Huerta.

It should be borne in mind, however, that Luis Rosales did not yet know Ruiz Alonso and that he was not a witness to the latter's alleged visit or visits to the Huerta de San Vicente. We cannot, therefore, take his evidence on this point as being conclusive, however convenient it might be to do so.

The rebels also carried out several searches in a nearby villa, the Huerta del Tamarit, which belonged to Federico's uncle, Francisco García Rodríguez. The poet loved this villa even more than the Huerta de San Vicente, he once confessed to his cousin and good friend Clotilde García Picossi, daughter of Francisco

García. Clotilde García is today the owner of the Tamarit, and she described the searches to me:

We were virtually under siege, and had respite only at night. There was a threshing-floor just in front of the house, and we used to sit there in the evening because they never came then – the maize was very high, as was the tobacco, and they were scared to come at night because anyone could have hidden there and opened fire on them. They came during the day – many, many times – to search the house, because they were looking for Federico.

But Federico never set foot here. My uncle wanted him to come but I said: 'Uncle Federico, he'll be as badly off here as in your house, because they'll search my house just as they do yours, so don't send him here!' They looked for him everywhere, and they came here as well. And they asked if we knew where he was, several times.

One of the searches was fantastic. We had some large water jars in a corner of one of the rooms because in those days there was no piped water. The jars were always full of water, which was brought in a tank. And they even searched the jars! As if Federico was going to be there! They stuck their arms into the jars!

They virtually took over the house. There was a terrace (which since then we have blocked up because it gave us the shivers) and they would go up to it, and onto the roof, in case there was anyone there, to shoot him. My brother was here, but they never saw him. The tobacco plants were very tall, and when we saw the cars coming from the terrace, full of Falangists, the men hid in the tobacco and we stayed where we were: we were the ones who coped with them. They would come in several cars, raising a cloud of dust behind them. And when we saw the dust we thought we'd die of fear.

Here they mistreated no-one. They told my sister that their leader was Captain Rojas. It was he who pointed his gun at her when she said: 'He's not here! Federico's not here!' Captain Rojas, the Casas Viejas one.* That's what they said, but we didn't know him personally. That day they entered the house and began to search. My brother had just come from the Canaries, he was going to get married and had a case full of wedding clothes. Since they couldn't open the case,

* Captain Manuel Rojas had been responsible for the killing in cold blood of fourteen Anarchist prisoners in the Andalusian village of Casas Viejas in 1933.

which was locked, they slashed it with their bayonets. Perhaps they thought they'd find Federico inside? And out spilled all the new clothes all over the floor.[14]

How did Lorca's enemies discover where he was hiding? It seems certain that they threatened the family into revealing his whereabouts. According to Angelina Cordobilla, Concha García Lorca was to 'blame' for giving the game away, although it would be fairer to say that she had no option in the matter:

Angelina: His sister Concha was to blame. The gentleman who took Señor Federico away told his sister that on no account were they to say anything, that if they were asked where he was they were to say that he had fled across country. Since in those days everybody was running away, and ending up heaven knows where, he said: 'Even if they say that they'll kill your father, don't tell them where he is, say that you don't know.'
Author: Ah yes, that was Rosales.
Angelina: That's right. He said: 'Listen, even if they say they'll kill your father, don't tell them anything, don't say where he is.'

When the men returned, asking this time for Federico, Concha found herself in the position foreseen by Luis Rosales. Federico had clearly gone, and the bullies prepared to take away his father instead. Isabel Roldán recalls:

As they were taking my uncle off down the path to the car, and he refused to tell them where Federico was, Concha, seeing that they were taking her father away, cried out: 'All right, he's in such and such a place.' It was Concha who said it, because they were taking her father away down the path. I wasn't there but my cousin Paquita, Clotilde's sister, told me.[15]

In my interview with Luis Rosales in 1966 he told me much the same:

They went to the Huerta to arrest him, and finding that he was no longer there demanded an explanation. The family told them that he was in my house, a well-known house, and that there was no question of his having fled. They said that everyone knew who I was.

The poet's enemies had now tracked him down and his time was quickly running out.

TEN

Lorca with the Rosales

The Rosales's spacious house was situated at 1 Angulo Street, only 300 yards from the entrance to the Civil Government where Commandant Valdés Guzmán now held sway.

Miguel Rosales Vallecillos, the father, was proprietor of a thriving store, the Almacenes La Esperanza, in the animated Plaza de Bib-Rambla, where jousts used to be held in Moorish times. Don Miguel was one of the best-known merchants in the town and people respected him for his kindness and probity. According to Luis Rosales, his father was a 'liberal conservative' in politics and decidedly anti-Falangist. Luis's mother, on the other hand, approved of the political ideas of her Falangist sons José and Antonio, and before the rising helped them by sewing uniforms and preparing insignias.[1]

The five sons of Miguel and Esperanza Rosales had each a markedly individualistic personality, and it would be a mistake to imagine that they formed a homogenous group, in politics or any other sense.

Gerardo, the youngest (1915–1968), had artistic talent and became an original painter and poet. He was never a Falangist and, on the outbreak of the war, joined the Nationalist Army. When I met him in Granada in 1965, only a few years before his death, he was a judge by profession.

Luis (born in 1910), Federico's friend, had published an intelligent essay on Lorca's *Gypsy Ballads* in the highly reputed Madrid review *Cruz y Raya*, edited by José Bergamín, in May 1934. He was already showing his ability as a poet before the war, publishing his first book, *Abril*, in 1935. He is now a distinguished poet and critic, and member of the Royal Spanish Academy.

Luis had an extremely close relationship with his younger brother Gerardo, much closer than with his other brothers. And like Gerardo he had little interest in politics. Forced by circumstances rather than by conviction he joined the Falange on the afternoon of 20 July 1936, and was with Narciso Perales when the rebels occupied Radio Granada. In the early days of the war Luis was put in charge of the organisation of Falange HQ, installed in the disused convent of San Jerónimo, but soon he was transferred to the front lines. After Federico's death he was promoted head of the Motril sector.[2]

José (1911–1978), Antonio (1908–1958) and Miguel Rosales (1904–1976) did not share the artistic tastes of Gerardo and Luis, but this did not prevent them from being able to turn out some improvised Andalusian verses from time to time. All three were lovers of wine, women, song and nightlife, and passionately anti-Republican. José and Antonio, as we have seen, had joined the Falange in the early days and played an important role in the conspiracy against the Republic. Both had had brushes with the Republican police, and José spent a brief period in gaol.

José Rosales, who was famous in Granada for his pranks and affectionately known as 'Pepiniqui', possessed undeniable charm. He remained faithful until the end of his life to the ideals of the old, pre-war Falange, and when I saw him two days before his death he was reading – and discussing with great enthusiasm – a book on the ideas of the party's founder, José Antonio Primo de Rivera.

Antonio Rosales is remembered in Granada as a fanatical Falangist, and it is sometimes said there that he belonged to the infamous 'Black Squad'. This accusation is, I believe, false. Luis Rosales has told me:

My brother Antonio was a fanatical Falangist, it's true, but a Falangist in the style of Narciso Perales, who was a great friend of his. He was a fanatical Falangist, but not an assassin. He was never involved in any of that, nor had he any connection with the place where the killings were organised, that is to say the Civil Government.[3]

Miguel Rosales, the eldest brother, had not been a Falangist before the rising, and in fact, as Luis has pointed out, was a Monarchist.[4] During my many conversations with Miguel in Granada between 1966 and 1967 he boasted that he had taken part in the events of 20 July 1936, exclaiming on one occasion: 'A lot of the original Falangists didn't have the courage to take to the street, but I did, even though I had only just joined the party.' Luis Rosales and his sister Esperanza insist, however, that this was all an invention, since Miguel joined the Falange several weeks after the rising.[5] An ironic, inventive man with more than a dash of *machismo*, Miguel no doubt enjoyed himself entertaining foreign investigators with a mixture of truth and fiction.

Today (I am writing in December 1978) only Luis, of the five brothers, is still alive. I have also been able to talk to his sister Esperanza, who knows more than anyone about the week which Federico spent in Angulo Street in August 1936.

Luis and Esperanza have described their old house to me in great detail. It no longer belongs to the family and, since the war, has undergone important modifications.

The ample building, built in typical Granadine style, comprised, in 1936, two upper floors and a spacious ground floor with a charming patio, slender columns, fountain, fine marble staircase, numerous rooms occupied by the family in summer, Luis's library and the servants' quarters.

On the second floor lived Aunt Luisa Camacho, sister of Mrs Rosales. Here they installed Federico. Luis explains:

The first and second floors were completely separate, and had different doors. The second floor had its own street door, just before the main entrance to the house, so that Federico was completely isolated up there. There was a door between the two parts of the house, but only we could open it. It was a different flat, with its own completely separate entrance. As a rule you had to enter it from the street, so that Federico was quite cut off.[6]

In 1936 there was a flat roof over Aunt Luisa's quarters, but a few years ago more rooms were built on top of this, changing the appearance of the house considerably. The street entrance to Aunt Luisa's staircase has also disappeared, as has the nearby window of what was Luis's library, both having been replaced by a garage with a metal door.

When Federico arrived at the Rosales's house he was frightened and anxious, but little by little he regained his calm. The three women of the house (Aunt Luisa, Mrs Rosales and Esperanza) did all in their power to put the poet at his ease, and Esperanza has assured me that soon he felt at home among them. Two other women lived in the building: an ancient cook and a one-eyed servant called Basilisa. When Republican planes appeared over Granada, Federico and the women would go down to shelter in a room on the ground floor where the water jars were stored and which the ever-inventive poet had baptised the 'bombario'. There he would joke with his five female companions and assure them that no bombs would fall on a house containing so many nice people.

It is crucial to understand that, during the week Federico spent with the Rosales, there were hardly ever any men in the house. Miguel and José were married, with their own flats, and even before the rising rarely went to Angulo Street. Gerardo, Luis and Antonio lived there theoretically, but in practice were almost always absent during the opening months of the war. During the first fifteen days, moreover, Luis hardly slept a single night at home. As for the father, Don Miguel Rosales, he went out every morning and afternoon to look after his shop.

As a result, Federico rarely saw the Rosales brothers, and it is quite untrue that he 'ate with the family', as if nothing unusual were happening in Granada. Luis again:

He lived on the second floor with Aunt Luisa, alone. My sister Esperanza went up frequently to see him. He ate up there and was never downstairs, in our part of the house. Federico never saw any-body with guns, never. And he never ate with us. We were never at home – it was no time for playing chess! – and he didn't eat with my father. Well, he may have done one day, that's different – on account of their friendship – but he was never with us downstairs. Always upstairs.[7]

Luis only returned home late each night, if he returned, and then he would go up to Aunt Luisa's flat to see Federico:

It was I who went up, since I was his friend, and as soon as I arrived at night I used to go up and talk to him. None of my brothers was ever with me on those occasions, not even Pepe or Gerardo. . . . I repeat that the first and second floors of the house were completely separate, so that, when we were visited by people like Cecilio Cirre and José Díaz Pla, Federico didn't know.[8]

But did Federico know that he was not the only person being protected by the Rosales? And that the family was doing its best to save the lives of other 'Reds'? I believe that he did, no matter how cut-off he may have been upstairs, for he saw Esperanza frequently and she must have told him that other people were hiding downstairs. Since some ill-informed commentators have actually gone into print alleging that Don Miguel Rosales in-formed on his own guest Federico, it should be stressed that he put his life at stake, and his fortune, by helping not only the famous poet but several other left-wing Republicans in danger of being shot by Valdés and his henchmen. In the early days of the rising, the Nationalist authorities in Granada published a de-cree in which they stated that anyone caught sheltering a 'Red' would be shot. This was no idle threat, as several generous and courageous families found to their cost, and Don Miguel Rosa-les's bravery and sense of decency in protecting Republicans should not be minimised. Luis Rosales has told me:

In my father's house, and with his permission (because of course I couldn't do anything like that in my father's house without his permis-sion) Federico wasn't the only one. There were lots of people, not only three, four, five or six. There were nights, the early nights, when there were more than five people in the house. And there were lots of nights, because all those early nights there was someone to be saved. During the first fifteen days there was someone in our house every single night.[9]

One night a distant relative of the Rosales turned up at the house, a Falangist called Antonio López Font. Esperanza Rosales recalls that, during supper, López Font announced, as if it were the most natural thing in the world, 'tonight we're going to round some of them up'. On being asked *who* was going to be rounded up, López Font gave the names of three 'Reds' who had been denounced by neighbours for listening to the Republican radio (a 'crime' punishable by death): Manuel López Banús (a friend of Lorca), Manuel Contreras Chena and Eduardo Ruiz Chena. López Font had no idea that the three men were friends of Luis Rosales, nor of the impact that his words produced on the latter. Luis made an instantaneous decision. 'Father,' he said, rising to his feet, 'I'm terribly sorry but I haven't got time to finish my supper. They're waiting for me at HQ.' He went at once to warn his friends of the danger, and that night the three of them slept in Angulo Street.[10]

Now, is this the truth or have the Rosales made it all up in order to improve their image in the eyes of the world? I put the question to Manuel Contreras Chena who, in 1936, was a leading member of the Communist Party in Granada and an obvious case for elimination. Contreras Chena raised himself in his hospital bed (he was recovering from a serious operation) and looked me full in the face. 'I swear to you', he said, 'that I owe my life to the Rosales. I asked other people, other right-wing people, to take me in that night and they refused. But the Rosales took me in and I owe my life to them.' Contreras Chena added other details of his stay with the Rosales that fitted perfectly with what Esperanza, quite independently, had told me.[11]

Manuel López Banús is still alive, and no doubt could also testify to the Rosales's courage and generosity.

Eduardo Ruiz Chena was not so fortunate: a few weeks after he left the Rosales he was caught in another part of the province, brought back to Granada and shot.[12]

There was an old Pleyel piano in Aunt Luisa's flat at which Federico would sit during these long, claustrophobic days and play Spanish folksongs. Often he would tell Aunt Luisa and Esperanza stories about his experiences in South America, Cuba and New York, or recite poems to them. Gerardo Rosales told me in 1966 about the lasting impression made on him by Federico's recitations of the medieval monk-poet Gonzalo de Berceo, and Aunt Luisa told Claude Couffon that he had recited some of these poems (*Miracles of Our Lady*) to her from memory.[13]

Esperanza Rosales had never met Lorca before, and she retains an indelible memory of his charm and kindness. Enrique, Esperanza's fiancé, had been stranded in Madrid when the rebellion began, and she had had no news from him. Federico, despite his own anxieties, tried to raise her spirits. One day he said to her: 'Don't worry, Esperanza. Nothing will happen to him and when all this is over the three of us will go together to the opening night of my next play.'

Esperanza feels sure that Federico must have gone down to the first floor from time to time to telephone his parents at the Huerta, although after so many years she cannot be absolutely certain of this. What *is* certain is that the telephone was working normally at that time (Esperanza does not think that it was tapped), so that we can be fairly sure that there must have been some contact between the poet and his family during the eight days he spent with the Rosales.

Esperanza remembers that Federico read the newspaper voraciously, and that she took it up to him every morning. Since *El Defensor de Granada* and the *Noticiero Granadino* were closed down on the first day of the rebellion, and the Seville edition of *ABC* was not to reach Granada until after 18 August 1936 (the date on which normal communications with Seville were re-established), we can be quite sure that the newspaper devoured by Federico was *Ideal*. Which means that he was perfectly aware of the great danger his brother-in-law Manuel Fernández-Montesinos was running in the gaol, for *Ideal*, as we have seen, often referred to the executions of prisoners that were taking place in alleged reprisal for Republican bombing.

Federico listened all day long to Aunt Luisa's radio, tuning in to both Nationalist and Republican programmes. To Esperanza, whom he nicknamed *La divina carcelera* ('The Divine Gaoler'), he would exclaim 'And what crazy things have *you* heard today? Listen to this one that *I* heard!' And they would swap 'news items'. 'It was impossible', recalls Esperanza, 'to believe anything you heard on the radio those days, you just couldn't distinguish any longer between truth and fiction.' Was Federico listening to Radio Granada on the night of 7 August 1936, one wonders, when the letter signed by his brother-in-law Fernández-Montesinos and other prisoners protesting against the bombings was broadcast? We cannot say, but since the letter was published the following morning in *Ideal*, as will be recalled, there can be no doubt that Federico must have known it. It is difficult to imagine that the poet would not have asked the Rosales to see if they could intervene on Montesinos's behalf.

Esperanza Rosales remembers that Federico spent some time writing, although she has no idea what. When he was arrested these papers were taken to his father by Don Miguel Rosales.[14]

In these last days before his death, Federico spoke to Luis Rosales at some length about his literary projects. Luis recalls these conversations clearly:

What he was planning then (and he may have been working at it, although I don't think so) was a book called *Garden of Sonnets*. That's what he was planning. If he wrote anything while he was with us (which I'm not sure that he did), it would have been in connection with this project. He also very much wanted to write a sort of *Lost Paradise*, a long, narrative epic poem to be called *Adam*. He was always talking to me about this poem, it was a constant idea of his during the last years of his life – during the last two years of his life at least he was always saying to me 'No, no, my *great* work is going to be *Adam*.'[15]

One other related matter should be briefly mentioned here. It was frequently maintained by Nationalist propagandists that Luis and Federico collaborated at this time in the composition of a hymn in honour of the Falange fallen. During my conversation with Luis in 1966 he categorically denied that such had been their intention:

Federico wanted to collaborate with me in composing an elegy to *all* the dead of Spain, not just those of the Falange or of Granada. He at no time considered writing a 'Falangist' hymn. I myself have never, never said this. If they say that I did, either they have misunderstood me or have deliberately chosen to twist my words.[16]

In 1978 Luis Rosales stands by this statement.

Everything we know about Lorca's stay with the Rosales suggests that until the morning of 16 August 1936 he felt relatively secure in Angulo Street, despite his general state of anxiety. But early that day, before dawn, Manuel Fernández-Montesinos was shot in the cemetery along with twenty-nine other victims, and there is no doubt that Federico was immediately informed of his brother-in-law's death. Esperanza Rosales has a clear memory of the poet's distress on hearing the news, and remembers him exclaiming in a broken voice, 'Poor, poor Concha! What will happen to her and the children!' How did Federico learn the terrible news? Again we cannot be sure, but Esperanza thinks it likely that his parents telephoned to tell him what had happened.

Isabel Roldán, Federico's cousin, recalls how the family heard of Manuel Fernández-Montesinos's death:

It was a priest who brought the first news. The priest who took his confession went to see Manolo Montesinos's mother, Doña Pilar. He went to tell her. She had always lived with Manolo, in San Antón Street. Federico's parents, my uncle and aunt, were also there then. Concha was still at Clotilde's *huerta*. The priest arrived and said what had happened and I remember that my aunt said, 'Let him in but don't let my husband see him!' and the priest went to Doña Pilar's room. She was very old, very decrepit. The priest gave her Manolo's last farewell or message because Manolo had asked him to go and see his mother.[17]

Federico's mother Vicenta now went to the Huerta del Tamarit – the one owned by Francisco García and which the poet so admired – to break the tragic news to Concha. In August 1978, Clotilde García Picossi, her face eloquent with pity, sat by the door of the Tamarit and recalled the unforgettable arrival of Lorca's mother at the Huerta:

Aunt Vicenta came to tell Conchita what had happened. Over there, in that corner, sat my cousin Concha, in a dreadful state, the poor thing, because she'd had no news of Manolo. She was sick with worry and fear. She no sooner set eyes on her mother, on her expression, than she knew. The two of them, with those sorrowful faces, were like two Marys.[18]

That afternoon Concha, her three children and Angelina the nanny moved to the flat in San Antón Street. And that same afternoon Federico was arrested at the Rosales's house.

Federico García Lorca during his triumphant visit to Buenos Aires, 1933 or 1934 (courtesy of Isabel García Lorca)

Lorca on the terrace of the Huerta de San Vicente with Constantino Ruiz Carnero, editor of *El Defensor de Granada* and an early victim of the repression (1935?) (courtesy of the late José García Carrillo)

The Huerta de San Vicente

The author with César Torres Martínez, Civil Governor of Granada immediately before the rising, in 1977 (courtesy of *Fotografía Magar*)

The Rosales's house in Angulo Street, Granada

Angelina, the Fernández-Montesinos's servant, who saw Lorca in the Civil Government Building (courtesy of *Triumfo* and Antonio Ramos Espejo)

(Below) The *Colonia* (now demolished), at Víznar, where Lorca spent his last hours

Part of the wall of Granada cemetery, where thousands of Republican sympathisers were shot between 1936 and 1939

Fuente Grande: all that remains of the old olive grove where Lorca was shot; at the left, the ditch referred to by the grave-digger (courtesy of *Triumfo* and José Monleón)

(*Above*) The cover of Ramón Ruiz Alonso's book, published in 1937

(*Below*) Federico García Lorca's death certificate

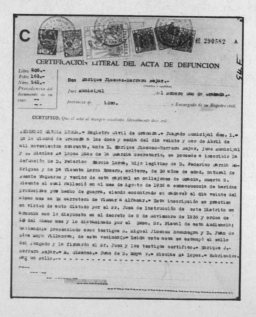

ELEVEN

Lorca in the Civil Government Building

On the morning of Sunday 16 August 1936 a prisoner, more fortunate than Manuel Fernández-Montesinos, was freed from Granada gaol: Dr José Rodríguez Contreras.

A few days earlier he had spoken to the ex-mayor reminding him of the recommendations he had made to him on 18 July, when he insisted that Nestares, Pelayo and other well-known conspirators should be immediately arrested. 'What fools we all were!' muttered Montesinos. 'What fools! But it's too late now.'

Rodríguez Contreras recalls:

The military judge they had appointed for me said, 'Your case is going well and one of these days we'll release you.' 'That's good,' I replied, 'but release me by day because I'm not leaving here at night.' The point is that, when people were acquitted by the courts, they were released at night. The bastards would wait for them at the prison door and kill them down by the River Beiro.* After they had been acquitted! Not many people were acquitted, but when they were they killed them afterwards. So I told him, 'No fear. If you're going to release me, do it by day.'

And that's what happened. On 16 August my brother, and my lawyer José Alvarez de Cienfuegos, arrived at the prison with papers for my release from the Military Commandery.

In short, I was freed at twelve o'clock. I stuck my mattress on top of the car and soon was driving down Duquesa Street (from the San Juan de Dios end) towards my house, which was in Horno de Haza

* The small River Beiro, which is dry in summer, flows towards Granada from the Sierra de Víznar.

Street. As I passed the Civil Government an Assault Guard, José María Vialard Márquez, a friend of mine, stepped into the street. He was an old-guard Falangist, a friend of Valdés and a member of his group that met in the Bar Jandilla, but a good bloke. He made me stop the car, not realising who was inside. When he saw me he said, 'Sorry, Pepe, but you've got to go back.' 'Why?' 'We've been given orders that no cars are to be allowed into the Plaza de la Trinidad, Tablas Street and that area. They're arresting the poet García Lorca, who's in Angulo Street with the Rosales. They've gone to arrest him. Orders are that the whole block has to be surrounded and that no cars are to go down there.'

So I turned back, went round by Misericordia Street and reached my house that way. It would have been about one o'clock.

Rodríguez Contreras is convinced that he saw Vialard Márquez at about this time of day:

I'm quite sure of it. When you've been released from gaol you can never forget at what time. It was around one o'clock, because I was freed at twelve. They released prisoners in two batches: either before lunch or before supper.[1]

The doctor's narrative is confirmed by the account given to me by the Granadine sculptor Eduardo Carretero:

It would not be quite accurate to say that I actually witnessed Lorca's arrest. I learnt later that that was what I saw. I was walking down Tablas Street from the Plaza de la Trinidad when I saw a lot of people and soldiers with guns. They were even on the rooftops. I was scared because I thought there was going to be shooting, that something was going to happen. Fear prevented me from running, fear makes you go slowly, as if nothing unusual is happening. I was sixteen. At the time it seemed to be just another of those things that one saw regularly in the street. I didn't lend it much importance at the time, but I realised later what it was. There were a lot of people, a lot of guards. I retain a clear memory of afternoon light.[2]

There is not the slightest doubt that the poet's arrest, carried out on 16 August 1936, was an official, large-scale operation. Not only was the street surrounded, but armed men were placed on the rooftops to prevent a possible escape by that unlikely route. The Civil Government was determined to arrest Lorca.

As is now widely known, the person who arrived at the Rosales's house with an order for Lorca's detention was Ramón Ruiz Alonso, the ex-deputy of the CEDA, whose career we discussed earlier. Ruiz Alonso himself has admitted that he was present on that occasion, so it will be worthwhile to listen first to his account, which was surreptitiously tape-recorded in 1967:*

I am going to speak to you with utter sincerity, as if I were about to die. The moment will come, however, when I can add nothing further, not because I want to hide something but because I honestly know no more. I am going to speak to you with complete honesty, as if I were about to die, as if I were before God. I am a Catholic, Apostolic and Roman ... and I'm going to speak to you as truthfully as if I were about to be judged this very moment by Our Lord. What happened was as follows, but don't ask me for the exact dates or times of the day because I honestly don't remember: the sixteenth, the seventeeth – I don't know exactly. Well, one day ... one of my assignments in Granada at the time was with the Civil Government. I used to go there every day and they gave me their orders. I had been an MP, and in the war I have my service record, all perfectly in order, fighting under military command and obeying orders. Well, one day I went to the Civil Government and the Civil Governor himself wasn't there. Actually he was visiting the trenches on the Jaén front. When the Governor was absent his place was taken by a Lieutenant-Colonel of the Civil Guard called Velasco.[3] He said to me: 'We've got a tricky job for you, Ruiz Alonso. We've discovered that García Lorca is hiding in such-and-such a street, number so-and-so.'† I should explain to you that

* The interview took place on 20 March 1967 in Ruiz Alonso's office at the Instituto Balmes in Madrid, where at that time the ex-deputy of the CEDA was secretary of the Seminar on Industrial and Human Relations. A small, not very efficient tape-recorder was used, and the quality of the recording is not always perfect. Gaps are indicated by square brackets, within which the sense of Ruiz Alonso's words is supplied where possible.

† 'Resulta que en la calle tal número tal se encuentra el señor García Lorca.' Ruiz Alonso did not seem to recall the name of the street where the Rosales lived, or the number of the house.

at that time in Granada, in those circumstances, the poet – God rest him! – was, well, considerably disliked because, obviously, well, they used his plays, you know, in the workers' club for [...]*. Then he said to me: 'Look, this gentleman has got to come here to the Civil Government. The Governor has told me that he wants him here by the time he gets back. But it's terribly important to get him here without anyone laying hands on him or interfering with him in any way, so the Governor has told me that he is to be brought in by a person of standing. You're that person.'

Now obviously – and I don't want you to interpret this as pride on my part; no, I'm a down-to-earth chap myself and I believe in calling a spade a spade – yes, it's true, I *did* enjoy considerable prestige in Granada, for my integrity, for my work, for the work I had done throughout the province (I was an MP and a linotypist on the newspaper *Ideal*). Yes, it's true, I *did* enjoy considerable prestige. As I prepared to set off to the house belonging to ...† Velasco [said to me]: 'You can take all the men you need as protection', [to which I replied] that my name was protection enough. As I went along Duquesa Street – the Civil Government wasn't then where it is now, it was in Duquesa Street – I had to pass in front of Police HQ. A policeman standing at an upstairs balcony saw me and asked: 'Where are you off to, Ramón?' 'To such-and-such a street, number so-and-so.' He replied: 'Ah, yes, to X's house.'

Now I was rather surprised at this since, well, X was none other than the *Provincial Chief of the Falange, Rosales, the Provincial Chief of the Falange*. I was surprised because I just couldn't believe that the Chief of the Falange was sheltering Lorca. I couldn't make head or tail of the thing [...] so I said to myself: 'I'm not going to *his* house [...]', and off I go instead to Falange HQ. 'Where is the Provincial Chief?' I demanded. I asked to see him and said to him: 'I've been given this assignment. They've told me that García Lorca is in your house. Tell me if he is or isn't. If you assure me that he's not, I'll go back and tell them: "It's turned out that the house you told me belongs

* Ruiz Alonso told me at this point that in the Granada Workers' Club Lorca's rural tragedy *Blood Wedding* (*Bodas de sangre*) was adapted for political purposes and renamed *Dynamite Wedding* (*Bodas de dinamita*). Can there be any truth in this extraordinary assertion?
† Here Ruiz Alonso holds back Rosales's name in order to maintain suspense and give added effect to the final 'revelation'.

to ... I've spoken to him – a natural thing to do under the circumstances – and he's informed me that Señor García Lorca is not there.
So you can take whatever steps are necessary."' Then he said to
me: 'Look, Ramón, I'm not going to lie to you, Lorca *is* there. What
will we do?' 'I don't know.' 'Do you think they'll harm him?'
'I don't think so.' 'Well, if they assure me that he's to be accompanied by an important person, well, then I see no objection.' 'At
all events', I said to him, 'I have an idea. You go home and have
a family meeting about it. Decide what you like. Meanwhile I'll wait
here and then you can call me and tell me what you've agreed.' 'Fair
enough.'

After quite a long time he came back. 'Well, Ramón,' he said, 'we've
decided that perhaps it would be the best thing, you know [...]. But
how did they find out that he was there?' 'I've no idea, none at all.
Well, shall we go?'

When we arrived they were just finishing an afternoon cup of chocolate. I hadn't met Señor García Lorca before – God rest his soul!
[I knew a little about his books but I'd never actually met him.]
They introduced us: 'How do you do? How are you?' 'Well, now,'
I said to him, 'how do you feel about all this?' 'The family think
that the best thing is for me to go with you', he replied, '[but why
do they want me?]'. 'I don't know. All I know is that they've
told me that your safe arrival at the Civil Government is to be
guaranteed ... I have no other duty [...].' 'Well,' he said, 'in that
case let's go.'

We arrived at the Civil Government. Going up the stairs I couldn't
prevent one of the men there from trying to give Señor García a blow
with a rifle butt, but then I stepped between them. I tell you this to
show you that I carried out my orders to the letter, carried them
out honourably according to the dictates of my conscience,
my conscience. I took him to a room there, accompanied by the
Provincial Chief of the Falange, Señor Rosales – the three of us
went together to the Civil Government. Once they were there I went
to see the Governor, or rather Lieutenant-Colonel Velasco, who was
acting Civil Governor. 'Lieutenant-Colonel Velasco,' I said, 'the
gentleman you entrusted to me and who I had to find is here with
Señor Rosales, in whose house he was staying.' 'Yes, yes, I knew he
was there,' he replied. 'Do you need me further?' I asked. 'No,' he
answered, 'but I want to congratulate you on the way you have

carried out your assignment.' 'Thank you very much, sir. Good day.'

Then I returned to the room where I had left the others. 'Well, what has the acting Governor told you?' they asked. 'That you have to wait here. Nothing can be done until the Civil Governor, Señor Valdés, gets back from the front. I've done all I have to do. Can I be of any further assistance to you?' Señor García Lorca offered me some cigarettes but I replied that I didn't smoke. I had a word with the orderly and told him that Señor García Lorca would like a plate of chicken broth. 'Anything else I can do for you?' I enquired. 'No, thank you,' said Señor García Lorca. 'All I want is to thank you very much indeed and to be allowed to embrace you for having looked after me so well and brought me safely from the Rosales's house. I'll never be able to thank you sufficiently for your kindness.' 'Well, if I can do nothing more I'll be off,' I said. Then I went back to Lieutenant-Colonel Velasco. 'I'm off now, sir,' I said. 'Are you sure that I can be of no further use?' 'Quite sure, thank you,' he replied, 'see you tomorrow.' 'See you tomorrow.'

Next morning I returned to the Civil Government as I did every morning – it was one of my obligations – and they told me that Señor García Lorca was no longer there. *I swear to you before God that I know nothing more.* I have heard ... they told me ... I suspect that ... it seems that ... I swear, with my hand on the Gospels, that I can tell you no more, because I know no more. I have told you *everything*. I swear to you now, as if I were swearing before a crucifix, that this is the whole truth. I swear this, as I said before, as if I were to appear this minute before God. I left him in the hands of the Provincial Chief of the Falange, Señor Rosales, in the room. This is the only part I played in the proceedings from beginning to end.

I have argued that we do not have enough evidence to enable us to assert with confidence that Ruiz Alonso first went to detain Lorca at the Huerta de San Vicente before finally arriving at the Rosales's house in Angulo Street. In theory, therefore, when Ruiz Alonso insisted in another of our conversations that he knew nothing of this he may well have been telling the truth. But it is indisputable that his declaration, while it confirms his participation in Lorca's arrest, also contains more than one detail that casts doubt on its veracity.

The first major inconsistency concerns the way in which the arrest was carried out. Ruiz Alonso claims that he set off on foot from the Civil Government and that he refused the armed support offered by Velasco ('My name is protection enough'). But, as we have seen, there is irrefutable evidence that it was a large-scale operation.

Ruiz Alonso asserts that, when he discovered to his surprise that Lorca was being protected by no less a family than the Rosales, he changed direction and went to Falange HQ and demanded to see the Provincial Chief, 'Señor Rosales'. This claim is at complete variance with the accounts given to me independently by Esperanza, Miguel, José and Luis Rosales. According to them, Ruiz Alonso went directly to Angulo Street, accompanied by two other members of Acción Popular, Luis García Alix Fernández and Juan Luis Trescastro. Esperanza recalls clearly, moreover, that when Ruiz Alonso arrived he was wearing a blue overall (*mono*) sporting the yoke and arrows of the Falangist emblem.[4]

None of the Rosales menfolk were in the house at the time, and Mrs Rosales showed remarkable courage and presence of mind in standing up to the ex-deputy of the CEDA. When he had explained his purpose, and perhaps showed her an order for Lorca's detention, she refused point-blank to allow him to take Federico away. Did he not realise that two of her sons were prominent Falangists? What was the meaning of posting soldiers in the street? Fearing that they might kill Federico there and then if she let them take him away, she insisted that first she must telephone her sons. Ruiz Alonso demurred, and for half an hour, or perhaps longer, Mrs Rosales tried desperately to contact them, without success. Finally she located Miguel, who was on duty in Falange HQ, and told him what was happening.

Although Esperanza Rosales believes that Ruiz Alonso waited in the house until Miguel arrived, it seems more likely that the ex-deputy drove to pick him up. Miguel (whose evidence, admittedly, was not always trustworthy) insisted during our conversations in 1965 and 1966 that he saw Ruiz Alonso at Falange

HQ, and that the latter showed him an order for Lorca's arrest. Miguel claimed that he and Ruiz Alonso returned together to Angulo Street, and that there was no question of the ex-deputy's remaining alone at Falange HQ while the family made up its mind about what to do.

Miguel maintained that, in the car with Ruiz Alonso, were two of his Acción Popular colleagues, García Alix and Trescastro, and two other men whom he did not know. Perhaps these were Sánchez Rubio and Antonio Godoy Abellán who, according to José Rosales, also accompanied Ruiz Alonso that afternoon.[5] The car (Miguel recalled that it was an Oakland) belonged to Trescastro, and had been requisitioned at the beginning of the rebellion.

As they returned to Angulo Street, Miguel asked Ruiz Alonso what charges had been preferred against Federico. 'He did more damage with his pen than others with their guns,' replied the ex-deputy, adding that the poet was a 'Russian agent'.

Ruiz Alonso is incorrect, as the reader is aware, in asserting that at Falange HQ he talked to the 'Provincial Chief'. None of the Rosales brothers ever held that important position, which was occupied at the time by Dr Antonio Robles Jiménez. Miguel, the Rosales to whom Ruiz Alonso undoubtedly spoke, never had any position of note in the Falange.

From the second-floor windows of the house, which look directly into the narrow street, Federico must have seen not only what was happening below but the soldiers posted on the roof-tops. Moreover, although as we have said, Aunt Luisa's flat was quite independent of the rest of the house, it had inner windows which opened onto the central courtyard, and perhaps Federico heard snatches of the conversation taking place below between Mrs Rosales and Ruiz Alonso. His worst suspicions would have been confirmed when Esperanza ran up the stairs, opened the communicating door between the two parts of the house and told him that Ruiz Alonso had come with an order for his arrest.

Esperanza insists that, on hearing the news, Federico remained calm, or at least showed no external signs of terror.

On top of the old Pleyel piano stood an image of the Sacred Heart to which Aunt Luisa was much attached. When Federico had dressed and was ready to go downstairs, she said, 'Let's pray, the three of us, in front of the image. Then nothing will happen.' And they did. Federico said goodbye tenderly to Luisa Camacho and went down the stairs to the first floor where Ruiz Alonso and Miguel were waiting for him.

There he took his leave of Mrs Rosales and her daughter, thanking them for their kindness and saying to Esperanza, his 'Divine Gaoler', 'I'm not going to shake your hand because I don't want you to think that we're not going to see each other again.'

They never did see each other again.

Miguel told me that in the car Federico was trembling with fear, and that, as they drove the short distance to the Civil Government – via the Plaza de la Trinidad and Trinidad Street – Federico kept begging him to intervene on his behalf with Valdés and to try and find Pepe.

In my second interview with Ruiz Alonso, he denied that they *drove* to the Civil Government, alleging that such a procedure would have been ridiculous given the proximity of Duquesa Street.[6] But, once again, the evidence of various witnesses demonstrates either that the ex-deputy is lying or that he is mistaken. The best proof comes from Juan Luis Trescastro, the owner of the Oakland, who was certainly with Ruiz Alonso that afternoon. Trescastro, who died in 1947, never made any secret of the fact that he had participated in Lorca's arrest, nor that his Oakland had been used on that occasion.[7] It seems that Trescastro's chauffeur, Manuel Casares, was similarly explicit.[8]

Miguel Rosales confirmed that, when they arrived at the Civil Government, Valdés was absent. It was clear that, until his return, little could be done.

Meanwhile, Federico was searched and locked into one of the rooms used as temporary cells. Miguel tried to reassure him, promising that he would return as soon as possible with José and that nothing would happen to him. But Miguel was worried, fearing in particular that Federico might be interrogated by 'Italobalbo', one of Valdes's most brutal accomplices.

On leaving the Civil Government, Miguel returned to Falange HQ and tried to contact José by telephone. To no avail. José was inspecting the outposts of the *vega*, and would not return to Granada until that night. Nor could Miguel contact Luis or Antonio, both of whom were at the front.

When Luis Rosales returned home that evening he was shocked to hear that Federico had been arrested and taken to the Civil Government. Luis immediately decided to confront Valdés, and set out for Duquesa Street in the company of José and other Falangists, including Cecilio Cirre. They found that Valdés was not in the Civil Government. Luis recalled in 1966:

There must have been a hundred people in the room. It was packed. Among them was Ramón Ruiz Alonso, whom I didn't yet know by sight. I knew no one there.[9] I said, with violent hatred: 'Who is this Ruiz Alonso who went to our house, a Falangist house, this afternoon, to remove without either a verbal or a written warrant someone staying under the roof of his superiors?'[10] I stressed the 'this Ruiz Alonso', and repeated my question a couple of times. Then – I was speaking with passion, with hatred in my voice – one of the individuals present stepped forward: 'I am *this* Ruiz Alonso,' he declared. I demanded of him before the whole gathering (there were a hundred people there who could confirm the accuracy of this) how he had dared to go to my house without a warrant, and to arrest my guest. He replied that he had acted on his own initiative. I said to him: 'You don't know what you're saying. Repeat it!' I was aware of the poignancy of the moment and wanted to be sure that both I and those present remembered the exact words spoken. So I repeated the question three times, and he replied each time: 'I acted on my own initiative.' Then I said to him: 'Salute and get out!' 'Who *me*?' he replied. Cecilio Cirre was great, and got hold of Ruiz Alonso and shook him. To avoid more trouble Cirre said to him: 'You're speaking to a superior. Now salute and get out!' Finally Ruiz Alonso left.[11]

Ruiz Alonso categorically denied that there was any such scene in the Civil Government that night. When I repeated Luis Rosales's account he burst out, 'It's all lies! I went home after leaving Lorca with Rosales and stayed there.' Cecilio Cirre, however, confirmed Luis Rosales's account in a conversation I had with him in Granada in 1966.

Luis Rosales next made a statement before Lieutenant-Colonel Velasco, Valdés's second-in-command, in which he explained why he had taken Federico to his house:

In my statement I pointed out that Lorca had been threatened at his home on the outskirts of Granada, that he had sought my help, that he was politically innocuous and that, as a poet myself and as a man, I could not refuse my assistance to a friend who was being unjustifiably persecuted. I said that I would do the same thing again.[12]

That night, at a quarter to ten, Valdés returned to the Civil Government. He had spent the day, not visiting the trenches on the Jaén front, as Ruiz Alonso claimed in our interview, but in Lanjarón where, according to *Ideal*, the enthusiasm of the people had prevented him from inspecting other towns in the Alpujarras.[13]

On 26 August 1978, two days before his death, José Rosales made an important declaration to me in Granada, claiming that he not only talked to Valdés that night in the Civil Government but saw with his own eyes the accusation against Lorca *signed by Ruiz Alonso* which had led to the poet's arrest. Our conversation was tape-recorded:

Rosales: Without the written accusation they couldn't arrest him. Ruiz Alonso had to accuse him formally and make me and the rest of my family look like assassins. We were all absent, at the front. In the document he said that Lorca was an agent of Radio Moscow, that there were Russian spies in our house, that Federico had been Fernando de los Ríos's secretary. My brother Luis will remember the accusation better than I do.
Author: Are you saying that you actually saw the accusation? A written, signed accusation?
Rosales: Written and signed, and my brother Luis also.[14]

Author: By Ramón Ruiz Alonso?

Rosales: Of course.

Author: That's incredible!

Rosales: Incredible? Not at all! If Ruiz Alonso hadn't denounced us, how could he have taken Federico away? He wanted to damage our reputation, that's what I believe: he says that we're traitors and denounces us. I've tried to find the document but with no success – a lot of papers were lost....

Author: Was the accusation type-written?

Rosales: Yes. Colonel Velasco, that's the man who took it all down. Then the Governor returned, and said to me, 'If it wasn't for this accusation, Pepé, I'd let you take him away with you.'

Author: Valdés said that?

Rosales: Yes, 'but I can't, because look what it says.' And right enough, it said the lot, two or three sheets of it.

Author: Two or three sheets?

Rosales: Yes, attacking us. In my opinion Ruiz Alonso is the only person responsible for the death of Federico.

Author: And that night in the Civil Government, when you went with Luis and with Cecilio Cirre, I think it was, what happened, because there was a large room there full of people, wasn't there?

Rosales: Yes, and they didn't want to know me.... I went and pushed Valdés's door open and said to him, 'No one surrounds my house, least of all the CEDA.' I was ready to shoot whoever was responsible, and Valdés told me to send for Ruiz Alonso and shoot him in the road. But I didn't want to kill him. '*You* give the order and *you* kill him, I replied ... because for Valdés nobody's life was sacred.

Seven years earlier, in 1971, José Rosales had told the well-known Granadine lawyer Antonio Jiménez Blanco that Valdés was accompanied that night in the Civil Government by the brothers José and Manuel Jiménez de Parga, the police chief Julio Romero Funes and the lawyer José Díaz Pla. According to this earlier version, Valdés told José Rosales that nothing would happen to Federico and that he could go and see him.[15]

José did so, and talked to the poet for a few moments, promising that he would return the following morning to take him away.[16] It appears that another Falangist, Julián Fernández

Amigo, also saw Federico that night,[17] as did a young Falangist known as 'El Bene', whom Mrs Rosales sent with blankets and food.[18]

Luis Rosales, on the other hand, did not see the poet that night, or ever again. Nor did he see Valdés. After the scene with Ruiz Alonso, José Díaz Pla, Local Chief of the Granada Falange and a lawyer by profession, helped Luis to draw up a careful legal declaration stating his reasons for sheltering Lorca, for it was obvious that Valdés would turn his attentions to him next. Luis sent a copy of this document to each of the following authorities in Granada: the Civil Governor (Valdés), the Military Commander (General González Espinosa), the Provincial Chief of the Falange (Dr Antonio Robles Jiménez), the Mayor (Lieutenant-Colonel Miguel del Campo) and Díaz Pla himself. Rosales believes that a copy of this document may still exist in Granada, although the possibility is a slim one: many Civil War papers have been lost or destroyed.[19]

When Ruiz Alonso took Federico away, Mrs Rosales immediately telephoned the poet's family to tell them what had happened. She also managed to contact her husband who, without returning home, went at once to see Federico's father. Esperanza Rosales believes that the two men then went straightaway to consult the lawyer Manuel Pérez Serrabona about the possibility of his defending Federico. 'We all thought that Federico would be tried', recalls Esperanza, 'and that therefore there would be the possibility of a legal defence.' One must assume that Pérez Serrabona did his best on behalf of the poet, since after the latter's death he continued to act as the family's lawyer.

The following morning, Monday 17 August, José Rosales went to the Military Commandery and obtained an order for Lorca's release. As he made his way to the Civil Government José was relieved, since – in theory at any rate – the Military Commander was Valdés's superior.[20] But a shock was in store for him: Valdés told José that it was too late, and that Federico had been taken away during the night. 'And now', added the Civil Governor, 'we're going to see about your baby brother Luis.' José Rosales accepted that Lorca was no longer in the Civil Government (we do not know how he reacted on hearing the news) and, until his death in 1978, he could never be convinced of the contrary.[21] Yet it is certain that Federico was still in the Civil Government building that morning.

When the poet was removed from Angulo Street, Mrs Rosales, as I have said, immediately telephoned his family, by then installed in San Antón Street. The following morning, 18 August, Federico's mother sent Angelina, the Montesinos's nanny, to the Civil Government with food, tobacco and clean linen for the poet.

My long conversation with Angelina and her daughter in 1966 convinced me that Valdés lied to José Rosales on the morning of 17 August when he told him that Lorca was no longer in the Civil Government:

Author: So you went to the Civil Government with food for Federico?
Angelina: Yes, I saw him twice.
Author: About what time in the day did you go?
Angelina: In the morning.
Author: What did you take him?
Angelina: I took him a flask of hot coffee, a basket with food, tobacco.
Author: With a name tag?
Angelina: No.
Daughter: No, not in the Civil Government, because there weren't any prisoners there. When my mother went to take food to Don Manuel in the gaol, she had to put a name tag on the basket.*
Author: I see. So you took him a flask of coffee and a basket of food?
Angelina: That's right.
Author: How many times a day did you go?
Angelina: Only once, in the morning.
Author: You're absolutely sure?

---

* Angelina took food to Manuel Fernández-Montesinos in the provincial gaol every day until his execution on 16 August 1936. This explains her unshakeable confidence that Montesino's death and Lorca's arrest took place on the same day. 'How could I ever forget it?' she said to me. 'Don Manuel in the morning and Señorito Federico that afternoon.'

Angelina: Of course. How could I forget? It nearly killed me. I was terrified. The first day I was sent I arrived trembling at the Civil Government. I asked the guards at the door: 'Is Señor García Lorca here?' 'Who are you looking for, what do you want?' they replied. 'I'm looking for Señor García Lorca.' 'And what do you want *him* for?' 'I've been sent with food.' 'I'm sorry, it's forbidden.' 'But why is it forbidden?' Then the other guard said: 'Oh, leave her alone, she's their servant. It's all right, you can go up.' I replied: 'But I can't go up by myself. Won't one of you go with me?' They took me upstairs to where Señor García Lorca was locked up. I was terrified!

Author: I bet you were!

Daughter: They were terrible days.

Angelina: Even servants weren't safe. They'd shoot you for anything. Then one of the guards opened the omelette like this [*making the appropriate gesture*] to see if there was anything inside.* Señor Federico was locked in an upstairs room all by himself. There was no one else there, he was all alone. In the room there was a table, an inkwell, a pen and some writing paper – and a chair.

Author: Was he writing, then?

Angelina: No, the things were just there. And a man at the door said: 'What a tragedy! What a tragedy for the son and for his father!' When I went in Federico said: 'Angelina! It's you!' and I said: 'You poor child!' 'Why have you come?' he asked, and I told him that his mother had sent me. While I was talking to him – you won't get me into trouble for saying this, will you? I'm terrified. . . .

Daughter: Everyone knows about it, Mamma. He knows more than you're going to tell him!

Angelina: Well, I was inside with Señor Federico and – they were at the door, pointing guns at us!

Author: They had you covered?

Daughter: But that sort of thing is natural in wartime, Mamma!

Angelina: They wanted to see if I slipped him something.

Author: How long did you stay?

Angelina: Only a few minutes. He didn't want to eat anything.

Author: And you went there again the next day?

Angelina: Yes, and he hadn't eaten anything. Then, the third day, as I left the house in San Antón Street, a man said to me: 'The person

* In Spain omelettes are often eaten cold, placed between the halves of a loaf of bread.

you're going to see in the Civil Government is no longer there.' But I knew nobody in Granada, I didn't know who he was, and I continued on my way. When I arrived at the Civil Government, they said to me: 'Señor García Lorca is no longer here.' 'Won't you tell me where he is?' I asked. 'We don't know.' 'Have they taken him to the prison?' 'We don't know.'

Daughter: A nice lot!

Angelina: I said: 'Can you tell me if he's left anything upstairs?' 'We don't know. Go up and see for yourself.' 'One of you'll have to go with me', I replied. We went up to the room. It was empty. He'd only left the flask and a napkin.

Author: Nothing else?

Angelina: Not a thing. Then I left the Civil Government and set out for the gaol, right across town.

Author: Still carrying the basket and the things you collected in the Civil Government?

Angelina: Everything. I went to the gaol, and I asked them: 'Can you tell me if a gentleman called Señor García Lorca has been brought here from the Civil Government?' 'We don't know,' they replied, 'but come back later and we'll tell you – perhaps he's in one of the cells.' So I left the basket there and the tobacco. I returned the next day. Of course, he wasn't there. They'd already killed him....

Ten years after I tape-recorded this conversation with Angelina, the old lady, now ninety years old, repeated the account almost word-for-word to a journalist, underlining the fact that she had seen the poet *twice*:

I went two days: the 17th and the 18th. The third day, as I was setting off with the basket for Señor Federico, a man stopped me and said, 'The person you're taking that to is no longer there.'[22]

It seems almost certain, then, that Lorca spent two and a half days in the Civil Government, from the afternoon of 16 August until the night of the 18th or early hours of the 19th.

Why did the Civil Governor lie to Rosales that morning, saying that Lorca was no longer there? The question is difficult to answer, but it seems that Valdés may have wanted time to think – without interruption from the Rosales. It would be a mistake to suppose that the Civil Governor was unaware of Lorca's importance or the damage that his death might do to the Nationalist cause at home and abroad, for he had been living in Granada since 1931 and knew perfectly well who Lorca was, who his friends were and what sentiments the poet had expressed in the Republican press.

By the time Federico arrived in the Civil Government Valdés had already given his assent to many executions. At least 236 people had been shot in the cemetery by 16 August, and by all accounts Valdés had no qualms about signing death warrants. A Falangist priest in Granada said to me one day, 'Valdés would have killed Jesus and His Holy Mother if he'd got the chance.' The Civil Governor hardly slept during the first month of the Movement or even bothered to change his clothes. He was in a state of extreme nervous tension, and Miguel Rosales recalled that he incessantly drank cups of black coffee to stop himself from falling asleep on his feet. He was also suffering from the internal complaint which eventually killed him. Valdés could not be expected to show mercy to anyone; only expediency might make him change his mind. Perhaps this is why he hesitated with Lorca, since it was most unusual for an 'undesirable' to be kept more than a few hours in the Civil Government before being taken out and shot.

Valdés must have given the order for Lorca's execution at some point in time between the evening of 16 August and the early hours of the morning of 19 August.

I believe that the fatal decision was taken after 10 p.m. on 18 August, and with the official blessing of the supreme Nationalist authority in Andalusia. One of the members of the Civil Governor's clique was a man called Germán Fernández Ramos, who before the rising had played cards with Valdés in the Bar Jandilla and Café Royal. Fernández Ramos told a close friend how the order for Lorca's death was given. Valdés had a radio in the Civil Government which he used every night to contact his immediate superior, General Queipo de Llano, after the latter's customary harangue on Radio Seville. Valdés was worried about Lorca and one night – I believe that it must have been 19 August – he told Queipo that the poet had been arrested. 'What am I to do with him?' he asked, 'I've already had him here for two days.' Queipo's reply was immediate. 'Give him coffee,' he rasped, 'plenty of coffee.' It was the savage General's favourite euphemism when ordering an execution. The Civil Governor did as he was told and next morning Lorca was dead.[23]

There is further evidence that Queipo de Llano was involved in Lorca's death, evidence concerning the rumoured assassination of the playwright Jacinto Benavente, who had received the Nobel Prize in 1921 and was a figure of great prestige in Spain.

When Gerald Brenan visited Granada in 1949 people told him repeatedly that Lorca's death had been ordered in reprisal for that of Benavente at the hands of the 'Reds' in Madrid, which had been announced on the Nationalist radio.[24] The first reference to this theory of the poet's death that I have found comes in the Madrid weekly review *Estampa* of 26 September 1936:

One day somebody announced in the gathering [of young Nationalists] that Benavente had been shot in Barcelona, and that the mayor of El Escorial had done the same with the Quintero brothers. And one of the young bucks commented: 'While the Reds do this, we here have respected the life of García Lorca, knowing as we do that he's one of them. We're going to have to do something about it.'[25]

The fact is, however, that the first allusion to Jacinto Benavente's death that it has been possible to find in the press appeared in the Seville morning newspaper *El Correo de Andalucía* on 19 August 1936, that is to say a few hours *after* Lorca's assassination and three days *after* his arrest:

They Are Killing Great Writers Too
Among the victims of Marxist barbarism are great writers such as Benavente, the Quinteros and Muñoz Seca (p. 7).

The same note appeared again in *El Correo de Andalucía* the following day, 20 August, and that night Queipo de Llano gave widespread publicity to the lie in his broadcast. What he said was published in *Ideal* on 21 August:

Amongst the delicacies which they [the Reds] have reserved for us figures that of having shot Benavente, the Quintero brothers, Muñoz Seca, Zuloaga and even poor Zamora. This is to say that these scum were determined not to leave anyone alive who excelled in anything. What must they be thinking in the civilised world of the men who have shot Benavente? When will the country recover from the loss of figures as outstanding as Benavente, the Quintero brothers and Zuloaga? (p. 2.)

But all the 'victims' of Marxist barbarity named by Queipo de Llano were alive and well, and the allegations had no basis whatsoever in fact. The whole thing was an exercise in deceitful propaganda.[26]

I would like to repeat that the first news of the 'deaths' of Benavente, the Quintero brothers and Muñoz Seca that I have been able to find appeared in *El Correo de Andalucía*, a newspaper controlled by Queipo de Llano, on 19 August 1936. The fact that these four men were all, like Lorca, *dramatists*, is too close a coincidence not to be connected with his death. It seems to me likely that, during the small hours of 19 August, after Queipo de Llano had given the order to shoot the Granadine poet, the fake news of the assassinations of the four playwrights was concocted in order to counteract any outcry which might ensue once Lorca's death was known. And this fake news was published only a few hours after Lorca was shot.

But whatever the part played by Queipo de Llano in the decision to eliminate Lorca, Valdés must still be held most responsible for what happened, as indeed he must for the deaths of many hundreds of other innocent *granadinos*. For no matter what accusations had been made against the poet, by Ramón Ruiz Alonso or other persons (we shall review this question in Chapter Thirteen), it is obvious that Valdés, had he so wished, could have saved him. But Valdés was not given to acts of clemency, least of all on behalf of 'Red intellectuals'.

In April 1937 Valdés was relieved of his post as Civil Governor by Franco, almost certainly on the instances of those Granada Nationalists who felt that too many people were being executed. He died on 5 March 1939, before the end of the war, and never made any public statement about Lorca's death.[27]

Shortly after the event, however, he denied in private that he had any knowledge of the poet's execution. One evening towards the end of August 1936, Miguel Cerón, a conservative business-man who had been an intimate friend of Federico, was having a drink with some friends in the Café Royal. Sitting at another table was Valdés with a group of henchmen, including the Jiménez de Parga brothers. The Civil Governor greeted Cerón and his friends, who were discussing the Españoles Patriotas civilian militia of which Cerón had been made a Colonel and asked for a contribu-tion to a proposed blood bank. After a few moments of super-ficial conversation someone said, quite informally: 'You know, Valdés, that was a great mistake you made with Federico García Lorca.' 'García Lorca?' the Civil Governor replied. 'We didn't kill García Lorca! He's just disappeared, that's all.'[28]

We will probably never know if there was a final confrontation between Valdés and Federico on 18 August 1936. Only one thing is certain: the poet was taken from the Civil Government and driven to the place of execution either late that night or in the early hours of 19 August.

TWELVE

Death at Dawn: Fuente Grande

The Tower of the Vela commands a magnificent prospect of the *vega* of Granada and its circle of mountains, and affords a fascinating view of the town itself. In his book, *Impressions and Landscapes* (1918), the young Lorca evoked the colours, forms and sounds of a Granadine evening experienced from this vantage point:

The sun drops out of sight and from the Sierra innumerable cascades of musical colours come tumbling down onto the town and the hillside ... and the musical colour fuses with the ripples of sound ... Everything is resonant with melody, age-old sorrow, weeping. A terrible, irremediable sadness immerses the clustered houses of the Albaicín and the proud, reddish-green declivities of the Alhambra and Generalife ... and the colour varies each minute and, with the colour, the sounds.... There are pink sounds, red sounds, yellow sounds and sounds impossible to define in terms of sound or colour ... then a great blue chord ... and the nocturnal symphony of the bells strikes up.[1]

Beyond the Albaicín, the rounded, earthy hills move up once more from the edge of the *vega*, this time to end abruptly in the distance at the foot of a long, stark mountain which, seen from Granada, appears to be without growth of any sort. The sharp dividing line between rock and vegetation is what most strikes the eye, and it produces an impression of cruel transition. This is the Sierra de Alfacar, the first in a line of parallel and increasingly lofty ranges which stretch north to Jaén, and whose highest peak, in the Sierra de Harana, rises to 6,000 feet.

It was at the foot of this Sierra, at a point just on the line between rock and vegetation, that Federico García Lorca was shot.

Two villages, separated by little more than a mile as the crow
flies, stand on the slopes below the mountain: Alfacar and
Víznar. Alfacar (the name derives from the Arabic for 'potter')
is situated several hundred feet lower than Víznar, from which
it is separated by a sloping valley of olive groves. The village is
famous in Granada for its excellent bread, but remarkable for
little else. Víznar—here the word descends from the Arabic version
of a still earlier place-name – is an attractive little hamlet of steep
streets with dazzlingly white houses, against whose front walls
strings of orange capsicums and pots of geraniums afford a brilliant contrast. While Granada swelters in the heat of summer,
Víznar is fanned by cool breezes, and it was doubtless for this
reason that the rich Archbishop Moscoso y Peralta built his palace
here at the end of the eighteenth century when he returned from
South America.

At the outbreak of the war in July 1936, Víznar was rapidly
converted into one of the Granada Nationalists' military outposts, because it was evident to the rebels that the village would
become a position of considerable importance in the struggle to
resist Republican incursions from the hilly country to the north-
east of the capital. The area behind Alfacar and Víznar, indeed,
remained more or less in Republican hands during the war, which
explains why the Nationalists strove to make the foothill villages
as impregnable as possible.

The commander of this military sector was the Falangist Captain José María Nestares, who has already been mentioned. Nestares established his HQ in Archbishop Moscoso's palace, and
it was from here that he directed the military organisation of the
area. Some years later a plaque was set up just inside the palace's
front entrance to commemorate its role during the war:

The barracks of the First Granada Spanish Falange was established
in this palace on 29 July 1936. Inside these walls it grew to become
the First Bandera, then the First Tercio of the Tradionalist Spanish

Falange of Granada, which in fierce combats maintained the security of our capital against the Marxist onslaught.

But Víznar was not only a military position. Had it been that alone its name would not be so notorious today. Víznar is remembered because it was above all a Nationalist execution place, a Calvary for many hundreds of men and women liquidated by the rebels. Nestares was in constant touch with Valdés in Granada (only five miles of bumpy, unsurfaced road link Víznar with the capital) and every night cars would arrive from the Civil Government and villages in the *vega* with batches of 'undesirables' to be shot at dawn. The cars from Granada had first to pass in front of Archbishop Moscoso's palace, and sometimes they would stop to exchange papers with the Falange HQ – then they set off up the hill.

Hugging the wall of the palace, a narrow street leads out of Víznar's little square, climbing steeply. On the right, the houses of the village. On the left, suddenly, the ground falls away past the palace walls down the hillside towards Alfacar. In the distance is the *vega*, with the Sierra de Elvira jutting out of it like an extinct volcano. Where the houses end, the street, now little more than a cart track, is joined above the village by the rough road that winds across the undulating countryside that lies between Víznar and the main road from Granada to Murcia.

The ground is now level. Directly ahead rises the Sierra de Alfacar; on its highest point stands a tall cross. And there is the abrupt transition from vegetation to rock which catches the attention from Granada, although it can now be seen that small clumps of pine and hardy plants manage to grow in the occasional loamy pockets between the boulders.

To the left, the vast sweep of the *vega*. Not a sound of human activity disturbs the silence, only the quiet gurgle from the *acequia* (watercourse) which runs just below the road.

The *acequia* now passes into an old, mill-like building half hidden among trees, and comes out on the other side. This building served as a summer residence for school-children before the rising and was known as *La Colonia* (The Colony) to local inhabitants. When the Falangists converted Víznar into a military position at the end of July 1936 the *Colonia* became a makeshift prison, and here the cars came each evening with groups of condemned men and women.

A party of fourteen freemasons, lucky to escape with their lives, had been brought to the *Colonia* from Granada to dig the victims' graves. Among them were Manuel Plaza, three men surnamed Henares, Lopera and Bocanegra, a certain Fernando (no one remembers his surname) and A. M. The latter, who has given me a full account of how the *Colonia* operated, prefers to remain anonymous.

With the masons worked a lad of seventeen, M. C., who had been taken to Víznar for execution. Some local ladies intervened on his behalf with Nestares who, in this instance, showed clemency. M. C. has asked me not to give his name, and it is easy to understand his desire to remain anonymous, for M. C. buried García Lorca and knows that, once his identity were known, he would be harassed by journalists. In 1966 and 1978 I visited Víznar with M. C., whose vivid account of his experiences there confirmed what I had been told by A. M. and added many more details.

Nestares had also taken to Víznar four 'Reds' whom, for personal reasons, he wanted to protect: two professors from the University, Joaquín García Labella and Jesús Yoldi Bereau, and the town councillors Manuel Salinas and Francisco Rubio Callejón. He dressed them in Falangist uniforms, but to no avail: during his temporary absence from Víznar one day, Valdés sent a car from Granada to pick them up and shortly afterwards they were shot in the cemetery.

Although Captain Nestares was principally concerned with the military organisation of the Víznar area, there is no doubt that he also controlled the *Colonia*. It is regrettable, therefore, that he should have died, in May 1977, before the freer atmosphere in Spain made it possible to interview him openly about his involvement in the Víznar killings.[2]

The gaol was on the ground floor of the building, and the victims would usually arrive at 1 or 2 a.m. to be locked up there until early morning. If they so desired, the parish priest of Víznar, José Crovetto Bustamente, would hear their last confession. Upstairs were the quarters of various soldiers and Assault Guards, the grave-diggers and two women protected by Nestares: a certain Alicia and an attractive girl called María Luisa Alcalde González, who had been an active member of International Red Aid in Granada. The women looked after the cooking and the general domestic organisation of the *Colonia*. With them often was a young English woman, Frances Turner – 'La Fanny', as she was known – whose parents lived near to the Alhambra and seem to have been of decidedly right-wing views. Frances Turner was a close friend of Nestares, and is well remembered in Granada for her striking good looks and habit of wearing a swastika on her blue Falangist shirt.

A. M. and M. C. insist that the men in charge of the killings at the *Colonia* were all volunteers, with the exception of some Assault Guards forced by Nestares to participate in the executions as a punishment. Many of the volunteers belonged to the 'Black Squad', and all of them were men who enjoyed killing for killing's sake. Among them were the individuals known as 'El Motrileño', 'El Cuchillero', 'Jamuga', 'El Sevilla' (who killed himself while cleaning his gun) – I have been unable to identify their surnames – a certain Gonzalo, Benavides 'El Verdugo', Sergeant Mariano, Moles, Hernández, Corporal Ayllón and José Arenas.

The prisoners were usually shot before sunrise (although often killings took place during the day and even at night) and the bodies were left where they fell until the grave-diggers arrived some time later.

Did García Lorca spend the last hours of his life in the *Colonia*? The information obtained in the 1950s by the Italian author Enzo Cobelli, and later by Vila-San-Juan, suggests that he did. Cobelli spoke to a man who claimed to have been on guard outside the room where Federico and other condemned men were imprisoned, and it was presumably from him that he received the following description:

Throughout the night of 19 August [sic], Federico García Lorca keeps up his cellmates' spirits. He talks and smokes despairingly (the poet always smoked a great deal – sweet tobacco which he had sent in huge quantities from abroad because he didn't like the Spanish 'black' brand). In the morning, when they came for him, he understood immediately that they were taking him on the 'paseo' (the walk of death). He asked at once for a priest, but unfortunately the parish priest of Víznar (when I saw him he was over eighty-five), who had been there all night, had left because they told him that there would not be any executions.[3]

Vila-San-Juan, for his part, spoke to a certain J. G., an ex-Assault-Guard who claimed that he was on duty at the *Colonia* the night that García Lorca arrived. J. G. had seen the poet in the company of the Socialist leader Fernando de los Ríos, and recognised him immediately.[4]

A. M. and M. C. insist that if Lorca had arrived at the *Colonia* before nightfall (at which time the grave-diggers were locked into their rooms), or if he had spent more than one night there, they would certainly have known of it, the more so since García Labella, Yoldi, Salinas and Rubio Callejón were all acquainted with the poet. But A. M. and M. C. were unaware of Lorca's presence downstairs, which suggests that at most he can have spent but a few hours in the building.

Lorca did not die alone.

When, in 1966, I eventually located M. C., the grave-digger who buried the poet, he remembered the names of two other victims shot that morning: the bullfighters, or more correctly *banderilleros*, Joaquín Arcollas Cabezas and Francisco Galadí Mergal. Both men were well-known in Granada, as much for their skill in the ring as for their political activities. According to Gollonet and Morales, Cabezas and Galadí had been in charge of the surveillance under which Valdés's house had been placed just before the rising. They were also among the principal organisers of the abortive column which was to have marched in relief of Cordoba. So the rebels felt they had good cause to take revenge.

M. C. could not remember the name of another victim that morning, a one-legged schoolmaster from the village of Cogollos Vega. Investigation quickly revealed, however, that the man in question was the schoolmaster, not of Cogollos Vega, but of another nearby village, Pulianas: a small error on the part of M. C. which convinced me that he was telling the truth.

In Pulianas the villagers remembered the schoolmaster with great affection: his name was Dióscoro Galindo González. According to his death certificate, Galindo died on 18 August, 1936, whereas it is almost certain that Lorca was shot on 19 August. But the certificates were drawn up several years after the deaths, and one cannot have automatic confidence in their accuracy. What is certain is that Dióscoro's family have assured me that they knew very soon that their father had been shot and buried with Lorca.[5]

If one proceeds along 'The Archbishop's Road', as it is sometimes called locally, leaving the *Colonia* behind and still accompanied by the *acequia* that winds on around the valley, crossed at intervals by attractive little stone bridges, one arrives after a few minutes' walk at a sharp loop in the road where it passes over a small gorge. The *acequia* rushes across a narrow aqueduct below the road, and above, to the right, one observes a slope of bluish clay and pebbles, dotted with pine trees, which stretches back up the hillside towards the first rocky outcrop of the Sierra de Alfacar.

This is the *barranco* of Víznar, somewhat melodramatically described by Couffon and Schonberg. Only a few dozen paces from the road, hundreds of bodies lie buried in the shale.

After passing through a clump of pines one comes out on to a flatter patch of grassy hillock and dips, comprising an area of perhaps 4,000 square yards. This ground covers the bodies of most of the victims despatched by the killers at the *Colonia*. Shallow graves were dug all over the slope, the bodies were tossed in and a thin covering of stones and soil was thrown over them. When Gerald Brenan visited the site in 1949 he found that 'the entire area was pitted with low hollows and mounds, at the head of each of which had been placed a small stone. I began to count them, but gave up when I saw that the number ran into hundreds'.[6] By the early 1950s the evidence afforded by these headstones had been removed, though, for Schonberg comments that he saw not one during his visits to the place.[7]

No pine trees grew in the *barranco* in 1936. Those which are there now were planted by the Forestry Department after the war, and according to Couffon the whole area was landscaped in order to mask the outlines of the graves. But in many cases these were still clearly visible in 1967 .[8]

The largest pit in the *barranco* – it must hold at least a hundred bodies – was dug in what is in the summer the dry, soft bed of a rush-edged dip, and in the rainy season becomes a pool full of toads. Here it was easy for the grave-diggers to excavate a deep trench into which successive layers of corpses could be laid. The prisoners were brought to the pit tied together with rope or wire, and shot in the nape of the neck with pistols. They were then piled in heaps to await burial. There is no conclusive evidence that they were tortured before execution, or that they were ordered to run and then shot in the back (the infamous 'shot while trying to escape' procedure), although these charges are frequently made in Granada. Nor were the prisoners forced to dig their own graves.

In the early days of the Granada repression the men at the *Colonia* did not despatch their victims in the *barranco*, but in the olive groves that clothe the slopes of this wide valley. Federico was one of these early victims and, contrary to what has often been said, is not buried in the *pozos* (as the sinister pits in the *barranco* are known to local inhabitants).

The road now curves on around the valley, with the *acequia* still beside it, and in a few moments one arrives at a group of modern bungalows standing on its right, an unexpected sight in this otherwise lonely spot. The bungalows are faced across the road by a clump of pines and just beyond these is the famous, horsehoe-shaped *Fuente Grande*.

The Fuente Grande has an intriguing history. The Arabs, noting the water-bubbles which rise continually from the depths of the spring, called it Ainadamar, 'The Fountain of Tears', a name by which the pool is still known. Ainadamar was apparently more vigorous in the past than it is now, for when Richard Ford visited it between 1831 and 1833 he found 'a vast spring of water which bubbles up in a column several feet high'.[9] The water is abundant and excellent to drink and the Arabs, always skilled in matters of irrigation, decided to construct a canal to carry it to Granada. The *acequia de Ainadamar* still flows around the valley to Víznar, drops down the slope to El Fargue and skirts the hills to the Albaicín, where for centuries it supplied the whole quarter. But a new piped system was installed in Granada a few years ago, and the canal lost its former importance. Today it serves only to nourish the geraniums and jasmines of the Albaicín's gardens.

The Arabs admired the loveliness of the spring's surroundings, and a sizeable colony of summer residences soon appeared near the pool. No vestiges of the villas remain above ground, but several compositions by Arab poets in praise of Ainadamar's beauty have survived, most notably that by Abū 'l-Barakāt al-Balafīqī, who died in 1372:[*]

Is it my separation from Ainadamar, stopping the pulsation of my blood, which has dried up the flow of tears from the well of my eyes?

Its water moans in sadness like the moaning of one who, enslaved by love, has lost his heart.

Beside it the birds sing melodies comparable to those of the

[*] Judge, historian and poet, born in Almería; one of the literary men who adorned the Granadine court at the zenith of its splendour in the fourteenth century. I am most grateful to my friend Dr James Dickie of Lancaster University for his researches concerning Ainadamar, undertaken on my behalf. He located this poem in al-Maqqarī, *Nafh al-Tīb* (Cairo, 1949), VII, p. 401. The translation is his, as are those of other Arabic descriptions of Ainadamar reproduced in Appendix D.

Mausilt,* reminding me of the now distant past into which I entered in my youth; and the moons of that place,† beautiful as Joseph, would make every Moslem abandon his faith for that of love.

It seems appropriate that the Fuente Grande, praised by the Islamic poets of Granada, should continue, six hundred years later, to bubble up its clear waters only a few hundred yards from the unacknowledged resting place of Granada's greatest poet. For it was to this spot that the killers drove Federico García Lorca and his three fellow prisoners in the dawn of 19 August 1936; here that they took the poet who had dared to say that the fall of Moorish Granada to Ferdinand and Isabella, the 'Catholic Monarchs', was a disaster.[10]

In 1966 I visited Fuente Grande with M. C., and he showed me the place where the corpses awaited him that morning, to the right of the chalets which have been built beside the road from Alfacar to Víznar, not far from the pool. Here there was an ancient olive grove in 1936, most of which was cut down to make way for the chalets. Two trees remain, and close to one of them the four men were shot and buried.

The prisoners had been taken to Fuente Grande from the *Colonia* by car. M. C. arrived not long afterwards on foot. He noticed immediately that one of the victims had only one leg, and when he returned to the *Colonia* they told him that this was the nationalist schoolteacher Galindo González.[11] M. C. had also noticed that one of the dead men was wearing a loose tie ('you know, one of those artist's ties'): in the *Colonia* they told him that the 'artist' was none other than the poet Federico García Lorca. As for Cabezas and Galadí, M. C. knew them by sight.

On 24 August 1978 I returned to Fuente Grande with M. C., who repeated all the details he had given to me in 1966 and added new ones. This time there was no fear of being arrested by the Civil Guard who used to patrol the road between Víznar and

* A reference to Ishāq al-Mausilī (that is, from Mosul), the most famous of all Arab musicians.
† In plain words, the local women.

Alfacar on the look-out for snoopers, and took several people into custody for daring to enquire about Lorca's grave. M. C. was relaxed and communicative, and he led me again to the spot to the right of the chalets, where the old olive tree still stands. Close to it there is a ditch, which M. C. remembers well. As he talked, in a dreamy monologue, I switched on the cassette recorder:

This is where it was, I'm certain.... There were more olive trees then, where the pines are now.... There were no pines then. Here the only ones buried are the schoolteacher from Pulianas, Galadí and Cabezas, and Lorca. There were no more here. Only these ones.... On this patch of ground here, yes, this is where it was ... maybe a bit further up, a bit further down, but here.... In the winter a stream flows down the ditch.... This is where it was. There were far more olive trees then, but they rooted them out to plant the pines.... There was nothing around here then, nothing – only the little house beside the Fuente. No bar, no swimming pool, nothing.... The pines are recent.... There was nothing here then.

From Angelina Cordobilla, who as we know took food and clothing to Federico in the Civil Government, the poet's family learnt immediately that he had been removed from the building. The great composer Manuel de Falla did not know this, however, and that morning he made his way down to the town from his *carmen* below the Alhambra to intercede for Federico with Valdés. Falla was a tiny, timid man, and it is difficult to overestimate his courage on this occasion. In the Civil Government he was informed that Lorca was already dead, and it seems that he himself was in danger of being shot, despite his fervid and well-known Catholicism and his fame as a composer. Falla, crushed by the dreadful news, made his way to the Fernández-Montesinos's flat in San Antón Street, knowing that Federico's parents were there. The poet's cousin, Isabel Roldán, opened the door:

Poor Don Manuel, he escaped by the skin of his teeth. He went to intercede for Federico, and they put him in the patio, to shoot him.

They ordered him into the patio, but an officer arrived who saved him and who took him out to the street. Valdés sent him to the patio. Pérez Aguilera, a very right-wing person (his father was a retired Civil Guard), told us this. Don Manuel got out of the building after being mistreated, and went to San Antón Street. I opened the door and I said to him: 'Don Manuel, they don't know what has happened.' He went to the flat to say that he had tried to intercede for Federico but that they wouldn't even let him speak. I opened the door, and when I saw his agonised face I said to him: 'Don Manuel, they know nothing, but go on up.' He stayed for a while and said nothing.[12]

The account which Falla gave to José Mora Guarnido in Buenos Aires some years later coincides in its essentials with Isabel Roldán's, although the composer did not tell Mora Guarnido that he had been in danger of his life in the Civil Government.[13]

A few days later an Assault Guard knocked on the door of the flat in San Antón Street. Isabel Roldán continues:

It happened three or four days after Federico's death. An Assault Guard arrived with a letter from Federico. He must have left it behind when, at the last moment, they said to him 'make a donation', a donation to the Army, 1,000 pesetas. I opened the door to the policeman, and I couldn't tell the family not to make a donation because they didn't yet know that Federico was dead. They didn't know for a very long time because we didn't tell them. The note only said 'Dear Father, please give the bearer of this letter a donation of 1,000 pesetas for the Armed Forces. Love. Federico,' that's all it said, written in his own hand.[14]

Angelina Cordobilla also remembered, with extreme indignation, the arrival of this pathetic letter:

A man came with a letter from Señor Federico which they made him sign and which said, I think: 'Dear Father, please give this man 1,000 pesetas.' And he'd already been dead for days, they'd taken him out and shot him near the Fuente in Víznar![15]

This letter, which seems not to have been preserved, almost certainly the poet's last manuscript, a shocking indictme of the fact that, in Nationalist Granada, even condemned men had to contribute to the Cause.

In Federico García Lorca's death certificate, drawn up in 1940 by the civil servants of the new regime, we read that '... he died in the month of August 1936 from war-wounds, his body having been found on the 20th day [sic] of the same month on the road from Víznar to Alfacar.'*

* Lorca's death certificate is kept in the Audiencia of Granada, Juzgado no. 1.

THIRTEEN

Why Did They Kill Lorca?

García Lorca was eliminated, along with thousands of other victims, by a system of terror set up with the express purpose of crushing all possible resistance by the Granadine populace to the Nationalist Movement. Seen in the context of the repression of Granada, Lorca's death was no more special than that of the dozens of other eminent men shot by the rebels, including five professors (Vila Hernández, García Labella, Yoldi Bereau, García Duarte, Palanco Romero), town councillors, lawyers, doctors and schoolteachers. The insurgents had made up their minds to kill as many left-wing sympathisers as they could lay their hands on, and it is difficult to believe that Lorca, who was well-known for his anti-Fascist declarations to the Press, his rejection of traditionalist Spain and his friendship with leading Republicans, could have escaped from the holocaust.

Yet someone must have initiated the proceedings that led to the poet's death. Was that man Ramón Ruiz Alonso, as the Rosales claim?

Almost all those who have written on the subject believe that he was, although widely different interpretations of the motivations behind his action are given.

Brenan (1950)[1] and Couffon (1951)[2] repeat the theory prevalent in Granada according to which Ruiz Alonso exacted Lorca's death in reprisal for that of Jacinto Benavente. As we have seen, this hypothesis is untenable.

'Schonberg' (the pseudonym of Baron Louis Stinglhamber) (1956) believes that Lorca was the victim of a homosexual vendetta between himself, Ruiz Alonso, the Granadine painter Gabriel Morcillo and Luis Rosales. For 'Schonberg' there were no political factors at work in Lorca's death: it was a strictly personal affair, a sordid 'settling of accounts between homosexuals'. It is little wonder that this theory, which we disprove in Appendix C, was seized upon with such delight by Franco's propagandists.[3]

The Italian writer Enzo Cobelli (1959) affirms that Lorca was but a mere pawn in a violent power struggle being fought out between Valdés (Civil Governor), Nestares (the Army – Cobelli is unaware that Nestares, like Valdés, was both an 'old guard' Falangist and an army officer) and the Falange. Ruiz Alonso, 'a born informer', was persuaded, according to Cobelli, to arrest Lorca and hand him over to Nestares for execution. Valdés hoped in this way to discredit the Army. The theory is based on a serious misunderstanding of the situation in Granada at the time and need concern us no further.[4]

A far more convincing and well-documented explanation was put forward by Marcelle Auclair in 1968. It was that Ruiz Alonso, on discovering that his political enemies the Falangist Rosales were protecting a 'Red', denounced them to Valdés, whose sympathies lay more with the CEDA than the Falange (despite the fact that he was a Falangist). Ruiz Alonso alleged that the Rosales were betraying the Movement, and had little difficulty in convincing Valdés that he must take action against them. The Civil Governor decided to make an example of the Rosales by arresting Lorca. By this theory (which fits in closely with the declaration made to me by José Rosales in 1978, during which Rosales claimed to have seen the accusation signed by Ruiz Alonso), Lorca's death was basically the result of political rivalry between Ruiz Alonso (Acción Popular) and the Rosales (Falange).[5]

I mentioned earlier the altercation between Luis Rosales and Valdés that took place just a few days before the rising. It is possible that Luis's clumsy behaviour that day may have played a part in Valdés's decision to teach the family a lesson. What is certain is that Luis's life was in danger on account of the Lorca affair. He was expelled from the Falange by the brutal Captain Rojas, now one of the party's top men in Granada, and an investigation into his conduct was opened. Luis recalls:

They told me to stop wearing my Falangist shirt. For several days I was completely alone, and the only person who stood by me was Díaz Pla. As a result of what had happened they imposed a huge fine on me – I don't remember how much, 50,000 or 75,000 pesetas – and eventually accepted me back into their ranks. They gave me a fine instead of killing me, or putting me in gaol, or what have you. It was my father, of course, who had to pay up.[6]

At this time everyone in Granada was contributing money and valuables to the Nationalist cause, and the lists of subscribers appeared daily in *Ideal*. People were afraid of not being seen to contribute to the financing of the Movement,* and it is of interest that the name of the Rosales's father appears in *Ideal*'s lists on precisely 19 August 1936:

Don Miguel Rosales Vallecillos and his wife, a necklace and two brooches, three pairs of earrings, two lady's watches, a gentleman's watch and chain, three tiepins, a pair of spectacles, a crucifix, two bracelets, a signet ring, two rings and ten gold coins of various weights.[7]

Luis himself figures in the lists on 20 August: 'The Falangist Luis Rosales Camacho, a signet ring'[8] and these entries would seem to confirm partially what Esperanza Rosales, Luis's sister, has told me, namely that the fine imposed on the family was made to seem like a voluntary contribution to the war cause.[9]

Luis Rosales was saved from further persecution by the intervention of a leading Falangist, Narciso Perales, to whom José

---

* They were also afraid of not being thought good Catholics. Soon after the beginning of the rising people began to sport Catholic badges on their lapels. These were known as *santos*, and on one occasion a member of the 'Black Squad' was heard to remark: 'What a lot of bloody Catholics we have around here. I know what I'd do to them!' (Conversation with Miguel Cerón, Granada, February 1966.)

Antonio Primo de Rivera had awarded the party's highest decoration, the *palma de plata*, for his part in events before the rising. Few people in Granada were aware of Perales's distinguished Falangist background, and when the rising broke out he did not push himself to the fore. He was, in fact, subordinate to Luis Rosales in the opening days of the insurrection and with him on 20 July when the Nationalists occupied Radio Granada. He was thus in a position to observe Rosales's conduct at first hand. Shortly before Federico's arrest, Perales went to visit the HQ of the Andalusian Falange in Seville, and when he returned to Granada it was with the authority that corresponded to his rank. He found then that Lorca had already been killed, but was in time to intervene with Valdés on Luis Rosales's behalf. Perales claims to have saved Luis's life by insisting that he was 'one of the few genuine Falangists that he had seen in Granada,' and believes that, if he had arrived back a few days earlier, he would have been able to save Lorca.[10]

It soon became known in Madrid that Luis Rosales had risked losing his life for having attempted to save Lorca. According to the President of the Granada branch of the Federation of University Students, who managed to escape from the town:

The Fascists arrested Rosales, who was about to be executed. But his brother, who is a prominent Falangist, intervened, and finally the poet was fined 25,000 pesetas.[11]

There can be no doubt, therefore, that Luis Rosales got into serious trouble for having helped Lorca, and this should be borne in mind by those who continue to insinuate that he did not do enough to save his friend.

The Rosales's Falangist colleague Cecilio Cirre told Marcelle Auclair that José was also in danger as a result of what had happened. And José, as we know, was an important Falangist.[12]

Valdés, it becomes increasingly clear, was above all a military man, despite the fact that he also belonged to the Falange. The Civil Governor knew perfectly well that, without the Army, there could have been no rising against the Republic, and that the role of the Falange, while important, had been secondary. As a result, and given what we know of his aggressive personality, it is not surprising that he should have felt perfectly justified in dealing sternly with his former comrades, nor that he should have read Ruiz Alonso's accusation, or listened to it, with anger.

And, as for Ruiz Alonso, all the information at our disposal suggests that, once Lorca's enemies had tracked him down to the Rosales's house in Angulo Street, the ex-deputy of the CEDA decided to take charge of the matter, with a double end in view: to improve his 'image' in the eyes of Valdés by denouncing a notorious 'Red', and to damage the reputation of a well-known Falangist family.

We must not forget, however, that Lorca was being harassed before he fled to the Rosales's house and that his enemies returned to the Huerta several times before they discovered that he was with the Rosales. If Ruiz Alonso himself did not go the Huerta – and there is not a shred of evidence to suggest that he did – there is no doubt that others ransacked the house and demanded to know where the poet had gone. And since it is obvious that the poet's pursuers could not have anticipated his removal to Angulo Street, one may conclude that the subsequent embarrassment of the Rosales family was an unforeseen consequence of the determination of Lorca's enemies to lay their hands on him whatever the obstacles.

In my last conversation with José Rosales in Granada, two days before he died in 1978, he claimed that in Valdés's office he was shown the accusation signed by Ruiz Alonso. An accusation which said, among other things, that Lorca was a Russian agent, a correspondent of Radio Moscow and so forth, and that the Rosales were sheltering Russian spies in their house.

Now, can we have any faith in José Rosales's declaration? Might the whole thing not be a red herring, designed to remove any lingering suspicion that the behaviour of the Rosales might not have been spotless, and to throw all the blame for Lorca's death onto Ruiz Alonso? If someone were to exhume the accusatory document (and it may still exist in some military archive in Granada), the mystery would be solved once and for all. In the meantime I believe that it really was signed by Ramón Ruiz Alonso.

In my conversations with Ruiz Alonso he denied categorically that he was responsible for the denunciation that led to Lorca's death, just as he denied that he had played any part in the visits to the Huerta de San Vicente. According to the ex-deputy, his role was limited strictly to carrying out Valdés's order that he was to escort the poet from the Rosales's house to the Civil Government. But, as we have seen, there are many details in Ruiz Alonso's declaration that simply do not fit the facts and which lead us to doubt its general veracity.

Let us examine Ruiz Alonso's activities in Granada at this time more closely.

Throughout our conversations, Ruiz Alonso insisted time and again on his Catholic rectitude and on the cleanliness of his conscience before God. One afternoon he declared:

For me all men's lives are equally valuable, whatever the colour of their skins – red, yellow, green or blue. We're all human beings made in the image and likeness of God.

But on the night of 19 August 1936, not many hours after Lorca had been shot, Ruiz Alonso expressed somewhat less enlightened views over Radio Granada, in a talk entitled *Listen, Spanish Proletariat*. Luckily for us this broadcast was published the following morning in *Ideal*:

You who, ever since you were a child, have treasured an ideal in your heart and are ready to die for it....

You who, hardened struggler, know full well the cruel bitterness of life, and have passed the best days of your youth in deep sadness....

You who have always liked people to talk to you in tough, straightforward language....

You who have suffered hunger and persecution because you insisted on following leaders who were rogues and traitors, men who always hide in the shadows, waiting for the best moment to assault banks and who then run away, leaving you abandoned, while the bullets tear through your flesh at the battlefronts....

Listen: the Marxist leaders, the scum, have engulfed you in tyranny and condemned you to slavery.

The men who call themselves your saviours are hypocrites and liars; they trample on your backs and live and prosper at the expense of your sweat and honest toil. At your expense, and wrapping themselves like cowards in the cloak of a prostituted companionship and brotherhood, they exacted from you in the workers' clubs contributions robbed from your salaries, and lived at their ease by exercising over you an abject, hateful and criminal despotism. Meanwhile your children were dying from hunger as a result of politically orientated and systematic strikes.

Sinister Red committees, made up of professional bullies and killers, forced you to join their union if you didn't want sorrow and poverty to invade your homes.

Spain is now standing squarely on her own feet to prevent the high prerogative of Human Liberty from being besmirched by the first scoundrel with a pistol to appear, or by a threat from the first street brawler to come along.

Indalecio Prieto, Largo Caballero, Fernando de los Ríos, Manuel Azaña, Casares Quiroga, Alejandro Otero ... I accuse you before the whole world.*

More than this: before the generations which in the new Spain will build altars where Justice will be offered genuine homage.

Workers of Spain, my friends, brothers who listen to me – beyond the Alpujarras,† perhaps, or beyond the sturdy walls of the Alhambra, or perhaps even across the seas...shout with me now, shout until you are hoarse:

I accuse you.

I accuse you of having stained the glorious flag of the Spanish proletariat and – you vipers! – of having poisoned the souls of the workers.

* Republican politicians. Casares Quiroga was Prime Minister when the rising began. Alejandro Otero, a distinguished gynaecologist, was the Socialist leader most hated by the Granada Right, with the possible exception of Fernando de los Ríos; both men were fortunate that the war did not find them in Granada.
† The Alpujarras, a high valley nestling among the southern slopes of the Sierra Nevada, lovingly described by Gerald Brenan in *South from Granada*.

I accuse you of having sullied the high ideals of redemption with the blood of our exploited companions, with the lives of our unyielding companions who retained in spite of everything their manly pride.

Rebellious proletariat:

Undefeated and undefeatable rebellion!

Rise up against them!

Your leaders ... are hypocrites, because they deceived you.

Your leaders ... are farcical, because it was nothing but a farce they enacted, while you, blinded, left bits of your life behind in the struggle for bread, bread which you won by the sweat of your brow and which they savoured with relish.

Your leaders ... are criminals and bandits because they have bathed their hands in innocent blood and brought bereavement to an infinite number of humble, honest families.

Your leaders ... are the aborted offspring of Humanity.

There is not and cannot be a Spanish mother capable of giving birth to these monsters who have made crime one of their principal weapons and assassination a way of life.

They always attack from behind!

The declaration of war was the result of an assassination from behind. A bullet in the neck of our glorious Calvo Sotelo.* They carry on the struggle with the same perfidious tactics: Dimas Madariaga falls, treacherously assassinated from behind.†

José Calvo Sotelo and Dimas Madariaga!

Your throne is on high above the stars.

Spanish proletariat: on your feet!

My incautious, idealistic fellow workers, who go on believing in an impossible utopia: you are still in time. But tomorrow may be too late.

Wake up and think over this:

The Fatherland which witnessed your birth...

Your holy mothers...

Your virtuous wives...

Your innocent, unsuspecting, virtuous children...

* This was untrue, since by the date of Calvo Sotelo's assassination (13 July 1936) the plans for the Nationalist rising were already well advanced.
† Dimas Madariaga, a founder member of Acción Popular and CEDA deputy to the Cortes for Toledo, was killed in the first month of the Civil War.

You who have always liked people to talk to you in tough, straight-
forward language, listen:
A sword's blade is strong and well-tempered.
The traitors' throats will be bathed in their own blood.
Make way for the new Spain! (p. 8.)

The speech affords us a valuable insight into the workings of
Ruiz Alonso's – and by extension Acción Popular's – mind at
the time of Lorca's death, and shows clearly that impenitent Republican supporters could expect no mercy from *him*.

One of the Republicans most loathed by the Right in Granada
was the brilliant Socialist minister Fernando de los Ríos, who
had been Professor of Political Law at Granada University for
many years before moving to Madrid. In 1916 Don Fernando had
listened astonished as the young Lorca sat playing Beethoven on
the piano in the Arts Centre, and prophesied an outstanding
future for him. The professor had become a close friend of the
family, and some years later his daughter Laura married Francisco García Lorca, Federico's younger brother. The friendship
was well known in Granada, and when the Huerta de San Vicente
was ransacked after Federico had fled to Angulo Street, it seems
that the men claimed that they were searching for letters from
Don Fernando.[13]

Ruiz Alonso hated de los Ríos, as can be seen from the
reference to him and other Republican leaders in the above
broadcast. In his book he writes:

I was a working man, a compositor, and a deputy to the Cortes for
Granada!
But:
Ramón Lamoneda was also a deputy to the Cortes for Granada,
a working man and a compositor!
He was a Socialist: President of the National Federation of Graphic
Arts. His name figured on the list of candidates beside that of a Jew:
Fernando de los Ríos; he [Lamoneda] was the leader of the typo-
graphical workers of Spain. Mine figured in another list beside that
of a genius and a brave man: General Varela (p. 134).[14]

Ruiz Alonso knew perfectly well that Fernando de los Ríos, despite the Jewish antecedents of his distinguished family and his undeniably Hebraic features, was not a Jew. But no matter. For the Catholic Ruiz Alonso, inspired by the fanatical anti-Semitism rife among the Nationalists at the time, a Jew, unlike a Spanish general, cannot be either a genius or a brave man.[15] By such comments Ruiz Alonso reveals throughout his Fascist manual an attitude of mind and a Catholicism radically different to the one which he claimed for himself in our conversations in 1967.

José Rosales told me that, among the accusations made against Lorca, was the charge that he had been Fernando de los Ríos's secretary. If this was so it would have been an added incentive to Valdés to rid himself of the poet.[16]

It is often said in Granada that another of the charges against Lorca was his membership of the Association of Friends of the Soviet Union (and again we have seen that, according to José Rosales, the accusation contained references to Lorca's pro-Russian activities). Can we forget at this point that, in 1933, Ruiz Alonso belonged to the JONS and was possibly one of the men who wrecked the HQ of the Friends of the Soviet Union in Madrid? (See p. 63.) Ruiz Alonso's loathing of Russia is evident throughout his book, and there can be no doubt that the man was capable of denouncing anyone he suspected of entertaining friendly sentiments towards that country.

It is also frequently said in Granada that Lorca was killed because he belonged to International Red Aid (*Socorro Rojo Internacional*). This, too, is plausible, and we have seen that on several occasions Federico expressed his solidarity with SRI: reading poems in the Madrid Socialist Workers' Club (*Casa del Pueblo*) during the Luis Carlos Prestes meeting in March 1936; publishing a message to the workers of Spain in the 1 May 1936 issue of the organisation's magazine *¡Ayuda!* and, a few days before the rising began, making a contribution to Red Aid's funds in Granada. If the document of accusation ever turns up, I should not be surprised to find a reference to *Socorro Rojo Internacional* among the charges laid against the poet.

Until recently I believed that Ruiz Alonso had not been involved in any other unpleasant incidents in Granada. But José Rosales told me in our last conversation that one day the ex-deputy boasted openly of having shot a 'Red' who was accused of having raped a young girl. Ruiz Alonso told Rosales:

After I blew his brains out I went to confession. I didn't have to do any penance.

And during my last visit to Granada I heard other similar accounts which, through lack of corroboration, I prefer not to print here.

I am persuaded however, despite all the evidence against Ruiz Alonso, that the proceedings which led to Lorca's death were initiated not only by him but by other members of Acción Popular. In particular by Juan Luis Trescastro, Luis García Alix Fernández and Jesús Casas Fernández. Let us discuss these men briefly.

Various witnesses have declared that during Lorca's arrest Ruiz Alonso was accompanied by Juan Luis Trescastro, who died in 1947. Trescastro, a well-off landowner, braggart and womaniser, apparently talked freely about his participation in Lorca's arrest and death, as has been said, and never made any secret of the fact that his car was used that afternoon to take the poet from Angulo Street to the Civil Government. Lorca's friend Miguel Cerón told me in 1966 that Trescastro died obsessed by the memory of his activities during the Granada repression, and in particular of his involvement in the the poet's death. He insisted, however, that it was Ruiz Alonso and not he who had informed Valdés that the Rosales were sheltering Lorca.

Then there is the testimony of Trescastro's doctor, whom I met in Granada in 1971. He once brought up the subject of Lorca's death in the presence of Trescastro without knowing of the latter's involvement in it. Trescastro burst out:

I was one of the people who went to get Lorca in the Rosales's house. We were sick and tired of queers in Granada.[17]

Moreover, Trescastro boasted that he had actually participated in the killing of the poet in Víznar. One morning – probably
that of 19 August 1936 – Angel Saldaña, one of the few Granada
town councillors to escape the Nationalist purge (see Appendix
A), was sitting in the Bar Pasaje, familiarly known as 'La
Pajarera', when Trescastro swaggered in and exclaimed for
everyone to hear:

We've just killed Federico García Lorca. We left him in a ditch and
I fired two bullets into his arse for being a queer.[18]

That same day the Granadine painter Gabriel Morcillo was
having a drink in another café, the Royal, when Trescastro came
up to him and announced:

Don Gabriel, we bumped off your friend the poet with the big fat head
this morning.[19]

The fact that Trescastro (an archetypal Spanish *macho*)
boasted in the streets and bars of Granada that he had participated in Lorca's death does not prove that he did so, but taking
all we know about him it does seem that his involvement in the
arrest is beyond doubt.

Then there is Luis García Alix Fernández, whom unfortunately
I never met and who died in a car crash on 7 March 1971. Luis
García's presence that afternoon in Angulo Street is also well
attested, and it should be noted that he was Secretary of the
Granada branch of Acción Popular, a person of some position.

When I returned to Granada in 1971 I was introduced to a man
who had been an Assault Guard before the war, a loyal Republican who had had no option but to join the rebels. He told me
that he was on guard in Valdés's office one day when Lorca's
presence in the Rosales's house was denounced to the Civil Governor by another member of Acción Popular, Jesús Casas Fernández, a lawyer renowned in Granada for his fanatical Catholicism.
Casas Fernández lived in 4 Tablas Street, in a large corner house

adjoining that of the Rosales, and had become aware that Lorca was in hiding next door. Outraged that a Falangist family should protect such a notorious Republican, Casas Fernández went immediately to Valdés, who then consulted with his henchmen and decided to have the poet arrested. Casas Fernández died some years ago, and I possess no further evidence to substantiate this charge against him, but the Assault Guard's account is convincing (I have been able to verify that Casas Fernández did indeed live next door to the Rosales), and adds further weight to the case against Acción Popular.[20]

In Granada in August 1936 a person with Lorca's reputation and friends could not expect to escape death.

A man who had been a 'friend' of the poet before the Movement said to Miguel Cerón in 1936, 'If they've killed Federico they must have known what they were doing',[21] and a Granadine acquaintance of Mme Auclair told her that an individual there who now sings the poet's praises said to him a few years ago, 'If I had had a pistol and Federico were there in front of me, my hand wouldn't have trembled.'[22]

I have not the slightest doubt that Ruiz Alonso and his friends in Acción Popular detested Lorca and all he stood for, whatever they may say about him now, years later, when he is acclaimed as an outstanding poet and playwright, and I believe that enough evidence has been adduced in the course of this book to suggest strongly that the Granada branch of Acción Popular was responsible for the original denunciation that led to Lorca's arrest and death. The fact that Ruiz Alonso was accompanied to Angulo Street by Juan Luis Trescastro and Luis García Alix, both prominent members of Acción Popular; that Trescastro admitted to the part played by him in Lorca's arrest and actual death; that Ruiz Alonso's conversations with me in Madrid revealed many fundamental inconsistencies which could not be attributed merely to a fading memory; that Ruiz Alonso hated Fernando de los Ríos, with whose name that of Lorca was so closely connected; that he admits that Lorca was disliked in Granada on account of his contacts with the Left; that in all probability Jesús

Fernández, another member of Acción Popular, also denounced Lorca – all these and other details already discussed do not *prove* that Ruiz Alonso and Acción Popular were the first to decide that Lorca should die, but they certainly make it the most likely hypothesis.

That Lorca was much disliked by traditionalist Spanish Catholics is beyond doubt. As an example of the feelings he aroused, the following quotation from an article published in London by the Marquis de Merry de Val in 1937 may be found appropriate. The Marquis is attacking a Statement issued in November 1936 by the Spanish Embassy, and his remarks demonstrate that he, at least, has no doubt that Lorca was a fervent, *political* adversary of Catholic Spain and that, as such, he deserved to die:

We encounter the same *suppressio veri* in the individual cases specified by the Statement. The 'Socialist' (read 'Communist') lawyers J. A. Manso, Rufilanchas, and Landovre, as also the poet García Lorca, whose literary merits were outshone by his political zeal, were all dangerous agitators who abused their talent and superior education to lead the ignorant masses astray for their own personal profit. In common with the other persons named, they were executed after a trial by court-martial.[23]

Lorca, whose liberal sympathies were well known and whose opinion of the reactionary middle class in Granada had been read there with anger when it appeared in the Madrid press just before the rising, could expect little mercy from the self-appointed guardians of the Faith who were now devoting themselves to ferreting out and destroying all those whom, with Merry del Val, they accused of being 'dangerous agitators'.

But this is not to say that Ramón Ruiz Alonso and his fellow members of Acción Popular were alone responsible for the death of the poet, as the Falange would have us believe. The fact that Lorca was taken to the Civil Government instead of being immediately shot in the street or by some roadside on the outskirts of the town – the usual fate of the victims of the 'Black Squad', for example – shows that in arresting him Ruiz Alonso was acting with the official blessing of no less an authority than the Falangist Civil Governor himself, and it is undeniable that responsibility for what was to happen to Lorca passed out of Ruiz Alonso's hands once he had left him in Duquesa Street.* Henceforth Federico was at the mercy of Valdés. And Valdés – with the probable connivance of Queipo de Llano – chose to have him shot. Whoever first decided that Lorca should be arrested, and the evidence points to Ruiz Alonso and Acción Popular, the death itself was carried out officially, on the orders of Valdés.

Lorca spent two and a half days in the Civil Government, and it seems that no one in authority attempted to save him, despite the fact that his presence in Duquesa Street must have been well known and that the poet's father did everything in his power to obtain a reprieve. There was one man who could certainly have intervened: Monsignor Agustín Parrado y García, Cardinal Archbishop of Granada and one of the most influential prelates in Spain. But no help could be expected from a man who never once protested publicly about the mass killings that were taking place daily in the cemetery, and under whose direction the clergy in Granada had sided with the rebels from the start, identifying the Generals' insurrection with a Holy Crusade against the enemies of Christ and the 'true' Spain, the Spain of Ferdinand and Isabella, the Spain of sword and mitre.

In the last analysis, Federico, along with many of his friends and thousands of the humbler citizens of the Granada he loved so deeply, fell victim to the hatred of the Catholic Church and those whom he had termed 'the worst bourgeoisie in Spain'.[24]

* Ramón Ruiz Alonso left Granada shortly after the failure of the Pérez del Pulgar Batallion (see pp. 95–6). According to a note published in *ABC*, Seville, on 2 April 1937, entitled 'Nationalist Propaganda at the Combat Fronts,' Ruiz Alonso was by that time collaborating with Vicente Gay, head of Franco's propaganda department. Like Ruiz Alonso, Gay was a fanatical Catholic, anti-Semitic and an enemy of Fernando de los Ríos (see his book *Estampas rojas y caballeros blancos*, Burgos, 1937, *passim*).

FOURTEEN

Lorca's Assassination:
Press and Propaganda from 1936
until the Death of Franco

Lorca's death was first announced in the Republican, not the Nationalist, press. The news took several days to reach Madrid, as was to be expected: Granada was cut off from the Republican zone, and rebel radio stations were careful to avoid any immediate reference to the event.

The first newspaper to mention the possible death of the poet was *El Diario de Albacete*, which, on Sunday 30 August 1936, asked on its front page:

Has García Lorca been assassinated?
Guadix. Rumours from the Córdoba front, which up to now have not been disproved, reveal the possible shooting of the great poet Federico García Lorca, on the orders of Colonel Cascajo.*

García Lorca, one of our most outstanding contemporary literary figures, appears to have been under arrest in Córdoba and to have been killed during one of the latest insurgent razzias, on which they habitually embark when they have suffered a setback.

The rumour reached Madrid at once. On 1 September, the evening newspaper *La Voz* reproduced the first paragraph of the *Diario de Albacete*'s despatch, and next day the Republican press of the entire country expressed its concern for the safety of the

* Colonel Cascajo was commander of the Nationalist forces that took Córdoba.

poet. Federico's friend Carlos Morla Lynch has recalled the moment when he heard the terrible news:

In the Plaza Mayor, which, like the rest of the city, was full of militia-men, I was having my shoes cleaned in order to be able to give a few pennies to the last shoecleaner 'who still drags his box from here to there'.

Some newspaper sellers passed, shouting: 'Federico García Lorca! Federico García Lorca! Executed in Granada!'

It was as though I'd been hit over the head with a club. My ears buzzed, my sight was affected and I rested my hand on the shoulder of the lad who knelt in front of me, to steady myself.

Then I reacted and began to run, to run, to run.... Where? I've no idea, in any direction.... Here, there, beserk.... And all the time I said to myself: 'No, no, it isn't true, it isn't true, it isn't true!'[1]

We need not reproduce here the many notes and commentaries on Lorca's rumoured death that appeared at this time in the press, since for the most part they added no new facts and limited themselves to the expression of horror, indignation or disbelief (see the bibliography). Soon, however, more information became available, and it became increasingly likely that the poet had indeed been killed.

On 8 September 1936 several Madrid newspapers reproduced disturbing details from an interview with a Republican who had escaped from Granada to Guadix. This man was an intimate friend of Manuel Fernández-Montesinos, and he had not the slightest doubt that both Montesinos and his brother-in-law García Lorca had been shot. The front-page headline of *La Voz* read: 'THE EXECUTION OF THE GREAT POET GARCÍA LORCA HAS BEEN CONFIRMED.'

But many people still refused to accept that the poet could really have been shot. It seemed impossible. On 9 September *El Sol* wrote:

On the Alleged Assassination of García Lorca

Some colleagues in Madrid and the provinces give as proven the assassination of our glorious poet Federico García Lorca. Personally

this paper has hesitated, and still hesitates, to accept this tragic confirmation because, although we may lack positively favourable news,
it is nevertheless true to say that the evidence is not conclusive.

The information most likely to be accurate, proceeding from the
Ministry of War and the Security Department, is not definitive, while
on the other hand that which arrives from Andalusian sources is full
of contradictions, it being variously affirmed that the assassination by
the miserable insurgent forces took place in Córdoba, Guadix and
Granada. A person just back from the siege of Córdoba tells us that
the rumours circulating there located the assassination, without rhyme
or reason, in Guadix. From there the event is transferred to Granada
while, according to other sources, the great poet of the *Gypsy Ballads*
was staying with his parents in their Huerta del Tamarit.*

It is quite likely that rumours about this foul deed, of which the
traitors are perfectly capable, are based solely on the proven fact of
the execution of Manuel Fernández Montesinos, Socialist mayor of
Granada and husband of the poet's elder sister. Let us hope that we
are not wrong, although we can expect anything from the vileness
of soul characteristic of the accursed breed now bathing Andalusia
and all Spain in blood!

The Nationalist press, aware that the fact of Lorca's death
could no longer be concealed, embarked at this point on a de-
liberate policy of misrepresentation.[2]

On 10 September 1936 *La Provincia* of Huelva declared:

RADIO STATIONS CAPTURED BY THE REDS

Barcelona. Radio Unión and Radio Asociación are in the hands of
the Central Committee of the Catalan Anti-Fascist militia.
The poet García Lorca was to have given a poetry reading last night
over these stations but the reading failed to take place. (p. 2.)

On the same day another Huelvan paper published a different
account, making no bones about its dislike of Lorca:

* The Huerta del Tamarit belonged to Federico's uncle, not his father. It is situated about half a mile away from the Huerta de San Vicente.

THEY ARE KILLING EACH OTHER ALREADY!
HAS FEDERICO GARCÍA LORCA BEEN
ASSASSINATED?

Madrid, 9 September. It seems that the body of Federico García Lorca has been discovered among the numerous corpses that litter the streets of Madrid day in, day out.

Chaos amongst the Marxists has become so total that they no longer respect even each other.

Unable to escape from the Red fury, the author of *Gypsy Ballads* gained nothing from having been the 'coreligionist' of Azaña in politics, in literature and in – how could one put it? – in doubtful sexuality.[3]

On 19 September 1936 the Nationalist press throughout Spain (with the notable exception of *ABC* in Seville) stated unequivocally that Lorca had been assassinated by the 'Reds' and stressed his connections with the Republic.

The *Diario de Huelva* announced:

THE POET FEDERICO GARCÍA LORCA
SHOT IN BARCELONA

Barcelona. Today it has become known that the celebrated poet Federico García Lorca was assassinated by several extremists [i.e. 'Reds'] on 16 August. As the result of a denunciation he was discovered in the house of a businessman where he had been in hiding since the beginning of the revolution. (p. 10.)

The same report figured in *La Provincia* of Huelva under the headline FEDERICO GARCÍA LORCA SHOT IN BARCELONA, while the *Diario de Burgos*, the most authoritative rebel newspaper, affirmed that the poet had been killed in the capital:

GARCÍA LORCA HAS BEEN SHOT

Paris. It is known that the poet García Lorca has been shot in Madrid by Marxist elements.

In French literary circles the news has caused a shock since the poet's left-wing ideas were well known.

Two days later, on 21 September, another Burgos daily, *El Castellano*, announced:

THE POET GARCÍA LORCA SHOT WITH THE WORKERS

Barcelona. A man from Barcelona who has succeeded in escaping from Granada confirms that the poet García Lorca was shot on 16 August.

He was arrested in the house of a businessman called González. 200 workers were shot along with the poet.

García Lorca was spending the summer in his native village, Fuente Vaqueros, and the rising caught him in Granada where he had gone to take part in a music congress.

A strangely ambiguous report, this, which evidently emanated from the same source as that published a few days earlier in the *Diario de Huelva* but seemed also to suggest that the poet was executed by the authorities in Granada.

ABC, the Sevillan daily, now controlled by Queipo de Llano, avoided any direct reference to Lorca's death. The first, oblique allusion to it appeared in a piece of double-think published on 27 September 1936:

The arrest of the Duke of Canalejas. Benavente. García Lorca

In a Red newspaper we read that the Duke of Canalejas has been arrested on leaving an embassy where he was hiding. The papers also mention the arrest of Fascist spies and name well-known people in that connection. And they insert an alleged letter from Don Jacinto Benavente, whom they claim is in Valencia. A trick in connection with the death of García Lorca – may he rest in peace.

With regard to Benavente, we note, an intention to mislead the public. We hope that he is still alive. It would be ridiculous to start a quarrel about it. Before long the truth will be established and confirmed. What we *can* affirm is that the letter doesn't look at all like one by Don Jacinto. Or else the illustrious author of *Holy Russia* is in a state of nerves – *Holy Russia*, the only work by him that the newspapers remember when, to create a fuss, they join the names of García Lorca – may his soul rest in peace – and Benavente, to whom all

honour if he's alive and honour to his memory if he has succumbed.
M. SÁNCHEZ DEL ARCO

It can be seen from the above piece that the Nationalists now at least conceded that Lorca had indeed been killed, while at the same time deliberately avoiding all reference to the actual circumstances of his death. The journalist evidently assumes that his readers are already acquainted with the fact of the death, and this suggests that an official version of how it took place had been broadcast over the Nationalist radio.*

By the beginning of October 1936 the Republican press was reluctantly forced to conclude that the rumours about the assassination were based on fact. On October 2 *El Sol* published this report:

MORE DETAILS ABOUT THE SHOOTING OF GARCÍA LORCA

The president of the Granada FUE† has managed to escape from that city to Murcia, where he has made new declarations that confirm the outrages committed by the Fascists in the city by the Darro. The Granadine student has provided fresh information about the shooting of the great poet García Lorca. The author of *Yerma* was warned by various friends of the danger he was running on account of his connections with the Left, so he sought refuge in the house of another Granadine poet, Rosales, where he stayed until his presence there was denounced by a servant in league with the rebels. For having had García Lorca in his house, Rosales was on the point of being shot against the cemetery wall....

The European press was becoming increasingly interested in Lorca's death (in London *The Times* carried brief reports on 12, 14 and 23 September and 5 October), and it was at this point that H. G. Wells (a former guest of Lorca and his friends in

---

* Many people in Granada have told me independently that they heard the Nationalist radio announce that Lorca had been killed accidentally by a stray bullet or bomb.
† Federación Universitaria Española, the left-wing students' union.

Granada) sent his famous telegram to the military authorities of the town. On the front page of *El Sol*, 14 October 1936, we read:

A Plea from Wells

The rebel governor of Granada says that he does not know the whereabouts of García Lorca

London, 13. The writer H. G. Wells, president of the PEN Club in London, has sent the following message to the military authorities in Granada: 'H. G. Wells, president of the PEN Club in London, anxiously desires news of his distinguished colleague Federico García Lorca and will greatly appreciate courtesy of reply.'

The reply was as follows: 'Colonel Governor of Granada to H. G. Wells. I do not know whereabouts of Don Federico García Lorca.' Signed Colonel Espinosa.

El Sol followed the publication of the telegrams with a further article on 15 October in which it launched a vitriolic attack on Espinosa and went on to connect the name of Ramón Ruiz Alonso for the first time with the assassination, an interesting detail that shows how widely known the participation of the 'domesticated worker' in Lorca's arrest had already become:

Espinosa knows nothing about it. Or rather he chooses not to know anything about it, which unfortunately seems to confirm the treacherous death of the Spanish poet.

[...] Ex-Colonel Espinosa probably did not even know who García Lorca was. A reader in his moments of leisure of pseudo-pornographic novels and a devourer of all that foul, nauseous literature put out by our wretched right-wing scribblers, he never had either the opportunity or the desire to enter into communion with García Lorca's splendid work, pregnant with popular and poetic essences of a rare quality.

Ex-Colonel Espinosa will certainly have found out now, after receiving Wells's telegram, that there was once a poet called Federico García Lorca, and that he was murdered by the rabble led by Ruiz Alonso, the well-known paid assassin in the hire of Gil Robles, for the simple fact of having put his distinguished pen at the service of the people. Faced with a *fait accompli*, ex-Colonel Espinosa decided that the most graceful attitude was to pretend that he knew nothing about it. (p. 4.)

The death of the poet was becoming an increasing embarrassment to the Nationalists, and it was inevitable that they should now seek to exonerate themselves in the eyes of world opinion. To do this they would have to claim Lorca as 'one of their own' and either deny that they had taken any part in the killing or else ascribe it to the 'Reds'. Since it had become abundantly clear that Lorca could not have been shot by Republican extremists, Franco's propagandists decided to lay all the blame on unspecified assassins 'acting on their own initiative'. Only the Marquis de Merry de Val was unwise enough to state publicly that Lorca had been shot officially (see p. 181) and his mistake was never repeated.

The Falange quickly began to foster the legend that before his death Lorca was actively in sympathy with the aims of José Antonio Primo de Rivera (who had died some months after the poet, executed in Alicante by the Republicans).

On 11 March 1937 an article entitled 'They have killed Imperial Spain's greatest poet' appeared in the Falangist paper *Unidad* of San Sebastián. The author, Luis Hurtado, writes in the overblown style (quite untranslatable) of Spanish political rhetoric, and particularly the Falangist variety, and insists not only on the party's innocence in Lorca's death but that Lorca himself was virtually a Falangist:

I swear solemnly, by the friendship we once shared and by my blood shed in the noblest of tempests on the battlefield, that neither the Falange nor the Spanish Army had any part in your death. The Falange always forgives; and forgets. You would have been its greatest poet; for your sentiments were those of the Falange: you wanted Fatherland, Bread and Justice for all. Whoever dares to deny this is a liar, and his denial is the surest proof that he never wanted anything to do with you [...]. The crime was in Granada, and there was no light to brighten the sky which you now possess. The hundred thousand violins of jealousy took away your life for ever [...]. And yet I cannot resign myself to the belief that you are really dead; you cannot die. The Falange is waiting for you; its welcome is Biblical: Comrade, your faith has saved you. No one could have synthesised like you the religious and poetic doctrines of the Falange, glossing their clauses, their aspirations. They have killed Imperial Spain's greatest poet. The Spanish Falange, arms stretched in salute, pays homage to your memory.

Understandably, Hurtado's article infuriated Lorca's Republican friends, and shortly afterwards a riposte appeared in the Valencian journal *Hora de España*:

We would never have believed it possible that these despicable writers, Franco's vile 'singers of praise', could have gone so far, with their total lack of honesty, as to laud their victims when they think it is in their interests or those of their leaders to do so. The whole world has reacted with indignation to the cowardly assassination; they, for their part, have apparently received orders to confuse the issue as much as possible, burning incense before the memory of the dead poet and seeking, as far as possible, to blame the 'Reds' for the crime....[4]

Some months later another acount of Lorca's death became available to those who were genuinely concerned to find out how the poet had died. On 15 September 1937 the Valencian paper *Adelante* published a sensational article entitled '*The crime was in Granada*: I witnessed the assassination of García Lorca ...' which claimed to be the report of an interview given to the journalist Vicente Vidal Corella by a Civil Guard forced to participate in Lorca's execution. The man had allegedly managed to escape to Valencia where he stated that the poet was executed by a group of Civil Guards near Padul, on the road from Granada to Motril. In December 1937 the essential part of this interview was reproduced by the Costa Rican newspaper *Repertorio americano*, thereby spreading throughout South America the legend that Lorca had been shot by the Civil Guard.[5] Virtually the same account was published in Havana in 1939 and later in Brooklyn in 1940 by J. Rubia Barcia, who had also spoken to the escaped guard.[6] A small detail of Rubia Barcia's version reveals that the story about the Civil Guard's participation in Lorca's death was quite untrustworthy, but despite this it is still widely believed.*

Shortly before the contents of the *Adelante* article were disseminated in South America, the Nationalist authorities had decided that something should be done to counteract the wide, anti-Franco press coverage that was being given to the Lorca affair. Accordingly when the correspondent of the Mexican daily newspaper *La Prensa* guardedly asked General Franco in November 1937 for his views on the subject in the course of a long interview, the Caudillo had the text of his official reply ready. In answer to the question 'Have you [the Nationalists] shot any writers of world reputation?' he replied:

There has been a lot of talk outside Spain about a Granadine writer whose fame has spread far and wide, although I could not personally judge its dimensions; there has been a lot of talk about him because the Reds have used his name for propaganda purposes. The fact of the matter is that, in the early days of the revolution, this writer died in Granada mixed up with the rebels ['*mezclado con los revoltosos*']: one of the inevitable accidents of war. Granada was cut off for many days, and the idiocy of the Republican authorities who distributed arms to the people gave rise to the disturbances in one of which the Granadine poet lost his life.†

As a poet his death is most regrettable, and Red propaganda has made much capital out of the accident, exploiting the sensibility of the intellectual world; on the other hand these people never mention the following men who were assassinated in cold blood and with a brutality that would terrify even the most equanimous person: Don José Calvo Sotelo, Don Víctor Pradera, Don José Polo Benito, the Duke of Canalejas, Don Honorio Maura, Don Francisco Valdés, Don Rufino Blanco, Don Manuel Bueno, Don José María Albiñana, Don Ramiro de Maeztu, Don Pedro Muñoz Seca, Don Pedro Mourlane

---

* For a discussion of this version of Lorca's death, see Appendix B.
† Franco well knew that this was a lie. As we have seen, the Republican authorities in Granada did not distribute weapons to the workers.

Michelena, Don Antonio Bermúdez Cañete, Don Rafael Salazar Alonso, Don Alfonso Rodríguez Santamaría (President of the Press Association), Don Melquiades Alvarez, Don Enrique Estévez Ortega, Don Federico Salmón, Father Zacarías G. Villadas, Don Fernando de la Quandra Salcedo, Don Gregorio de Balparda, and so many others whose enumeration would make my reply interminable. I say it again: we have shot no poets.[7]*

Franco and his aides must have realised that his propagation of this version of Lorca's death had been an imprudence, and when the interview was reproduced in the official edition of Franco's collected declarations to the press the editors thought it politic to remove the Caudillo's last sentence.[8]

Shortly after Franco's *La Prensa* interview his brother-in-law, Ramón Serrano Suñer, was appointed Minister of the Interior and Falange Propaganda Chief. Serrano had been head of the JAP (*Juventudes de Acción Popular*), the CEDA youth organisation, before the Nationalist rising and it was he who engineered its defection to the Falange in April 1936 after the CEDA's ineffectiveness had finally discouraged its younger members. When Serrano escaped from Madrid's Model Gaol in 1937 he made his way to Salamanca, where he quickly became one of Franco's closest accomplices. He was the principal architect of the famous Decree of Unification promulgated on 19 April 1937, whereby all the parties of the Right were fused into one state organisation, the *Falange Española Tradicionalista de las JONS* which, to be sure, bore little resemblance to José Antonio Primo de Rivera's original movement. Franco, who had not been a Falangist before the rising, proclaimed himself National Chief of the new 'party' and put Serrano Suñer in charge of his propaganda machine. Serrano was thus in a position to control all news published in Nationalist Spain. He was also responsible for promoting abroad a climate of opinion favourable to Franco.

Ten years passed before Serrano Suñer himself made any

---

* I have not personally investigated these cases, the enumeration of which does not absolve the Nationalists of the death of Lorca.

public reference to Lorca's death. Perhaps he had learned a lesson from the Caudillo's mistake. During these years it was positively dangerous to talk openly about Lorca in Spain, and none of his books was tolerated, nor were his plays produced in Spanish theatres. But at last worldwide interest in the poet forced the regime to reconsider its position and in the early 1950s the thaw started.[9]

Since it was well known that Ramón Ruiz Alonso and other members of Acción Popular had participated in Lorca's arrest, and since, moreover, the CEDA no longer existed, the Franco authorities had little difficulty in deciding where to lay the blame for his death. Gerald Brenan takes up the story:

The first open blow in this controversy had already [by December 1948] been struck by the Falangist ex-minister, Serrano Suñer. In December 1947 he gave an interview to a Mexican journalist, Alfonso Junco, in which he asserted that the man who had given the order to kill Lorca was the Catholic Conservative deputy to the Cortes, Ramón Ruiz Alonso. Such an accusation could not of course be published in the Spanish press, but it conveyed accurately enough what the Falangists were saying. They were organising a whispering campaign to claim the poet for their friend and lay the blame for his death on the Clericals.[10]

Alfonso Junco has denied that his interview with Serrano Suñer was ever published,[11] and it has become clear that the interview referred to by Brenan was given, not to Junco but to another Mexican journalist, Armando Chávez Camacho, editor of *El Universal gráfico*. The interview appeared on 2 January 1948 and contained the following allusion to Lorca's death:

We knew a little about the death of García Lorca. Wanting to know more, we enquired. Serrano Suñer told us:
'I will complete your information. The leader of the group that took Lorca from his house and killed him was the right-wing deputy and ex-typographer Ramón Ruiz Alonso. He is still alive and kicking, and nobody molests him, in spite of the fact that the crime was stupid

and unjust and that it did us great harm, for Lorca was an outstanding poet.'[12]

Serrano Suñer was far from happy that such a charge should be imputed to him in print, for he well knew that Lorca had been executed officially in Granada and that Ruiz Alonso, 'still alive and kicking' as he was, might be prepared to blurt out the truth publicly, were he to be openly blamed for Lorca's death. Serrano, therefore, wrote to Chávez Camacho to 'clarify' what he had said during their 'private' conversation. On 3 March 1948 Chávez published the most significant part of this letter in *El Universal gráfico*. It is a document of considerable interest, for while an interviewee can claim that his views have been misreported (as Serrano does), a letter affords no such loophole:

My dear friend,
[...] both of us lamented, in our private conversation, the tragic error committed by Nationalist Spain in the matter of the great Granadine poet's death. I argued that the crime had been deplored by many of us who were (and some who still are) leaders of the National Cause, which had itself no part in the crime, this being the work of a group of 'uncontrollables', the sort that take part, as a matter of course, in all upheavals. I was concerned to point out – and this without any equivocation – that not a single Falangist had participated in the crime.

And I'll go further now and add, if I didn't say it then, that it was precisely the few Falangists there were in Granada who acted as friends and protectors of the poet, whose adhesion to the Cause they envisaged. His death was brought about by those who least understood the generous, Spanish ambition of the Movement, elements possessed of a provincial and not easily definable rancour, and who were, needless to say, anti-Falangist.

As proof of this I explained to you how public opinion had connected with the perpetrators of the Granada crime the name of a CEDA deputy who was naturally assumed to be in close touch with the militia of Acción Popular who arrested García Lorca, although certainly without the intention of leading him to his tragic destiny. The arrest took place in the house of the Falangist poet Rosales, who was protecting him. As a result the story that the Acción Popular militia and the deputy in question were responsible for the poet's death was no more than a rumour that I adduced as proof of the anti-Falangist character that public opinion gave to the crime from the first moment....

Serrano Suñer was careful to preclude all acrimony with Ruiz Alonso himself, and the ex-deputy of the CEDA showed me a letter from Serrano, dated March 1948, which contains more or less the same sentiments as those expressed soon afterwards in his letter to *El Universal gráfico*. Having denied that he ever accused Ruiz Alonso of Lorca's death, Serrano goes on to tell him – Ruiz Alonso! – that:

The death of Federico García Lorca was the work of a group of 'uncontrollables' during the confused situation of the first moments of the Civil War but not, as has been said throughout the world, the work of Falangist uncontrollables.

He adds:

Federico García Lorca was not in the enemy camp; in fact he was coming over to us when stupidity and rancour went out to meet him on the way.

It was not long before another prominent Nationalist apologist referred, in equally imprecise and misleading terms, to the poet's death. This time it was the turn of José María Pemán, a member of the Spanish Academy, who exclaimed testily in an editorial in *ABC*:

I do not think it will come as a surprise to anyone when I say that the death of Federico García Lorca, the great Granadine poet, is still one of the accusations most commonly levelled against Spain throughout the whole of Spanish-speaking America. It is also clear that, in spite of the continued bandying of this topic for polemical purposes, the simple truth is making itself known, namely that the poet's death was a vile and unfortunate episode, totally foreign to all official responsibility and initiative ['un episodio vil y desgraciado, totalmente ajeno a toda responsabilidad e iniciativa oficial'].... [13]

The ambiguity of this last sentence was doubtless intentional: it could mean either that Lorca's death was not carried out by the official authorities in Granada at the time or that those authorities who carried it out acted in a totally irresponsible fashion. Such casuistry has typified Nationalist writing on the subject.

Nowhere is this better shown than in *La estafeta literaria*, the regime's 'official' literary review, which has occupied itself more than once with the subject of Lorca's death.

The 1950s witnessed the appearance of three significant pieces of research on the death, each involving personal investigations in Granada, and each the work of a non-Spaniard. Gerald Brenan was the first in the field with his chapter on Granada and Víznar in *The Face of Spain*, and this account was reproduced shortly afterwards in a French literary journal. [14] Meanwhile Claude Couffon had been carrying out a more detailed piece of literary detective work, and the resultant article was featured in *Le Figaro Littéraire* on 18 August 1951. [15] Then, on 29 September 1956, the same magazine printed Jean-Louis Schonberg's 'homosexual' thesis under the following heading:

ENFIN, LA VÉRITÉ SUR LA MORT DE LORCA!
UN ASSASSINAT, CERTES, MAIS DONT LA
POLITIQUE N'A PAS ÉTÉ LE MOBILE.

At last the Nationalists had been presented with a convenient explanation of the poet's death, one all the more useful inasmuch as it was the product of a foreign pen. Brenan and Couffon had blown holes in the regime's previous propaganda, and their accounts were therefore totally unserviceable, but here was an article that lent support to the Nationalist argument that Lorca's death had been caused by individuals acting independently of official control. On 13 October 1956, a mere fortnight after the publication of Schonberg's article, *La estafeta literaria* carried the following banner headline on its front page:

THE FIGARO LITTÉRAIRE CONFESSES: AT LAST,
THE TRUTH ABOUT GARCÍA LORCA'S DEATH!
'THE MOTIVATION HAD NOTHING TO DO
WITH POLITICS'.

As the reader can see, the magazine is careful to omit from its headline version the phrase 'an assassination, certainly'. Its treatment of the substance of Schonberg's article is similarly devious, and reveals in every line a determination to distort the facts of Lorca's death. When one considers that Schonberg's article is itself most untrustworthy, the efforts of the propagandists seem even more clumsy:

At last, we for our part exclaim, the bluff has been called! Twenty years using García Lorca's death as a political instrument! Not that such a gambit is unique or original, of course: it can be seen on an international scale. But there we are, the death of the Granadine poet was available for exploitation without scruples or honesty, even if it meant committing a conscientious, vile and systematic swindle against people of good faith. Those public ceremonies, those solemn recitals of his work, that constant flaunting of his name as a victim, those crocodile tears – who could ever forget them?

Meanwhile in Spain, the true, honourable Spain, all the facts were there, waiting to tell the embarrassing truth which would show up the conspiracy for what it was. There is only one truth, and the person who has truth on his side is the best person to reveal and demonstrate it. And here, in Spain, all the facts were there to reveal and demonstrate that truth. But, of course, nobody was interested in this outside Spain. How could the ripped garments be sewn up? Or the big political issues?

'DE POLITIQUE, PAS DE [sic] QUESTION'

Now, at last, a French writer, J. L. Schomberg [sic], author of the most complete and fully documented biography of the poet, has been in Spain several times between 1953 and 1956, has travelled all over

Andalusia, visited villages adjacent to Granada and spoken to whomever he considered either useful or necessary. He has searched in archives and visited the relevant places. Finally, after all this, he has arrived at the following conclusion:

'De politique, pas question. La politique, c'était alors la purge qui vous évacuait sans préambule'. In other words, there was no question of a political motive. That is what this special correspondent writes in the third paragraph of the fifth column on page five of the *Figaro littéraire*, 29 September 1956.

Twenty years to admit the truth. Is truth so difficult to find? The point is, of course, that the problem or snag did not lie in finding the truth, but rather in allowing it to become known.

'L'AMOUR OSCUR* [sic], VOILÀ LE FOND DE L'AFFAIRE'

Bit by bit the writer and journalist tries to uncover the motives.† Blackmail? Revenge? Perhaps both, he replies openly and in print. But by whom? He also answers this:

'Reste alors la vengeance; la vengeance de l'amour oscur [sic].' Homosexual love's revenge, he writes in the first paragraph, column six of the fifth page.

From the time he wrote the *Ode to Walt Whitman* García Lorca knew perfectly well – continues the French writer and meticulous biographer – that he was the object of terrible hatreds. He was not unaware of the cesspool of humanity, full of pederasts, where they waited for him. 'Murderers of doves! No quarter! Death glints in your eyes. May the "pure", the "Classicals", shut the doors of the bacchanalia against you.'‡ And the journalist and biographer concludes: 'And here we have the crux of the matter.'

HATRED IN EXCHANGE FOR SCORN

It is true that politically he had nothing to fear. True that he knew he had nothing to fear from the authorities. The authorities and the

---

* That is, homosexual love.
† Here the *Estafeta* hurriedly passes over Schonberg's account of the Nationalist repression of Granada, which certainly could not have been reproduced in Spain.
‡ Disjointed quotations from Lorca's *Ode to Walt Whitman*.

Falange were also his friends. He had taken refuge in the house belonging to the Rosales brothers. 'Ah, si Luis, l'ami qui adorait Lorca, avait été là.' And the Socialists and the Republicans. He was friendly with everyone. 'But it would be an error ', he continues, 'to imagine that Federico, friendly with everyone, only attracted friendship in return. Beneath his affable manner he knew how to cultivate disdain. To this disdain the "impures" replied with hatred.'

'The accusation which led to the designation of Lorca's pursuer and executioner rested initially on nothing more than a personal vengeance which was completely independent of political, literary, religious or social considerations.'* 'This homosexual underworld, the bar in Elvira Street which gave him the key to two poems,† the gypsyism and the gypsy lads, all these lower levels of society that Lorca frequented as one of the confraternity, were treated by him with contempt, despite his personal nobility of character. It was precisely for this pride in his own superiority that they made him pay.'

It is to this conclusion that the writer and biographer J. L. Schomberg [sic] has come after a long and meticulous investigation into the places and people able to furnish him with the information he was seeking. At last the disreputable clique responsible for cooking up that deceitful tissue of lies has had its bluff – its political bluff – called.

At last, after twenty years! 'Voilà!'

This characteristic piece of Nationalist journalism was discussed widely in Spain and provoked the indignation of a leading ex-Falangist, the poet Dionisio Ridruejo. Ridruejo had been Director General of Propaganda (he was dismissed in May 1941) and was a close friend of Luis Rosales, from whom he had received a detailed account of Lorca's arrest. He now wrote an angry and courageous letter to the Minister of Information and Tourism, Gabriel Arias Salgado, which, according to Fernando Vázquez Ocaña, was 're-produced or discussed the world over'.[16]

It was not, though, reproduced in Spain, and subsequent numbers of La Estafeta literaria made no allusion whatsoever to the controversy. Nor indeed could they, for Ridruejo had placed

* Schonberg had referred openly at this point to Ramón Ruiz Alonso.
† Here the anonymous Estafeta journalist reveals again his shaky knowledge of French. Schonberg had written: 'Cette pègre de l'amour obscur, ce bar de la rue d'Elvira *qui donne la clef de deux chansons....*' (my italics).

the blame for the poet's death squarely on the shoulders of the rebel authorities in Granada:

Dear friend,

I cannot and will not allow to pass in silence and without protest the publication of an article that appeared recently in *La Estafeta literaria* and in which, for despicable reasons, some paragraphs of the article on Federico García Lorca's death published by M. Schonberg in the *Figaro Littéraire* are reproduced and discussed. The *Estafeta* article is the kind that dishonours both its author, its publisher and those who read it without anger. I ask you to judge for yourself: the aim of the article is to wipe from the Nationalist Movement the stain cast on it by the poet's death; but the attempt fails and the author of the article, even were he an idiot, would have realised this. It is precisely what people have always said that remains true: that a system of political terrorism killed a man who, even from the most fanatical standpoint, ought to have been considered innocent. The article confirms his innocence, dissipates the possibility of a subjective justification based on a revolutionary necessity, while failing, at the same time, to disprove the fact that the poet died at the hands of the agents of the political repression of Granada, without anyone saying boo to them.

Why, then, this article? To my mind for only one reason: because the publication of Schonberg's paragraphs was a way of casting a shadow, a suggestion of moral degeneracy, on the memory of the victim. It was not so much a question of establishing that the reasons for his death, as hinted by the French writer, were not political as of proclaiming that they were 'homosexual'. Doubtless the editor of the *Estafeta*, Juan Aparicio, thought, with 'Christian' insight, that by diminishing the stature of the victim he would make the crime or the error more forgiveable.

It seems to me that this is going too far, that it is really a disgusting business and that all the laws of honour, pity and common decency have been trampled underfoot. I ask myself and you if the way Spaniards think is to be dictated by people capable of such foul behaviour. If this is to be so, we have sunk too low to command any respect at all....[17]

Unlike Ridruejo, the Falangist journalist Rafael García Serrano was happy to prolong the official campaign of misrepresentation.

In 1953 he had published a book which described the visit to South America of the Song and Dance Troupe of the Nationalist regime. In it García Serrano refers to Lorca's death (about which he was frequently quizzed by the poet's admirers) and, doubtless taking his cue from Serrano Suñer, ascribes total blame for the event to the CEDA and Ramón Ruiz Alonso, whom he is careful not to mention by name:

What is certain is that Lorca's death cannot be attributed to the Falange. He had taken refuge in a house belonging to two Falangists, in the hope of surviving those first confused moments which occur in all revolutions. The brother of the poet Luis Rosales was the provincial chief of the Granada Militia.* It was there that García Lorca found shelter. It has been asserted that he was composing an *Ode to the Falangist Dead*, and if this story has any basis in fact, it would be a good thing if Luis Rosales, who knows a great deal about the matter, were to say so. It was a group of right-wing militiamen, commanded by a certain CEDA deputy [...] who, taking advantage of the absence of the Chief of Militia and his brother, led García Lorca to face a Civil Guard firing squad, because the CEDA never had the guts to take firm decisions itself.[18]

The only original detail in García Serrano's tirade against the CEDA is his allegation that Lorca was shot by the Civil Guard. Such a charge had never been made in a Nationalist publication and it must have considerably angered the force, no member of which had in fact intervened in the killing.

Twelve years later García Serrano returned, undeterred, to the subject of Lorca's death, publishing on 7 May 1965 a vicious leading article in *ABC* entitled 'A Note to Mme Auclair'. The French writer, who had been a close friend of the poet, was in Spain at the time, collecting material for a book on his life and work. Her opposition to the Franco regime was well known. García Serrano begins pleasantly: Mme Auclair is interested in Lorca's travelling theatre, La Barraca, and he will give her the name and

* This is inaccurate, as we have seen. José Rosales was never Provincial Chief of the Granada Falange Militia.

address of a friend who was a member of the company. But at the end of the article he reveals that his information will unfortunately be of little use to Mme Auclair because the friend in question was assassinated during the war – by the Reds. García Serrano repeats yet again the official story of Lorca's death and concludes:

That mistake for which we have all paid so dearly can be attributed only to the confused cruelty of a civil war that had just begun. The Rosales brothers and their comrades did all they could to obtain the reprieve that was so often impossible in the enemy zone, where no one complained. . . .

In the course of his 'Note to Mme Auclair' the Falangist journalist refers to a recent article in *La Estafeta literaria* which provided new details about Lorca's death. The item turns out to be a blatantly biased gloss on an account of Lorca's death by Saint-Paulien, which itself derives almost in its entirety from Jean-Louis Schonberg.[19] I reproduce some paragraphs from the article as a final example of this journal's lack of intellectual honesty (shown further by the fact that it does not even take the trouble to give the source of Saint-Paulien's and Werrie's pieces):[20]

Our excellent friend Federico García Lorca, the poet in New York who protests against the anglicisation of the Hispanic world [?] – a protest more important than the 'local colour' of his work which is so pleasing to those in search of 'typical Spanish' [sic] – was fortunate to live intensely, to know success in the fullness of youth and to find favour with the gods.

But he was unlucky in that dark passions cut down his life when his poet's heart was full of promise, of verses taking shape, verses which he was never able to utter. After his treacherous death at the hands of the small men, his fame spread like a train of gunpowder across the hesitant and writhing continents of Europe and the Americas. Poor Federico was converted overnight into an anti-Fascist hero, into the genius immolated by the Granada Fascists. [. . .]

But there are also learned men determined to tell the historical truth. In France, as far as Lorca is concerned, this truth has been highlighted by many people. The most recent to do so are Paul Werrie and Saint-Paulien.

Saint-Paulien, a fine *lorquista*,[21] accumulated a large amount of documentation in Spain, talking to people of all ideologies who knew Lorca or were his intimate friends. The legend of his death, he says, is a hoax as prodigious as that of *The Shoemaker's Wife*.*

Lorca, writes Saint-Paulien, adducing numerous proofs, was politically innocuous, and never committed himself with regard to the Republic, despite the fact that it financed the *Barraca*; in his latter days he showed much interest in the Falange. José Antonio offered him an important post.† But Federico drew back and limited himself to cultivating the friendship of well-known Falangists such as Iturriaga and the Rosales brothers. [...]

Saint-Paulien utilises the information collected by himself, quotes Federico's biographers González Caballero [sic] and J. L. Schonberg, and has recourse to Lorca's letters published in the *Revista de Indias* in Bogotá.

These well-known facts are analysed, given new life and described by Saint-Paulien in their full horror, the material and psychological horror of lives, deaths and crimes inspired by passion.

Let us have the decency not to mix or confound these things with a political crime that never existed.[22]

No more need be said to demonstrate the lack of seriousness shown by *La Estafeta literaria* in its allusions to Lorca's death.

A year later, in the autumn of 1966, the Buenos Aires publishers Codex launched a weekly series of illustrated brochures on the Spanish Civil War. The series was distributed throughout the Spanish-speaking world and became immediately available to readers in Spain.

The tenth episode, *Andalusia: Confusion and Tragedy*, appeared on Spanish bookstands in November 1966. Largely dedicated to Queipo de Llano's putsch in Seville, the number also

---

* A meaningless reference to Lorca's play *La zapatera prodigiosa*.
† Saint-Paulien states, p. 8, that there is in existence a correspondence between José Antonio Primo de Rivera and Lorca, and that one of the poet's letters to the Falange chief begins 'My dear friend'. I have found no evidence in support of this assertion, and it is hard to believe that, if the letters really existed, the Falange would have delayed their publication.

devoted considerable space to Lorca.[23] Most of the information on the poet's death was a rehash of Hugh Thomas's brief and rather inaccurate synthesis,[24] and as a result no mention was made of Lorca's detention in the Civil Government.

The explanation of Lorca's death ascribed to Ramón Pérez de Ayala, the Republic's ambassador in London, however, was startlingly new and provoked much comment. Although the editors claimed not to lend much credence to the account they nevertheless decided to publish it, ostensibly as one more example of the multiplicity of rumours surrounding the poet's death, but perhaps also to call in question the reputation of the Communist poet Rafael Alberti. Pérez de Ayala's version reads:

García Lorca, who, because of his connections with the Left, had gone, frightened, into hiding at the house of his great friend Luis Rosales, the Falangist poet, seldom sallied forth from his hiding place.* When he did so he was watched attentively by the excitable Nationalist militiamen, who regarded Federico with suspicion. It appears that on one of these occasions they questioned him and asked him where he was off to. Lorca replied that he was going to hand over some letters for friends and relatives in the Republican zone, which a well-known messenger had promised to deliver. The militiamen, probably Falangists, accepted his story with some scepticism. Some days later the voice of Rafael Alberti was heard over Madrid Radio referring to the great poet Federico García Lorca who was a prisoner of the insurgent traitors but who had not lost faith in the ultimate victory [of the Republic], and who for this reason had sent some lines of poetry to his friends in Madrid which he, Alberti, was now going to read there and then over the microphone. Alberti proceeded to read some tremendous lines in which the rebel leaders were insulted in the most vile language; the poem could evidently not be imputed to Lorca, who was always correct and elegant in his expression. The lines bore the clear stamp of Alberti himself, who ended his broadcast by thanking Lorca for sending them and hoping for his speedy release.

It appears that the militiamen and Falangists who heard the broadcast in the Granada zone were incensed with García Lorca,

* According to the Rosales, Federico never once left their house during his stay there: such an action would have been unthinkable in the circumstances.

considering that he had tricked them. [...] This alleged act on the part of Lorca unleashed the fury of his fanatical accusers, who put him to death during a confused spell of disorder and terror which has never been satisfactorily clarified....[25]

Alberti reacted quickly to this grotesque account and initiated legal proceedings against Codex. He had in fact been in hiding in Ibiza until 15 August 1936, when the island was liberated by the Bayo Expedition, and could hardly have reached Madrid before Lorca's death.

The Codex affair was widely covered in the Spanish press and, while most journalists were sensible enough to dismiss the accusations against Alberti, the customary evasiveness about the poet's death was again in evidence. We can be content with one example. Jaime Capmany, writing in *Arriba*, concluded:

We must approach this version of the death of the great poet Federico García Lorca with the same scepticism as the many and varied accounts which up to now have circulated in books, periodicals and newspapers both in Spain and abroad. The death of Federico García Lorca continues to be one of the enigmas of the first days of our war; a painful enigma, the clarification of which can now only have an historical meaning. These were days of general disorder and collective lunacy, and if for many months everything was possible in one zone, it is not surprising that for a few hours or a few days everything was possible in Granada, including the death of García Lorca.[26]

Lorca's 'reinstatement' became virtually official on Sunday 6 November 1966, when *ABC*, the most widely read newspaper in Spain, published a 'homage' to the poet on the occasion of the thirtieth anniversary of his death.

The only reference in that issue to the death itself is to be found in an article by Edgar Neville, 'The Works of Federico, the Nation's Property'. The sentiments are predictable and require little comment:

Federico was killed by the disorder of the early moments, when evil men on both sides took advantage of the confusion to give free rein to their worst instincts and to revenge themselves on their enemies or on other people's success. It was a small-town crime, one might almost say a personal one, just like those that were committed on the other side against thousands of innocent creatures, some of them poets or authors, writers who had nothing to do with politics and who wanted nothing to do with them....

Referring to the 'evil men' responsible for Federico's death, Neville concludes:

It seems that some of those implicated have already died, but others are around still and wriggle out of their responsibility whenever anyone tries to shame them publicly.[27]

Which is, of course, an apt description of what the regime itself had been successfully doing for the last thirty years.

Six years passed before there was any further reference in the Spanish press to Lorca's death. Then, suddenly, a new controversy flared up. On 23 March 1972, a plaque commemorating the foundation of the Falange was fixed to the front of Madrid's Teatro de la Comedia, where the party was launched in 1933. The Nuria Espert production of Lorca's *Yerma* (which was received with acclaim in London some weeks later) was playing in the Comedia at the time, and the coincidence did not go unnoticed.

The day after the commemoration, the Catholic newspaper *Ya* published photographs of the ceremony which showed the plaque and the *Yerma* poster in close proximity, and Luis Apostúa commented in his daily column:

Other important political events yesterday were the reception of Archbishop Monsignor González as a Councillor of State and the uncovering of a plaque commemorating the foundation of the Falange on the front of the Teatro de la Comedia, where a drama by Federico García Lorca, who died in 1936, is currently playing. The Falange's return to an active role is evident ['*El retorno a la escena activa de Falange es bien visible*'].[28]

The Falange had no doubt that the last sentence was double-edged, and that evening Antonio Gibello, editor of *El Alcázar*, took up the challenge on the party's behalf. He informed Apostúa that Lorca, hounded by militant Acción Popular youths, had taken refuge in a Falangist house, accused the CEDA of the poet's death and ended his article with a veiled allusion to Ramón Ruiz Alonso and the newspaper on which the latter worked in Granada, *Ideal* (which is owned by Editorial Católica, the publishing company which also controls *Ya*).[29]

Next morning the Falangist daily, *Arriba*, added its voice of protest,[30] and Luis Apostúa proclaimed his innocence in *Ya*. How could the Falangists have read such a polemical intention into that innocuous sentence? Such an interpretation of what he had written was as absurd as it was gratuitous:

The return of the Falange to an active political role had already been noted with approval several times in *Ya*, because we believe that the future of Spain depends on the open functioning of authentic political groups.

Moreover, insisted Apostúa, he knew perfectly well that the Falange was not responsible for the poet's death. Indeed, he knew as well as anyone who *was* responsible.[31]

Next day an unsigned leading article in *Ya* reaffirmed the newspaper's absolute incomprehension of Gibello's charges.[32]

On 27 March Gibello fired his Parthian shot from the battlements of *El Alcázar*. He accepted Apostúa's clarifications but had one final query: if Apostúa really knew who killed García Lorca, would it not be a mark of courtesy to inform *Ya*'s readers, who must surely be *avid* for the facts?[33]

It was understandable that among all these innuendos and counter-accusations someone should have thought to ask Luis Rosales for his opinion. On 29 March *ABC* published the following letter:

To the editor of ABC

My dear friend,

Having been encouraged in an article by the well-known journalist Emilio Romero in your paper *Pueblo* to make a public statement concerning what I know about the death of Federico García Lorca,[34] I wish now to say the following:

That painful event has exerted a decisive influence on my life and mode of being. To it I owe my deepest experience. As a result there is nothing I have desired more since 1936 than the opportunity to make a full and unconditional declaration in Spain about these matters. This I have already done more than once outside Spain.

Thanking you in advance for printing these lines.

Yours sincerely,

LUIS ROSALES

This letter highlighted the trivial nature of the controversy which was just then spluttering out in the Madrid press and proved that it was still impossible to write openly, 'unconditionally', about Lorca's death in Spain.

Or almost so, for a few weeks later a book appeared that contained the most daring account of it yet published in the country.[35] In his chapter 'Who killed García Lorca?', the author, José Luis Vila-San-Juan, had pieced the story together from Thomas, Brenan, Marcelle Auclair and myself, and was the first writer to state openly in Spain that the Nationalist repression of Granada had been 'very severe' and that Lorca was arrested on the orders of Valdés and imprisoned in the Civil Government before his execution. Blame had been laid publicly on the shoulders of the *authorities* in Granada for the first time, although Ramón Ruiz Alonso was still seen as the principal culprit.* Not only that: the author casually noted in passing that Valdés was an 'old guard' member of the Falange, which is precisely what the party had been trying to hide for thirty-seven years. Serrano Suñer's 1948 assurance that 'not a single Falangist participated in the crime' and the party's insistence on its spotless innocence in the Lorca affair could now be seen to be less than honest.

---

* Ruiz Alonso responded by initiating legal proceedings against Vila-San-Juan, without, so far as I know, any positive results to date. See *Sábado gráfico*, Madrid, 21 October 1972.

Vila-San-Juan had set the cat of intellectual honesty amongst the pigeons of deceit, and it is hard to believe that he had no official backing for his exposé, particularly in view of the fact that his chapter on Lorca was reproduced shortly afterwards in a glossy weekly.[36]

Moreover, some weeks later the Madrid newspaper *Informaciones* gave Luis Rosales the opportunity he had been seeking. In an interview published on 17 August (the anniversary of Lorca's imprisonment), Rosales at last told his story, or part of it, in his own country and – most unexpectedly – quotations from the original Spanish-language edition of the present book were reproduced, notably a passage indicating that Lorca was shot officially on the orders of Valdés.[37]

Clearly the authorities had decided on a change of approach, and this was confirmed a month later when, on 23 September 1972, José María Pemán of the Spanish Academy (whose contribution in 1948 to the Lorca debate has already been discussed) stated in *ABC* that, in his opinion, my book was written 'with intellectual integrity and without bias' and should therefore be made available in Spain.[38]

With the publication, in 1975, of the books on Lorca's death by Eduardo Castro[39] and José Luis Vila-San-Juan[40] – both of them appeared shortly before the demise of General Franco in November of that year – the basic facts about what had taken place forty years earlier in Granada became widely known. In particular that Lorca had been but one victim among thousands and that his death had been ordered officially.

Today Lorca can be seen not only as one of the greatest Spanish poets of all time but as the supreme symbol of the suffering, havoc and death wrought on the people of Spain by the Nationalist allies of Hitler and Mussolini.

But old attitudes die hard, particularly, it seems, in Granada. On 19 August 1978, the anniversary of Lorca's assassination, the Granadine newspaper *Patria*, founded by the Falange, recalled that forty-two years earlier 'A group of uncontrolled persons killed the writer, poet and dramatist Federico García Lorca' (p. 2).

AFTERWORD
TO THE PENGUIN EDITION

Since the publication of the revised English edition of this book (1979), and of the Spanish editions of 1978 and 1981, little new information concerning Lorca's death has been unearthed—or, at least, brought to the attention of the public. This is disappointing. One had hoped that, freed from the restrictions operating under the Franco dictatorship, some Spaniard (and preferably a *granadino*) would undertake to fill in the few missing gaps in the picture, completing our knowledge of how the great poet met his end.

There was, in fact, an excellent candidate for the post. I refer to Eduardo Molina Fajardo. Molina, for many years editor of the Granada Falangist newspaper *Patria,* founded at the beginning of the Civil War, was basically a liberal, despite professional appearances to the contrary. A gifted local historian, intrigued by all aspects of Granada's life and culture, he had written several useful books, the most notable of which, perhaps, was his slim volume on Manuel de Falla and the *cante jondo* festival (held in the Alhambra in June 1922). Molina could not fail to be deeply interested in Lorca; and for twenty years he amassed information on the poet's death, information to which, as a Falangist, he had privileged access. Under Franco his findings could not, of course, be published; but after the aged Caudillo's demise in 1975 Molina announced openly that he would shortly give to the world the results of his investigation into Lorca's last days.

Those results were not forthcoming, however. Year after year Molina fobbed off enquirers with the excuse that the book was *almost* ready, but not quite. And, in early November 1979, he died suddenly before the work had appeared.

It then transpired that not only was the book not finished but that all the author had left behind was a huge, unmanageable pile of notes and filing cards, as well as a series of interviews (we don't even know if they were tape recorded) with such personages as Luis Rosales, Ramón Ruiz Alonso and others involved, in one way or another, in the events surrounding the poet's arrest and assassination. Molina's widow hastened to state that, notwithstanding her husband's death, the book would be published; and insisted that she would permit no one outside the immediate family to inspect the dead man's papers.

That was almost three years ago. Molina's study has not yet seen the light of day, and the publishers with whom he signed the contract for the book, Plaza and Janés of Barcelona (recently acquired by the German group Bertelsmann), prefer not to discuss the matter. It is my hope that, whatever its imperfections, Molina's research may yet be published, for there can be no doubt that he collected a considerable amount of new information on Lorca's death, and perhaps even obtained documents, or copies of documents, proceeding from military archives.

In this latter respect, it now seems certain that such documents existed. Earlier this year I met in Granada a young man who, in 1972, was working in the city's military headquarters. He assured me that one day, while the archives were being cleared out, he suddenly found himself holding a sizable file on the outside of which was inscribed: 'FEDERICO GARCIA LORCA.' The temptation to remove the dossier, or photocopy it, was strong, but not so strong as the fear which, by my informant's own admission, immediately overwhelmed him. My man missed his historic opportunity, and has regretted it bitterly ever since. It is just possible, however, that the file was not destroyed but sent to Seville where, along with other military documents from Granada, it may have been deposited in the military archives of that city. So far attempts to locate it have failed. Probably the only hope is that Eduardo Molina Fajardo may have had access to the dossier before it was removed, in which case it is all the more imperative that his research be published. The missing file could well contain, or may have contained, vital information about the charges levelled at the poet; its destruction would be a tragedy.

As regards the causes of Lorca's death, it is today generally recognised in Spain that these were largely political. The story, put out by the Franco regime, that the motives were strictly personal, and even homosexual, are now accepted only by a small minority of ultra-right-wing hardliners. As the poet's brother Francisco pointed out in his study (posthumous, alas) of Lorca and his world, it was virtually impossible to be apolitical in the heady, passionate and dangerous days of the Spanish Republic, and even less so in the months leading up to July 1936.[1] The poet, by closely identifying himself with the Popular Front, had made his position more than clear. His numerous public condemnations of Fascism were well known in Granada, as was his friendship with eminent men of the Left such as Fernando de los Ríos (Socialist Minister of Education under Azaña) or the Communist poet Rafael Alberti. Moreover, the Right had never forgiven Lorca for his play *Yerma,* particularly the exchange:

Yerma: In that case, God help me!
Old Woman: No, not God, I've never liked God. When are people going to realise that there's no such person?

As an indication of the feeling *Yerma* elicited in certain quarters (the play was staged in Madrid in December 1934), the following commentary, published at that time, needs no comment:

The Gay Fraternity

At the recent première in the Español, mixing with those members of the audience who, in good faith but utterly mistakenly, were present in the theatre, there was gathered together an odd confraternity whose leader is the author of *Yerma.*

In the passages, in the foyer, in the bar, during the intervals, our ears were offended by effeminate voices. [. . .] It was a repellent spectacle. As repellent as the repulsive, filthy phrases and scenes of the play, incompatible with human dignity and, naturally, with art.

No decent women could sit and watch the play, which ought to be brought to the attention of the Law, because it constitutes an offence against public decency.[2]

Lorca had left-wing views, even though he belonged to no political party; he had made his dislike of Fascism clear; he was homosexual; he was famous, and hence widely envied; and he had the wrong friends. Any one of these contingencies would have made things difficult for him in Nationalist Granada. All things taken together, his death warrant was already signed the evening he boarded the train for Andalusia.

There is one interesting item which should be added to previous editions of this book. It is that Franco's references to Lorca's death, published by the Mexican daily *La Prensa* (see pp. 192–3 of the present edition), were reproduced in Nationalist Spain by *ABC* (Seville), on 6 January 1938, under the heading 'Destruction of a Lie'. In the article, signed by *ABC*'s correspondent in Valparaíso, Chile, it was alleged that Lorca's death at the hands of the Granada authorities was a lie concocted by the actress Margarita Xirgu, a close friend of the poet. This was a monstrous libel—but excellent propaganda.

A few days after the appearance of the article, the insurance agent Manuel Marín Forero (whose brother Enrique, a Granada town councillor, was executed some months earlier) visited Lorca's father, don Federico García Rodríguez, at the Huerta de San Vicente. Don Federico was holding a copy of *ABC* in his hand. 'Look what they say about my son!', he exclaimed, with tears in his eyes. 'The lying blackguards!'.[3]

In 1980 the Granada County Council purchased several acres surrounding the spot where Lorca and his fellow unfortunates were killed that morning in August 1936, not far from the Fuente Grande in Alfacar. Extensive enquiries had first been made concerning the exact location in which the crime was committed, and these confirmed my own earlier investigations. One witness in particular, who had passed along the road shortly after the shooting, knew Lorca personally and was able to testify to the exact position in which he saw the poet's body. His account tallied closely with that of the grave digger M. C., with whom I had visited the site in 1966 and again in 1978.

The County Council then held an international competition for ideas as to how the area could best be adapted as a memorial park to the victims of the repression, and preserved for posterity. The winning scheme, which has recently been initiated, fosters the natural vegetation and flora of the hillside; several rows of poplars have been planted (the *chopo* was one of Lorca's favourite trees); and the old olive, close to which lie the remains of the four men, has been pruned and tended. In a few years the park will be opened to the public as both a symbol of reconciliation among Spaniards, and a warning to future generations.

The fact that the Granada County Council, when plans to purchase the Alfacar site were put in motion, was presided over by a conservative, speaks eloquently of the extent to which the political atmosphere has changed in Spain. Such a gesture would have been unthinkable only eight years ago. It is clear that this nation is determined that never again shall it be rent by the obscenity of civil war.

Ian Gibson
Madrid
September 1982

APPENDIX A

A complete list of town councillors holding office in Granada between February and July 1936 and of those executed

This list was published by *Ideal* on 10 July 1936. By that date only the first twenty-four councillors on the list still held office. All those marked with an asterisk were executed. Alejandro Otero, who was particularly loathed by the Nationalists, was lucky to be out of Granada when the rising began.

*Manuel Fernández-Montesinos (Socialist)
Francisco Gómez Román (Independent)
*Rafael Gómez Juárez (Socialist)
*Juan Fernández Rosillo (Socialist)
*Constantino Ruiz Carnero (Left Republican)
*Rafael Baquero Sanmartín (Left Republican)
*Antonio Dalmases Miquel (Socialist)
*Francisco Ramírez Caballero (Socialist)
*José Valenzuela Marín (Socialist)
Miguel Lozano Gómez (Left Republican)
*Enrique Marín Forero (Left Republican)
Antonio Ortega Molina (Independent)
*Jesús Yoldi Bereau (Left Republican)
Alejandro Otero (Left Republican)
*Maximiliano Hernández (Socialist)
*Francisco Rubio Callejón (Left Republican)
*Virgilio Castilla (Socialist)
*Juan Comino (Socialist)
*José Megías Manzano (Socialist)
Cristóbal López Mezquita (Independent)
*Manuel Salinas (Left Republican)
*Wenceslao Guerrero (Socialist)
Rafael Jiménez Romero (Independent)

*Luis Fajardo (Left Republican)
*Rafael García Duarte (Socialist)
  Antonio Alvarez Cienfuegos (CEDA)
  Federico García Ponce (Socialist)
  José Martín Barrales (Left Republican)
  José Pareja Yévenes (Left Republican)
  Eduardo Moreno Velasco (CEDA)
  Claudio Hernández López (Left Republican)
  Juan Félix Sanz Blanco (CEDA)
  Angel Saldaña (Independent)
  Carlos Morenilla (CEDA)
  José Antonio Tello Ruiz (CEDA)
  Indalecio Romero de la Cruz (CEDA)
*Ricardo Corro Moncho (Left Republican)
*José Palanco Romero (Left Republican)
*Francisco Menoyo Baños (Socialist)
*Pablo Cortés Fauré (Socialist)
  Eduardo Molina Díaz (CEDA)
  Germán García Gil de Gibaja (CEDA)
  Fermín Garrido Quintana (CEDA)

APPENDIX B

The Origins of a Rumour: Federico García Lorca and the Spanish Civil Guard

It was probably inevitable that Lorca's death should have been attributed to the Civil Guard.

His *Ballad of the Spanish Civil Guard* had become one of the most famous poems in the language and lines from it were on everybody's tongue:

> The horses are black.
> The horseshoes are black.
> On their capes shine
> Stains of ink and wax.
> Their skulls are made of lead,
> that is why they cannot weep.
> Up the road they come
> with their souls of patent leather....

The poem evokes the traditional struggle between the Civil Guard (founded in 1844 to suppress banditry) and the gypsies, whose lawlessness and refusal to be assimilated into Spanish society have always made them particularly odious to the authorities. In the ballad a band of forty *civiles* attacks an unsuspecting gypsy village busily celebrating Christmas Eve. But Lorca's poem is far more than a mere concession to Andalusian local colour: for him the gypsy symbolises the deepest elements in the human personality, the ultimate source of laughter and tears, while the brutal Civil Guard embodies the oppressive forces of 'civilisation' which seek to stamp out vitality and spontaneity. The poem has, therefore, a relevance far beyond the confines of Southern Spain.

The Civil Guard was offended by it. In 1936 (eight years after the appearance of the *Gypsy Ballads*) a case was brought against Lorca by a man from Tarragona who claimed that the poet had grossly insulted the force. 'He would be satisfied with little less than my head', laughed Federico afterwards. The poet had no difficulty in persuading the judge of his 'innocence', but the incident revealed the extent to which his work was capable of irritating the Spanish reactionary mentality.[1]

When Federico's death began to be known in Spain it was natural to assume that the Civil Guard had been implicated.

What started out as an assumption soon attained the status of accepted fact. On 15 September 1937 the Valencian Socialist daily *Adelante* carried a sensational article on its front page which was to have immediate repercussions throughout the Spanish-speaking world:

THE CRIME WAS IN GRANADA, HIS GRANADA. 'I SAW GARCÍA LORCA BEING ASSASSINATED' ...

'Federico was chased by a hail of bullets from the Civil Guard as he upheld, before dying, the justness of our struggle', relates a witness to that crime.

He did not want to tell me his name because he has five brothers and a mother in the other Spain. The black Spain of crimes and treachery. And crime and treachery would visit the five boys and the poor old woman who have remained behind, thinking about the other son, absent from their side. But even though we may not know his name it's all the same. What matters is to hear the true, spine-chilling account of that terrible crime: the assassination of our poet Federico García Lorca.

The man is from Granada. Along with him are several others who have escaped from the enemy zone and now live in this happy, welcoming Valencian barracks where the atmosphere of hatred that permeated those where the treacherous plot against the Spanish people was hatched is entirely lacking.

At my side a young lad notices my curiosity and draws my attention to the strange uniforms of the soldiers, some of whom are mere boys, almost children.

'Did you escape too?'

'Yes, but not just now. Those chaps are from the Aragonese fronts. I got here from Granada.'

'García Lorca's Granada....'

'Yes.'

The lad suddenly looks upset, stops talking and lowers his head.

'Did you know García Lorca, then?'

'No, but I've read a lot of his books. I knew his work and quite a lot about his life.... The awful thing is that I also know how he died.'

'Did you see him in front of the firing-squad?'

'Federico García Lorca didn't die that way. His death was something I'll never forget, something so monstrous, so criminal, that I'll always remember it. Even when I close my eyes I can still see it. Federico was mown down as he ran by the Civil Guard's bullets.'

The terrible room in the Civil Guard barracks

'I was a member of the Civil Guard in Granada. Although I was totally uninterested in politics I sympathised with the Cause of the ordinary people because I'm an ordinary chap myself. And even if I hadn't sympathised with the Cause, I would have been forced to do so by the terrible succession of crimes and assassinations committed in the early days of the rebellion. Crimes carried out with sadistic refinement, with ghastly cruelty, all over the place and at all hours of the day. So much so that all the things I could tell you about the people assassinated and the form the assassinations took would be only a pale imitation of the truth.... That awful room in the barracks, full of inquisitorial instruments of torture! It was ghastly. I could never have believed that the human spirit could sink so low – and with such a refinement of cruelty. There were truncheons, iron clubs, knives, tongs.... Someone had even devised a club bristling with razor-sharp blades with which he used to beat his victims to make them divulge where the workers were hiding – the workers were terrified by the crimes committed against so many of their comrades and had hidden wherever they could in an effort to escape from the worst sort of death.

Luckily I managed to pretend that I was unwell, and so avoided having to live through all that horror or to take part in crimes.

'Their skulls are made of lead, that is why they cannot weep.'

That day I was on guard duty. I saw this young man entering the barracks. He was pale, but walked with serenity. It was Federico García Lorca. When I saw him I understood at once that a tremendous tragedy was about to occur. García Lorca signed his death warrant the day he put his name to the famous ballad about the Civil Guard....

They told me they had found him in the French Legation. They tricked him into leaving the building and then arrested him. He got no more of a trial than any of the other victims before him, naturally, and that same night he left the barracks escorted by a picket of Civil Guards. It's terrible to have to admit it, but I was one of them. The cars pulled off along the road to Padul. The sinister convoy stopped about ten miles from Granada. It was eight o'clock. The headlamps lit up the man walking to his death. His silhouette stood out against the depths of the night. The picket formed up behind the lamps, where the victim couldn't see it.

García Lorca walked steadily, with magnificent serenity. Suddenly he stopped, and turned to face us, as if wanting to speak. This caused a great surprise, especially to Lieutenant Medina, who was in command of the picket.

And he spoke. García Lorca spoke with firmness and a steady voice. His words betrayed no weakness and he begged no forgiveness. They were manly words in defence of what he had always loved: liberty. And he praised the people's Cause, which was his, and the good work they were doing in the face of such barbarity and crime.

Those words spoken with the fire of passion made a tremendous impression on the men with the guns. For me it was like a penetrating light that burned into my brain. The poet continued speaking....

But he never finished. Something terrible, something monstrous and criminal happened: Lieutenant Medina, shouting dreadful curses, fired his pistol and urged his Civil Guards on against the poet.

The spectacle was appalling. Clubbing him with rifle-butts, firing at him (some of us stood petrified with terror at the sight), they hurled themselves on García Lorca, who ran followed by a tremendous hail of bullets. He fell about a hundred yards away and they went after him to finish him off. But Federico stood up again, pouring blood, and with terrible eyes stared at the men, who drew back in horror. All the Civil Guards got back into their cars and only the Lieutenant remained with him, pistol in hand. García Lorca closed his eyes for the last time and slumped to the ground that was already saturated with his blood.

Medina stepped rapidly forward and emptied three rounds of bullets into poor Federico's body.

There they left the poet, unburied, outside Granada, *his* Granada....

VICENTE VIDAL CORELLA[2]

On 10 December 1937 the substance of this article was reproduced in the course of a speech delivered before the Democratic Anti-Fascist League of Costa Rica by Vicente Saenz. The speech was published a few days later in the influential Costa Rican weekly, *Repertorio americano*, and was widely read and discussed in Central and South America.[3]

But there was more to come, for Vidal Corella was not the only journalist who had talked to the Civil Guard from Granada. So too had J. Rubia Barcia, a teacher from Granada who had known Lorca. Rubia Barcia delayed two years before publishing his version of the Civil Guard's declaration, which first appeared, in Havana, in 1939. Adopting the 'omniscient narrator' technique, he describes Lorca's arrival at the Civil Guard barracks:

Sergeant Remacho, head of the local Civil Guard 'Black Squad', was waiting for him. Young, tall and corpulent, he affords a striking contrast to the physical weakness of the author of *Gypsy Ballads*.* In this room there are

---

* Properly, Romacho. Romacho was also a Falangist, and is listed by Gollonet and Morales with Valdés's early accomplices. In Granada one hears frequently of his brutality during the repression.

pizzles, pincers and clubs which have been used on other occasions to force useless declarations out of condemned men. Until eight that night they remain together.

Meanwhile groups of Civil Guards chat in the courtyard. Some, a small minority, leave, unable to bear the screams of the victims under torture. Others, among whom Francisco Ubiña Jiménez, an ex-schoolteacher, stands out, make witty comments each time a scream of pain is heard. The scene is interrupted by the arrival of Staff-Sergeant Tomás Olmo. It is time for the list [of those to be shot]. The Civil Guards are already drawn up and the trucks await their load of men to be killed that night. Federico García Lorca will doubtless be among them. But the plans are changed. Better for him to go alone, by himself, with five *civiles* under the command of Lieutenant Medina. These will be the men entrusted with the execution.

Everything is ready. The only person missing is the prisoner himself, who now appears escorted by two Civil Guards who hold his arms. Blood is flowing from his face and hands. Nevertheless he maintains his dignity. He is shoved and jostled into the truck, which moves off. In it are the Civil Guards Francisco Ubiña Jiménez, the bloodthirsty ex-schoolteacher; Burgos, who used to be a clerk in the Military Commandery; Carrión, no less celebrated than the first man for his ferocity; and finally the new recruits, Corpas Jiménez and José Vázquez Plaza, who are unable to conceal their terror as newcomers to the assassination business. Sitting with them is the sadistic Lieutenant Medina, the father of three priests.*

They stop about half a mile from Padul, on the road from Granada. The moment has arrived. Night has already fallen and the headlamps are on. The prisoner is ordered to walk six yards away from the truck....

The description of the shooting that follows corresponds almost exactly to that given by Vidal Corella and indeed a comparison of the two writers' versions reveals quite clearly that they spoke to the same man. Rubia Barcia's article was reproduced a year later in New York* and shortly afterwards John A. Crow referred closely in another article on the poet's death to Vidal Corella's original *Adelante* account as quoted by Vicente Saenz in *Repertorio americano.*[5]

But there was a snag that those who repeated the story about the Civil Guard's complicity in the poet's execution had failed to notice. The 1940 publication of Rubia Barcia's article was introduced by the following explanation:

One day during the wartime summer of 1937 the author of this article, a friend of Federico García Lorca, was summoned to the Almirante Barracks

---

* I have not investigated these allegations. Ubiña and Burgos, I gather, still live in Granada. It can be deduced that either Corpas Jiménez or Vázquez Plaza is the escaped Civil Guard.

in Valencia, which at that time had been converted into a provisional gaol
for prisoners and escapees from the Nationalist zone, to hear the unsolicited
confession of a Civil Guard who had been a member of the picket that shot
the great Granadine poet. Seemingly a simple, straightforward country type,
he had passed over to the loyal troops after being forced to commit this
and other crimes that were repugnant to his conscience. *He did not know
the first thing about the poet, but one afternoon, in the 'Cultural Corner'
of the barracks ['Rincón de Cultura'], he saw a picture of him which he
recognised; unable to conceal his emotion, he exclaimed: 'We killed that
man as well.'* And then, with a moving simplicity, he began to speak....
[my italics]

Thus it is evident that, on 19 August 1936, the date of Lorca's death, the Civil
Guard in question did not know the poet by sight or even, apparently, by reputation. In 1937 he had seen a photograph in Valencia of a man who resembled
a prisoner whose execution he witnessed *a year earlier*, had been told that it
was of the famous poet Federico García Lorca, and had gone on to conclude
that he had been present at the execution. The legend of the Civil Guard's participation in Lorca's death was the result, first, of a faulty piece of identification
made one year after the event and, second, of an over-readiness on the part of
two journalists to give credence to an unsubstantiated declaration.

One question remains unanswered: who was the *real* victim of that night's
brutal killing by the Civil Guard? We will probably never know.

APPENDIX C

'Jean-Louis Schonberg' and his 'Homosexual Jealousy' Thesis Concerning Lorca's Death

In his book *Federico García Lorca. L'homme – L'oeuvre* (Paris, Plon, 1956), Jean-Louis Schonberg offered the first coherent explanation of why the poet was killed. His chapter on the death appeared separately in *Le Figaro Littéraire* a few weeks before the book's publication and produced widespread interest in France and Spain (see pp. 197–201).[1]

Having denied, on the flimsiest of evidence, that the death had a political motive, Schonberg concludes: 'Reste alors la vengeance; la vengeance de l'amour obscur' (p. 106). The *non sequitur* is obvious and the second inference strikes one as particularly unjustified, for even if Lorca had been killed in revenge that revenge need not necessarily have had a homosexual basis. It might, for example, have been motivated by jealousy – jealousy of the poet's talents, his fame, etc.

Determined to prove that the assassination was the outcome of a homosexual rivalry, Schonberg proceeds to build up the details of his case.

The first question he must answer is: who was Lorca's homosexual rival? He tackles the matter obliquely. To start with we are told that the murder squads were recruited from the low world of 'communistes retournés et de pédérastes' (p. 107). It is difficult to see what evil qualities Communists and pederasts share as a matter of course, and in fact there is simply no evidence that the Granada killers, whatever their individual political histories, were noted for their pederastic inclinations. Schonberg insinuates that these men entertained a violent, homosexual hatred of Lorca which was then exploited by someone who was determined that he should die. He reminds us that in his *Ode to Walt Whitman* the poet had established a distinction between 'pure' and 'impure' homosexuals, accusing the latter of being 'assassins of doves', and goes on to affirm that it was precisely because Lorca had spurned the 'impure' members of the homosexual confraternity in Granada that they decided to kill him, just as they did another 'pure' homosexual, Constantino Ruiz Carnero.[2]

Now, whose was the sinister mind behind all this? Schonberg begins by insinuating that the culprit was Ramón Ruiz Alonso and it follows that he must make Ruiz Alonso not only a homosexual but an 'impure' one at that:

---

* Pseudonym of Baron Louis Stinglhamber.

Parmi ces loups, doit-on compter le chef lui-même des bandes noires, Ramón Ruiz Alonso, sur qui deux témoignages laissent peser le soupçon d'inversion sexuelle? (p. 107)

I have already insisted that Ramón Ruiz Alonso was not a member of these squads, let alone the 'chef lui-même'. As regards the man's alleged homosexuality there can be little doubt either. In Granada, a town well known for its active disapproval of those who cannot or will not conform to the demands of conventional sexuality, I never once heard such a charge. On the the contrary, Ruiz Alonso is remembered as a lady's man. When I informed him that doubts had been cast on his virility, he burst out:

I can assure you that I am and always have been very virile, very virile. So he thinks I'm a queer! If M. Schonberg wants proof of my interest in women let's see him send me his wife and daughters for a fortnight. They could take him back some accurate documentation on my sexual preferences!

This crude sally, typical of the man, would of course be inadequate proof in itself (many a Spanish *macho* with hidden insecurities must have made similar claims) but the fact remains that if Ruiz Alonso has homosexual tendencies he has also been capable of fathering two famous daughters, the film actresses Emma Penella and Elisa Montes. The 'suspicions' of Schonberg's 'two witnesses' are in my opinion without foundation and, if Ruiz Alonso was jealous of Lorca at all, it is likely to have been for other reasons.

Schonberg proceeds to describe how this homosexual Ruiz Alonso, discovering that Lorca was hiding in the Rosales's house, had his 'black squad' cordon off the street. I have shown that Lorca's arrest was not effected by the murder squads, however, but by a formidable array of militia and police acting on instructions from the Civil Government. Once again Schonberg is either misinformed or else imposing his assumptions on what really happened: since the members of the squads were all perverts it *must* have been they who arrested the poet.

According to Schonberg this group of homosexuals, turncoat Communists and pederasts frequented a bar in Elvira Street. Federico was a member of the confraternity, but because he was 'noble' and 'pure' he scorned the others and so they decided to kill him:

C'est justement cette morgue supérieure qu'on lui a fait payer. Le meurtre de Lorca, couvert par la politique, absous par la complicité du clergé de Grenade, qui ne risqua ni une intervention ni une protestation contre l'odieux massacre des innocents, sort d'une guerre de hannetons. C'est un règlement de comptes entre invertis. (p. 113)

A settling of accounts between homosexual rivals. But who was Lorca's enemy? At the end of his tortuous exposition Schonberg finally gets to the point and makes a totally unexpected and unsubstantiated accusation:

Un règlement où la jalousie, la perversité de don Gabriel Morcillo, peintre d'éphèbes, ne restèrent pas plus étrangères qu'au crime du bar de la rue Elvira commis par un de ses élèves. Entre Lorca et Morcillo s'était creusé une cassure empoisonnée, traîtresse....Mais devenu personnage officiel et peintre du Régime, pour avoir su à temps retourner sa veste, Morcillo est tabou. D'autres que lui se sauvèrent, au même prix, le prix d'une délation. (pp. 113–14)

Schonberg made it quite clear in his reply to a letter by Claude Couffon criticising his article (both letters were published by Le Figaro Littéraire on 13 October 1956), moreover, that he stood by his accusation:

Quant au dénonciateur, nommé en toutes lettres, le lecteur saura bien le trouver.[3]

So the well-known Granadine painter Gabriel Morcillo was responsible for Lorca's death. Ramón Ruiz Alonso was involved in the arrest and entertained a homosexual jealousy towards the poet, but Morcillo was the original informer, the homosexual rival who was determined to 'settle accounts'.

The charge is a serious one, all the more so since Schonberg produces not a shred of evidence to support his allegations. Federico, in fact, had never been a close friend of Morcillo, as Schonberg implies when he talks of the poisoned rift that opened between them, although it is true that the painter did have the reputation in Granada of being a homosexual (despite which he was married with a family). I met no one in the town who ever suggested that Morcillo was in any way involved in the poet's death. Indeed several friends of both Morcillo and Lorca, especially Miguel Cerón, rejected Schonberg's accusation as monstrous. Some months after the publication of the Spanish-language edition of this book an acquaintance wrote from Granada:

Gabriel Morcillo heard the news of Lorca's death in the Café Royal. He himself told me about it. He was drinking a beer when Trescastro himself came up to him on purpose and said: 'Don Gabriel, we bumped off your friend the poet with the big fat head this morning.' Morcillo says that his hand trembled and that he got back to his carmen as quickly as possible and hid in his garden for two months. I know him well. Schonberg's disgusting accusation is nonsense. Like all the other artists and intellectuals in Granada, Morcillo was terrified.

Who was the source of Schonberg's information about Morcillo? Why does he not provide us with the evidence on which his accusation rests? Moreover the other murder referred to by Schonberg, the one committed in the infamous bar in Elvira Street (which I have been unable to identify), had nothing to do with Morcillo either. The student in question, who apparently murdered an old homosexual, was the protégé, not of Morcillo, but of a South American painter who was living in Granada at the time (some ten years or so ago). Schonberg has accused Morcillo of Lorca's death without producing any evidence. Such a procedure is intolerable.

In a footnote appended to the above exposition, Schonberg tells us that:

Le dossier de Lorca aux archives du ministère de l'Intérieur confirme le nôtre. Un récent article de la *Tribune de Genève* à propos de la représentation de *Yerma*, s'exprime dans le même sens. (p. 114)

The first sentence of this footnote would lead the unsuspecting reader to the conclusion that Schonberg has himself seen the dossier to which he so confidently refers. Yet in the later Swiss edition of his book, *A la recherche de Lorca* (Neuchâtel, A la Baconnière, 1966), we learn that this is not so. In this book, which is little more than a re-working of the original French edition, Schonberg appends two new paragraphs to his homosexual 'settling of accounts' explanation of the poet's death.

In the first of these he refers again to the file on Lorca kept in the Ministry of the Interior in Madrid, and informs the reader that, although he himself has not seen the dossier, the information he possesses about it proceeds from a completely trustworthy source. (p. 120)

The second sentence of the footnote refers to an article that appeared in the *Tribune de Genève* 'à propos de la représentation de *Yerma*' shortly before the publication of the French edition of Schonberg's book, in October 1956. The author does not refer the reader to the exact article in question, and a search through the paper's files is therefore necessary if one wants to judge for oneself to what extent it 'confirms' his thesis. Two brief articles on Lorca appeared at about that time in the *Tribune*, but only one of them referred to the current production of *Yerma* in Geneva. This was published on 8 December 1955, under the title '*Yerma* à la Comédie', and made no allusion whatsoever to Lorca's death. It seems, therefore, that Schonberg's reference must be to the second article. Entitled 'Une fleur de sel et d'intelligence' à la bouche/ Il y a vingt ans/ FEDERICO GARCÍA LORCA,' it appeared on 31 May 1956, signed by Jacques Givet. But this short article, which contains an obtuse and skimpy commentary on the poet's last days, is based neither on personal research nor on an adequate knowledge of Lorca's work. Givet seems to be quite unaware of the investigations of Brenan, Couffon and Schonberg himself, and claims that little is known about the circumstances of the poet's death except that he was executed without a trial. He does assert, however – and this is probably what drew Schonberg's attention – that:

Il serait hasardeux d'affirmer, comme on s'est risqué à le faire, qu'on a voulu tuer en lui le poète de la révolution espagnole, puisqu'il n'était pas, politiquement parlant, engagé dans la bataille.

Is Schonberg referring to Givet's article, which in no sense 'confirms' his own theories? Or to another item, published about the same time but which has escaped one's notice despite a careful search? It would be helpful if Schonberg could indicate exactly which article in the *Tribune de Genève* 's'exprime dans le même sens' as the Ministry of the Interior dossier which he himself has not seen.

Having investigated these pieces of so-called confirmation which Schonberg adduces in support of his 'homosexual' thesis we can now proceed to consider his further clarifications.

In the Second Preface to the Mexican edition of his book, *Federico García Lorca. El hombre – La obra* (Mexico, Compañía General de Ediciones, SA, 1959), Schonberg seeks to defend himself against those critics who have shown their dissatisfaction with certain aspects of the French 1956 edition, and produces three new pieces of 'corroboration' with which to confound them.

First, he announces that he has received a 'signed' letter from a man who knew Lorca, Luis Rosales and other members of that group, and who confirms that the account he has read in Schonberg's book is accurate. The author then goes on to reveal that the source of his corresponent's information about Lorca's arrest and death is – Luis Rosales! This would lead us to expect that Rosales's version and that of Schonberg coincide, but nothing could be further from the truth. Rosales has told me that he completely rejects Schonberg's thesis, along with numerous other details of his account. Rosales can hardly have told Schonberg's anonymous correspondent that Lorca was killed for homosexual motives, therefore, since he has never held this opinion, and he certainly has never imputed the responsibility for Lorca's death to the painter Gabriel Morcillo, as Schonberg does. Thus the letter is worthless as confirmation of the latter's thesis.

Schonberg's next reference is to a note published in the Jesuit literary journal *Brotéria. Revista contemporânea* (Lisbon, no. 5 (1956), pp. 480–1). The author of this snippet, which is entitled 'A morte de García Lorca', is a certain 'M.A.' who claims to have himself investigated Lorca's death in Granada. He has come to the same conclusion as Schonberg, he informs us, and proceeds disdainfully to dismiss Couffon's *Figaro* article as a 'novel'. M.A. brings no new information whatsoever to bear on the subject of Lorca's death, in spite of his alleged personal researches, and his 36-line note cannot therefore be taken as a worthwhile 'confirmation' of Schonberg's thesis.

The final piece of new 'evidence' with which Schonberg seeks to combat the opinions of his critics is, without a doubt, the most flimsy:

To these true testimonies which confirm our own, should we add the confession of a famous singer, an old friend of Lorca's, whose confidences pertaining to the poet's death were well-known in Parisian literary circles? (p. 18)

The reader can decide for himself what might be a fitting reply to that question. This leaves the additional material contained in the Swiss edition of Schonberg's book, which has already been briefly mentioned in passing. Here Gabriel Morcillo is no longer named in full as the man responsible for the poet's death: he is now designated 'Don G.M' (p. 119). And Schonberg has discovered what the Ministry of the Interior's file on Lorca, which he himself has not seen, says about the reasons for his death:

Au dire de qui l'a su, et qui l'atteste sous la garantie d'une voix tout-à-fait autorisée et peu suspecte, outre le coup dans le dos de M., un autre bras, celui du Commandeur [Valdés?], s'est exercé par l'entremise de Ruiz Alonso. Moins odieuse que la première, pour autant qu'une vengeance puisse trouver son excuse, c'était la vindicte du père outragé d'un triste adolescent entraîné dans le vice par Lorca; pour joindre sur sa tête, au drame de la trahison, celui de l'assouvissement d'une justice immanente. De Thesée cette fois, l'ombre irritée, sur le coupable s'abattait. (p. 120)

It seems certain that there is indeed an official dossier on Lorca in the Ministry of the Interior, and it may even contain these accusations. But it would be ludicrous to imagine that such a file, compiled by the very people who for more than thirty years have been seeking to exculpate the Movement for the poet's death could possibly be trustworthy. By repeating these charges without producing any supporting evidence, Schonberg has further weakened his case. In fact he has totally failed to substantiate his a priori theories concerning the alleged homosexual motives for the poet's death. His arguments cannot withstand close scrutiny, his research is careless and it can be seen that he seeks to shift the ultimate responsibility for Lorca's death from the leaders of the rising in Granada onto the shoulders of private individuals acting more or less on their own initiative. It was for this reason that his 'revelations' were received with such delight in Spain and, as we have seen (in Chapter Fourteen), Franco's propagandists lost no time in appropriating for their own purposes the essential details of his account. Thanks to Schonberg, Lorca's death could, from 1956 onwards, be explained away as a sordid 'affaire de moeurs' (p. 113) and the Nationalist authorities in Granada be freed of responsibility for the crime.

APPENDIX D

Further References by Arab Authors to Ainadamar*

1. *Ibn al-Khaṭīb* (1313–74). The greatest of Granada's Arab historians, vizier to Mohammed V and teacher of the poet Ibn Zamrak, whose odes cover the walls of the Alhambra, Ibn al-Khaṭīb himself possessed a palace in Ainadamar. First, his prose description of the spot:

Concerning the Fountain of Tears, it is inclined towards the South Spring† and located on the skirts of Mount Alfacar. It overflows with water which is channelled along the road, and enjoys a marvellous situation, blessed with pleasant orchards and incomparable gardens, a temperate climate and the sweetness of its water, in addition to the several prospects it commands. There are to be found well-guarded palaces and well-attended places of worship, lofty residences and fortified buildings amidst a landscape verdant with myrtle. The idle rich have foregathered there to the cost of the learned and the wise who formerly dwelt there, and have drawn on their resources to expend them therein. State employees have vied one with another enviously in the purchase of property until, in the course of time, it has become the talk of the world, beauty finding in it its own reflection such that mention of it is frequent in poetry and on the tongues of the eloquent amongst those who abide there and those who go to visit it.[1]

After this enthusiastic description, Ibn al-Khaṭīb cites verses from two of his own poems, the second of which he had inscribed inside a dome of his palace near the pool:

Oh Ainadamar, how many years like pearls shed in the course of our acquaintance could you perhaps restore! When your soft breezes blow cold and damp during the night, an ardent passion for you agitates me.

---

* I am indebted to my friend Dr James Dickie of Lancaster University for the information and translations contained in this appendix, and remember with pleasure our many visits together to Ainadamar.
† Perhaps this was what is today called the *Fuente Chica* ('Small Pool') in Alfacar.

If Ainadamar were a real eye,* then....†

Neither has it ever ceased to be a race-course for the horses of orgy and amusement, nor its soft accommodation to form an abundant pasture.

[So brilliant is it that] the Pleiades themselves want to be its residence; the Dog-star wants to praise it [for its abundance even in the canicular heat] and al-Mu"‡ to watch over it.

2. *The alfaquí Abū 'l-Qāsim ibn Qūṭīya.* Lines from three poems quoted by Ibn al-Khaṭīb:

I spent the night in Ainadamar, feasting in its pastures, and in its dwelling places I had my fill of love.

Whenever the East Wind blows it carries me its scent and evokes the spectre of the lost loved one.

It was a night of amorous union in Ainadamar when its stars amongst all others presaged good fortune,

in which one could behold beauty unrolling its mystery and the shadow of hopes long on the hills.

We spent the night, and there were flowers in the garden of the cheeks and cheeks amongst the roses in the garden,

and red were our apples and full and swollen our pomegranates in the centre of the breasts;

and a violent passion and a beautiful woman learned from our livers§ the limits and extent of love.

Of a certainty, Ainadamar enchains the beholder's eyes, so free your eye in contemplation of its....¶

and pause at that spot, if you are inclined to love, for on its hills wild cows pasture;

and shake therein the hand of the narcissus in greeting, kissing the cheeks of companionship amidst the flowers;

and take them freely in the valleys and on the mounds where they shall assuage the thirst of your thoughts.

---

* '*Ain* means both eye and spring in Arabic'. (Translator's note.)
† Scribal errors render the Arabic text unintelligible at this point. (Translator's note.)
‡ Al-Mu" is a star or constellation, and to indentify it with certainty one would have to consult astronomical treatises. It does not figure in the dictionaries. (Translator's note.)
§ 'To the Arabs the liver is the seat of love'. (Translator's note.)
¶ See note (†).

Such a spring is a wine matured by Time itself, so fear not, in drinking
of it, that there befall you the vicissitudes of the times.

It could speak to you of Chosroes and of Sāsān before him, and could
inform you about a mortal vine become immortal.*

O tempora, o mores! Not a vestige of Ainadamar's palaces remain above
ground today. The spring's resources have been exploited by modern entrepreneurs, however, and a swimming pool was built a few years ago near the
Fuente Grande. There is now a hotel, and bungalows are in demand in the
vicinity. Ainadamar has been rediscovered by a new generation of *granadinos*,
most of whom must be unaware of its Arab or more sinister, recent associations,
and at weekends the place is alive with picnickers from the capital.

---

* Sāsān gave his name to the Sassanian Dynasty of the neo-Persian empire,
founded by Ardashir I in AD 226, and of which Chosroes I (531–97) was the
most powerful ruler. The Sassanian empire was conquered by the Arabs in 637,
less than a century before they invaded the Iberian Peninsula.

APPENDIX E

An Anonymous Ballad on the Death of García Lorca

One afternoon in the summer of 1966, Dr Sanford Shepard, Professor of Spanish at Oberlin College, USA, and his wife Helen were walking in the garden of their delightful *carmen* in Granada. Among the flowers Mrs Shepard noticed a soiled piece of paper with writing on it. Picking it up, she was surprised to find herself reading a poem on Lorca's death, scribbled in longhand on a sheet of notepaper bearing the heading 'The National Institute of Social Security Employees' Confraternity of Our Lady of Perpetual Succour' ('Hermandad de Nra. Sra. del Perpetuo Socorro de Funcionarios del Instituto Nacional de Previsión').

The poem narrates the burial of the poet by grief-stricken gypsies on the slopes of the Cerro del Aceituno (The Hill of the Olive Tree), which rises behind the Albaicín and is crowned by the Church of Saint Michael. Lorca, in his *Ballad of Saint Michael*, had evoked the pilgrimage which winds up through the Albaicín every 29 September to reach the church and pay homage to the dazzling image of the Archangel by Bernardo Mora, and somehow it seems appropriate that the anonymous ballad should locate the poet's burial place there. The elegy has little artistic merit, but is touching in its simplicity:

> Calle Real de Cartuja
> y la Cuesta de Alhacaba,
> Plaza Larga y Albaicín,
> a hombros de seis gitanas.
>
> Por siete cuestas arriba
> al filo de la mañana,
> va Federico García
> a hombros de seis gitanas.
>
> Al Cerro del Aceituno
> se lo llevan a enterrar
> solo gitanos delante
> solo gitanos detrás,
> y solo suena en el aire
> un cante, la soleá.

> Soleá con la soleá
> (escarcha) en aquella aurora
> (moja) tus huesos llorando
> Soleá, Soleá Montoya.

Up Real de Cartuja Street and Alhacaba Hill, through Larga Square and the Albaicín, on the shoulders of six gypsy women.

Up the seven hills goes Federico García, just as dawn is breaking, on the shoulders of six gypsy women.

To the Cerro del Aceituno they take him to be buried, with only gypsies in front and only gypsies behind and only one strain sounding in the air, the soleá.

The soleá, oh the soleá, (frost) in the dawn (wets) your bones with its weeping, Soleá, Soleá Montoya.*

---

* The *soleá* (the Andalusian pronunciation of the world *soledad*, solitude) is a flamenco song that expresses grief and suffering. Soledad Montoya, an embodiment of the soleá, appears in Lorca's ballad *Romance de la pena negra*.

NOTES

Throughout the notes, Federico García Lorca, *Obras completas* (Madrid, Aguilar, 20th edition, two vols., 1977) is referred to as 'Aguilar' and *El Defensor de Granada* as *El Defensor*.

CHAPTER ONE

1. Richard Ford, *A Handbook for Travellers in Spain* (London, John Murray, 1845), p. 367.
2. To be more precise, Lorca's mother was born on 25 July 1870 at 10 p.m., in 1 Solarillo Street, Granada. Her parents were Vicente Lorca, a native of Granada, and Concepción Romero, from Atarfe in the *vega*. Details from the Register of Births for Granada, 1870, no. 126, kept in the Town Hall.
3. Aguilar, II, pp. 1,021–2.
4. *Id.*, II, pp. 1,040–1.
5. *Id.*, I, p. 158.
6. Karl Baedeker, *Spain and Portugal. Handbook for Travellers* (Leipzig, 2nd edition, 1901), pp. 379–80.
7. Victor Hugo, *Grenade*, in *Les Orientales* (1829).
8. Aguilar, I, p. 1,011.
9. Ford, p. 363.
10. Aguilar, I, pp. 968–9.
11. José Mora Guarnido, *Federico García Lorca. Testimonio para una biografía* (Buenos Aires, Losada, 1958).
12. J. B. Trend, 'A Poet of Arabia', in *Alfonso the Sage and Other Spanish Essays* (London, Constable, 1926), pp. 155–61.
13. Conversation with Miguel Cerón, Granada, July 1971.
14. Aguilar, II, p. 939.
15. *Id.*, I, p. 1,184.
16. *Id.*, I, p. 1,180.

CHAPTER TWO

1. The *Nuevo Ripalda enriquecido con varios apéndices* (14th edition, 1927), quoted by J. B. Trend, *The Origins of Modern Spain* (Cambridge, 1934), p. 63.

2. Gerald Brenan, *The Spanish Labyrinth* (Cambridge, 1960), p. 53.

3. *Id.*, p. 236: 'A bare two weeks after the proclamation of the Republic, the Cardinal Primate of Spain, Mgr Segura, had issued a violently militant pastoral against the Government.'

4. All details from José Venegas, *Las elecciones del Frente Popular* (Buenos Aires, Patronato Hispano–Argentino de Cultura, 1942).

5. The Electoral Law of 1932 had given the vote to Spanish women for the first time, and it has sometimes been suggested that the Left's defeat at the polls in 1933 was partly due to the fact that the Catholic women of Spain voted against the government that had enfranchised them. One of the Socialist candidates for Granada in 1933, for example, has described how even the nuns in that constituency were given a special dispensation by the ecclesiastical authorities to issue forth from the perpetual seclusion of their convents and vote against the Republic (María Martínez Sierra, *Una mujer por caminos de España*, Buenos Aires, Losada, 1952, p. 87). The author almost seems to imply that the good sisters' votes were decisive. The truth is probably that the female vote made little difference, if any, to the outcome of the election. In the vast majority of cases the women would have voted with their menfolk, the only result of their participation in the election being to increase the number of votes cast for all the parties. See Venegas, p. 19.

6. Brenan, p. 265.

7. *Id.*, p. 267.

8. *Id.*

9. *Id.*, p. 269.

10. Gabriel Jackson, *The Spanish Republic and the Civil War. 1931–1939* (Princeton University Press, 1965), pp. 146–8.

11. *El Defensor*, 21 November 1933.

12. Marcelle Auclair, *Enfances et mort de Garcia Lorca* (Paris, Seuil, 1968), pp. 330–2.

CHAPTER THREE

1. *El Defensor*, 17 February 1936, p. 4.

2. *Id.*, 19 February 1936, p. 4.

3. *Id.*, 17, 18, 19 February 1936, *passim*.

4. Brenan, p. 298.

5. *Id.*, pp. 298–9.

6. *El Defensor*, 9 March 1936.

7. *Id.*, 22 February 1936.

8. *Id.*, 21 February 1936.

9. *Id.*, 10 March 1936.

10. A. Gollonet Megías and J. Morales López, *Rojo y azul en Granada* (Granada, 1937), p. 37. Henceforth, Gollonet and Morales.

11. *El Defensor*, 12 March 1936.

12. *Historia de la Cruzada Española*, the official Nationalist history of the war. Details in the Bibliography, section 4. All references are to Vol. III, book xi. Henceforth, *Cruzada*. This ref., p. 276.

13. *Cruzada*, p. 280.

14. Gollonet and Morales, pp. 41–7.

15. *Id.*, p. 47: 'The [new] Civil Governor is a faithful servant of the high officials of the Masonic Order and of Judaism'.

16. Herbert Rutledge Southworth, 'The Falange: An Analysis of Spain's Fascist Heritage', in *Spain in Crisis*, edited by Paul Preston (Hassocks, Sussex, The Harvester Press, 1976), p. 9.

17. Stanley Payne, *Falange. A History of Spanish Fascism* (Stanford University Press and Oxford, 1962), p. 95.

18. José María Gil Robles, *No fue posible la paz* (Barcelona, Ariel, 1968), p. 558.

19. *El Defensor*, 4 May 1936.

20. These details concerning Torres Martínez are taken from several conversations I had with the ex-Civil Governor of Granada in 1977.

21. *Cruzada*, p. 275.

22. Details from a potted biography of Valdés published in *Ideal*, 25 July 1936.

23. Conversation with José Rosales, Granada, April 1966.

24. Claude Couffon, 'Ce que fut la mort de Federico García Lorca', *Le Figaro Littéraire*, Paris, no. 278, 18 August 1951. The definitive version of Couffon's celebrated article, entitled 'Le crime a eu lieu à Grenade ...' is included in his *A Grenade, sur les pas de García Lorca* (Paris, Seghers, 1962), referred to henceforth as 'Couffon'.

25. 'Jean-Louis Schonberg', 'Enfin la vérité sur la mort de Lorca! Un assassinat, certes, mais dont la politique n'a pas été le mobile', *Le Figaro Littéraire*, no. 545, 29 September 1956. The article was reproduced in the author's book *Federico García Lorca. L'homme-L'oeuvre* (Paris, Plon, 1956), pp. 101–18, referred to henceforth as 'Schonberg'.

26. Gollonet and Morales, p. 53 *et seq.*; *Cruzada*, p. 276.

CHAPTER FOUR

1. In an advance sheet of the Communist-inspired review *Octubre*, 1 May 1933.

2. This was published in *Diario de Madrid*, 9 November 1935.

3. See especially *Mundo obrero*, Madrid, 11 February 1936, p. 5.

4. This event was covered by almost all the Madrid newspapers. See in particular *El Sol*, 15 February 1936, p. 8; *La Libertad*, 15 February, p. 4; and *Mundo obrero*, 15 February, p. 5.

5. See especially *El Socialista*, Madrid, 29 March 1936, p. 6.

6. The Spanish texts relating to these activities may be found in my book *Granada 1936 y el asesinato de Federico García Lorca* (Barcelona, Crítica, 1979).

7. The interview is reproduced in Aguilar, II, pp. 1,076–81. This quotation, pp. 1,079–80.

8. The interview appeared in *El Sol*, Madrid, 10 June 1936, and is reproduced in Aguilar, II, pp. 1,082–7. These quotations, pp. 1,083, 1,085.

9. Several *granadinos* told me in 1965 and 1966 that they remembered reading this interview in *El Sol* and hearing the angry comments that Lorca's reference to the town's middle class aroused.

10. Interview published in *La Voz*, Madrid, 7 April 1936 and reproduced in Aguilar, II, pp. 1,079–80.

11. The interview with Otero Seco is reproduced in Aguilar, II, pp. 1,088–90.

12. This is an extract from the unpublished memoirs of Antonio Rodríguez Espinosa, Lorca's first school-teacher. It was included by Marie Laffranque, in French translation, in her *Federico García Lorca* (Paris, Seghers, 'Théâtre de tous les temps', 1966), p. 110.

13. Carlos Morla Lynch, *En España con Federico García Lorca* (Madrid, Aguilar, 1958), pp. 491–2.

14. Marcelle Auclair, *Enfances et mort de García Lorca* (Paris, Seuil, 1968), p. 369.

15. *Id*.

16. Hugh Thomas, *The Spanish Civil War* (Harmondsworth, Penguin Books, 1965), pp. 145–6, 169–70.

17. Dámaso Alonso, *Poetas españoles contemporáneos* (Madrid, Gredos, 1978), pp. 160–1.

18. As for note 13, pp. 493–4.

19. Rafael Martínez Nadal, 'El último día de Federico García Lorca en Madrid', *Residencia. Revista de la Residencia de Estudiantes*, commemorative issue published in Mexico, December 1963. An English translation of the article may be found in Martínez Nadal's *Lorca's The Public. A Study of His Unfinished Play ('El Público') and of Love and Death in the Work of Federico García Lorca* (London, Calder and Boyars, 1974), pp. 11–17.

20. See note 12.

21. Conversation with Laura de los Ríos, widow of Francisco García Lorca, and Isabel García Lorca, Madrid, September 1978.

CHAPTER FIVE

1. The Falange was founded in the Teatro Comedia on 29 October 1933.

2. I visited Villaflores in October 1977.

3. Tape-recorded conversation with Ramón Ruiz Alonso in Madrid, April 1967.

4. See, for example, *Diario de Sesiones*, 10 May 1934, pp. 2,758–9 and 2,761–2.

5. Tomás Borrás, *Ramiro Ledesma Ramos* (Madrid, Editora Nacional, 1971), p. 428.

6. *Id.*

CHAPTER SIX

1. Thomas, pp. 131–4.

2. *Id.*, p. 134.

3. *Id.*, p. 135.

4. *Id.*, pp. 136–8; *Cruzada*, pp. 169–85.

5. *Ideal*, 19 July 1936, p. 2.

6. *Cruzada*, p. 183.

7. Thomas, p. 138.

8. *Cruzada*, pp. 278–9.

9. Tape-recorded conversation with Dr José Rodríguez Contreras, Granada, 23 August 1978.

10. Details from *Cruzada*, pp. 279–81.

11. *Cruzada*, pp. 281–2.

12. *Id.*

13. Details from *Cruzada*, pp. 282–4; Gollonet and Morales, p. 91.

14. Published in *Ideal*, July 21, p. 1.

15. *Cruzada*, p. 286.

16. *Ideal*, 21 July, p. 1.

17. *Ideal*, 21 July, p. 2.

18. Gollonet and Morales, p. 112.

19. *Id.*, pp. 120–1; *Cruzada*, p. 285.

20. Gollonet and Morales, p. 112.

21. Miguel Rosales told me in 1966 that he commanded this expedition to Seville.

22. Gollonet and Morales, pp. 113–14.

23. *Id.*, p. 113.

24. Gollonet and Morales, pp. 115–16.

25. *Id.*, p. 116.

26. *Ideal*, 21 July, p. 3.

27. *Id.*, p. 4.

28. *Cruzada*, p. 288.

29. *Ideal*, 22 July, p. 4.

30. *Ideal*, 22 July, p. 1.

31. *Id.*, 23 July, p. 4.

32. *Id.*, p. 3. According to the *Cruzada*, p. 297, these aeroplanes had been sent from Madrid to protect Republican bombers attacking Seville. Their pilots, unaware that Armilla was in rebel hands, were arrested on landing.
33. *Id.*, p. 3.
34. *Id.*
35. *Id.*, 24 July, p. 3.
36. *Cruzada*, p. 289.

CHAPTER SEVEN

1. *Ideal*, 26 July 1936, p. 3; *Cruzada*, p. 289.
2. *Ideal*, 30 July, p. 3; Gollonet and Morales, pp. 138–9.
3. Gollonet and Morales, pp. 138–40.
4. *Cruzada*, pp. 287–8.
5. Torres Martínez kindly made a copy of his sentence available to me in October 1977.
6. Tape-recorded conversation with César Torres Martínez, 15 October 1977.
7. *Id.*
8. *Cruzada*, p. 276.
9. *Ideal*, 22 July 1936, p. 5.
10. Gollonet and Morales, p. 165.
11. *Ideal*, 31 August and 3 September 1936.
12. Conversation with Ramón Ruiz Alonso, April 1967.
13. *Cruzada*, p. 289.
14. *Ideal*, 6 September 1936, p. 5.
15. *Cruzada*, p. 289; *Ideal*, 4 August 1936, pp. 1, 3–4.
16. Gollonet and Morales, p. 140; *Ideal*, 19 August 1936, p. 1.
17. Gollonet and Morales, pp. 140–1.
18. Couffon, p. 89.
19. I am grateful to Manuel Fernández-Montesinos García for his kindness in making this letter available to me for publication.

CHAPTER EIGHT

1. 'Mass Executions and Air Raids in Spain Related in Neville Diary. Granada Incidents of Civil War are described by *Herald Tribune* Bridge Editor; Victims of Firing Squad Hauled Alive to Cemetery', *New York Herald Tribune*, 30 August 1936, pp. 1 and 6.
2. *Id.*
3. Helen Nicholson, *Death in the Morning* (London, Loval Dickson, 1937), p. 33.
4. *Id.*, p. 82.

5. See note 1.
6. Gerald Brenan, *The Face of Spain* (London, The Turnstile Press, 1950), p. 130.
7. *Id.*, p. 135.
8. *Id.*, p. 132.
9. Conversation with José García Carrillo, Granada, 1966. García Carrillo was a close friend of Ruiz Carnero, and with him in prison.

CHAPTER NINE

1. Aguilar, II, p. 1,220.
2. Interview with Alfredo Rodríguez Orgaz, Madrid, 9 October 1978.
3. Tape-recorded interview with Isabel Roldán, Chinchón (Madrid), 22 September 1978.
4. 'Manuel Fernández-Montesinos, diputado por Granada y sobrino de Lorca. "Todavía queda gente que debe saber lo que pasó con mi tío"', interview given by Fernández-Montesinos to Eduardo Castro, *El País semanal*, Madrid, 30 July 1978, pp. 6-8.
5. As for note 3.
6. Couffon, pp. 90-1.
7. 'Schonberg', p. 106.
8. As for note 3.
9. Tape-recorded interview with Luis Rosales, Cercedilla (Madrid), 2 September 1966.
10. Unfortunately I did not manage to check this detail with Gerardo Rosales, who died in 1968.
11. Couffon, pp. 102-3.
12. 'Schonberg', p. 110.
13. See Franco Pierini, 'Incontro a Spoleto con la sorella di Federico. Quella notte a Granada ...,' *L'Europeo*, 17 July 1960. In the interview Concha talked about her brother's death without mentioning Ruiz Alonso.
14. Tape-recorded interview with Clotilde García Picossi, Huerta del Tamarit, Granada, 17 August 1978.
15. As for note 3.

CHAPTER TEN

1. Interview with Luis Rosales, Madrid, 6 October 1978.
2. Tape-recorded interview with Luis Rosales, Madrid, 22 October 1978.
3. *Id.*
4. *Id.*

5. Tape-recorded interview with Luis and Esperanza Rosales, Madrid, 7 November 1978.

6. Tape-recorded interview with Luis Rosales, Madrid, 22 October 1978.

7. *Id.*

8. *Id.*

9. *Id.*

10. Tape-recorded interview with Luis and Esperanza Rosales, Madrid, 7 November 1978.

11. Interview with Manuel Contreras Chena, Madrid, 26 October 1978.

12. *Id.*

13. Couffon, p. 99.

14. All these details are from Esperanza Rosales, see note 5.

15. See note 2.

16. Tape-recorded interview with Luis Rosales, Cercedilla (Madrid), 2 September 1966.

17. Tape-recorded interview with Isabel Roldán, Chinchón (Madrid), 22 September 1978.

18. Tape-recorded interview with Clotilde García Picossi, Huerta del Tamarit, Granada, 17 August 1978.

CHAPTER ELEVEN

1. Tape-recorded interview with José Rodríguez Contreras, Granada, 23 August 1978.

2. Tape-recorded interview with Eduardo Carretero, Chinchón (Madrid), 22 September 1978.

3. There are frequent references in *Ideal* to Velasco's deputisation for Valdés. On 18 August 1936, for example, we read, 'Lieutenant-Colonel Velasco received representatives of the press on behalf of the Civil Governor, who was absent from his desk owing to the unavoidable pressures of his position', p. 3.

4. All the details in this chapter deriving from Esperanza Rosales are taken from my tape-recorded interview with her, in Madrid, of 7 November 1978.

5. Declaration made by José Rosales to the well-known Granada lawyer Antonio Jiménez Blanco in 1971. See José Luis Vila-San-Juan, *García Lorca, asesinado: toda la verdad* (Barcelona, Planeta, 1975), pp. 190-3.

6. The interview took place in Madrid on 3 April 1967.

7. Interview with Miguel Cerón, Granada, 1966.

8. Interview with José Rodríguez Contreras, Granada, 1966.

9. Luis, as I have said earlier, had been living for several years in Madrid, and was out of touch with the political life of his home town.

10. Luis does not believe that there was a written warrant for Lorca's arrest,

and insists that Miguel was imagining this detail. I am inclined to believe, nonetheless, that there was a warrant.

11. Tape-recorded interview with Luis Rosales, Cercedilla (Madrid), 2 September 1966.

12. *Id.*

13. *Ideal*, 17 August 1936.

14. Luis told me on 6 October 1978 that, while he did not himself see the document, he remembers José telling him about it.

15. See note 5.

16. Vila-San-Juan, pp. 150–2.

17. Vila-San-Juan, p. 143.

18. The information concerning El Bene comes from Luis Rosales, and was first published by Couffon, p. 108. It has not been possible to trace this man.

19. See note 11.

20. José Rosales's statement concerning this order for Lorca's release was first given by Vila-San-Juan, p. 152. Rosales confirmed it during my conversation with him on 26 August 1978.

21. José Rosales said to me during our conversation on 26 August 1978, 'You believe that Federico was still there that morning, but I don't.'

22. Antonio Ramos Espejo, 'Los últimos días de Federico García Lorca. El testimonio de Angelina,' *Triunfo*, Madrid, 17 May 1975, pp. 27–8.

23. Details given to me in Granada on 20 September 1966 by the Socialist lawyer Antonio Pérez Funes, who died in 1971. Pérez Funes was convinced that Queipo ordered Valdés to shoot Lorca, and that this conversation really took place as described.

24. Gerald Brenan, *The Face of Spain* (London, The Turnstile Press, 1950), pp. 137–8.

25. Antonio de la Villa, 'Un evadido de Granada cuenta el fusilamiento de García Lorca,' *Estampa*, Madrid, 26 September 1936.

26. Jacinto Benavente, dramatist, 1866–1954; Joaquín Alvarez Quintero, dramatist, 1873–1944; Serafín Alvarez Quintero, dramatist, 1871–1938; Pedro Muñoz Seca, another dramatist, was assassinated in Madrid on 28 November 1936, three months after Lorca's death; Ricardo Zamora, a famous footballer, died in 1978. Who was 'Zuloaga'? According to *Ideal*, 23 August 1936, this was a certain José Zuloaga, 'a potter with a wide reputation'. But no such person existed, and it seems that 'José' Zuloaga, was an amalgam, intentional or otherwise, of the painter Ignacio Zuloaga, who died in 1945, and Juan Zuloaga, the latter's cousin (son of the famous potter Daniel Zuloaga), who died recently.

On 18 August 1936 *Ideal* made a passing reference to the death of Zamora in Madrid. On 22 August the newspaper published photographs of him and Benavente on its front page and of the Quintero brothers on p. 8; on August

23 *Ideal*'s front page carried photographs of 'José' Zuloaga and Pedro Muñoz Seca, the latter being designated in the caption as 'our most popular and productive national dramatist'.

27. I was repeatedly told on good authority in Granada that a deputation headed by Lieutenant Mariano Pelayo of the Civil Guard travelled to Burgos to complain to Franco about the continuing brutality of the repression being imposed by Valdés. On 22 April 1937 *Ideal* announced that the Civil Governor had resigned, and published a farewell message from him in which he apologised to the people of Granada for the severity he was forced to demonstrate during his occupancy of the Governorship but asserted that his conscience was clear before God.

On 14 June 1937 *Ideal* reported that Valdés was to be sent to Tetuán to take command of a unit of the Regulares (African Army). It is possible that he was later wounded in action, for it is stated on his tomb in Granada that he died 'for God and Country'. The main cause of his death, however, is almost certain to have been tuberculosis or cancer.

28. Conversation with Miguel Cerón, Granada, December 1965.

CHAPTER TWELVE

1. Aguilar, I, p. 920.
2. In the summer of 1966 I gave English lessons to Nestares's daughter at their Granada home, in the hope of eventually being able to discuss Lorca's death with him. Nestares's visiting card read 'Infantry Colonel (Retired)': that he never received further promotion was probably due to his serious mishandling of the famous Peñón da la Mata operation against a Republican position, in which hundreds of Nationalists lost their lives. The lessons were conducted in Nestares's study, which contains, among other mementoes of the war, a framed diploma from Hitler's chancellery which read: 'Im Namen des deutschen Reiches/Verleihe ich/dem Oberst-Leutnant/José María Nestares/ das Verdienstkreuz/des Ordens vom deutschen/Adler/erster Stufe/mit Schwerten/Berlin den 5 Juni/Der deutsche Reichskanzler'. Nestares's daughter repeated to me her father's version of Lorca's death: he was a friend of the poet, and when he heard about the arrest he rushed to Granada from Víznar to intervene on his behalf. But it was too late, and Lorca had already been killed 'by a certain individual acting on his own initiative'. When I plucked up the courage to approach the subject with Nestares, he shied away from the question. 'It was all a mistake', he said. 'The sort of mistake that occurs in all civil wars, when innocent people die because they just happen to be there when the trouble starts ... he was a friend of mine ... he had left-wing acquaintances ... it was all a mistake.' No more information was forthcoming and in the interests of safety I pursued the

matter no further: the rest of the discussion was devoted to less dangerous topics, such as furniture and Irish stamps (on which Nestares was an expert). Nestares was an influential man in Granada – and a rich one. He possessed a splendid house, half a dozen estates and a large block of apartments, 'El Ancla', in the summer resort of Almuñécar on the Granada coast, and was reputed to have become wealthy as a result of the appropriation of property belonging to the victims of the repression.

3. Enzo Cobelli, *García Lorca* (Mantua, Editrice La Gonzaghiana, 2nd edition, 1959), p. 78.

4. Vila-San-Juan, p. 157, note 87.

5. Conversations in Madrid and Barcelona, 1977 and 1978.

6. Brenan, *The Face of Spain*, p. 145.

7. 'Schonberg', p. 117.

8. Couffon, p. 114.

9. Richard Ford, *A Handbook for Travellers in Spain* (London, John Murray, 4th edition, 1869), p. 372.

10. Aguilar, II, p. 1,085.

11. With the passing of years M. C. forgot the name of the schoolteacher, and Pulianas became Cogollos Vega in his mind.

12. Tape-recorded interview with Isabel Roldán, Chinchón (Madrid), 22 September 1978.

13. José Mora Guarnido, *Federico García Lorca y su mundo* (Buenos Aires, Losada, 1958), pp. 199–201. Falla said to Mora Guarnido: 'It was a case of personal revenge. I know who was responsible, but my conscience forbids that I should reveal it ...', p. 200. Did the composer really know who was responsible for Lorca's death? Had he Ramón Ruiz Alonso in mind? It is impossible to answer these questions.

14. As for note 12.

15. Tape-recorded interview with Angelina Cordobilla, Granada, summer of 1966.

CHAPTER THIRTEEN

1. Gerald Brenan, *The Face of Spain* (London, The Turnstile Press, 1950), pp. 137–8.

2. Claude Couffon, p. 102.

3. 'Schonberg', pp. 104–22.

4. Enzo Gobelli, *García Lorca* (Mantua, Editrice La Gonzaghiana, 2nd edition, 1959), pp. 65–76.

5. Marcelle Auclair, *Enfances et mort de García Lorca* (Paris, Seuil, 1968), pp. 390–3.

6. Tape-recorded interview with Luis Rosales, Cercedilla (Madrid), 2 September 1966.

7. *Ideal*, 19 August 1936, p. 6.

8. *Id.*, 20 August, p. 4.

9. Interview with Esperanza Rosales, Madrid, September 1966.

10. Marcelle Auclair, pp. 442-3.

11. 'El presidente de la FUE de Granada confirma el fusilamiento de García Lorca', *Claridad*, Madrid, 2 October 1936, p. 2.

12. Marcelle Auclair, pp. 399-400.

13. Antonio de la Villa, 'Un evadido de Granada cuenta el fusilamiento de García Lorca', *Estampa*, Madrid, 26 September 1936.

14. Varela was one of the National Front candidates in the re-convened Granada election of May 1936.

15. The anti-Semitic strain in Nationalist propaganda has not yet, to my knowledge, been adequately appreciated. In the Seville edition of *ABC* it was particularly virulent.

16. Tape-recorded interview with José Rosales, Granada, 26 August 1978.

17. Personal communication from the doctor, whom I cannot yet name, Granada, July 1971.

18. Conversation with Angel Saldaña, Madrid, 27 May 1966.

19. Personal communication from the Granadine doctor and writer Manuel Orozco, to whom Morcillo recounted this episode.

20. A witness to my conversation with the ex-Assault Guard was Dr José Rodríguez Contreras.

21. Conversation with Miguel Cerón, Granada, 1966.

22. Letter to the author from Marcelle Auclair, 2 May 1968.

23. The Marquis de Merry del Val, 'Spain: Six of One and Half a Dozen of the Other', *The Nineteenth Century*, London, March 1937, p. 368.

24. See Chapter Four, note 8.

CHAPTER FOURTEEN

1. Carlos Morla Lynch, *En España con Federico García Lorca. (Paginas de un diario íntimo, 1926-1936)* (Madrid, Aguilar, 2nd edition, 1958), p. 496.

2. Angel del Río, *Federico García Lorca* (Hispanic Institute in the United States, 1941), p. 24, wrote that, shortly after the news of Lorca's death reached Madrid, the following United Press despatch appeared in the newspapers: 'A report from Murcia states that a copy of the Granadine daily, *Ideal*, dated 20 August, which arrived in that city, includes the names of the poet Federico García Lorca in the list [of executed prisoners] for 19 August'. Many later writers have accepted the accuracy of this report, yet *Ideal* made no such reference to the poet's death on 20 August 1936. Lists of executed prisoners rarely appeared in *Ideal*'s columns and allusions were never made to the

victims of the 'Black Squad'. Many years were to pass before *Ideal* printed Lorca's name.

3. This reference, quoted in French translation by Marcelle Auclair, p. 417, is probably from *El Diario de Huelva*. The snide allusion to Lorca's homosexuality is typical of the traditionalist, Catholic mentality of the Spanish Right which was responsible for his death. Cipriano Rivas Cherif – well-known theatre director, nephew of Manuel Azaña and close friend of Lorca – has written: 'From Geneva I was unable to pick up the wartime ravings of the Falangist Radio National, but someone with the precise job of listening to the enemy broadcasts heard, more than once, the voice of José María Pemán (not yet the voice of Pemán the Academician) labelling Federico, Margarita Xirgu [the Catalan actress who played many of Lorca's protagonists] and me as sexual inverts' ('Poesía y drama del gran Federico. La muerte y la pasión de García Lorca', in *Excelsior*, Mexico, 13 January 1957).

4. S.B., 'La muerte de García Lorca comentada por sus asesinos', in *Hora de España*, Valencia, no. 5, May 1937, pp. 71–2.

5. Vicente Saenz, 'Consideraciones sobre civilización occidental propósito de Federico García Lorca', in *Repertorio americano*, San José de Costa Rica, 18 December 1937.

6. J. Rubia Barcia, 'Cómo murió García Lorca', in *Nuestra España*, Havana, no. 2, 1939, pp. 67–72, and *España Libre*, Brooklyn, 1 March 1940.

7. Ricardo Saenz Hayes, 'Para *La Prensa* hizo el general Franco importantes declaraciones', in *La Prensa*, Mexico, 26 November 1937.

8. Francisco Franco, *Palabras del Caudillo*. 19 Abril, 1937–7 Diciembre, 1942 (Madrid, Editora Nacional, 1943), pp. 439–51.

9. The first edition of the Aguilar *Obras completas* of García Lorca appeared in 1954. The bibliography had been carefully vetted, and titles referring too obviously to the poet's death had been mutilated or omitted altogether. In the *Chronology* the final entry, for 1936, reads: 'August 19. Dies (*Muere*)'.

10. Brenan, *The Face of Spain*, p. 137.

11. In a conversation with the British Embassy in Mexico in July 1966 (letter to me from the Embassy, 22 July 1966).

12. Chávez Camacho reproduced the original article and Serrano Suñer's letter in his book *Misión de prensa en España* (Mexico, Editorial Jus, 1948), pp. 372–4.

13. José María Pemán, 'García Lorca', in *ABC*, 5 December 1948.

14. Gerald Brenan, 'La vérité sur la mort de Lorca', in *Les Nouvelles Littéraires*, 31 May 1951.

15. Couffon, see note 3, Chapter Seven.

16. Fernando Vázquez Ocaña, *García Lorca. Vida, cántico y muerte* (Mexico, Grijalbo, 1957; 2nd edition, 1962), p. 381.

17. The text of Ridruejo's letter is reproduced by Vázquez Ocaña (see note 16 above), pp. 381-2, and was probably taken from the Mexican newspaper *Excelsior*.

18. Rafael García Serrano, *Bailando hacia la Cruz del Sur* (Madrid, Gráficas Cies, 1953), pp. 330-1.

19. Saint-Paulien, 'Sur la vie et la mort de Federico García Lorca', in *Cahiers des Amis de Robert Brasillach*, Lausanne, no. 10, Noël 1964, pp. 7-10.

20. Paul Werrie has kindly supplied me with a copy of his article: 'Lettre d'Espagne: García Lorca a reparu sur scène à Madrid', in *Ecrits de Paris*, February 1961, pp. 91-5. It contains no allusion to Lorca's death.

21. I am not aware that Saint-Paulien has written anything else on Lorca.

22. *La estafeta literaria*, no. 314, 27 March 1965, p. 36.

23. *Crónica de la guerra española. No apta para irreconciliables* (Buenos Aires, Editorial Codex, 1966), no. 10, October 1966, pp. 224-5, 227, 237-8.

24. Thomas, pp. 169-70.

25. As for note 23 above, p. 227.

26. Jaime Capmany, 'Lorca y Alberti'. Unfortunately the cutting of this article, sent to me by a Madrid friend, is undated. It appeared in *Arriba* during the spring of 1966.

27. Edgar Neville, 'La obra de Federico, bien nacional', in *ABC*, Madrid, 6 November 1966, p. 2.

28. Luis Apostúa, 'Jornada española', in *Ya*, Madrid, 24 March 1972, p. 5.

29. Antonio Gibello, 'García Lorca y Luis Apostúa', in *El Alcázar*, Madrid, 24 March 1972, p. 2.

30. —'¿Qué pretenden?', in *Arriba*, Madrid, 25 March 1972, p. 3.

31. Luis Apostúa, 'Jornada española', in *Ya*, 25 March 1972, p. 5.

32. —'Esto pretendemos', in *Ya*, 26 March 1972.

33. Antonio Gibello, 'La verdad ocultada', in *El Alcázar*, 27 March 1972, p. 3.

34. Emilio Romero, 'La Guinda', in *Pueblo*, Madrid, 27 March 1972.

35. José Luis Vila-San-Juan, '¿Quién mató a Federico García Lorca?', Chapter Six of *¿Así fue? Enigmas de la guerra civil española* (Barcelona, Nauta, 1971, appeared April 1972), pp. 104-18.

36. *Sábado gráfico*, Madrid, no. 790, 22 July 1972, pp. 67-71.

37. Luis Rosales, interview with Manolo Alcalá entitled 'Luis Rosales recuerda los últimos días de Federico García Lorca', in *Informaciones*, Madrid, 17 August 1972, pp. 12-13.

38. José María Pemán, 'Las razones de la sinrazón', in *ABC*, Madrid, 23 September 1972.

39. Eduardo Castro, *Muerte en Granada: la tragedia de Federico García Lorca* (Madrid, Akal, 1975).

40. José Luis Vila-San-Juan, *García Lorca, asesinado: toda la verdad* (Barcelona, Planeta, 1975).

AFTERWORD TO THE PENGUIN EDITION

1. Francisco García Lorca, *Federico y su mundo* (Madrid, Alianza, 1981).
2. I have not yet been able to trace the source of this commentary, contained in a cutting sent to me by an anonymous collaborator.
3. Conversation with señor Marín Forero, Madrid, 1978.

APPENDIX B

1. Interview given to Antonio Otero in 1936. For details, see Chapter Four, note 11, above.
2. Vicente Vidal Corella, 'El crimen fue en Granada. "Yo he visto asesinar a García Lorca...." "Federico fue cazado a tiros por la Guardia Civil cuando defendía, antes de morir, la verdad de nuestra lucha," relata un testigo de aquel crimen', in *Adelante*, Valencia, 15 September 1937, p. 1.
3. For details see Chapter Fourteen, above.
4. J. Rubia Barcia, 'Cómo murió García Lorca', in *Nuestra España*, Havana, no. 2, 1939 and *España libre*, Brooklyn, 1 March 1940.
5. John A. Crow, 'The Death of García Lorca', in *Modern Language Forum*, Los Angeles, XXV (1940), pp. 177–87.

APPENDIX C

1. For details, see Chapter Three, note 25, above.
2. Constantino Ruiz Carnero was shot officially (see p. 110), not for any 'sexual' reason.
3. 'Enfin la vérité sur la mort de Lorca: une lettre de M. Claude Couffon et la réponse de M. J.-L. Schonberg', in *Le Figaro Littéraire*, 13 October 1956.

APPENDIX D

1. All quotations, verse and prose, are from Ibn al-Khaṭīb's history of Granada, *al-Iḥāṭafī akhbār Gharnāṭa*, ed. by 'Abd Allāh 'Inān (Cairo, 1955), I, pp. 127–8.

SELECTED BIBLIOGRAPHY

This biliography lists only those sources which I have consulted myself: it makes no claims to be exhaustive. Sources referred to in the text, appendices and notes are indicated by an asterisk.

1. *The principal Spanish-language editions of Lorca's work*
GARCÍA LORCA, FEDERICO, *Obras completas*. Introduced and selected by Guillermo de Torre (Buenos Aires, Losada, 1938–1942, 7 vols. Several later editions).
*GARCÍA LORCA, FEDERICO, *Obras completas*, ed. by Arturo del Hoyo (Madrid, Aguilar, 1954, and successive editions). In this book all references are to the 20th edition, two vols., 1977.

2. *English-language editions of Lorca's work*
There is no complete English-language translation of Lorca, and those which exist of separate works are unsatisfactory. Perhaps the best and most readily available texts for the English-speaking reader new to Lorca are the bilingual anthology of his poetry by J. G. Gili, with a sensible introduction (Penguin Books), and that edited by Donald M. Allen (New Directions), and the plays *Three Tragedies* (*Blood Wedding, Yerma, The House of Bernarda Alba*), translated by James Graham-Luján and Richard L. O'Connell and introduced by Francisco García Lorca (published by New Directions in the U.S.A. and Penguin Books in Britain).

3. *Principal sources consulted for general information on Granada*
*BAEDEKER, KARL, *Spain and Portugal. Handbook for Travellers* Leipzig, 2nd edition, 1901).
*BRENAN, GERALD, *South from Granada* (London, Hamish Hamilton, 1957).
*FORD, RICHARD, *A Handbook for Travellers in Spain* (London, John Murray, 1845, 2 vols.; Carbondale, Southern Illinois University Press, 1966).
GALLAS ENCINAS, GONZALO, *Granada. España en paz* (Madrid, Publicaciones Españolas, 1964).
GARCÍA GÓMEZ, EMILIO, *Silla del moro y nuevas escenas andaluzas* (Madrid, Revista de Occidente, 1948; Buenos Aires, Espasa-Calpe, 1954).

GALLEGO Y BURÍN, ANTONIO, *Guía de Granada* (Granada, 1946).

GÁMIR SANDOVAL, ALFONSO, *Los viajeros ingleses y norteamericanos en la Granada del siglo XIX* (Universidad de Granada, 1954).

MOLINA FAJARDO, EDUARDO, *Manuel de Falla y el 'cante jondo'* (Universidad de Granada, 1962).

*MORA GUARNIDO, JOSÉ, *Federico García Lorca y su mundo. Testimonio para una biografía* (Buenos Aires, Losada, 1958).

RUIZ CARNERO, CONSTANTINO, *Siluetas de 'Constancio'* (Granada, 1931).

SECO DE LUCENA, LUIS, *Anuario de Granada* (Granada, 1917).

SECO DE LUCENA, LUIS, *Granada. Guía breve* (Granada, 2nd edition, 1919).

SECO DE LUCENA, LUIS, *Mis memorias de Granada* (Granada, 1941).

*TREND, J. B., 'A Poet of Arabia', in *Alfonso the Sage and Other Spanish Essays* (London, Constable, 1926).

4. *Principal sources consulted in connection with the history of the Spanish Republic and the Civil War*

ARRARÁS, JOAQUÍN, *Historia de la Segunda República Española* (Madrid, Editora Nacional, 1957; 3rd edition, 1964).

BAHAMONDE Y SÁNCHEZ DE CASTRO, *Un año con Queipo. Memorias de un nacionalista* (Barcelona, 1938).

*BORRÁS, TOMÁS, *Ramiro Ledesma Ramos* (Madrid, Editora nacional, 1971).

*BRENAN, GERALD, *The Spanish Labyrinth* (Cambridge, 1943; in my book I refer throughout to the 1960 paperback edition).

CARR, RAYMOND, *Spain, 1808–1939* (Oxford, 1966).

CROZIER, BRIAN, *Franco. A Biographical History* (London, Eyre & Spottiswoode, 1967; Boston, Little, Brown, 1968).

Cruzada Española, Historia de la. Literary editor, Joaquín Arrarás; artistic editor, Carlos Saenz de Tejada. (Madrid, 1939–1943, 35 vols.) Vol. III, book xi, contains the official Nationalist version of the rising in Granada.

Defensor de Granada, El. Left-wing newspaper founded in 1879.

GARCÍA VENERO, MAXIMIANO, *Falange en la guerra de España; la Unificación y Hedilla* (Paris, Ruedo ibérico, 1967).

*GIL ROBLES, JOSÉ MARÍA, *No fue posible la paz* (Barcelona, Ariel, 1968).

*GOLLONET Y MEGÍAS, ANGEL, and MORALES LÓPEZ, JOSÉ, *Rojo y azul en Granada* (Granada, Prieto, 1937).

HILLS, GEORGE, *Franco. The Man and his Nation* (London, Robert Hale, 1967; New York, Macmillan, 1968).

Ideal. Granadine Catholic newspaper founded by Acción Popular in 1931. Still published.

* JACKSON, GABRIEL, *The Spanish Republic and the Civil War* (Princeton, 1965).

KOESTLER, ARTHUR, *Spanish Testament* (London, Gollancz, 1937).

MARTÍNEZ SIERRA, MARÍA, *Una mujer por caminos de España. Recuerdos de propagandista* (Buenos Aires, Losada, 1952).

ORTIZ DE VILLAJOS, CÁNDIDO, *Crónica de Granada en 1937, II año triunfal* (Granada, 1938).

*PAYNE, STANLEY, *Falange. A History of Spanish Fascism* (Stanford University Press and Oxford, 1962).

PAYNE, STANLEY, *Politics and the Military in Modern Spain* (Stanford University Press and Oxford, 1967).

PEERS, E. ALLISON, *The Spanish Tragedy, 1930–1936* (London, Methuen, 1936).

PRESTON, PAUL, *La destrucción de la democracia en España. Reacción, reforma y revolución en la Segunda República* (Madrid, Turner, 1978).

RIESENFELD, JANET, *Dancer in Madrid* (London, Harrap, 1938).

*RUIZ ALONSO, RAMÓN, *Corporativismo* (Salamanca, 1937).

SOUTHWORTH, HERBERT R., *Le mythe de la Croisade de Franco* (Paris, Ruedo ibérico, 1964).

SOUTHWORTH, HERBERT R., *Antifalange. Estudio crítico de 'Falange en la guerra de España' de M. García Venero* (Paris, Ruedo ibérico, 1967).

*SOUTHWORTH, HERBERT R., 'The Falange: An Analysis of Spain's Fascist Heritage', in Paul Preston (ed.), *Spain in Crisis* (Hassocks, Sussex, The Harvester Press, 1976), pp. 1–22.

TUÑÓN DE LARA, MANUEL, *La España del siglo XX* (Barcelona, Laia, 3 vols., 1977).

TUSSELL, JAVIER, *Las elecciones del Frente Popular* (Madrid, Cuadernos Para el Diálogo, 2 vols., 1971).

VENEGAS, JOSE, *Las elecciones del Frente Popular* (Buenos Aires, Patronato Hispano-Argentino de Cultura, 1942).

5. *Contemporary printed sources concerning the 'siege' and repression of Granada, arranged in chronological order*
—(1936), 'Cinco mil kilos de bombas sobre Granada', *Claridad*, Madrid, 11 August.
*NEVILLE, ROBERT (1936), 'Mass Executions and Air Raids in Spain Related in Neville Diary. Granada Incidents of Civil War are Described by *Herald Tribune* Bridge Editor; Victims of Firing Squad Hauled Alive to Cemetery', *New York Herald Tribune*, 30 August, pp. 1 and 6.

NEVILLE, ROBERT (1936), 'Llegan a Iznalloz muchos evadidos de Granada y pueblos en que los traidores fusilan a mujeres y niños', La Voz, Madrid, 2 September, p. 4.

—(1936), 'Mientras se estrecha el cerco sobre Granada', ABC, Madrid, 3 September, p. 7.

—(1936), 'Ante el próximo avance sobre Granada', ABC, Madrid, 9 September, p. 12.

VIDAL, ANTONIO (1936), 'Desde Guadix, Cuartel General del frente de Granada. Los fascistas emplean en Granada procedimientos criminales ...', Solidaridad obrera, Barcelona, 11 September, p. 2.

—(1936), 'Criminales! En Granada, por cada bomba que arrojan nuestros aviones, son fusilados diez hombres de izquierda', Solidaridad obrera, Barcelona, 16 September, p. 15.

—(1936), 'Los facciosos han fusilado a los masones de Granada después de hacerles cavar sus tumbas', La Voz, Madrid, 22 September, p. 2.

—(1936), 'En Granada han sido fusilados todos los masones', ABC, Madrid, 23 September, p. 9.

VIDAL, ANTONIO (1936), 'Los grandes crímenes del fascismo en Granada. En Granada son asesinados catedráticos, médicos, abogados y centenares de trabajadores, sin formación de causa. Interesante relato de dos testigos presenciales huidos hace pocos días de la capital', Solidaridad obrera, Barcelona, 29 September, p. 4.

—(1936), 'Granada bajo el terror. Los sicarios fascistas han perpetrado más de cinco mil asesinatos. Las mujeres, víctimas preferidas de sus ensañamientos', Claridad, Madrid, 14 October, p. 4.

—(1936), 'El terror fascista. En Granada han sido fusiladas muchas personas', La Libertad, Madrid, 26 October, p. 2.

—(1936), 'En los frentes de Andalucía. Más de mil cuatrocientos antifascistas fusilados en Granada', ABC, Madrid, 10 November, p. 10.

—(1936), 'En la Granada infernal de los fascistas. Ochenta y noventa fusilamientos diarios, martirios, envenenamientos, violaciones. ... Allí se ha dado cita toda la crueldad de una guerra emprendida contra un pueblo', Claridad, Madrid, 10 November, p. 7.

— (1936), 'Nuevo acto de cruel salvajismo en Granada', ABC, Madrid, 19 December, p. 4.

— (1937), 'Los crímenes de la "Escuadra Negra"', ABC, Madrid, 27 April, p. 9.

*NICHOLSON, HELEN (BARONESS DE ZGLINITZKI) (1937), Death in the Morning (London, Loval Dickson).

6. Newspaper references, articles and books consulted in connection with the death of García Lorca and the ensuing polemic. Arranged in chronological order.

*—(1936), '¿Ha sido asesinado García Lorca?', El Diarico de Albacete, 30 August, p. 1.

254

— (1936), '¿Han asesinado a García Lorca?', *ABC*, Madrid, 1 September, p. 16.

*— (1936), 'Una noticia increíble. Federico García Lorca', *La Voz*, Madrid, 1 September, p. 2.

— (1936), '¿Ha sido fusilado el gran poeta García Lorca?' *Heraldo de Madrid*, 1 September, p. 3.

— (1936), '¿Pero será posible? ¿Federico García Lorca, el inmenso poeta, asesinado por los facciosos?', *El Liberal*, Madrid, 2 September, p. 3.

— (1936), 'Los fascistas han fusilado a Federico García Lorca', *Solidaridad Obrera*, Barcelona, 5 September, p. 2.

GIL BELMONTE, L. (1936), 'En el frente de Guadix. Un amigo del conocido socialista granadino señor Fernández Montesinos, asesinado vilmente por los traidores, afirma que también han dado muerte los facciosos al gran poeta de fama universal Federico García Lorca', *Heraldo de Madrid*, 8 September, p. 5.

— (1936), 'Se confirma el asesinato de Federico García Lorca', *ABC*, Madrid, 8 September, p. 9.

*— (1936), 'La barbarie. Se ha confirmado la ejecución del gran poeta García Lorca', *La Voz*, Madrid, 8 September, p. 1.

*— (1936), 'Sobre el supuesto asesinato de Federico García Lorca', *El Sol*, Madrid, 9 September, p. 1.

— (1936), 'La ejecutoria de los bárbaros. Al asesinar a García Lorca pretendían matar al pensamiento', *Mundo obrero*, Madrid, 9 September, p. 1.

—(1936), 'Vuelve a asegurarse que el gran poeta García Lorca fue asesinado per los traidores', *El Liberal*, Madrid, 9 September, p. 1.

— (1936), '¿Ha sido fusilado per los traidores el gran poeta popular Federico García Lorca?', *Milicia Popular*, Madrid, 9 September, p. 3.

— (1936), 'El vil asesinato de García Lorca. Se confirma el monstruoso crimen', *El Liberal*, Madrid, 10 September, p. 3.

— (1936), 'Sobre el asesinato de García Lorca', *ABC*, Madrid, 10 September, p. 9.

— (1936), 'La Barraca y el asesinato de García Lorca', *ABC*, Madrid, 10 September, p. 14.

— (1936), 'Duelo por la muerte de Federico García Lorca. Una nota de "La Barraca"', *La Voz*, Madrid, 10 September, p. 3.

— (1936), 'Ante la noticia del asesinato de García Lorca. Un comunicado de la Asociación de Amigos de la Unión Soviética', *Heraldo de Madrid*, 10 September, p. 6.

— (1936), 'Emisoras intervenidas por los rojos', *La Provincia*, Huelva, 10 September, p. 2.

RODRÍGUEZ ESPINOSA, ANTONIO (1936), '"Sobre el monstruoso asesinato de Federico García Lorca. ¡Qué infamia!"', *El Liberal*, Madrid, 11 September, p. 3.

RODRIGUEZ ESPINOZA, ANTONIO (1936), reference to the death of Lorca in *The Times*, London, 12 September, p. 11, col. 1.

— (1936), 'La protesta de los autores por el asesinato de García Lorca', *El Liberal*, Madrid, 12 September, p. 6.

— (1936), 'Dolor por la muerte de García Lorca', *ABC*, Madrid, 13 September, p. 11.

— (1936), 'Condenación de los autores españoles por el asesinato de García Lorca', *El Liberal*, Madrid, 13 September, p. 5.

— (1936), referencia a la muerte del poeta en *The Times*, London, 14 September, p. 12, col. 4.

— (1936), 'Puerto Rico y su protesta por la muerte de García Lorca', *ABC*, Madrid, 15 September, p. 14.

CASTROVIDO, ROBERTO (1936), 'El poeta de "Mariana Pineda"', *El Liberal*, Madrid, 16 September, p. 4.

FERRAGUT, JUAN (1936), 'El fusilamiento de un gran poeta del pueblo. Federico García Lorca', *Mundo Gráfico*, Madrid, 16 September, p. 11.

— (1936), 'En Barcelona ha sido fusilado el poeta Federico García Lorca', *El Diario de Huelva*, 19 September, p. 10.

— (1936), 'García Lorca ha sido fusilado', *Diario de Burgos*, 19 September.

*— (1936), 'En Barcelona. Federico García Lorca, fusilado. Otros fusilamientos', *La Provincia*, Huelva, 19 September, p. 2.

— (1936), 'Nuestro homenaje a García Lorca', *Ayuda*, Madrid, 19 September, p. 1.

— (1936), 'Jacinto Benavente hace constar su protesta por el asesinato de García Lorca', *El Liberal*, Madrid, 20 September, p. 5.

— (1936), 'El poeta García Lorca fusilado con los obreros', *El Castellano*, Burgos, 21 September.

— (1936), 'Rivas Cherif tiene la impresión de que no ha muerto García Lorca', *Heraldo de Madrid*, 21 de September, p. 5.

— (1936), reference to the death of the poet in *The Times*, London, 23 September, p. 12, col. 5.

*VILLA, ANTONIO DE LA (1936), 'Un evadido de Granada cuenta el fusilamiento de García Lorca', *Estampa*, Madrid, 26 September.

*SÁNCHEZ DEL ARCO, M. (1936), 'Detención del duque de Canalejas. Benavente. García Lorca', *ABC*, Sevilla, 27 September, p. 4.

— (1936), 'La Alianza de Intelectuales celebra un gran acto de afirmación cultural antifascista. José Bergamín no cree en la muerte de García Lorca, pero sí en el . . . fusilamiento de Unamuno', *Heraldo de Madrid*, 28 September, p. 5.

CASTROVIDO, ROBERTO (1936), 'Dulce esperanza: ¿Vive el poeta García Lorca ?', *El Liberal*, Madrid, 29 de September, pp. 1 y 2.

— (1936), 'Un importante documento sobre la insurreción. El Colegio de Abogados de Madrid expone los casos de barbarie fascista que se han registrado en las poblaciones ocupadas por los facciosos', *Heraldo de Madrid*, 30 September, p. 5.

— (1936), 'Un llamamiento a los patriotas granadinos' [para la formación del batallón Mariana Pineda], *Heraldo de Madrid*, 30 September, p. 4.

— (1936), 'Detalles del asesinato de García Lorca. La odisea de un evadido de Granada', *ABC*, Madrid, 1 October, p. 9.

— (1936), 'La barbarie fascista. Un evadido de Granada confirma el fusilamiento del poeta García Lorca', *La Libertad*, Madrid, 2 October, p. 2.

*—(1936), 'Nuevos detalles del fusilamiento de García Lorca', *El Sol*, Madrid, 2 October, p. 3.

— (1936), 'El presidente de la FUE de Granada confirma el fusilamiento de García Lorca', *Claridad*, Madrid, 2 October, p. 2.

— (1936), 'Un evadido de Granada confirma el asesinato por los fascistas del gran poeta García Lorca', *Heraldo de Madrid*, 2 October, p. 3.

— (1936), 'Un grupo escolar llevará el nombre de García Lorca', *ABC*, Madrid, 3 October, p. 12.

— (1936), reference to the death of Lorca in *The Times*, London, 5 October, p. 11, col. 4.

— (1936), 'Un mitin del Socorro Rojo Internacional' [Isidoro Acevedo of SRI refers to the death of Lorca] *Heraldo de Madrid*, 5 October, p. 2.

— (1936), 'Después del crimen. Wells pregunta por García Lorca, y el gobernador militar rebelde de Granada contesta que ignora su paradero', *La Libertad*, Madrid, 14 October, p. 1.

*—(1936), 'Una gestión de Wells. El gobernador faccioso de Granada dice que ignora el paradero de García Lorca', *El Sol*, Madrid, 14 October, p. 1.

— (1936), 'La muerte de Federico García Lorca. El insigne Wells pide noticias de nuestro gran poeta nacional', *La Libertad*, Madrid, 15 October, p. 6.

*— (1936), 'Ante el asesinato del gran poeta español Federico García Lorca', *El Sol*, Madrid, 15 October, p. 4.

MACHADO, ANTONIO (1936), 'El crimen fue en Granada: a Federico García Lorca', *Ayuda*, Madrid, 17 October, p. 3. This great elegiac poem became immediately famous and was reprinted in many Republican newspapers and magazines.

TREND, J. B. (1936), ['Federico García Lorca'], letter on the death of the poet, *Times Literary Supplement*, London, 17 October, p. 839.

— (1936), 'Un grupo de intelectuales argentinos protesta por el asesinato de García Lorca en Granada', *Heraldo de Madrid*, 30 October, p. 4.

TORRES RIOSECO, A. (1936), 'El asesinato de García Lorca', *Repertorio americano*, San José de Costa Rica, 7 November, pp. 268–9.

*HURTADO ÁLVAREZ, LUIS (1937), 'A la España Imperial le han asesinado su mejor poeta', *Unidad*, San Sebastián, 11 March, p. 1.

*MACHADO, ANTONIO (1937), 'Carta a David Vigodsky', *Hora de España*, Valencia, núm. 4, April.

MERRY DEL VAL, THE MARQUIS DE (1937), 'Spain: Six of One and Half a Dozen of the Other', *The Nineteenth Century*, London, May, pp. 355–71.

QUINTANAR, MARQUÉS DE (1937), 'Los inocentes poetas', *ABC*, Seville, 27 May, pp. 3–4.

*S. B. [SÁNCHEZ BARBUDO] (1937), 'La muerte de García Lorca comentada por sus asesinos', *Hora de España*, Valencia. núm. 5, mayo, pp. 71–2.

RÍOS, FERNANDO DE LOS (1937), reference to Lorca's death in a lecture reprinted in *Hora de España*, Valencia, no. 8, August, pp. 25–9.

'EL BACHILLER ALCAÑICES' (1937), '*ABC* en Chile. Puerta cerrada', *ABC*, Seville, 31 August, p. 4.

*VIDAL CORELIA, Vicente (1937), ' "El crimen fue en Granada". "Yo he visto asesinar a García Lorca ...". "Federico fue cazade a tiros por la Guardia Civil cuando defendía, antes de morir, la verdad de nuestra lucha" relata un testigo de aquel crimen', *Adelante*, Valencia, 15 September, p. 1.

— (1937), 'Un testigo presencial relata cómo asesinaron los facciosos al inmortal García Lorca. "Se levantó, sangrando.... Con ojos terribles miró a todos, que retrocedieron espantados" ', *ABC*, Madrid, 17 September, p. 7.

— (1937), 'El asesinato de García Lorca. "Allí quedó el poeta insepulto, frente a su Granada." Relato de un testigo presencial', *Claridad*, Madrid, 17 September, p. 4.

— (1937), 'Como su amigo el Camborio. Pasión y muerte de Federico García Lorca', *Solidaridad Obrera*, Barcelona, 21 September.

RÍOS, FERNANDO DE LOS (1937), ' "Fusilaron a F. García Lorca porque él representaba el pensamiento español ..." ', Discurso pronunciado en el homenaje a Lorca organizado por la Sociedad Hispana de Nueva York, *La Prensa*, New York, 11 October.

*SAENZ HAYES, RICARDO (1937), 'Para *La Prensa* hizo el General Franco importantes declaraciones', *La Prensa*, Buenos Aires, 26 November.

*SAENZ, VICENTE (1937), 'Consideraciones sobre civilización occidental a propósito de Federico García Lorca', *Repertorio americano*, San José de Costa Rica, 18 December, pp. 353–7.

GONZÁLEZ CARBALHO, JOSÉ (1938), *Vida, obra y muerte de Federico García Lorca (escrita para ser leída en un acto recordatorio)* (Santiago de Chile, Ercilla; 2nd edition, 1941).

— (1938), 'García Lorca fue muerto por miembros del partido Acción Católica', *La Prensa*, New York, 27 July.

CAMPBELL, ROY (1939), *Flowering Rifle: A Poem from the Battlefield of Spain* (London, Longmans, Green & Company).

MARTÍNEZ NADAL, RAFAEL (1939), Introduction to *Poems. F. García*

Lorca, with English translations by Stephen Spender and J. L. Gili (London, Dolphin; 2nd edition, 1942).

*RUBIA BARCIA, J. (1939), 'Cómo murió García Lorca', *Nuestra España*, Havana, núm. 2. Reproduced in *España Libre*, Brooklyn, 1 March 1940, p. 2.

BERGAMÍN, JOSÉ (1940), Introduction to Lorca's *Poeta en Nueva York* (Mexico, Séneca and New York, W. W. Norton).

CROW, JOHN A. (1940), 'The Death of García Lorca', *Modern Language Forum*, Los Angeles, XXV, pp. 177–87.

*RÍO, ANGEL DEL (1941), *Federico García Lorca. Vida y obra* (New York, Hispanic Institute in the United States), pp. 23–4.

OTERO SECO, ANTONIO (1947), 'Así murió Federico García Lorca', *Iberia*, Bordeaux, V, May.

CAMACHO MONTOYA, GUILLERMO (1947), 'Por qué y cómo murió García Lorca', *El Siglo*, Bogotá, 15 November.

CHÁVEZ CAMACHO, ARMANDO (1948), 'La verdad sobre España', *El Universal Gráfico*, Mexico, 2 January.

*SERRANO SUÑER, RAMÓN (1948), ['Sobre la muerte del poeta García Lorca'], letter to Armando Chávez Camacho (see above), *El Universal Gráfico*, Mexico, 3 May.

*CHÁVEZ CAMACHO, ARMANDO (1948), *Misión de prensa en España* (Mexico, Jus), pp. 372–4.

*PEMÁN, JOSÉ MARÍA (1948), 'García Lorca', *ABC*, Madrid, 5 December.

*BRENAN, GERALD (1950), 'Granada', sixth chapter of *The Face of Spain* (London, The Turnstile Press), pp. 122–48.

*BRENAN, GERALD (1951), 'La vérité sur la mort de Lorca', *Les Nouvelles Littéraires*, Paris, 31 May (translation of the sixth chapter of *The Face of Spain*).

*COUFFON, CLAUDE (1951), 'Ce que fut la mort de Federico García Lorca', *Le Figaro Littéraire*, Paris, núm. 278, 18 August, p. 5.

COUFFON, CLAUDE (1953), *El crimen fue en Granada* (Ecuador, University of Quito).

*GARCÍA SERRANO, RAFAEL (1953), *Bailando hacia la Cruz del Sur* (Madrid, Gráficas Cies), pp. 330–1.

DALI, SALVADOR (1954), 'La morte di García Lorca', *Il Popolo*, 1 July, p. 3.

— (1956), 'La mort de Lorca', *L'Express*, Paris, 24 August, p. 17. First publication of extracts from Lorca's death certificate.

VEGA, ESTEBAN (1956), 'Federico García Lorca en el XX aniversario de su muerte', *Novedades*, Mexico, 16 September.

*'SCHONBERG, JEAN-LOUIS' (1956), 'Enfin, la vérité sur la mort de Lorca! Un assassinat, certes, mais dont la politique n'a pas été le mobile', *Le Figaro Littéraire*, Paris, no. 545, 29 September.

*'SCHONBERG, JEAN-LOUIS' and COUFFON, CLAUDE (1956), ['Enfin, la vérité sur la mort de Lorca: une lettre de M. Claude Couffon et la réponse de M. J.-L. Schonberg'], *Le Figaro Littéraire*, Paris, 13 October, pp. 1, 5–6.

*— (1956), '*Le Figaro Littéraire* confiesa: "!En fin, la verdad sobre la muerte de García Lorca!" "No fue la politica el móvil"', *La Estafeta literaria*, Madrid, 13 October, p. 1.

CHABROL, JEAN-PIERRE (1956), 'Grenade a retrouvé les assassins de Lorca', *Les Lettres Françaises*, Paris, 18 October.

*RIDRUEJO, DIONISIO (1956), letter to the Minister of Tourism and Information, Gabriel Arias Salgado, in protest against the article by Schonberg reproduced in *La Estafeta literaria* (see above), 22 October. Reproduced by Vázquez Ocaña (see below), pp. 381–2.

*'SCHONBERG, JEAN-LOUIS' (1956), 'Víznar', sixth chapter of *Federico García Lorca. L'homme – L'oeuvre* (Paris, Plon), pp. 101–22. Contains the same text as that published by 'Schonberg' in *Le Figaro Littéraire* (see above).

M. A. (1956), 'A morte de García Lorca', *Brotéria*, Lisbon, LXIII, November, pp. 480–1.

*RIVAS CHERIF, CIPRIANO (1957), 'Poesía y drama del gran Federico. La muerte y la pasión de García Lorca', *Excelsior*, Mexico, 6, 13 and 27 January. The first two articles reproduce a conversation with Luis Rosales.

*VÁZQUEZ OCAÑA, FERNANDO (1957), 'La muerte fue en Granada, en su Granada', chapter XV of *García Lorca. Vida, cántico y muerte* (Mexico, Grijalbo), pp. 364–89.

'ALBE' [R. JOOSTENS] (1958), *Andalusisch Dagboek* (Herk-de-Stad, Belgium, Drukkerij-Uitgeverij Brems, no date but almost certainly 1958). The author spoke to Miguel and Luis Rosales and their aunt, Luisa Camacho.

*MORA GUARNIDO, JOSÉ (1958), 'La muerte en la madrugada' and 'Los perros en el cementerio', chapters XVI and XVIII of *Federico García Lorca y su mundo. Testimonio para una biografía* (Buenos Aires, Losada), pp. 196–208, 216–38.

*MORLA LYNCH, CARLOS (1958), *En España con Federico García Lorca (Páginas de un diario íntimo, 1928–1936)* (Madrid, Aguilar), pp. 491–8.

*COBELLI, ENZO (1959), *García Lorca* (Mantua, Editrice La Gonzaghiana, 2nd edition), pp. 64–81.

LEÓN, MARÍA TERESA (1959), 'Doña Vicenta y su hijo', *El Nacional*, Caracas, 14 May.

*'SCHONBERG, JEAN-LOUIS' (1959), *Federico García Lorca. El hombre-La obra* (Mexico, Compañía General de Ediciones). Adds a few details to the original French edition.

PIERINI, FRANCO (1960), 'Incontro a Spoleto con la sorella di Federico. Quella notte a Granada. Conchita García Lorca ha raccontato per la prima volta ciò che avvenne quando alla famiglia vennero a dire: "lo hanno portato via"', *L'Europeo*, 17 July, pp. 74–6.

*WERRIE, PAUL (1961), 'Lettre d'Espagne: García Lorca a reparu sur scène à Madrid', *Ecrits de Paris*, February, pp. 91–5.

— (1961), 'Dramma in Andalusia: Ecco la morte di García Lorca', *Epoca*, Milan, 2 July, pp. 34–9.

LORENZ, GÜNTER (1961), *Federico García Lorca* (Karlsruhe, Stahlberg), pp. 133–68.

*THOMAS, HUGH (1961), *The Spanish Civil War* (London, Eyre & Spottiswoode), pp. 169–70.

*COUFFON, CLAUDE (1962), 'Le crime a eu lieu à Grenade ...', *A Grenade, sur les pas de García Lorca* (Paris, Seghers), pp. 59–123. The definitive version of Couffon's account.

BELAMICH, ANDRÉ (1962), 'Sur la mort de Lorca et ses causes', *Lorca* (Paris, Gallimard), pp. 254–8.

*MARTÍNEZ NADAL, RAFAEL (1963), 'El último día de Federico García Lorca en Madrid', *Residencia. Revista de la Residencia de Estudiantes*, commemorative issue published in Mexico, December, pp. 58–61. Martínez Nadal reprinted the article in '*El público: amor, teatro y caballos en la obra de Federico García Lorca* (Oxford), The Dolphin Book Co. Ltd., 1970), pp. 9–15 and, more recently, as a prologue to his edition of Lorca's *El público* (Barcelona, Seix Barral, 1978), pp. 13–21.

SOUTHWORTH, HERBERT R. (1964), 'Campbell et García Lorca', *Le mythe de la croisade de Franco* (Paris, Ruedo ibérico), pp. 119–22 and notes.

*SAINT-PAULIEN (1964), 'Sur la vie et la mort de Federico García Lorca', *Cahiers des Amis de Robert Brasillach*, Lausanne, no. 10, Noël, pp. 7–10. Reproduced with title '"Comparer la mort de García Lorca à celle de Brasillach constitue un blasphème"' (Saint-Paulien), in *Rivarol*, Paris, 14 January 1965.

*— (1965), 'Nuestro entrañable Federico García Lorca, el poeta en Nueva York ...', *La Estafeta literaria*, Madrid, no. 314, 27 March, p. 36.

*GARCÍA SERRANO, RAFAEL (1965), 'Nota para Mme Auclair', *ABC*, Madrid, 7 May.

CELAYA, GABRIEL (1966), 'Un recuerdo de Federico García Lorca', *Realidad. Revista de cultura y política*, Rome, no. 9, April.

*RODRÍGUEZ ESPINOSA, ANTONIO (1966), 'Souvenirs d'un vieil ami', fragments of the unpublished memoirs of Lorca's first teacher, translated by Marie Laffranque and published in her *Federico García Lorca* (Paris, Seghers, 'Théâtre de tous les temps', 1966), pp. 107–10.

LAFFRANQUE, MARIE (1966), 'Lorca, treinta años después. 1936–1966', *Le Socialiste*, Paris, 19 August.

*— (1966), *Crónica de la guerra española. No apta para irreconciliables* (Buenos Aires, Editorial Codex, no. 10, October), pp. 222–5, 227, 237–8.

*NEVILLE, EDGAR (1966), 'La obra de Federico, bien nacional', *ABC*, Madrid, 6 November, p. 2.

*'SCHONBERG, JEAN-LOUIS' (1966), *A la Recherche de Lorca* (Neuchâtel, A la Baconnière). A re-working of the original French edition.

GIMÉNEZ CABALLERO, ERNESTO (1966), 'Conmemoración de García Lorca en el Paraguay', *La Tribuna*, Asunción, Paraguay, 4 December.

PAYNE, STANLEY (1967), *Politics and the Military in Modern Spain* (Stanford University Press and Oxford), pp. 416–17 and notes pp. 526–7.

COUFFON, CLAUDE (1967), 'El crimen fue en Granada', in *Granada y García Lorca*, translated by Bernardo Kordon (Buenos Aires, Losada), pp. 77–132. Translation of the definitive version of Couffon's study *A Grenade, sur les pas de García Lorca* (1962) (see above).

*AUCLAIR, MARCELLE (1968), *Enfances et mort de García Lorca* (Paris, Seuil).

*GIBSON, IAN (1971), *La represión nacionalista de Granada en 1936 y la muerte de Federico García Lorca* (Paris, Ruedo ibérico).

GARCÍA LORCA, FRANCISCO (1971), interview with Max Aub about the death of Federico García Lorca, reproduced, with errors, by Aub in *La gallina ciega* (Mexico, Joaquín Mortiz), pp. 243–6.

ROSALES, LUIS (1972), interview with René Arteaga entitled 'Eran 50 o 60 "Patriotas" los que fueron por García Lorca', *Excelsior*, Mexico, 13 January.

*APOSTÚA, LUIS (1972), 'Jornada española', *Ya*, Madrid, 24 March, p. 5.

*GIBELLO, ANTONIO (1972), 'García Lorca y Luis Apostúa', *El Alcázar*, Madrid, 24 March, p. 2.

*— (1972), '¿Qué pretenden?', *Arriba*, Madrid, 25 March, p. 3.

*APOSTÚA, LUIS (1972), 'Jornada española', *Ya*, Madrid, 25 March, p. 5.

*— (1972), 'Esto pretendemos', *Ya*, Madrid, 26 March.

*GIBELLO, ANTONIO (1972), 'La verdad ocultada', *El Alcázar*, Madrid, 27 March, p. 3.

*ROMERO, EMILIO (1972), 'La guinda', *Pueblo*, Madrid, 27 March.

*ROSALES, LUIS (1972), letter to the editor, *ABC*, Madrid, 29 March, p. 14.

GIBSON, IAN (1972), 'The Murder of a Genius', *The Guardian*, London, 17 April, p. 8.

GRANELL, E. F. (1972), 'Lorca, víctima marcada por la Falange', *España libre*, New York, March–April.

*VILA-SAN-JUAN, JOSÉ LUIS (1972), '¿Quién mató a Federico García Lorca?', chapter six of *¿Así fue? Enigmas de la guerra civil española* (Barcelona, Nauta, 1971, appeared April 1972), pp. 104–18. The chapter was reproduced in *Sábado gráfico*, Madrid, no. 790, 22 July 1972, pp. 67–71.

*ROSALES, LUIS (1972), interview with Manolo Alcalá entitled 'Luis Rosales recuerda los últimos días de Federico García Lorca', *Informaciones*, Madrid, 17 August, pp. 12–13.

*ROSALES, LUIS (1972), interview with Tico Medina entitled 'Introducción a la muerte de Federico García Lorca', *ABC*, Madrid, 20 August, pp. 17–21.

*PEMÁN, JOSÉ MARÍA (1972), 'Las razones de la sinrazón', *ABC*, Madrid, 23 September.

— (1972), 'En torno a la muerte de García Lorca', *Sábado gráfico*, Madrid, 21 October.

MUÑIZ-ROMERO, CARLOS (1973), 'A vueltas con una muerte en clave', *Razón y fe*, Madrid, no. 901, February, pp. 139–45.

EISENBERG, DANIEL (1975), 'Una visita con Jean-Louis Schonberg', *Textos y documentos lorquianos* (published by the compiler, Florida State University, Tallahassee), pp. 37–50.

MONLEÓN, JOSÉ (1975), 'La muerte de Federico García Lorca', *Triunfo*, Madrid, 1 March, pp. 25–9.

*CASTRO, EDUARDO (1975), *Muerte en Granada: la tragedia de Federico García Lorca* (Madrid, Akal).

*VILA-SAN-JUAN, JOSÉ LUIS (1975), *García Lorca, asesinado: toda la verdad* (Barcelona, Planeta).

*RAMOS ESPEJO, ANTONIO (1975), 'Los últimos días de Federico García Lorca. El testimonio de Angelina', *Triunfo*, Madrid, 17 May, pp. 27–8.

GIBSON, IAN (1975), 'La muerte de García Lorca. Carta abierta a José Luis Vila-San-Juan por su libro "García Lorca, asesinado: toda la verdad"', *Triunfo*, Madrid, 31 May, pp. 38–9.

MONLEÓN, JOSÉ (1975), '¿Toda la verdad?', *Triunfo*, Madrid, 31 May, p. 40.

VILA-SAN-JUAN, JOSÉ LUIS (1975), replies to the last two articles listed above, *Triunfo*, Madrid, 14 June, p. 13.

GIBSON, IAN (1975), 'Gibson a Vila-San-Juan. La muerte de García Lorca', *Triunfo*, Madrid, 28 June, pp. 34–5.

MONLEÓN, JOSÉ (1975), 'Sobre el "cinismo histórico" y la carta de Vila-San-Juan', *Triunfo*, Madrid, 12 July, p. 23.

GIBSON, IAN (1975), interview about Lorca's death with Antonio Saraqueta, *Blanco y Negro*, Madrid, 12 July, pp. 5–7.

VILA-SAN-JUAN, JOSÉ LUIS (1975), 'El derecho al pataleo de Mr Gibson', *Blanco y Negro*, Madrid, 12 July, p. 6.

PERÉZ VERA, MARÍA DEL CARMEN (1975), 'Aclaraciones a Vila-San-Juan', letter concerning the Catholicism of her father, the Socialist lawyer Antonio Pérez Funes, *Triunfo*, Madrid, 16 August, pp. 34–5.

SUEIRO, DANIEL (1976), 'En los escenarios de los últimos días de Lorca', *Triunfo*, Madrid, 7 February, pp. 34–8.

GÓMEZ BURÓN, JOAQUÍN (1976), 'Al pie de un olivo próximo a Víznar. Aquí enterraron a García Lorca', *Personas*, Madrid, 11 April, pp. 34–8.

CASADO, MARISA (1976), 'García Lorca. Revelaciones sobre su muerte', *Gaceta ilustrada*, Madrid, 6 June, pp. 56-9.

NAVEROS, JOSÉ MIGUEL (1976), 'García Lorca y Falla. Cuarenta años de un fusilamiento y cien de un nacimiento', *Historia 16*, Madrid, September, pp. 138-40.

— (1976), '"No maté a García Lorca ni estuve jamás en Víznar" afirma "Perete"', *Ideal*, Granada, 27 November.

ZARZO HERNÁNDEZ, MANUEL 'PERETE' (1976), ['No fue "Perete"'], letter in which the ex-bullfighter "Perete" denies having taken part in the death of Lorca, *Historia 16*, Madrid, November.

RIDRUEJO, DIONISIO (1976), *Casi unas memorias*, edited by César Armando Gómez (Barcelona, Planeta), pp. 133-4.

SALGADO-ARAUJO, TENIENTE GENERAL (1976), *Mis conversaciones privadas con Franco* (Barcelona, Planeta), p. 78.

SUANES, HECTOR (1976), *Llanto por Federico García Lorca. La detención y la muerte del poeta en Granada y los más bellos poemas escritos a su memoria* (Buenos Aires, Ediciones del Libertador).

SOREL, ANDRÉS (1977), *Yo, García Lorca* (Madrid, Zero).

*GIBSON, IAN (1978), 'Lorca y el tren de Granada', *Triunfo*, Madrid, 8 April, pp. 26-7.

GUIJARRO, FERNANDO (1978), '¿Dónde está Federico?', *Tierras del sur*, Sevilla, August, pp. 4-7.

ROSALES, LUIS (1978), interview with Félix Grande entitled 'Luis Rosales: "Yo no invento nada, vivo"', *El País*, Madrid, 'Arte y pensamiento', 17 September, pp. I, VI-VII.

FRANCO, ENRIQUE (1978), 'El día que Falla se fue de Granada. En torno a Hermenegildo Lanz', *El País*, Madrid, 'Arte y pensamiento', 23 July, p. IX.

*FERNÁNDEZ-MONTESINGS, MANUEL (1978), interview with Eduardo Castro entitled 'Manuel Fernández-Montesinos, diputado por Granada y sobrino de Lorca. "Todavía quede gente que debe saber lo que pasó con mi tío"', *El País semanal*, Madrid, 30 July, pp. 6-8.

ATIENZA RIVERO, EMILIO (1978), 'Las coordenadas históricas del destino de Federico García Lorca', *Tiempo de historia*, Madrid, November, pp. 26-39.

JIMÉNEZ, SERAFÍN (1979), 'Un episodio inédito de la Guerra Civil. García Lorca no pudo ser liberado por las locuras de un militar republicano', *Blanco y Negro*, Madrid, 10-16 January, pp. 24-7.

ROSALES, LUIS (1979), interview with Ian Gibson entitled 'Los últimos días de García Lorca: Luis Rosales aclara su actuación y la de su familia', *Triunfo*, Madrid, 24 February, pp. 40-3.

Index

Names of books, paintings, etc, are indexed in italics, followed by their creator's name in brackets, except in the case of the works of García Lorca, whose name has not been added to the titles.

À la recherche de Lorca (Schonberg), 227

Abril (Rosales), 126

Abū l-Barakāt a;-Balafīquī, 163

Acción Obrerista: premises burnt, 40; Ruiz Alonso in Cortes, 64

Acción Popular, 30; founding *Ideal* newspaper, 33; premises burnt, 40; militia during war, 95

Adam, 132

Aerodrome, *see* Armilla aerodrome

Afán de Ribera, Luis Gerardo, 47

Ainadamar, 163; references by Arab authors, 230–2

Alameda, Cafe, 21

Albaicín, 16; resistance to Nationalists, 84, 85–6, 87; women and children evacuated, 87–8; artillery bombardment, 88; invaded by soldiers and Falangists, 88

Alberti, Rafael, 52, 205–6

Alcalde González, María Luisa, 159

Alcántara, José, 92

Alfacar, 156

Alfonso XIII, King of Spain, deposed, 26

Alguacil González, Julio, 47

Alhambra, 16–17; allowed to become ruin, 18

Alonso, Dámaso, 58

Alvarez, Captain, 72; treachery, 73; promises Assault Guards' support for rising, 76

Alvarez Arenas, General Elíseo, 42

Alvarez de Cienfuegos, José, 135

Alvarez del Vayo, Julio, 53

Alvarez Quintero, Joaquin, 243

Alvarez Quintero, Serafin, 243

Anarchist Syndicates, closed down, 33

Ángulo Montes, Francisco, 92

Anti-Semitism, 177

Apostúa, Luis, 207–8

Arcollas Cabezas, Joaquín, 160

Arias Salgado, Gabriel, 200

Armilla aerodrome, taken by rebels, 81

Army: importance to Spain's political life, 67; Military Commandery during war, 91–3 *see also* Garrison

Arrese, José Luis de, 47

Assassination squads, 109 *see also* 'Black Squad'

Assault Guards, 72; join rebellion, 76, 80–1; protection for Civil Government, 81–2; during war, 94

Association of Friends of the Soviet Union, 63, 177

Asturian miners rising, 31–2, 64; García Lorca's defence of, 33–4

Auclair, Marcelle, 169, 202–3

¡Ayuda! (magazine of International Red Aid), 54, 177

Azaña, Manuel, 26, 28, 53

Ballad of Saint Michael, 233

Ballad of the Spanish Civil Guard, see Gypsy Ballads

Bandurria, 14

La Barraca (travelling theatre company), 23–4, 55

Barranco de Buco offensive, wounded prisoners shot, 99

Barrios, Angel, 20

Bécquer, Gustavo Adolfo, 23

Benavente, Jacinto, 152, 187, 243

Bergamín, José, 125

'Black biennium', 26

'Black Squad', 93; structure and practices, 97–9; victims unknown, 109; involved in Víznar executions, 159

Blood Wedding, 15; success in Buenos Aires, 24

Bombing, of Granada, 90

Borrás, Tomás, 62

Borrow, George, 17

Brenan, Gerald, 20n; on Acción Popular, 30; on total of burials following executions, 108; on burial of execution victims, 109
British Consulate, 104
Burín, Antonio Gallego, 20

'C., M.': buried García Lorca, 158; account of group shot with García Lorca, 164–5
Calvo Sotelo, José, 175
Campins, Aura, General Miguel, 49; contact with Civil Government, 70–2; instructed to relieve Córdoba, 74; unaware of Army decision to take to streets, 77–8; forced to sign proclamation of war, 78–9; statement to *Ideal*, 79–80; executed, 86n
Campo, Lt.-Col. Miguel del, takes over as mayor of Granada, 83
Cañadas, Miguel, 98
Cante jondo, 17
Cante Jondo Festival (1922), 17–18
Capmany, Jaime, 206
Carlists, *see* Requetés
Carmen (country house), 20n
Carretero, Eduardo, 136
Casares, Manuel, 143
Casas Fernández, Jesús, involvement in García Lorca's arrest and death, 179–80
Casas Viejas killings, 122n
Cascajo, Colonel, 183
Cassou, Jean, 54
Castilla, Virgilio, 74, 77, 81; arrested 82–3; condemned to death, 92–3
Castillo, José, assassinated by Fallangists, 58
Castro, Eduardo, 210
Catholic Church: traditionalists identified with, 27; church attacked during 24-hour strike, 40; hatred of Left wing, 182
Cemetery: site of executions, 104–10; caretaker driven insane, 106–7; register of burials, 107, 108; extension, 109
Cerón, Miguel, 170n; part of Granada's artistic community, 21; embarrassed by García Lorca's visits, 22–3; conversation with Valdés on García Lorca's death, 154

Ceuta, army revolt in, 67
Chávez Camacho, Armando, 194–5
Cienfuegos, Alberto A. de, 20, 24
Cirre, Cecilio: in command of sector of Granada, 48; goes to Civil Government in search of García Lorca, 144; confirmation of Luis Rosales's story, 145
Civil Government: bad relations with garrison, 45–6; protected by Assault Guards, 81–2; taken by rebels, 82; during war, 93
Civil Governor (of Granada): changes in 1936, 37, 42, 46; political status, 38
Civil Guard, 42; loyalty trusted by Torres Martínez, 72; during war, 94; implicated in García Lorca's death, 191–2, 218-23
Cobelli, Enzo, 159, 167n, 169
Codex (Buenos Aires publisher), 204–6
La Colonia (Víznar): used as gaol before executions, 158, 159
Confederación Española de Derechas Autónomas (CEDA): emergence as Catholic party, 30; right wing characteristics, 31; participation in 1934 government, 31; Right wing of party attracted by Fascism, 32; begins to lose support, 44
Contrevas Chena, Manuel, 130
Córdoba, taken by insurgents, 74
Cordobilla González, Angelina: on García Lorca's terror of bombs, 114; on search at Huerta de San Vicente, 116; how García Lorca's hiding place was discovered, 123; takes food to García Lorca in prison, 148–50; on letter received posthumously from García Lorca, 166
Corporativism (Ruiz Alonso), 61
Cortes (Spanish parliament): method of allocation of seats, 29; distribution of seats (1936), 36–7
Couffon, Claude, 49, 197; on methods of the 'Black Squad', 98–9; on threatening letter sent to García Lorca, 118
Courts-martial, 92–3
Cristóbal, Juan, 20

Crovetto Bustamente, José, 159
Crow, John A., 222

Darío, Rubén, 52
Darro river, 13
The Daughters of Jephthah (Segura), 18
Davenhill, Maravillas, 104
Davenhill, William, 20, 104
Death in the Morning (Nicholson), 106
El Debate (newspaper), 30, 63
Debussy, Claude, 18
Defensa Armada de Granada, during war, 96
El Defensor de Granada (newspaper), 20; expression of Left wing views, 33; article on García Lorca, 33–4; account of 24-hour strike (March 1936), 39–40; report of García Lorca's return to Granada, 60
Díaz Pla, José, 47, 146–7
Diego, Gerardo, 21
Díez Pastor, Fulgencio, 58
Dimas Madariaga, 175
Domíngues Berrueta, Don Martin, 19, 20
Doré, Gustav, 17
Dumas, Alexandre, père, 17

Economy, Spanish, in early 1930s, 28
Electoral Law (1932), 28–9; effect of enfranchising women, 236
Embíz, Pedro and Antonio, 98
Españoles Patriotas, 96
Espinosa, Colonel, 189
Executions: of gunmen firing on police, 82; of resistors in the Albaicín, 88; in reprisal for Republican bombings, 90; part played by Civil Guard, 94; of imprisoned 'undesirables', 100; outside Granada cemetery, 104–5; recollections of foreign residents, 104–9; monthly numbers, 109; of distinguished residents, 110, 111; at Víznar, 157
Explosives factory captured, 81

The Face of Spain (Brenan), 197
Falange: rise in popularity (from 1936), 32; merger with JONS, 32; gunmen fire on workers and families, 39; support from Catholic middle class, 43–4; part in conspiracy to overthrow Republic, 47; organisation in Granada for rising, 47–8; 'old shirt' members, 48n; recruitment during war, 94–5; responsible for many deaths, 95; merger with Españoles Patriotas, 96; commemorative plaque on Madrid theatre, 207
Falla, Manuel de, 17, 20; disagreement with García Lorca, 119; news of García Lorca's death, 165
El Fargue explosives factory, captured, 81
Fascism: attraction for Right of CEDA, 32; opposed by García Lorca, 51
Fernández, Captain, 93
Fernández Amigo, Cristóbal, 98
Fernández Amigo, Julián, 146–7
Fernández Montesinos, José, 20
Fernández-Montesinos, Manuel: elected mayor, 46; refuses to take action at start of rising, 74; arrested, 83, 113; protest against bombings, 132; shot, 103, 133, 185; news of death broken to family, 133–4; tomb, 110
Fernández-Montesinos García, Manuel, 116–17, 118
Fernández Ramos, Germán, 151
Firearms: not distributed to people of Madrid, 68, or Granada, 71; very few in workers' possession, 89
Folk music, 14, 17
Ford, Richard, 17
Foreign Legion, see Spanish Foreign Legion
Foxá, Agustín de, 58
Franco Bahamonde, Francisco: seizes control of Canary Islands, 67; Nationalist Movement manifesto announced, 67; interview for La Prensa, 192–3
Freemasons, used to dig graves at Víznar, 158
Friends of Latin America, 53
Friends of Portugal, 53
Fuente Grande, 163; site of García Lorca's execution, 164

Galadí Mergal, Francisco, 160

Galindo González, Dióscoro, 153, 161, 164

Gallo (review), 24

Gámir Sandoval, Alfonso, 20

Gaol, conditions for 'undesirables', 99–103

García Alix Fernández, Luis, 141; involvement in García Lorca's arrest and death, 179

García Arquelladas, José, 107, 109

García de Campo, Aurelio Matilla, 37

García Duarte, Rafael, 110

García Fernández, José, 111

García Labella, Joaquín, 111; shot, 158

García Lorca, Concha: wife of Manuel Fernández-Montesinos, 46; blamed for giving away García Lorca's hiding place, 123; widowed, 134

García Lorca, Federico: birth, 14; education, 18; musical education, 18–19; considered to be homosexual, 22–3; moves to Madrid, 23; appointed to travelling theatre company, 23–4; in South America, 24; political views, 51; attendance at political functions, 52–4; intention to visit Mexico, 56; return to Granada from Madrid, 59–60; staying at Huerta de San Vicente, 113; terror of bombs, 114; beaten up, 116–17, 118; in hiding at Rosales's home, 125–34; ways of passing the time in hiding, 131; plans for future literary projects, 132–3; projected elegy to the dead of Spain, 133; arrest, 134, 136, Ruiz Alonso's account of, 137–40; taken to Civil Government, 143; seen after arrest by Falangists, 146–7; defence arranged, 147; moved from Civil Government, 147–50; order given for execution, 151; last night in gaol, 160; execution, 154; others shot at same time, 160–1; letter authorising donation to Army delivered posthumously, 166; death certificate, 167; death seen as one of many, 168; theoretical reasons for his death, 168–9; newspaper reports,

183–90; works banned in Spain, 194; official 'reinstatement', 206; anonymous ballad on his death, 23–4

García Picossi, Clothilde, 121–3

García Rodríguez, Baldomero, 14

García Rodríguez, Enrique, 14

García Rodríguez, Federico, 14; return to Granada from Madrid, 113; bullied by rebels, 120

García Rodríguez, Francisco, owner of Huerta del Tamarit, 121–2

García Rodríguez, Narciso, 14

García Ruiz, Manuel, 98

García Serrano, Rafael, 201–2; 'A Note to Mme Auclair', 202–3

García Valdecasas, Don Alfonso, 61

Garden of Sonnets, 132

Garrison, 41–2; bad relations with Civil Government, 45–6; Nationalist rising planned, 49–50; Gen. Campins in command, 69–70; believed by Campins to be loyal to Republic, 70–1

Gautier, Théophile, 17

Genil river, 13

Gibello, Antonio, 207–8

Gil Robles, José María, 30–2, 44; schoolmate of Ruiz Alonso, 61; influence on Ruiz Alonso's career, 63

Glinka, Michael Ivanovich, 17

Godoy Abellán, Antonio, 93, 98, 142

Gollonet, Megias A., and Morales Lopez, J., 41, 42, 70, 80, 84

Góngora, Manuel de, 20, 24

González Espinosa, General Antonio, 91, 147

Granada: García Lorca's family moves to, 16; Moorish background, 16–17; pleasant atmosphere of town, 19–20; artistic community in early 1920s, 20; influence on García Lorca, 24; clashes between landowners and peasants, 32–3; right-wing election victories (1933 and 1936), 33; left-wing demonstration following 1936 election, 37; 1936 election result anulled, 44; life in town normalised by Torres Martínez, 46; Falangist organisation for rising, 47–8; García Lorca's attitude to Ferdinand and Isabella's capture of (1492), 55; firearms not issued to Republicans, 71; artillery placed in strategic positions, 80; centre completely in rebel hands, 84; whole city controlled by rebels, 89; bombed by Republicans, 90; attempt by Republican militia to capture, 91; town councillors in 1936, 216-7, and those executed, 110, 216-7, see also Albaicín; Cemetery; Garrison; Vega Granada University, García Lorca's attendance at, 18

Guillén, Jorge, 58

Gypsy Ballads, 23; critical essay by Rosales, 125; 'Ballad of the Spanish Civil Guard', 218, cause of García Lorca being summoned, 56-7

Hernando, Teófilo, 53
Herrera Oria, Angel, 30, 63
Herrero Vaquero, Alicia ('The Lady with the Fan'), 103, 109
Homosexuality: Granada's attitude to, 22-3; as reason for García Lorca's death, 199-200; Schonberg's thesis, 224-29
Hórques, Miguel, 98
The House of Bernarda Alba, read by García Lorca to friends, 57, 58
Huerta de San Vicente, 112-23
Huerta del Tamarit, 185
Hurtado, Luis, 190

Iberia (Debussy), 18
Ideal (Granada daily newspaper): importance in political struggle, 33, 47; offices wrecked, 40; announcement of García Lorca's return to Granada, 60; on rising in Seville, 73; Campin's statement, 79-80; on easy success of rising, 84; on the surrender of the Albaicín, 88; letter from men in Provincial Gaol, 101-2; paper read by García Lorca while in hiding, 131-2
Impressions and Landscapes, 19, 155
Inglis, Henry, 17
International Red Aid, 53, 54; García Lorca's membership a possible cause of death, 177
Irving, Washington, 17

Italobalbo, 93
Iturriaga, Enrique de, 48

Jabera (flamenco song), 14
Jackson, Gabriel, 31
Jiménez Blanco, Antonio, 146
Jiménez Callejas, Francisco ('El pajarero'), 98
Jiménez de Parga, José and Manuel, 93, 146
Jofré, Rafael, 99
Jota aragonesa (Glinka), 17
Junco, Alfonso, 194
Juntas de Ofensiva Nacional-Sindicalista (JONS), 32; Ruiz Alonso becomes a member, 62-3; attack on headquarters of Friends of the Soviet Union, 63

Kipling, Rudyard, 21

'The Lady with the Fan', see Herrero Vaquero, Alicia
Lamoneda, Ramón, 176
Landowska, Wanda, 21
Lanz, Hermenegildo, 21
Ledesma Ramos, Ramiro, 62
Left Republican party, meeting in Granada, 74
Lenormand, Henri-René, 54
León, María Teresa, 52
León Maestre, Colonel Basilio: conspirator in rising, 49; consultation on details, 73; conspires to bluff Campins, 74; becomes Military Commander, 86; replaced as Military Commander, 91
Lerroux, Alejandro, 31
Libro de poemas, 23
Llanos Medina, General, 42, 49
López Banús, Manuel, 130
López Font, Antonio, 130
López Peralta brothers, 98
Lorca Romero, Vicenta, 14-15

'M., A.', 158
Machado, Antonio, 53
Madrid, Lorca's time in, 23; politics and art intertwined, 51
Málaga, in hands of Popular Front, 69
Malraux, André, 54
María Pemán, José, 196-7, 210

Mariana Pineda, 24

Mariano Pelayo, Lieutenant, 73, 91; role in conspiracy, 50; becomes a leader of conspiracy, 75–6; organises informer, 103; retaliation for letter bomb, 109

Marín Forero, Enrique, 92

Martínez Fajardo, Lieutenant. 81, 82

Martínez Nadal, Rafael, 59

Megías Manzano, José, 111

Melilla garrison revolt, 67

Mérimée, Prosper, 17

Merry de Val, Marquis de, 181, 190

Miguel del Camp, Lt.-Col., 147

Military Commandery, 91–3

Military decree (21 July 1936), 86–7

Military presence, *see* Garrison

Militia, civilian, 90

Miranda, Captain, 83

Moorish background of Granada, 16–17

Mora Guarnido, José, 21, 166

Morales, Perico, 70, 98

Morales, Lopez, J., *see* Gollonet Megías A., and Morales Lopez, J.

Morcillo, Gabriel, 179, 226-7

Morla Lynch, Carlos, 57, 58–9; receives news of García Lorca's death, 184

El Movimiento (Nacional), *see* Nationalist Movement

Mundo obrero (newspaper), 52, 53

Muñoz Jiménez, Colonel Antonio, 50, 73, 74; confrontation with Campins, 77–8

Muñoz Seca, Pedro, 243

Musical talent of Garcías, 14

Musicians associated with Granada, 17–18

National Front: list of candidates for second 1936 election, 44; failure in Granada, 45

Nationalist Movement: manifesto announced, 67; subscription lists, 170

Neruda, Pablo, 58

Nestares, José María: participant in plotting rising, 50; known as enemy of Republicans, 72; visit to Munoz and Leon, 74–5; persuades police to rebel, 82; has headquarters in Víznar, 156, 158; account of García Lorca's death, 244

Neville, Edgar, 206–7

Neville, Robert, 104–5, 107

New York, García Lorca's visit to, 23

Nicholson, Helen, 105–7

Noticiero Granadino (newspaper), announcement of García Lorca's return to Granada, 60

Ode to the Holy Sacrament, 119

Ode to Walt Whitman, 199, 224

Oliber, Eusebio, 58

Olmo, Tomás, 222

Orgaz Yoldi, General: seizes control of the Canary Islands, 67; arrival in Granada, 90

Ortiz, Manuel Angeles, 20

Ossorio, Angel, 53

Ossuary, at Granada cemetery, 111

Otero Seco, Antonio, 56

Palanco Romero, José, 20, 111

Parrado y García, Monsignor Agustín, 182

Payne, Stanley, 43

Perales, Narciso, 126; protects Rosales, 170–1

Perea Ruiz, Gabriel, 115–18

Pérez de Ayala, Ramon, 205

Pérez del Pulgar Battalion, 95–6

Pérez Funes, Antonio, 100

Pérez Serrabona, Manuel, 108, 147

La Peurta del Vino (Debussy), 18

Pinos Puente, 115, 116

Pizzaro, Miguel, 21

The Poet in New York, 23, 53

Police: during war, 94; join the rebels, 82

Political structure of population, 26–7

Popular Front, 26; narrow victory in 1936 election, 36; great success at second 1936 election, 45; support of artistic community, 51–2; manifesto, 52–3; representatives from France in Madrid, 54.

Prestes, Luis Carlos, 53

Prieto, Indalecio, 115

Primo de Rivera, José Antonio, 32, 42, 126

270

Primo de Rivera, General Miguel, 26, 28

Prisoners: 'undesirables', 99; conditions in Granada prison, 99–103

Proclamation of war, 78–9

Progressives (Spanish political wing), 26, 27

Queipo de Llano, General, 49; seizes control of Sevillan garrison, 68, 69; overall command of Granada, 91; orders García Lorca's execution, 151–2

Quiroga, Casares, 46; error of judgement during military uprising, 68

Radio Granada: taken by rebels, 83; broadcast on Albaicín resistance, 86

Regulares, sent to Granada, 97

Requetés, 95

Residencia de Estudiantes, Madrid, 23

Revillagigedo, Conde de, 30

Reyes, Saturnino, 111

Ridruejo, Dionisio, 200–1

Rimas (Bécquer), 23

Ríos, Fernando de los: member of artistic community, 20; accompanies García Lorca to New York, 23; addresses meeting in sports stadium, 37; warning of Fascism, 57; letters to García Lorca sought at Huerta de San Vicente, 121; hated by the Right, 176, 177

Roberts, David, 17

Robles Jiménez, Antonio, 47, 147

Rodríguez Bouzo, Commandant, 76

Rodríguez Contreras, José, 74; freed from gaol, 135–6

Rodríguez Espinosa, Antonio, 57; García Lorca's farewell visit, 59

Rodríguez Murciano, Francisco, 17; chocolate factory set alight, 40

Rodríguez Orgaz, Alfredo, 114–15

Rojas, Captain Manuel, 122

Roldán, Isabel, 115–16, 117, 123, 133, 165

Romacho, Sergeant, 92, 221

Romance de la pena negra, 234n

Romera, Torres, 37

Romero Funes, Julio, 93, 94, 146

Rosaleny, Commandant, 83

Rosales, Antonio, 125, 126; fanatical Falangist, 126–7

Rosales, Esperanza, 127; on arrest of García Lorca, 142–3; on arranging García Lorca's legal defence, 147

Rosales, Gerardo, 125, 126

Rosales, José, 125, 126; saw signed accusation against García Lorca, 145–6, 172

Rosales, Luis: shelters García Lorca, 119–20, 123–4, 127–9; development as poet, 125–6; shelter for other 'Reds', 129; tries to contact Governor on García Lorca's behalf, 144; statement on reasons for sheltering Lorca, 147; betrayed by Ruiz Alonso, 169; expelled from Falange, 170; letter to *ABC*, March 1972, 208–9; 'quoted' by Schonberg, 228

Rosales, Miguel, 126, 127; help to several Republicans, 129; role during García Lorca's arrest, 141–2

Rosales Camacho, Antonio, 47

Rosales Camacho, José, 47, 48

Rosales Vallecillos, Miguel, 125, 126

Rubinstein, Arthur, 21

Rubia Barcia, J., 192, 221–2

Rubio, Sanchéz, 142

Rubio Callejón, Francisco, 158

Ruiz Alonso, Ramón, 60; early life, 61; work as draughtsman, 61–2; bricklayer, 62; attracted to Fascism, 62; joins JONS, 62–3; elected to Cortes, 64; joins Acción Popular, 64; Fascist ideals, 64–5; motor accident, 65–6; working with Valdés, 93; attempt to form Acción Popular militia, 95; in Pérez del Pulgar Battalion, 95–6; implicated in capture of García Lorca, 120–1; account of arrest of García Lorca, 137–40; inconsistencies, 141–2; confronted by Luis Rosales, 144–5; believed to be responsible for García Lorca's death, 108; denies involvement in denunciation, 173; radio talk after García Lorca's death, 173–6; newspapers make connection with García Lorca's death, 189; implicated by Serrano Suñer, 194–5; legal proceedings against Vila-San-Juan,

Ruiz Alonso, Ramón—*contd*
209n; Schonberg's assertion of homosexuality, 225
Ruiz Carnera, Constantino, 20, 38, 224; on García Lorca's return to Granada, 60; executed, 110
Ruiz Chena, Eduardo, 130; captured and shot, 131
Rus Romero, Antonio, 77, 81; arrested, 83; shot, 92

Saenz, Vicente, 222
Saldaña, Angel, 179
Salinas, Manuel, 158
Salinas, Pedro, 58
El Salvador church, set alight, 40
Salvatierra, Captain, 83
San Gregorio el Bajo, convent set on fire, 40
Santa Cruz, Juan José de, 110–11; shot, 92
Schonberg, Jean-Louis (pseudonym of Baron Louis Stinglhamber), 168–9, 197–8; homosexual jealousy theses, 224-29
Segovia, Andrés, 20
Segura, Antonio, 18–19
Serna, Ismael G. de la, 20
Serrano Suñer, Ramón: appointed Minister of the Interior, 193; propaganda on García Lorca's death, 194–6
Seville: military link with Granada, 41; seized by General Queipo, 68, 69
Shepard, Sanford, 233
Sierra de Alfacar, 155; site of García Lorca's execution, 156
Socialist workers' clubs, shut down, 33
El Socialisto (newspaper), 52
El Sol (newspaper), 53
Soriano Lapresa, Francisco, 21, 22
Sotelo, Calvo, kidnapped and assassinated, 58
Soto de Roma, 13
Southworth, Herbert Rutledge, 43
Spain: loss of overseas colonies, 14; 1933 election, 29–30; Republican governments (1930s), 26; election (1936), 36; parliamentary organisation, see Electoral Law (1932)
Spanish Civil War brochure series, 204
Spanish Foreign Legion, 96–7

Spying, by Republicans, 103
Strike, 24-hour, in Granada, 39
Summer Night in Madrid (Glinka), 17
Surnames, Spanish convention, 15n

Tafall, Ossorio, 46
Tetuan, army revolt, 67
Theatre, social role, 54–5, 56
Thomas, Hugh, 205
Torre, Guillermo de, 58
Torres Martínez, César, 44, 46; on events at time of military revolt, 70–2; uncertain of Campins' loyalty, 81; house detention, 83; tried and sentenced to life imprisonment, 92; on life in Granada gaol, 100–1
Torture, used by Civil Guard, 93
Traditionalists (Spanish political wing), 27
Trend, John, 21–2
Trescastro, Juan Luis, 141, 143; involvement in García Lorca's arrest and death, 178–9
Turner, Frances, 159

Ubiña Jiménez, Francisco, 222
Unification, Decree of, 193
Universal Union of Peace, manifesto, 53

Valdés Guzmán, José: appointed Chief of Militia, 47; background and rise to prominence, 48; position in Granada hierarchy, 49; night of 19/20 July 1936 spent in Military Commandery, 76; assumed Civil Governorship, 83; behaviour as Civil Governor, 93; return to Granada from Lanjaron visit, 145; conversation with José Rosales, 146; Luis Rosales sends statement on sheltering Lorca, 147; under strain during early days of war, 151; gives order for García Lorca's execution, 151; no longer Civil Governor, 154; military outlook, 171–2; officially responsible for García Lorca's death, 182; said to be 'old guard' Falangist, 209; transfer and subsequent death, 244
Valle-Inclán, Ramón del, 52
Vázquez Ocaña, Fernando, 200

Vega: fertility of, 13; social structure of inhabitants, 15–16; irrigation regulated by ringing 'La Vela', 18n
Vega, Ernesto, 42, 45
La Vela (bell), 18
Velasco, Lt.-Col., 145
Vilard Márquez, José María, 136
Vico Escamilla, José, 98
Vidal Corella, Vicente, 191, 221
Vidal Pagán, Lt.-Col. Fernando, 72, 81; instructed to collect weapons for workers, 75; loyalty to Republic reaffirmed, 77; arrested, 83
Vila, Salvador, 111
Vila-San-Juan, José Luis, 159, 160, 209–10
Vílchez, Carlos Jiménez, 98
Villa-Abrille, General, 68
Villoslada, José, 111
Víznar, 50, 156; execution place, 157; burial ground, 161–2
see also La Colonia
La Voz (newspaper), 53

Wellington, Arthur Wellesley, 1st Duke of, 13
Wells, H. G., 21; telegram to Granada military authorities, 189

Xirgu, Margaritu, 60

Yerma: success of first night, 34; performed in Madrid, March 1972, 207
Yoldi Bereau, Jesús, 111; shot, 158

Zamora, Alcalá, 31
Zamora, Ricardo, 153, 243
Zuloaga, 'José' (Ignacio and Juan), 153, 243

For a complete list of books available from Penguin in the United States, write to Dept. DG, Penguin Books, 299 Murray Hill Parkway, East Rutherford, New Jersey 07073.

For a complete list of books available from Penguin in Canada, write to Penguin Books Canada Limited, 2801 John Street, Markham, Ontario L3R 1B4.

If you live in the British Isles, write to Dept. EP, Penguin Books Ltd, Harmondsworth, Middlesex.